RESURRECTION KILL

Also by Laura Joh Rowland

Sano Ichiro

The Iris Fan
The Shogun's Daughter
The Incense Game
The Rōnin's Mistress
The Cloud Pavilion
The Fire Kimono
The Snow Empress
Red Chrysanthemum
The Assassin's Touch
The Perfumed Sleeve
The Dragon King's Palace
The Pillow Book of Lady Wisteria
Black Lotus
The Samurai's Wife
The Concubine's Tattoo
The Way of the Traitor
Bundori
Shinjū

The Secret Adventures of Charlotte Brontë

Bedlam
The Secret Adventures of Charlotte Brontë

Victorian Mystery

River of Fallen Angels
Garden of Sins
Portrait of Peril
The Woman in the Veil
The Hangman's Secret
A Mortal Likeness
The Ripper's Shadow

RESURRECTION KILL

A NOVEL

LAURA JOH ROWLAND

CROOKED LANE

NEW YORK

Published in the United States by Crooked Lane Books, an imprint of The Quick Brown Fox & Company LLC.

Crooked Lane Books and its logo are trademarks of The Quick Brown Fox & Company LLC.

Library of Congress Catalog-in-Publication data available upon request.

ISBN (hardcover): 979-8-89242-711-1
ISBN (paperback): 979-8-89242-712-8
ISBN (ebook): 979-8-89242-713-5

Cover design by Lauren Harms
Cover image ID 345839159 (green castle arch) © Artem Bolshakov | Dreamstime.com

Printed in the United States.

www.crookedlanebooks.com

Crooked Lane Books
34 West 27th St., 10th Floor
New York, NY 10001

First Edition: October 2026

The authorized representative in the EU for product safety and compliance is eucomply OÜPärnu mnt 139b-14, 11317 Tallinn, Estonia, hello@eucompliancepartner.com, +33757690241

10 9 8 7 6 5 4 3 2 1

To Marty, my forever man

CHAPTER

1

New York State, July 1953

A SIREN BLARES THROUGH the loudspeaker in the conference room where I sit with the four other new psychiatrists. A staticky voice repeats, "Code 1, East Drive." Startled, we look to the man at the head of the table.

Tall, dignified, and silver-haired, Superintendent Adrian Van Pelt raises his voice over the siren. "Welcome to your first day as residents at Resurrection Kill Hospital." His manner is calm, faintly amused, his black suit impeccably tailored. "You might as well see what you're getting into."

Beckoning, he strides out the door. We hurry after him along the wide hall, down the grand staircase. In the foyer, one resident catches up with Superintendent Van Pelt and opens the door. With his blond crewcut and conventional handsomeness, he looks like a movie star. The only other woman besides myself trots at his heels. She's bespectacled, her reddish-brown hair coiled in a bun, and her skirt stretches across wide hips. I lag behind the other men. One is slender and older than the rest of us, his hairline receding; shadows underscore his deep-set eyes. The other looks Japanese, with straight black hair and an upright posture that adds to his less than average height. My colleagues are eager beavers, but I hesitate. I should join the front of the charge because first impressions are lasting, and my career depends on the success of my residency; I mustn't look timid. But I need to avoid drawing close attention.

This is my colleagues' first day here. But not mine.

Twelve years ago, when I was fourteen, I was a patient at Resurrection Kill Hospital.

The people with me don't know. Nobody must ever know.

The heavy carved door set with stained glass starts to swing shut in my face. The others are already outside, and the Japanese-looking man holds it open for me. He's the only person who noticed that I've lagged behind. I take a deep breath, walk through the door, nod my thanks at him, and emerge into bright sunshine. The warm summer air smells of roses and freshly cut grass. I pause on the steps of the mansion that serves as the administration building. Around me as far as I can see spreads the hospital's campus, located five miles from Resurrection—the town from which it took its name—and about fifty miles upstate from New York City. *Kill* is the Dutch word for a stream, and the campus nestles in a curve of Resurrection Kill, a tributary of the Hudson River. Founded in 1885, the hospital was built by an architect inspired by Frederick Law Olmstead, designer of Central Park and other landmark sites. Buildings constructed mostly in the nineteenth century, in various styles, cluster together at the middle of a hundred and thirty acres of gently rolling hills landscaped with gardens and surrounded by woods. I don't recognize anything, which disappoints but doesn't surprise me.

The five months I spent here in 1941 are a black void in my memory, lit only by occasional, disturbing flashbacks. I returned to complete my training but also to reconstruct my past. I became a psychiatrist because I want to help the mentally ill, but I also need to find out what happened to me here and why I forgot it all.

I catch up with Superintendent Van Pelt and the other residents on the main road that winds through the campus. Redbrick buildings from the Victorian era, separated by lawns and gardens, line the road. People who look to be patients or visitors stroll in the gardens.

Yesterday, I had planned to arrive in time to move into my quarters, take a walk before dark, and search for scenes that evoked memories, but the drive from the city took longer than I expected due to heavy traffic, and my car had a flat tire. After getting the car towed and the tire fixed at a garage, I reached the hospital too late to explore the campus. Now I lift my gaze to the treetops, to the slate roofs of the other buildings, to the smokestacks that rise from a power plant to the cloudless blue sky. It's as if I've never been here before. I focus on Superintendent Van Pelt, at the head of our little parade. He moves with a rapid, athletic gait, as if the passage of his sixty years has diminished neither his strength nor his energy. I think I remember him, but perhaps my mind is filling the void with false memories.

The sounds of automobile horns and racing engines interrupt my thoughts. A male voice shouts through a megaphone: "Stop!" We round a curve in the road. A dark green pickup truck speeds toward us, followed by a white sedan. A second white sedan comes from the opposite direction, on a collision course with the truck. I gasp, bracing myself for the crash. The other residents exclaim in alarm. Brakes screech as the second sedan slews around to block the road. The green truck veers to avoid hitting the sedan and comes straight at us. We scatter out of its way. The truck jumps the curb, rolls over grass, and crunches to a halt. Rakes, shovels, and buckets rattle in its bed. On the road, the first sedan stops near the second. Both have the hospital's insignia—an oak tree spreading limbs over the letters RKH—and the word "Security" printed in green on the doors. The drivers, men clad in dark green uniforms, spring from the cars. They rush to the truck, whose front wheels have plowed over a ring of stones and low bushes that surround a flower bed. The truck's back wheels spin, churning up grass and dirt as its driver guns the engine. The flower bed, bright with pink, mauve, and blue hydrangeas, is set in the lawn in the curve of a semicircular drive. The drive fronts a building, three stories of red brick and white-framed windows, the roof ornate with gables, dormers, and chimneys. A sign outside reads "Serenity House."

Could it be where I lived when I was a patient?

Nurses in white dresses and caps and orderlies in blue uniforms run out of the building and flock around the truck. The security guards are trying to open the truck's doors, which are locked. One guard says, "It's Rosemary Kirkpatrick. She sneaked out of Haven House and stole a groundskeeper's truck."

"Rosemary is a problem patient," Superintendent Van Pelt informs our band of residents.

A guard strikes the truck's passenger side window with his truncheon. The glass breaks. A shrill voice screams from inside the vehicle: "Go away, you bastards!"

The truck's engine revs; the wheels spin faster, in vain. The guard reaches through the broken window, unlocks and opens the door. The engine dies as he turns the key in the ignition. He and his partner reach inside the truck and pull Rosemary Kirkpatrick out. She flails so wildly that all I can see of her is a tangle of thin limbs, pink garment, and long, dark hair. Shrieking curses that would put a sailor to shame, she kicks one guard in the groin. He howls and doubles over. She pulls free of the other guard, leaving the ripped sleeve of her dress in his hands, and runs . . . straight to me.

My heart clenches. Rosemary's face is small, her features delicate, her complexion pale within the frame of unruly black hair. She's just a girl, no more than sixteen or seventeen.

Everyone else is in motion—guards, nurses, and orderlies chasing Rosemary; the other residents backing away from her; Superintendent Van Pelt raising his hand, opening his mouth to issue commands. But Rosemary's gaze snares mine, and I'm rooted to the spot. It's as if she's singled me out of the crowd, with some primal instinct that sensed—what? A sympathetic ally? A fellow mental case? She clutches my arms, her fingers hard against the gabardine of my suit jacket, digging into my flesh. Her eyes are wide, startlingly green, and fringed with long black lashes.

"Help me!" she cries.

I instinctively grasp her arms—whether to break her hold on me or try to soothe her, I don't know. Her arms are thin but strong. Her anguish strikes a deep chord in me.

"Get me out of here!" she begs. "Please!"

My lips move involuntarily, and my mind echoes with the sound of my own voice crying out the same words. An eerie shiver ripples through me. The scene around me blurs, and my heart drums hard and fast through a tide of vertigo. Locked together, Rosemary and I seem to spin a hundred and eighty degrees, switching places. *The nurses and orderlies are after me, not her.* I see us from a vantage point high above—her dark-haired and half-naked in the tatters of her pink dress; myself with a brown pageboy, trim gray suit, and black pumps. I forget which of us is the doctor, which is the fugitive inmate. A flash of memory like a lightning bolt illuminates the dark void.

I once also accosted some stranger in my own desperate attempt to escape this hospital.

The orderlies yank Rosemary away from me, and our hands cling together for one last instant. Mouth wide with terror, she looks like she's drowning, a riptide pulling her away from her rescuer. I feel the same expression locked on my own face, as if we are mirror images. *Please don't let them take me back there! I don't want to go!*

"Calm down, Rosemary, that's a good girl," Superintendent Van Pelt says, his gentle, firm tone laced with condescending tolerance.

Rosemary screams as the orderlies wrestle her to the ground. A guard speaks into a walkie-talkie. The other residents look on with stoic expressions that mask whatever excitement or alarm they may be feeling. I rearrange my own face to match theirs as I take deep breaths to quell my panic.

The superintendent walks over to the fray, confident as a zookeeper accustomed to wild beasts. A nurse places a hypodermic syringe in his hand. While the orderlies hold Rosemary down, he stabs the needle into her thigh and pushes the plunger. Her screams dwindle to whimpers; the fight goes out of her. Her eyes roll up inside her head, and her body relaxes into drugged sleep. The orderlies step back, panting and wiping sweat off their brows. Superintendent Van Pelt gives the syringe back to the nurse and dusts off his hands. An ambulance arrives. The attendants bring a gurney, lift the unconscious Rosemary onto it, strap her down, and load her into the ambulance.

"I'll see her back to the ward," Superintendent Van Pelt tells our group of residents. "Wait for me in the conference room."

He climbs into the passenger seat of the ambulance and rides away. We retrace our steps to the administration building, the handsome blond man first, the other woman a step behind him, then the thin older man, then the Japanese-looking man and me, walking together.

"Are you all right?" My companion sounds concerned; he noticed my distress.

My cheeks warm. The other residents seem oblivious, and I'm glad he spoke quietly and didn't call their attention to me. "I'm fine."

I'm shaken and trembling inside, but my voice is cool, calm, the product of training and discipline. I can't afford to seem weak, lest the others shun me out of contempt. Triumph revives my strength. I've started to remember. Just as I'd hoped, coming back to Resurrection Kill Hospital has cracked open the void. After twelve years, light is shining through. I look from side to side and backward, eager to see what else might be revealed.

In the middle of the flower bed that Rosemary Kirkpatrick drove the truck into is a statue of a woman. Her stone skin is green with moss, her face hidden by ivy. What would she see if the ivy were torn away? Would she rather remain blind and ignorant?

CHAPTER

2

THE MANSION, BUILT in 1820, is the oldest part of Resurrection Kill Hospital—commonly referred to as RKH—and was the original home of the family who founded the institution on their estate. For some years after the family vacated it, the long, three-story redbrick structure housed patients, men on the north side, women on the south. It now contains administrative offices and common rooms on the first floor and staff apartments above. Last night I moved into one of the apartments, my home for the next three years. I was told that I'm lucky; my name was picked out of a hat during the drawing for the apartment. The other residents have to live in the staff dormitories, which are far less grand. White Corinthian columns above the entrance enclose a second-floor balcony and support a triangular pediment with a half-moon window. As our group of residents approaches the door, the men introduce themselves to one another with businesslike handshakes.

The Japanese-looking man is Dr. Daniel Tanaka. He has a broad, strong face with a serious expression in watchful eyes. The older man is Dr. Joseph Mandel.

"Dr. Ronald Norton," says the handsome blond man. He indicates the woman near his side. "This is my wife."

"I'm Dr. Jean Norton. It's so nice to meet you," she says with a nervous, ingratiating smile. She and her husband make an incongruous couple, as if the hero in a romantic comedy had chosen the glamorous heroine's plain friend.

Dr. Mandel addresses Ronald Norton in a formal tone inflected by a European accent. "I did not see you yesterday. Have you not moved in yet?"

"Nah, we don't want to live in some poky furnished rooms. We're renting a house in town." Ronald Norton's breezy manner connotes wealth, privilege, and snobbery.

Jean Norton hurries to explain, "What he means is, we need more privacy than we would have here."

I too crave privacy, and lodging at RKH will be like living in a fishbowl, but it's free, and I can't afford off-campus accommodations. Nearly broke, I'll have to scrimp until my first paycheck.

"Are you from Germany?" Ronald Norton asks Dr. Mandel, suddenly unfriendly. It's been eight years since the war ended, but there's still lingering hostility toward Germans.

"Yes." Polite but cold, Dr. Mandel explains, "My family emigrated to the United States to escape persecution."

He's Jewish, then. If the war interrupted his education, that would explain why he's older than the typical medical resident. Ronald Norton frowns in distaste that smacks of anti-Semitism.

"I earned my medical degree at New York Medical College," Dr. Mandel says, establishing his credentials, his right to be one of us. "Where did you earn yours?"

Ronald Norton pauses. "Jennings College." His chagrin says he knows that his alma mater, which I've never heard of, is inferior.

Jean Norton tries to smooth over the awkward moment. "It's a small college in Ohio. We studied there together."

Her husband turns to Dr. Tanaka. "Where are you from?"

"Los Angeles," Dr. Tanaka says.

"No, where are you *really* from?" Ronald Norton says impatiently.

"My family is from Japan, if that's what you mean." Dr. Tanaka's expression combines irritation, amusement, and resignation, as if he's been asked the same question ad nauseum. "But I was born in California."

"Right. Sorry." Ronald Norton's manner is unapologetic, and it's clear that he's also prejudiced against the Japanese.

"Were you in an internment camp during the war?" Dr. Mandel asks.

I wince. He's as tactless in his own way as Ronald Norton.

"My whole family was," Dr. Tanaka says calmly, adding, "My bachelor's and medical degrees are from Temple University in Philadelphia."

Ronald Norton's grimace acknowledges that Dr. Tanaka has won their one-upmanship contest. "Aren't we the motley crew."

"What he means is, it's nice to have a group with such varied backgrounds," Jean Norton hurries to say.

I think he actually means that we're an ill-assorted group stuck together at a hospital that's near the bottom of the list of choices for psychiatric residency. The top places likely refuse to accept Jewish war refugees and Japanese Americans, and married couples are hard-pressed to find residencies together even without the handicap of second-rate medical degrees.

Dr. Tanaka offers his hand to me. "We haven't been introduced. I'm Daniel Tanaka."

He's the only one to bother including me in the conversation, and I'm grateful. "Claire Kendall," I say.

As we shake hands, his grip is warm and firm. "An honor to meet you." His smile reveals kindness and a sense of humor behind the serious facade.

I find myself liking him, and I tamp down the emotion. I didn't come here to make friends, especially with a man. Gossip runs wild in hospitals, and I can't afford a bad reputation. Besides, it's risky to let anyone get to know me. My history as a mental patient wouldn't do me any favors with my peers—or with the entire medical establishment.

The other residents acknowledge my acquaintance with polite murmurs. Ronald Norton turns his scrutiny on me. "So where are you from? Where'd you go to school?"

His bold blue eyes sparkle with interest as he looks me up and down. His wife frowns. I feel a tinge of dismay. Unwanted advances have been a part of my life as a medical student and intern, and the last thing I need is a sticky situation here.

"I'm from Michigan. I graduated from Radcliffe, then Columbia Medical School."

Daniel Tanaka smiles and nods in approbation, but displeasure shows on the others' faces as they peg me for a rich girl whose qualifications top theirs.

"What the hell are you doing *here*?" Ronald Norton demands.

"It's hard for women to get residencies." His wife sounds not only eager to soothe his ruffled feathers but to think I must have done something wrong to end up at RKH.

I neglect to mention that I was accepted by Mount Sinai Hospital in New York City and completed a yearlong internship there before I transferred to RKH. "I want to work with troubled girls. Resurrection Kill has a special program."

Ronald Norton laughs with sardonic humor. "If what we just saw is any example, you have your work cut out for you."

I also don't mention that while I really *do* want to specialize in helping troubled girls, it's not my only reason for being here. RKH is the portal to my past. Having crossed the threshold, I must confront whatever memories I can unearth here.

* * *

Inside the mansion, the spacious, high-ceilinged foyer contains a desk for the receptionist and an alcove for the switchboard operator. An antique chandelier hangs above a round table that holds a model of the hospital—tiny buildings amid trees and ponds on sculpted hills. On the walls are framed maps, blueprints, and photos of the hospital throughout the years. Open doors lead to a dining room, lounge, and ballroom. No nurses, orderlies, or patients are in sight. The mansion is like a historic house converted into a museum and open for guided tours. We ascend the staircase that leads to a high gallery and walk along a wide corridor. When we reach the conference room, two women dressed in black uniforms and white aprons are setting out a coffee urn and silver trays of doughnuts, muffins, and sweet rolls. We help ourselves. I only have black coffee. I skipped breakfast, and nervousness has shrunk my empty stomach. Daniel Tanaka and Jean Norton limit themselves to one pastry, but Ronald Norton and Dr. Mandel each take three. As I set my cup on the table, Superintendent Van Pelt arrives with a stocky, balding man in a white laboratory coat, and a woman. The woman is statuesque and elegant, her beautiful features as severe as the cut of her slim dark blue suit. A black toque crowns her sleek, platinum blonde chignon.

Ronald Norton whistles under his breath. His wife shushes him. Superintendent Van Pelt frowns at me as if trying to place me. I freeze, my heart suddenly racing.

He snaps his fingers and points me toward the coffee urn. "White with two sugars."

He thinks I'm a secretary. He's the kind of man to whom his female subordinates are barely distinguishable from one another. This is just the latest in a series of slights I've endured from men since I started medical school—the professors who ignored my raised hand in lecture halls, male students who interrupted me during classes or blatantly told me I didn't belong there. My face burns.

Ronald Norton grins; he likes seeing the Radcliffe/Columbia graduate taken down a notch. Jean gives me a wry look; the same things must have happened to her. We're both interlopers in a man's world. Dr. Mandel gazes at me as if waiting for me to fetch the coffee and wondering why I'm not moving. Daniel Tanaka tactfully looks away, pretending he didn't hear the superintendent.

My second reaction is relief that douses the flames of humiliation. Superintendent Van Pelt didn't recognize me. He doesn't remember me from when I was a patient.

An actual secretary brings him his coffee. He doesn't acknowledge his mistake or apologize to me. Sipping the coffee, he stands at the head of the table, his two colleagues flanking him. When he invites us to be seated, my fellow residents and I take the same chairs we were sitting in before the emergency siren sounded. The Nortons are on Superintendent Van Pelt's right facing Daniel Tanaka, Joseph Mandel, and me. We open the notebooks and take up the pens we'd left on the table.

"It's my pleasure to welcome you to Resurrection Kill Hospital," Superintendent Van Pelt says. "Today you enter into the venerable tradition that began in 1885 when my grandfather, Dr. Cornelius Van Pelt, founded the hospital." He gestures toward a portrait on the wall, a dark oil painting of a man with old-fashioned garb and hairstyle. "Cornelius bequeathed his fortune and his estate to establish an alternative to the squalid madhouses where mentally disturbed folk were chained up and suffered gross physical and psychological torment. Here, those poor unfortunates received kind, moral, humane treatment in a pastoral environment that enabled them to rise from the hell of insanity into restored mental health." He lifts his arms toward the fresco of cherubs in heaven on the ceiling. "Hence, the name 'Resurrection' is appropriate. From the late nineteenth century through the early twentieth, when the states erected massive, prison-like asylums, we've accommodated our patients in an atmosphere that's remained wholesome and inspiring." He beams. "I am proud to be the third superintendent."

I know all this because I've read all the material I could find about RKH. There wasn't much—only scientific research papers, the brochure used to attract new patients, and a book, *The History of Resurrection Kill Hospital*, written by the previous superintendent and published in 1935.

"Today, Resurrection Kill Hospital has three hundred patients," Superintendent Van Pelt says. "We've pioneered many innovative treatments for the mentally ill. Resurrection Kill Hospital is at the forefront of modern psychiatry."

I know that's untrue. RKH has fallen behind institutions like Austen Riggs and Silver Hill. No one on its staff has published a paper in the last decade, and my advisor at the Manhattan Psychoanalytic Academy, where I did a special training course, tried to dissuade me from doing my residency here. "Why that backwater, when you have your pick of the best places?" Dr. Koffka asked me. When I expressed my interest in working with troubled girls, she shook her head. "You are making a big mistake." I couldn't tell her my real reason. Even then I was afraid she was right.

"By joining our staff, you join the leading edge of the march toward healing the mentally afflicted and advancing our profession," Superintendent Van Pelt says. "And now I'm sure you're all eager to meet your new colleagues and get to work." He indicates the woman beside him. "This is Dr. Mara Van Pelt, chief administrator of Resurrection Kill Hospital."

She inclines her sleek blonde head and gives us a smile that warms her severe features. She's older than I thought at first—perhaps fifty. Her dark blue eyes gleam with intelligence. As we take turns stating our names, I have a feeling she knows everything about us from our residency applications and maybe more. I don't remember her. Does she remember my younger self?

"You may call me Dr. Mara. Everyone here does." Her husky voice contrasts with her cool elegance.

Superintendent Van Pelt smiles at her. "Dr. Mara happens to be my dear wife."

The brochure doesn't mention her. I see my surprise reflected on the faces of the other residents; hospitals led by married couples aren't common.

"And this is Dr. Robert Bullard," the superintendent says. "He's our chief of staff. You'll report directly to him."

"Welcome aboard," Dr. Bullard says cheerfully.

The other residents smile as they murmur their thanks, glad to work for someone amiable and down to earth. I don't remember him. He's in his thirties and probably wasn't at RKH when I was a patient. Out of ingrained caution, I reserve judgment about him and Dr. Mara.

"The first order of business is to get you suited up." Dr. Bullard lifts a stack of folded white laboratory coats from the credenza and passes them out.

As we stand and put them on, there's an atmosphere of military camaraderie, as if we're donning armor for battle. Dr. Bullard gives us badges that display the green RKH insignia. Before I clip my badge on the pocket of my lab coat, I touch the typed letters of my name, *Dr. Claire Kendall.* It's not the name I had twelve years ago. The coat, badge, and my current name are all forms of camouflage. So are my horn-rimmed spectacles with the plain glass lenses and my hair dyed several shades darker than my natural honey blonde. I've taken pains to ensure that I look nothing like the girl who was a patient here in 1941. I could be fired for not disclosing my true identity. My record as a former mental patient would end my career before it starts. Four years of medical school and my dream of becoming a psychiatrist would go down the drain.

Dr. Bullard gives us each a ring of keys to the hospital buildings. When we're seated again, Dr. Mara says, "Here are your schedules."

She hands out stapled sheaves of mimeographed typewritten pages. They list the events we're required to attend. The first is this morning, a tour of the hospital and orientation at the wards where we'll be working. The second is a cocktail reception and formal dinner in the mansion tonight.

"You'll each have thirty patients," Dr. Mara says.

Ronald Norton asks the question on all of our minds. "Why so many?"

"What he means is, how can we treat each patient effectively without neglecting others?" Jean says.

Superintendent Van Pelt chuckles. "You'll learn. We all did."

It's no secret that interns and residents are cheap labor for hospitals, which take on as few of us as possible, underpaying and overworking us. I'm used to the heavy caseload at Mount Sinai, the long shifts and little sleep, but I'd hoped residency would be easier. Now I see that my job won't leave much time or energy for anything else.

"Who gets the gal that just stole the truck?" Ronald Norton asks.

"Rosemary Kirkpatrick has been assigned to Dr. Kendall." Dr. Mara smiles sympathetically at me.

The other residents look relieved. My stomach churns with mixed feelings. I remember my strange sense of connection with Rosemary, and I'm eager to try to help her, but if all my patients are as difficult as she promises to be, then my official business here won't be any easier than my personal business.

"What's she in for?" Ronald Norton sounds as if he's talking about a convict in prison.

"Sexual deviance." Superintendent Van Pelt shakes his head in pity. "The girl is a lesbian. Her parents sent her here to be converted to a normal woman."

CHAPTER 3

Dear Celia,

Wouldn't you know, I blew it again. When they sent me to this loony bin, my plan was to cooperate with the head-shrinkers so that I could leave and come back to you. I figured I'd pretend that liking girls was just a phase, and presto! I'm a normal, boy-crazy seventeen-year-old. But I just can't stay out of trouble. There's something in me that won't follow rules. I started misbehaving right from the start, and as Dad says, "The road to hell is paved with good intentions."

In my letters I've told you everything that's happened to me since I got here. Sharing it with you made the bad stuff seem not so bad, and I thought you'd like to know what I've been up to. Nobody is supposed to know about certain things that have happened here at RKH, but I do, and I can't help wanting to find out more. You always said I was too daring for my own good, and I imagined you someday saying "I told you so," *but being impressed with me in spite of yourself.*

Every day for three months I've hoped for a letter from you. I've been wondering, why don't you write? What's happened to you? Don't you care about me anymore?

Yesterday I found out.

Nurse Norris is a real witch. She hates me because I'm a pervert and sassy too. When I went to the nurse's station to ask for a stamp, she sneered and said, "Don't waste your time writing letters to your girlfriend. Your parents ordered us not to mail them. We just tear them up and throw them in the trash."

Oh, God. You never got my letters! That's why you never answered. Do you even know where I am? What have your parents told you? That I was sent away to some foreign country? Or that I'm dead?

Nurse Norris grinned. I guess she enjoyed getting back at me for the time when she wouldn't let me go downstairs for lunch because I wasn't wearing a dress and I told her to shove her broomstick up her ass. I wanted to strangle her, but I could tell she wanted me to try so she could have me transferred to the lockdown house. According to the girls who've been there, you're kept in a padded room and injected with medicine that turns you into a zombie. Those are the girls who will never really be normal again, if they ever were in the first place. They'll always be stuck in here or someplace worse. I don't want to be one of them. So I managed to swallow my anger, turned around, and walked back to my room.

The walls seem to close in on me. I pressed my pillow against my mouth so I wouldn't scream. I couldn't stand being here for one more minute, knowing you must think I've forgotten you and I don't love you anymore. I was desperate to see you and explain about the letters. Getting out of this house is no problem, I do it all the time, at night, when nobody's around, but how would I get to you? RKH is in the middle of nowhere. I thought of bribing someone on the staff to take me. They might if I paid them enough. But my money is tied up in a trust fund that I can't touch until I'm eighteen, and the only cash I have is a few dollars locked in the safe at the nurse's station. I cried because I was trapped.

But today I got my chance.

After breakfast, the plumber came to fix a leaky pipe. One of the girls was scared of him, and she threw a fit. That kept the nurses and orderlies busy. They didn't notice me when I followed the plumber down the stairs and out the back door. In the parking lot, I saw a groundskeeper drive up in his truck. He parked and walked toward the house, leaving the engine running. I ran to the truck, jumped inside, threw it into gear, stomped on the gas pedal, and drove away. Mother thinks ladies shouldn't drive. Luckily, my brother Ted taught me how. He said that if I were a boy, I could grow up to drive in the Indy 500. I would like to do that. There are lots of things I wish I could do. I wish Ted would come and visit me. None of the family does.

The groundskeeper yelled, "Hey!" and started chasing me.

He got really small in the rearview mirror really fast. I lost him altogether when I fishtailed around a curve. But before I reached the gate, a guard in a car zoomed up behind me, calling "Stop!" through his megaphone. Another car came straight toward me. I slammed on the brakes and jerked the wheel. I almost hit a bunch of people. The truck ran off the road and crashed.

To make a short story shorter, I got caught.

Now I'm writing to you in my head. It's the only way I can talk to you, and maybe somehow you'll hear me. At the moment, I couldn't write with a pencil and paper even if my letter was going to be mailed to you. I'm flat on my back, my arms pinned to my sides and my legs straight out and stuck together. I can barely twitch my toes or fingers, and I'm so sleepy that I can't open my eyes. Talking to you is the only thing keeping me awake.

I miss you.

I love you.

Rory

CHAPTER

4

Dr. Bullard takes our group of residents on a tour of the hospital. We ride around the campus in a tram, three open-air cars pulled by a tractor. We sit in the first car, which has seats for twelve people. The other cars are occupied by nurses, doctors, and other staff members. The tractor driver stops wherever they ask to be let off. Dr. Bullard explains that the tram operates from six AM to eight PM. April first through November first.

"It's a pleasant way to travel between buildings in the daytime in good weather," he says. "At night and in the winter, we use the underground tunnels."

Hearing the word *tunnels* makes my throat contract. I have a phobia of tunnels. In the city, I forego the subway, traveling by taxi and bus despite the expense and the traffic jams. Tunnels never bothered me before I came to RKH as a patient. Is whatever happened to me then at the root of my phobia? That's one mystery I came here to solve.

The campus is peaceful, the trees and grass lushly green, the flower beds bright. The kill flows around the western and southern part of the grounds, and its waters sparkle between the trees that line the road along which we're currently motoring. Birds soar in a blue sky dotted with puffy white clouds; their song spangles the air. We've seen the laboratory, gymnasiums, conservatory, and power plant.

Now, as we chug along a road by the apple orchard and the farm, Dr. Bullard says the farm once provided enough beef, mutton, pork, chicken, and dairy products to feed the entire staff and patient population, but during the war, labor was so scarce that most of the farm was shut down, the livestock sold. Today RKH only grows apples and vegetables, and the stable has a few horses for riding.

Dr. Bullard then tells us about the patients. Seventy percent of them are female. Manic-depression, schizophrenia, and dementia are the most common diagnoses.

"I'll show you around the houses where you'll be working," Dr. Bullard tells us. "I encourage you to visit the other houses, to familiarize yourselves with RKH's entire operation."

My muscles tighten with anxiety. We circle the perimeter of the campus, where dense woods encroach and overgrown shrubbery obscures several buildings with boarded-up windows.

"The patient census decreased during the war because of the shortage of medical personnel," Dr. Bullard says. "It's never bounced back to its prewar level. RKH had to close some buildings."

Not even this sanctuary for the mentally ill was spared the war's effects. Jean Norton points at the slate roofs of three houses visible amid the treetops. "What are those buildings?"

"The private cottages," Dr. Bullard says.

I remember their names from the brochure: Faith, Hope, and Charity. We don't stop; none of us have patients there. I've spoken very little today, and I don't want to be labeled a quiet one, an introvert. I know from past experience that introversion is too often misconstrued as boringness or stupidity.

"Who lives in the cottages?" I ask.

"Two are vacant," Dr. Bullard says. "The other is occupied by an individual who's attended by private nurses, doctors, and servants. That's one reason the cottages are called 'private.' The other is that the patients in them prefer not to have their identities known to anyone who doesn't need to know."

The tram halts on the drive below a large building. L-shaped, three stories high, and constructed of red brick, it resembles the hulking, gargantuan state asylums to which RKH is supposedly a more humane alternative. Black shutters frame windows crisscrossed with iron bars.

"This is your stop, boys," Dr. Bullard says.

Doctors Tanaka, Ronald Norton, and Mandel climb down from the tram. Jean Norton says, "I thought my husband and I would be working in the same place."

"Mercy House is a maximum-security ward for the most disturbed male patients," Dr. Bullard says. "They're a danger to themselves and others. We don't allow first-year female residents to work there."

"Oh." Jean sounds worried as well as disappointed.

Dr. Bullard steps out of the tram. "Excuse me, girls. I'll see the boys inside, then take you to your houses."

Jean and I watch her husband, the two other residents, and the last of the tram's other passengers mount the steps to Mercy House and disappear inside. Since I must avoid close relationships with the men, she's my only chance to form the kind of alliance that helps new doctors survive the crucible of internship and residency.

"Maybe you and your husband can work together in a few months," I say. "If this is like other hospitals, we'll rotate through the different wards."

She chews her lip and ignores me, lost in her own thoughts. We sit in silence for some twenty minutes until Dr. Bullard returns. Then we continue our drive. Apparently, the more disturbed patients are kept away from the less disturbed patients, who live in houses near the administration building. Our next stop is Grace House, another red-brick building, square with a pitched roof that sports a glass conservatory on top. A wide porch surrounded by white columns graces the front and side entrances, shadowed by second-floor balconies. It looks like the mansion of an affluent family.

"You'll be working here," Dr. Bullard tells Jean. "It's for chronically ill patients, most of them elderly."

As he escorts her to the door, her shoulders droop. Not only will she be separated from her husband during their shifts, she'll have the most hopeless cases.

"Last but not least." Dr. Bullard says when he returns to me. "On your application you expressed an interest in working with troubled girls, so I've assigned you to Haven House. It's the maximum-security ward for females under thirty. They do better when they're kept separate from the older patients."

"Thank you." I'm glad he's matched my assignment to my area of interest. "The brochure mentioned a special program for girls. Can you tell me about it?"

"It was suspended when the doctor in charge left last year," Dr. Bullard says.

"Oh." I'm dismayed to hear that RKH's special program currently consists of merely lumping the girls together in the same house.

"I hope you'll restart the program," Dr. Bullard says.

The idea is daunting to me, a complete novice, but I say, "I would be happy to." Unless I do it, there won't be any program, a detriment to the patients as well as to my professional goal.

The tram stops and Dr. Bullard says, "This is Haven House."

It's a rectangular structure, two stories high. Awnings over the windows and white-columned verandas at the corners refresh the old-fashioned Victorian architecture. The lane where the tram driver lets us off meanders around rose beds. Dr. Bullard speaks, but I barely hear him over the sudden ringing in my ears. The air shimmers as my vision blurs around the edges. All I can see, in clear, sharp detail, is Haven House, its redbrick walls and green-and-white-striped awnings glowing garishly, like a set in a Technicolor film. I'm caught in the same panicky vertigo that I felt during my encounter with Rosemary Kirkpatrick. The noise from the tractor's engine drowns in the thud of my accelerating heartbeat as a memory flares in the void, like a wildfire ignited by a cigarette tossed from a car window into a drought-stricken forest.

Haven House is where I lived while I was a patient here. It's the scene of whatever happened to me at RKH twelve years ago.

The excitement of recovering another memory immediately turns to dread. I feel a touch on my arm and recoil from Dr. Bullard, a dark silhouette against the nightmarish backdrop of Haven House. He gestures for me to step out of the tram. I obey, clutching my notebook to me like a shield. I don't want to go in there, because whatever happened to me here was very bad. I've suspected as much all along; now the certainty of it reverberates through me. Dr. Koffka once said amnesia is like scar tissue for psychological wounds. I'm breathless, trembling, nauseated. My body remembers even though my mind forgot.

How will I be able to work in this place? I can't predict when the flashbacks will come, what revelations they'll bring, or how I'll react to them. Fate has landed me exactly where I need to be, but how can I be a good doctor to my patients? I'm afraid that Dr. Koffka was correct: my coming here was a mistake, for both the hospital and myself.

I gulp deep breaths and concentrate on the hardness of the pavement under my feet, the rose-scented summer breeze that ruffles my hair. The ringing sound fades; the air stops shimmering; my vision clears; the panic dissipates. *Thank God.* As Dr. Bullard and I walk up the path to Haven House, it's just an ordinary building and I'm back in the present, a psychiatrist reporting for duty.

In the foyer, paneled walls enclose settees upholstered in floral velvet, potted ferns on wrought-iron stands, and antique coffee tables. Above a white marble fireplace, a gilt-framed mirror reflects vases of roses on the mantel. Persian carpets on the polished dark wood floor muffle our footsteps. A graceful arch curves over a wide staircase with carved balustrades. The loud ticking of a grandfather clock echoes the beating of my heart, which slows to its normal rhythm. Haven House seems like a time capsule from the Victorian era, with even the dust motes in the air preserved but unfamiliar. If I'm not ambushed by flashbacks at every turn, maybe I'll actually be able to focus on my job.

Dr. Bullard introduces me to the nurse at the reception desk. She's too young to have worked here while I was a patient. Dr. Bullard asks her to call the charge nurse, and as she telephones, his walkie-talkie squawks. He listens, then says, "A patient in the infirmary needs my attention. You'll have to excuse me."

He hurries away. So I won't be getting even the brief orientation he gave the other residents. Although it's common knowledge that in many hospitals interns and residents must swim or sink on their own, I didn't expect to be thrown into the deep end so soon.

A buxom middle-aged woman in a white uniform descends the staircase and approaches me. "Hello. I'm Enid Norris." Her white cap crowns short, stylishly waved brunette hair. Her large, bold features would be handsome on a man, and they're formidable on her, the charge nurse of Haven House.

I introduce myself, and we shake hands. Nurse Norris's smile and tone are friendly, but her eyes are hard. My heart sinks as I recognize her as one of those nurses who relish making interns' and residents' lives difficult. They resent us because we're newcomers and they have many more years of hospital experience, but we waltz in and take over. And we'll earn far more money and command far greater respect than they ever will. I don't blame them, but I dread the battles to come.

Nurse Norris unlocks a door on the right side of the foyer. "Welcome to Haven House."

Air that smells of industrial-strength disinfectant, cigarette smoke, and stale food rushes out at us. Nurse Norris leads me into a wide, unfurnished corridor with a beige linoleum floor, the walls painted dull brown the first four feet from the floor, cream above. The only period architectural features are the intricate plaster moldings and the antique light fixtures with etched-glass globes. The luxurious atmosphere of RKH stops here. Now I get my first taste of the fact that mental institutions aren't like regular hospitals, where many patients are confined to their beds. Haven House is all motion and noise. Girls and young women, clad in everything from shorts and T-shirts to capri pants, blouses, and dresses, wander up and down the hall. They talk to one another or themselves. Chatter blends with announcements from a loudspeaker and dance music playing on a radio somewhere. A red-haired woman tries to slip out the door before Nurse Norris closes it, screaming, "I can't stand all these crazy people any longer!"

Two aides drag her away. Other patients argue with orderlies. At Mount Sinai, I met mentally disturbed patients, but singly and never more than a few during a shift. So many all at once is overwhelming.

"The new residents get the most disturbed cases," Nurse Norris says with undisguised satisfaction.

"Because it's the best way to learn," I say.

"Because the staff doctors have given up on them. The hope is that new blood will bring new ideas and new chances." Nurse Norris laughs scornfully.

I begin to dislike her as much as she clearly dislikes me. She calls the three other nurses over and introduces me, saying their names too fast for me to remember. She shows me a room behind the nurse's station. It's like a closet, barely large enough for a chair and small desk. "This'll be your office while you're on duty."

I leave my notebook on the desk. She leads me on a tour, briskly passing and describing the facilities, obviously meaning to confuse me. Patients' rooms, each with a private bath, line one side of the corridor, across from the linen closet, utility room, and isolation rooms. The dining room, sitting room, and screened porch are at the end. Patients cluster at the nurse's station, voicing complaints and requests, making telephone calls, receiving mail. In the sitting room, they knit and watch television. An aide lights cigarettes for them, smoke hazing the air. A fat girl dances to the music from the radio, imitating a stripper. Other patients laugh and clap. I'm reminded of my college dormitory, but here, the merriment feels too volatile, dangerous.

"The layout on the other side of the house and on the second floor is the same as this but without a dining room," Nurse Norris says. "The attics are private suites. The kitchen, pantry, and supply room are in the basement. So is the entrance to the tunnels. I'll take you down there."

Tunnels. I stifle a shudder. "I'd like to meet the patients first."

Nurse Norris begins introducing patients as she breezes past them. She doesn't give them my name. When I ask her to slow down, she pauses, and hostility narrows her eyes.

"Suit yourself," she says.

The battle lines are drawn. I've made my first enemy at RKH.

She grudgingly introduces me to the patients in the sitting room. The first is Mrs. Andrea Bond, a small, thin woman in her late twenties, hunched over a notebook in which she writes frantically with a pencil. She lifts protuberant gray eyes and smiles. "Doctor, I'm so glad to meet you," she says, breathless and anxious. "Look—I've written down all my thoughts." She thrusts her notebook at me. Its lined pages are covered with tiny script.

"Later, dear," Nurse Norris says.

A woman hobbles toward us, her feet angled awkwardly. At first I think she's old, out of place at Haven House, but then I see that she's not only young but beautiful. Long, wavy blonde hair frames her heart-shaped face. A floral sundress flatters her full bust and tiny waist. She looks like an ingenue in a movie. She smiles, fluttering her hands. Her eyes are oddly innocent as she speaks in grunts, gurgles, and stammered monosyllables.

"This is Lulu Shelton," Nurse Norris says. "She wants us to admire her new dress. Yes, you look very pretty, dear."

Lulu Shelton giggles and hobbles away. Nurse Norris says, "She had a lobotomy about ten years ago."

"Why?" I ask, astonished because Lulu must have been little more than a child when she underwent a lobotomy—brain surgery—the most drastic psychiatric procedure.

"If you want to meet the other patients, you'd better hurry." Nurse Norris walks so fast that I have to run to catch up. "I haven't got all day."

Meeting the other patients takes ages because they're scattered around the ward, and many are eager to voice their complaints to the new doctor. Nurse Norris has to peel them off me. Soon I've stopped remembering their names, and I don't know what their diagnoses are because I haven't had a chance to read their files.

"Where's the office where I'll conduct psychotherapy sessions?" I ask.

Nurse Norris's expression shows pity for my naivete. "There's no office. You talk to the patients in their rooms. If you have time. Which you probably won't."

I unhappily realize that she's right. If I see each of my thirty patients every day, I'll have less than ten minutes to talk with each one, after I factor in the time spent on medical procedures, updating charts, writing reports, making rounds, attending training sessions, and other duties.

By the time Nurse Norris has shown me around the first and second floors of Haven House, it's noon. Patients head to the dining room for lunch while Nurse Norris shows me those who eat from trays in their rooms with aides supervising them because they're too disruptive to join the others.

"Judy Abbott refuses to eat because she thinks we're trying to poison her. She needs to be tube-fed. You'll have to insert the tube." Nurse Norris smiles with ill humor.

I've inserted feeding tubes before, but never under these circumstances. Judy is strapped to her bed. She yells curses while an aide holds her head still. As I force the tube through her nose and down her esophagus, she struggles and gags and tries to bite me. By the time the tube is in, I'm exhausted and sweating.

"You can go to the mansion for your lunch. Or you can eat here." Nurse Norris bends a challenging stare on me.

I have no appetite whatsoever. "I'd be happy to eat here."

CHAPTER

5

THE DINING ROOM is bright and sunny, the walls painted yellow, the windows hung with daffodil-print curtains. Yellow linen cloths cover the tables where the patients sit. Waitresses in hairnets, black uniforms, and white aprons serve coffee. We could be in a sorority house except for the nurses passing out small plastic cups that contain pills and an aide tying a bib around Lulu Shelton's neck. Nurse Norris leads me to a table occupied by other nurses.

"You're welcome to join us." Her tone is grudging.

I see two patients seated at a table by themselves. In their late teens or early twenties, they seemed among the most lucid I met today, and they're in the population I most want to help. "Thanks, but I'll sit over there."

Nurse Norris manages to look disapproving as well as glad of a respite from my company. "Suit yourself."

I approach the two patients and manage to recall their names. "Hello, Dot. Hello, Maureen."

"Oh, the new doctor." Dot is plump with a sweet voice, long, curling dark brown hair, and a pretty face. She wears blue dungarees and a pink ruffled blouse.

"Hi." Maureen is fat and plain. Her flesh bulges out of a sleeveless knit shift whose horizontal red-and-white stripes emphasize her heft. Her light brown hair is thin, straggly.

"May I join you?" I ask.

The girls look at each other, then at the empty seat next to Maureen, as if they're seeking permission from an invisible third party.

"Sure," Dot says.

I wonder if they suffer from hallucinations. Dr. Bullard said RKH has many cases of schizophrenia. Wishing I'd had time to read the girls' files first, I sit down beside Dot.

Our waitress says, "Hi, gals." She's an older woman with gray braids coiled under her hairnet. Filling our water glasses, she asks if we want milk, coffee, or tea, soup or salad.

"Milk and coffee. Soup and salad," Dot says.

"Me too," Maureen says.

I'm surprised by their big appetites, but the waitress only smiles before she departs.

"The insulin therapy makes us really, really hungry," Dot explains.

From lectures at med school I recall that insulin therapy involves injecting patients with massive doses of insulin to put them in a coma, then reviving them with glucose via a feeding tube. The coma supposedly relieves psychosis. But I didn't know that increased appetite and weight gain are side effects. I'm already learning new things on the job.

"I'm glad we have this chance to talk," I say. "Can you tell me a little about yourselves?"

"I'm a music major at Vassar," Dot says. "Or was. I had to drop out because I was having bad thoughts and hurting myself."

She tugs down the sleeves of her blouse to cover the scars on her wrists—signs of multiple suicide attempts. She spoke as casually as if about the weather, but I feel a stab of sympathy for her. My own wrists throb.

"I was at Smith," Maureen says. "I thought the girls in my dorm were trying to kill me, so I barricaded myself in the bathroom with my father's shotgun. The police came and got me out." Her manner is half chagrined, half mischievous.

I think she wanted to shock me, and she's succeeded. She and Dot are my fellow Seven Sisters girls. A shiver runs through me. It's been twelve years since I was a patient, but here I am at perhaps the very table where I once received my own plastic cups of pills with my meals. My sympathy for Dot and Maureen goes beyond the normal doctor-patient limit. I see them as if through a dark mirror, images of what I might have been at their age had I stayed longer at RKH.

The waitress serves our salads. I pick at mine. Dot and Maureen eat their salad and soup with gusto. I ask them, "How long have you been here?"

"Seven months," Dot says.

"Ten." Maureen adds, "I was in for three months the last time."

I'm dismayed because they seem on their way to becoming chronic, long-term patients. But they're young, and maybe their symptoms have improved. They're behaving quite normally now, except that Dot alternates one bite of salad with one mouthful of soup and one sip of milk, never varying the pattern, in what seems to be a neurotic ritual.

"How do you like it here?" I ask.

They look at each other, then at the empty seat. What do they see? Hallucinations aren't a good sign for their prognosis.

"It's okay," Dot says.

"It's haunted, you know." Maureen's gray eyes gleam with excitement.

I'm not surprised; old places are often said to be haunted. The library at Radcliffe supposedly harbors the ghost of alumna Margaret Coleman. I say, "Oh?" with an encouraging smile. A psychiatrist can engage patients via topics of interest to them.

Our waitress serves us chicken à la king, tomato aspic, and hot rolls, double portions for Dot and Maureen. I nibble my food. As the girls devour theirs, Dot tells the story.

"In 1885, three patients died. The first was Mr. Stanley Moore. He was a biologist from Yale. The second was Miss Jennie Washburn, a banker's daughter. And the third was Harvey Cutler, one of the doctors. Their ghosts have been here ever since." Her dark eyes sparkle as she and Maureen shovel food into their mouths. They must be testing me, trying to scare me or see how gullible I am.

"Any hospital this old must have had quite a few deaths." I try to seem sensible but also like a good sport.

"These weren't just deaths," Maureen says, her chin shiny with butter. "They were suicides."

She and Dot giggle at my consternation, which I can't hide. Dot says, "Stanley hanged himself from a chandelier. Jennie drowned herself in the bathtub. And Dr. Cutler shot himself in the apple orchard."

"Their ghosts roam around the hospital at night," Maureen says. "They whisper in the patients' ears, telling them to kill themselves."

It's a troubling story that doesn't appear in the book about Resurrection Kill Hospital. The girls watch me, eagerly awaiting my reaction. Is this a prank they play on the new staff? I don't want to seem rattled or to scold them and spoil the rapport I'm beginning to build, but if it's an actual legend that's going around the hospital, it's dangerous to vulnerable patients, and I must debunk it.

"Ghosts aren't real," I say.

"These are," Maureen insists. "I've seen them."

I think she believes she saw something. Hallucinations and paranoia are symptoms of schizophrenia. I decide to humor her until I've gained her trust.

"Where have you seen them?"

She starts to answer, but Dot says sternly, "Maureen." She casts a warning look at the empty chair.

Abashed, Maureen mutters, "Oh, just around the house."

She and Dot look down at their empty plates, avoiding my gaze. Dr. Koffka said that mental patients often lie—to get something they want, to hide compromising secrets, to minimize the severity of their illness. I've been working at RKH for less than three hours, and I've already heard my first lie.

* * *

After lunch, the first-floor nurse's station is temporarily deserted. When I rummage through the file cabinets, I find that it contains files for only the current patients.

"Looking for something?"

At the sound of Nurse Norris's voice, I slam the cabinet shut. "Just familiarizing myself with the records. Where are the files for former patients?"

She eyes me suspiciously. "Why do you want them?"

I give her the excuse I prepared just in case anyone asked. "I'm researching case histories for an article about past and current treatment protocols for girls with mental illness."

"Old records are kept in the basement of the library." Nurse Norris raises a quizzical eyebrow.

I change the subject before I have to embroider on my lie. "There's one patient I haven't seen. Where is Rosemary Kirkpatrick?"

Nurse Norris smirks; she seems glad the troublemaker is my patient. "She's in isolation."

Haven House has four isolation rooms, for patients who are experiencing violent upsets and need to be separated from the other patients. Nurse Norris unlocks the heavy wooden door whose small window has crisscrossed wire embedded in its glass. We enter a small cell with a gray linoleum floor and bare walls painted light blue. The cell is empty except for a metal hospital bed. It's as if a scene from a Victorian asylum were transplanted into Haven House. Light from the single window shines on Rosemary, who lies motionless on the bed, wrapped snugly in a white sheet from neck to toes like a mummy. A pink shower cap covers her hair. Her eyes are closed, her lips blue, her skin so pale that the freckles across her nose look as dark as spattered ink droplets. She inhales and exhales slow, shallow breaths.

"This is a cold pack," Nurse Norris says.

I feel the tight, immobilizing pressure of a sheet around me. Its icy dampness seeps into my bones. I was once in a cold pack, perhaps in this very room. Even as I begin to shiver, the memory fades. But I see in Rosemary my younger self as a patient—imprisoned, maltreated, and suffering. In the parlance of the great pioneering Viennese psychiatrist Dr. Sigmund Freud, she's my double—a doppelganger, a shadow from my past, a source of memory and terror.

"I didn't know hospitals still used this technique," I say, pretending I'm as ignorant of it as a new resident should be. "I've only seen photographs in old textbooks."

"There's a lot you don't know," Nurse Norris says with a superior smile. "Cold packs calm the patients down." She shakes her head at Rosemary. "To look at her, you'd never know that she's from such an important family." Seeing my puzzled expression, she explains, "Her father is John Kirkpatrick, a state senator in Albany. He's running for Congress. His wife, Josephine Shelley Kirkpatrick, is the heiress to a railroad fortune, and she's on the boards of all kinds of charities. Rosemary's four brothers are all lawyers or bankers, her three sisters are well married. Rosemary's the youngest, the misfit."

The girl's long black eyelashes flutter. We shouldn't discuss patients when they might be listening. I say to Nurse Norris, "Can you leave us alone for a while?"

She sniffs. "Good luck getting anywhere with her. Everyone else has tried and failed." She leaves, closing the door with exaggerated firmness.

I wait a moment while Rosemary lies still and silent. I say quietly, "Hello, Rosemary. I'm Dr. Kendall, your new psychiatrist."

For long seconds, her eyes remain closed. Then her lips move in a hoarse whisper. "My name is Rory."

I'm glad she's able and willing to talk. "Hello, Rory." Dr. Koffka said that in a first interview, it's important to meet patients where they are, which includes using the name they prefer. "Can you tell me what brought you here?"

Another long pause, then: "Haven't they told you?"

"I'd like to hear it from your point of view."

Displeasure wrinkles her brow. "Why should I tell you anything? I don't know you."

Dr. Koffka also said that psychotherapy requires some give and take. "Fair enough. I graduated from Columbia University Medical School. I'm starting my residency here."

Rory's eyes crack open, and she turns her head to stare incredulously at me. "You're a *beginner*? How are you supposed to help me?"

A good question. My training didn't include homosexual conversion therapy. "I'd like to try."

"I don't trust you." Her voice is bitter, raw with pain. "I don't trust anyone."

I have my own distrust of the hospital from which I left with amnesia, and if the cold pack is typical of how Rory is treated here, I can understand her attitude. To keep the conversation going, I ask, "Why not?"

"The other doctors make me look at pictures." Her expression turns accusing. "Are *you* going to make me look at pictures?"

I've no idea what "looking at pictures" entails, and I doubt I can countermand the other doctors' orders. "There are other possible therapies," I improvise. "For now, we can talk about anything you'd like."

Rory emits a snort of contemptuous disbelief. "Whatever I say, you'll tell everybody else, and they'll use it against me."

"No, I won't. It'll be confidential." I spoke impulsively and unwisely. Dr. Koffka said never to promise a patient anything that you can't guarantee. I'm supposed to report on my patients to Dr. Bullard, but if I don't gain Rory's trust, I can't help her. Putting a patient ahead of professional responsibilities means crossing a line, jeopardizing my career. And I'm a novice in a profession where the bar is set higher for women than men.

"Yeah, right." Whatever her mental problems, Rory isn't stupid or naive. Curling her lip in scorn, she turns her face away from me.

CHAPTER

6

At our table in the dining room of the mansion, Superintendent Van Pelt sits at one end, Dr. Mara at the other. I'm on Dr. Mara's right, with Ronald and Jean Norton beside me. Across from us sit Dr. Mandel, Dr. Bullard, and Daniel Tanaka. Chandeliers cast sparkling light over the white linen cloth, heavy silverware, and crystal goblets. Maroon velvet curtains frame tall windows that overlook the terrace and the garden, serene under the golden evening sun. The scent of roses blends with cigarette smoke. The other tables are filled with medical and administrative staff—some two hundred people. When we mingled during the cocktail reception, nobody seemed familiar. I met the senior residents, who are in their second and third years of training at RKH. Now, lively conversation echoes up to the high ceiling from all the tables except mine. While Superintendent Van Pelt chats with people who come over to pay their respects to him, Dr. Mara confers with the head waiter, and Dr. Bullard speaks into his walkie-talkie, the new residents sit silent, exhausted from our long first day.

Afternoon visiting hours cut into the time I'd planned to spend reading files. I met the patients' relatives and friends and listened to their concerns, which were many. RKH costs too much, the patients aren't getting better, what did I intend to do about it?

Nurse Norris told me, "They'll take up all your time if you let them. You'll never get anything done."

"They deserve my time," I said. "That's why I'm here."

She rolled her eyes.

All the while, Rory Kirkpatrick was on my mind. Even though her attitude put me off, I'm determined to help her. But how? And for whose sake? It's dangerous for a psychiatrist to identify too strongly with her patients. Confusing Rory's problems with my own could cause me to make mistakes in her treatment.

Waitresses pour white wine, and we residents drink eagerly. Ronald Norton nods in surprised appreciation and says, "This is top-notch stuff. Unlike everything else here."

Jean shushes him. She wears a green and yellow flowered dress that makes her complexion sallow. He's in a seersucker suit, as if for a garden party. I remember that they live off campus. They somehow found the time to go home and change clothes. Although I live here, I didn't have time to change out of my suit. The other residents are still in theirs too. The wine is good, tart and refreshing, and it relaxes my tense nerves.

Superintendent Van Pelt taps his knife against his glass. The room quiets down. He stands and says, "Good evening. We're gathered tonight to welcome our new residents." He introduces each of us by name. We stand and smile as the audience claps. "We at Resurrection Kill Hospital are a family of dedicated professionals, working together to help the mentally ill." I glance at the clock on the wall, then at my watch, wondering how long he's going to speak. "Today our family gained five new members. Here's to them." Hands raise glasses; everyone drinks. "I trust that we will all make them feel at home. Now let's enjoy our dinner."

Applause echoes as he sits down. Mine isn't the only sigh of relief. As the waitresses serve salads, he goes from table to table, greeting the staff. Dr. Mara is called away to the telephone and Dr. Bullard summoned to an emergency. We, the new family members, talk among ourselves and agree that since we'll be working together for three years, we should be on first name terms. Next, we try to get acquainted and determine whether we can be friends.

"What are you going to do after you're a full-fledged doctor, Claire?" Ronald Norton broaches the topic that inevitably comes up among interns and residents.

"I'd like to be a staff psychiatrist at a mental hospital," I say.

"Not me," Ronald says between bites of salad. "I'm going into private practice. That's where the money is. And the prestige. And the leisure time. I'm looking forward to golf on Wednesdays and the whole month of August off every year."

Joseph Mandel nods. Jean Norton looks uneasy, as if she dislikes her husband's attitude but doesn't want to say so. I'm aware that hospital psychiatrists are the unwanted stepchildren of the profession and they work the hardest for the lowest pay. It's no small sacrifice for a single woman with no marriage prospects who must earn her living in a man's world. But I didn't go into medicine for the money or the prestige.

"Patients in hospitals are the sickest ones who need psychiatric help the most," I say.

"I agree," Daniel Tanaka says. "I plan to work at a hospital and someday open a public clinic for people who can't afford places like RKH."

Jean and I smile at him. Ronald, clearly miffed because another man has won the ladies' admiration, changes the subject.

"RKH looks great from a distance," he says, "but if you look closer, you see the threadbare rugs, the faded upholstery, and the scuffed floors. They haven't redecorated in fifty years."

"I'm sure they've spent their budget on more important things," Jean says.

"They certainly did not spend it on research facilities," Dr. Mandel says. "The laboratory is very outdated. And there are too many hopeless cases on my ward."

"Face it—we're at a country club for people whose rich families want them out of sight, out of mind." Ronald Norton laughs glumly.

"They need psychiatric treatment just as much as if they were poor people in the kind of hospital that you probably wouldn't like any better than this one," Daniel Tanaka says.

Ronald Norton doesn't bother to answer, but anger narrows his eyes. He drains his wineglass and refills it from the bottle the waitress left on the table. The other residents look at me, waiting to see where I stand. Making critical remarks about one's employer is risky; such remarks have a way of reaching the wrong ears. And I, with my private purpose, am the one among us who can least afford to draw negative attention. But unless I contribute something to the conversation, they'll think I'm a dumb bump on a log.

"I'm concerned about the lack of time for psychotherapy," I say.

"No great loss," Ronald Norton says. "Psychotherapy in mental hospitals is worthless, if you ask me."

"She didn't ask you," Daniel Tanaka points out.

"What he means is, there are problems that psychotherapy can't solve," Jean hurries to explain.

"Bingo." The more wine he drinks, the more truculent her husband gets. "You can't talk people out of schizophrenia."

Annoyed at him, I feel compelled to defend my area of interest even though I don't want to embroil myself in an argument. "Psychotherapy can give patients valuable insight into their problems. And the bond that forms between doctor and patient can enhance the effectiveness of treatment."

Joseph Mandel nods. "I studied with disciples of Dr. Freud. There is much truth in his theory that unconscious memories, thoughts, and urges influence human behavior."

"Freud is fine in the office," Ronald Norton says. "I plan to interpret my clients' dreams and listen to their sexual fantasies all day long. But in a hospital, shock treatment, drugs, and lobotomy are the ticket."

He looks to his wife for support. She lowers her gaze. He says, "We've been all through this, honey. You know I'm right." He sets his empty glass on the table with a thud.

This is a matter under hot debate in the psychiatric profession. While I do believe that severe mental illness has biological components that require physical intervention, I myself am a case of a subject motivated by unconscious memories.

"Shock and lobotomy are barbaric," Joseph Mandel says. "They are like the experimental procedures that were used in the concentration camps."

Ronald Norton glares at him. "Are you calling me a Nazi?"

Temper burns in Joseph Mandel's deep-set eyes. "If the shoe fits . . ."

"I think combining psychotherapy with other treatments is the way to go," Daniel Tanaka says in an obvious attempt to smooth troubled waters. "It doesn't need to be all one or all the other." He and I exchange approving glances. "Why not use every weapon in our arsenal?"

Ronald Norton laughs nastily. "That's just what I would expect someone of your kind to say. Wishy-washy didn't win the war."

I gape in shock. As obnoxious as he is, I never expected him to go so far. Daniel Tanaka remains calm, but his features harden with the effort to control his temper. He says, "Bigotry and insensitivity don't make for a good psychiatrist."

Ronald Norton rises from his chair, his handsome face ugly with rage, and beckons Daniel Tanaka. "You want to come over here and say that?"

Daniel Tanaka and Joseph Mandel both rise, squaring their shoulders. Jean and I each fling out an arm in an instinctive, feminine urge to stop a fight. People at the other tables stare.

Not a minute too soon, Superintendent Van Pelt returns. He smiles and says, "Enjoying a lively discussion, I see." The men drop into their seats and force themselves to smile back. His eyes twinkle, and I'm sure he knows the men were butting heads like wild rams, taking out their frustrations on one another.

It's only our first day. How are we going to endure *three years* together?

No matter that RKH isn't a top-flight institution, we all worked hard to get here. That's the one thing we have in common. All our careers hinge on successfully completing our residencies. It's a pressure-cooker situation in which small disputes can blow up into a war.

Dr. Bullard and Dr. Mara return just as the main course arrives. It's prime rib with whipped potatoes, gravy, and creamed spinach. The waitresses pour red wine.

"I see where they spent the money," Ronald Norton mutters as he tucks into his food. "Not that I'm complaining."

The food is excellent, and my appetite comes back with each bite. Dr. Mara says, "I'm glad to have you with us, Dr. Kendall. How are you settling in?" She sounds genuinely interested.

"It's a bit overwhelming," I admit.

Dr. Mara chuckles sympathetically. "Believe me, I know. Working in a mental hospital is a challenge. And it's difficult being one of the few women in a profession dominated by men."

Her difficulties can't be anything compared to mine. Her husband is the superintendent and a member of the wealthy family that owns the hospital his ancestors founded.

Her smile says she knows what I'm thinking. "I didn't meet Adrian until I'd finished medical school, internship, and residency and I was working as a staff psychiatrist at Bellevue."

So she must have an idea of what I'm facing. "I suppose things were even more difficult then. How long have you worked here?"

"Twenty-one years." Dr. Mara laughs good-naturedly. "The stories I could tell you. Maybe I will someday. If you ever want to talk, just stop by my office."

"Thank you." My first day here has been like meeting different versions of myself: Rory, Dot and Maureen—the young mental patient; Jean Norton—the subservient wife I might be if I'd married during college; Dr. Mara—the established, confident professional I hope to be someday. Freud might have found me and my doppelgangers rich with material for psychoanalysis.

Superintendent Van Pelt dominates the rest of the conversation, regaling us with anecdotes at which we laugh, sometimes dutifully, sometimes with real amusement. My brief chat with Dr. Mara warms me, but I wonder what she remembers about the patients at Haven House in the summer of 1941. I don't know how to ask her without arousing her suspicion.

The meal drags on with coffee and cherry pie. I check my watch again. Ronald Norton asks snidely, "Is there someplace else you need to be?"

"Not at all." No need to mention the private expedition I have planned for tonight.

CHAPTER

7

When dinner is over, I make my farewells quickly and hurry up to the third floor of the mansion. My bed-sitting room is as large as the whole apartment I lived in during medical school in New York City. It's furnished comfortably but informally, with a rattan armchair and a bureau, nightstand, armoire, bookcase, and office desk and chair made of plain dark wood. A braided rug covers the parquet floor beside a single bed covered with a white chenille spread. In the spacious private bathroom, I fill the claw-footed white tub and settle in for a long soak.

The hot water relaxes my tense muscles, but my mind buzzes with nervous energy. The mansion is quiet; the walls are thick. If other rooms along the hall are occupied, I can't tell, but privacy is an illusion; I'm living in an institution where my superiors and colleagues can watch my comings and goings. I think of Rory Kirkpatrick and wonder if she's still in the cold pack. The memory of tight, wet sheets wrapped around me makes me claustrophobic, breathless. I wash quickly, climb out of the tub, dry myself, and dress in slacks and a blouse and walking shoes. Then I stand by the open window.

It's nine-thirty, the sky still faintly luminous. The full moon rides on gathering clouds. The cooling air smells of earth and pine. My room is at the back of the mansion, and I can see down to the terrace and across the garden to other buildings and beyond them, the woods.

Streetlights glow along the roads. An airplane drones overhead. Jittery with impatience, I wait until midnight. Then I put on my white laboratory coat and pocket my ring of keys to the hospital buildings. The coat will make me conspicuous but also give me an air of authority. I steal down the stairs, through the now deserted mansion, and out the door.

On our morning tour, I thought I'd learned my way around the campus, but soon I'm lost on curving, meandering roads. Wind scatters fallen leaves across my shadow, which appears and disappears as I pass through the pools of light beneath the widely spaced streetlamps. Owls hoot, reminding me that the land around RKH is wilderness, a natural barrier between the town and the mental patients.

A car draws up beside me. "Can I help you?" asks the driver, an older man in a dark green uniform and cap. His car sports the hospital's insignia. He's a security guard.

"Yes. I'm lost."

Suspicion draws his bushy eyebrows together. "Where are you going?"

"To the library."

His gaze lights on my white coat and my name badge, and his face clears. "Oh, you're one of the new docs. Hop in, I'll give you a lift."

The road he drives me along branches and circles. He stops the car by a path that leads to a one-story building. Up a low flight of stone steps, half hidden by shrubs, the library is classical revival in style, faced in beige stone. A lamp glows over an entrance framed by Ionic columns. After the guard gives me directions back to the mansion, I climb out of the car. Watching its taillights disappear, I fight an urge to run after it. The night presses in on me, and cicadas shrill like a warning signal as I walk up the path. This is what I came to RKH for, but I may not like what I find. I'm at the door, key ring in hand, when I hear a rustling noise in the bushes. I freeze, alarmed by sudden, primal instinct: *Someone's watching me.* But this isn't crime-ridden New York City; I'm perfectly safe. Then I hear giggles, their humor tinged with malicious mischief. They echo weirdly, and I recall the legend of the ghosts that haunt the hospital. Fumbling with the keys, I drop them twice before I find the one with the tag marked

"Library." I jam it into the lock, twist it with shaky fingers. Inside the building, I lock the door and lean my back against it, gasping until the panic subsides. Pocketing my keys, I look around.

The lamp over the entrance shines dimly through the fanlight set in the door. Archways on both sides of a narrow vestibule lead to rooms where bookshelves loom in the shadows. To my right, marble stairs descend into darkness. Urgency compels me toward them; fearful anticipation hobbles my feet. I flick the switch on the wall, and the stairs light up, beckoning me downward. At each step I pause to gather my courage and listen for any sounds of life. All I hear is a clock ticking somewhere. I hurry down the last few steps and find myself in a hall with doors to men's and women's lavatories and another marked "Tunnels."

Vertigo washes over me, and my vision begins to shimmer. I close my eyes and pant for a long moment until the vertigo recedes. Then I hasten down the passage, through the door labeled "Archives," and turn on the light. In the room, chairs surround a table equipped with green-shaded reading lamps. The walls are lined with file cabinets, one section labeled "Research." I skip it; I'm not here to read about old, obsolete experiments. The other section contains "Patient Records." I open the drawer of records for July 1941 and riffle through file folders, each labeled with a patient's name. My hand freezes on the one labeled "Lennox, Caroline."

My original name.

This folder contains the record of my time as a patient at RKH. Before I came back as a doctor, I couldn't have obtained it without asking for it and explaining why I wanted it, and unless I'd revealed that I was Caroline Lennox, it wouldn't have been released to me.

I've found a buried treasure chest only now to fear that it's Pandora's box.

As I pull out the folder, my knees wobble. I grope for a chair and fall into it, dropping the folder onto the table. I turn on the nearest lamp and open the folder. Its sharp edge slices my finger. I utter a little hiss of pain. As I wipe the blood from the cut with my handkerchief, my heart feels like it's beating in my throat, an anatomical impossibility. I open the folder. It contains few pages. My gaze rivets on a small photograph, black-and-white, stapled to the inside of the folder. It shows a teenage girl, her thin face framed by disheveled, chin-length blonde hair. Her puffy eyes are vacant and staring, her parted lips chapped. I've never seen this photograph, apparently taken of me the day I was admitted to RKH. My stomach contracts as if from a hard blow. In the photo, I'm wearing a white blouse with cross-stitch embroidery on the collar and yoke. The embroidery was blue; the blouse was my favorite that summer. I prop my elbows on the table, cradle my head in my hands, and stare at my younger self. She stares back at me across the distance of twelve years. My mind examines my recollection of that day.

My father helped me out of his black Cadillac. Half asleep, I staggered as we walked together. The pavement tilted beneath my feet. Trees slanted at a dizzying angle against a gray sky. My father caught my arm and dragged me along. Then came a blur of strange faces and muttering voices in a shadowy interior. A big, boxy wooden camera with a lens like the eye of a Cyclops pointed at me, and flashbulbs exploded in my face.

My only other clear memory from my time as a mental patient is of the day I left RKH. It was dark and cold. I wore my blue wool winter coat, and snowflakes glittered in the light from a streetlamp. My father put my suitcase in the trunk of the Cadillac and helped me into the front seat. Wide awake but confused, I looked at the brick building near the car. A nurse stood in a doorway decorated with multicolored Christmas lights. As my father and I drove off, she waved goodbye. Riding out through the gate, I looked backward at the illuminated sign that read "Resurrection Kill Hospital."

Those two memories are like parentheses with the words between them blacked out. Later, when I asked my father what had happened to me, he said, "It's over. Put it behind you." But I lost more than just the five months I spent at RKH. Most of the summer before I was admitted is lost to me. I know I had a nervous breakdown after my brother contracted tuberculosis, was sent to a sanitorium, and died there. I don't remember how I know. A veil of secrecy shrouded that period. My parents refused to discuss it. I supposed they were so grief-stricken by my brother's death that any mention of it was unbearably painful. Overwhelmed by my own grief, I stopped asking questions. I tried to put the past behind me, as my father had ordered. But I had panic attacks—fits of trembling, sweating, breathless terror so severe that I thought I would die. I also experienced a recurring nightmare in which I was traveling on my back through a tunnel with white tile walls, looking up at rusted pipes on the ceiling. Immobilized and terrified, I heard metal wheels rattling, voices echoing, and whirring fans. A blinding, sizzling, white explosion awakened me.

Dream interpretation is an important part of psychoanalysis. Since dreams aren't subject to the self-censorship that occurs when a person is awake, they can reveal thoughts, feelings, and desires without whitewashing. Freud called dream interpretation "the royal road to the unconscious mind." He said that tunnels symbolized female genitalia. A dream about them suggested a desire for sexual intercourse or a wish to return to the womb. I suppose that a burst of light at the end could symbolize orgasm or the shock of birth. Carl Jung, the Swiss psychiatrist, thought tunnels represented a journey to a confrontation with unresolved issues. But dream interpretation is subjective, and there's no "dream dictionary" in which you can look up "tunnels" and find an interpretation that applies to everyone. And my nightmare was so real that I thought it must stem from an actual event in my past. Its onset coincided with the beginning of my phobia.

Over the years, my panic attacks and nightmares grew less frequent. They plagued me during high school, occasionally recurred during college, but stopped by the time I entered medical school. My life was calm, like the surface of the ocean above dormant underwater volcanoes . . . until I decided to become a psychiatrist and underwent psychoanalysis with Dr. Emma Koffka as part of my training.

A tiny German-Jewish woman in her sixties, Dr. Koffka had obtained her medical degree from the University of Konigsberg. She worked with brain-injured soldiers during the first World War, then with patients in a sanitorium in Munich. Fleeing Nazi persecution, she emigrated to the United States and became a psychiatrist at Bellevue Hospital and an instructor at the Manhattan Psychoanalytic Academy. She had frizzy, gray-streaked dark hair and features that were sharp and austere but transformed by a wide smile that crinkled her whole face with laugh lines. Schooled in Freudian theory, Dr. Koffka believed that psychoanalysis was crucial to helping people understand and change their behavior by identifying and addressing the root causes of their psychological issues. She also believed that, in order to be a competent psychiatrist, one had to undergo psychoanalysis oneself.

"You must understand how it feels to stand in your client's shoes," she said. "And you must develop your self-awareness so that you will not confuse the client's issues with your own."

She taught me basic techniques for engaging with clients. One was the Rorschach test, in which the client is shown a series of ten inkblots and asked to describe what they resemble or suggest to him. His answers provide clues to his personality and emotions. Dr. Koffka considered the Rorschach too subjective to be a reliable diagnostic tool; she used it as an icebreaker when clients were too shy, inarticulate, or resistant to speak directly about themselves. In her office, we sat on the couch, side by side so that we couldn't make eye contact and she wouldn't influence me. She set the first card on the coffee table. The black inkblot printed on the white card was jagged and symmetrical.

"What do you see?" Dr. Koffka asked.

As I gazed at the inkblot, the air wavered, dissolving the bookshelves, the antique desk, the Persian rug, the sunny window, and Dr. Koffka. I had the strange sensation that my body had lost its solidity and my mind flowed freely into some other dimension. The inkblot expanded to fill my entire vision.

"I see two creatures, facing each other." My voice seemed to come from somewhere distant, outside of me.

"What are they?" Dr. Koffka asked.

They were wolves. Caught in their paws was a lamb flayed open down the middle. I was alarmed because I'd read up on the Rorschach, and I knew that most subjects see a butterfly in this inkblot. I also knew that the sort of images I saw were associated with mental disorders.

"They're butterflies," I said, "perched on a flower."

Dr. Koffka said nothing. Could she tell that I'd lied? She merely removed the card and laid down the next, a black inkblot that I interpreted as the figure of a man, angled as if seen from below, his hands on his hips, his huge feet planted on either side of a woman's head. A sense of menace set fear rocketing through me.

"It's a woman wearing a big hat." I struggled to keep my voice calm.

Dr. Koffka paused before showing me the next card. Gray, irregularly shaped blots surrounded a blank void. Suddenly I was in my nightmare of the white tunnel, the wheels rattling, the voices echoing. The void on the card burgeoned into the sizzling white explosion. I frantically tried to remember what normal people saw.

"They're heads in a circle. Girls, playing some sort of game." Instinctive realization dawned: Everything I'd seen in the inkblots related to RKH and that lost summer.

Dr. Koffka stacked the cards on the table, turned to me, and said quietly, "A psychiatrist must work out her own personal problems so that they do not affect her treatment of her clients." Then she waited in expectant silence.

I hated to deceive her. Even in my confused state, I knew I needed help, but if I confessed what I'd seen—and told her about my history—she might think I was unfit to be a psychiatrist and expel me from the academy, perhaps even prevent me from practicing medicine of any kind. All my work, all my hopes of helping the mentally ill, would be for nought.

It's over. Put it behind you.

I covered up my distress by starting a conversation about the pros and cons of the Rorschach test. Dr. Koffka never openly challenged me because she believed that aggressiveness only caused clients to retreat further into themselves. During my psychoanalysis, her remarks gently invited me to open up: *Healing others without first healing yourself can be as difficult as saving a drowning man when you can't swim.* The nightmare of the tunnel became a frequent, unwelcome visitor again. I realized I was broken and would never heal unless I understood what happened to me that summer. And how could I understand unless I remembered? So I came back to RKH, despite Dr. Koffka's advice not to train at a substandard institution, and now I can't predict whether the final outcome will be healing or new trauma.

I touch the folder on the table.

What secrets does it contain?

A scraping noise startles me. I look up and see a window near the ceiling, at ground level. Branches from bushes outside scrape the glass. It's not my imagination: Someone *is* watching me. They're trying to part the bushes and see inside the window. I can't afford to be caught and asked why I came to the library in the middle of the night and what I want with this particular file. If someone drew the connection between Caroline Lennox and me, it would end my residency, my career, and my chance to reconstruct my past.

I hurry to the cabinets. It takes me twenty long minutes to locate four suitable other files. I cram them and my own file under my white coat, then run up the stairs and out of the library, turning off the lights on my way. I lock the door and flee like a thief in the night.

CHAPTER

8

Dear Celia,

It's after midnight, and Haven House is quiet for the moment. Pretty soon somebody will start moaning or crying or screaming, and then everybody else will yell, "Shut up, I'm trying to sleep!" and the nurse will give her a shot and then it will be quiet again until somebody else starts up.

They took me out of the cold pack a few hours ago, and I'm sitting on my bed, feeling weak and twitchy but wide awake. The hall light shines through my open door. The door is always open. We're not allowed to have any privacy. Footsteps are coming down the hall. They're always checking on us. Tonight Fred is on duty. He's a big, muscular guy who fills the doorway as he peers in at me. He's about thirty years old but acts a lot younger. The kind of guy my dad calls "not the sharpest knife in the drawer." Well, if he were the sharpest, he wouldn't be working here. I'm always hearing the orderlies and nurses complain about how little they're paid. He grins and comes into my room, shutting the door.

I should have said the door is almost *always open.*

He sits down beside me and says, "Hi, baby." He kisses my cheek, a loud, wet, repulsive smack.

He thinks he's my boyfriend. I let him think so. I say, "Got a cigarette?"

He pulls the pack and lighter out of his pocket. My hands tremble as I put the cigarette in my mouth. He lights it, and I inhale greedily. The smoke calms my twitches. Fred puts his arm around me. He's warm and damp and stinks of sweat and stale aftershave, but I lean against him. Nobody else has hugged me since I've been here. Nobody touches me if they can help it. Some of the nurses are nice, but I think they've been warned not to touch me, because it might get me excited or turn them into lesbians. So it's kind of comforting to be hugged by someone who likes me, even though I don't like him. And I need to stay on his good side.

"Doris is out," Fred says.

Doris, the night nurse, has a boyfriend who's an orderly at Grace House. She sneaks out to see him, and she'll be gone for a couple of hours even though she's not supposed to leave Fred in charge of the ward for that long. I smile. This is a lucky break.

"I need some fresh air," I say.

"Oh, yeah?" Fred grins. He has small teeth between thick pink lips. "I need something else, baby."

We have a deal: He lets me go outside as long as I do my part of the bargain first. So I put my arms around his thick neck and stroke his bristly crewcut. When he kisses me, his tongue slides inside my mouth, and I almost gag. He tastes rotten, like he hasn't brushed his teeth today, and he's disgusting. But I need to be outside so badly that I would do anything, and after I stole the truck, my grounds privileges were revoked, and I'll be stuck indoors for God knows how long until they decide I've learned my lesson.

Fred's big, sweaty hands creep under my pajama shirt, up to my chest, and he moans. So far all he's done is feel me up, but he wants more every time. I'll just have to give it to him. It's not any worse than other things I have to put up with here. But as he fondles me, I wish it was you with me instead of him. I wish it so much that I start to cry.

Remember how you were always picking on me at school and saying mean things about me to your friends? I didn't fight back because I had a secret crush on you. You're so beautiful, with your red hair and amber eyes and creamy skin. Then that day I found you alone in the locker room after gym class. You looked at me with the same expression that I could feel on my face—pure, shameless wanting. I pressed you up against the lockers and kissed you on the mouth. And you kissed me back. That was our first kiss. Do you remember?

Fred grabs my hand and squeezes it around the hardness between his legs. I swallow tears. This is the first time he's made me touch him down there. He pumps for a minute, then he groans, and it's over, thank God. I wipe my eyes and smile at Fred, then I jam my bare feet into my moccasins. There's no time to waste on getting dressed. He stands up and grins, jingling the keys on the ring on his belt. He peeks out the door to make sure the nurse's station is vacant and none of the girls are up. We steal down the empty hall to Maureen Murray's room. She's a big lump in the bed, fast asleep. I tiptoe inside and tap her shoulder.

"Get up. We're going outside," I whisper.

Maureen stirs, blinks up at me, and yawns. "I'm so sleepy."

But she hauls herself out of bed, puts on her shoes, and follows me. So does Dot Powell when I awaken her. Maureen and Dot are my best friends here. Or rather, my only friends. They're not afraid of me, the pervert. Actually, Dot is more afraid of her own mind than anything else. She thinks that unless she does things a certain way, like brush her hair a hundred strokes starting at exactly nine o'clock every night, bad things will happen. Bad things are always happening somewhere, like fires or accidents, but she thinks they're her fault and she should be punished, and she cuts herself. Maureen is afraid of her hallucinations. Suppose a nurse comes walking toward her. Instead of the nurse, Maureen sees a bear or a dragon. So she goes berserk and starts yelling and hitting. You never know what'll set her off. The other girls avoid her because she scares them, and they avoid Dot because she hangs around with Maureen. I'm not afraid of Maureen, she's never gone off on me. She and Dot seem happy to do whatever I say, and the other girls treat us with respect. People call my dad "a leader among men." I guess I'm a leader among crazy girls.

Fred unlocks the door to the ward, looks to make sure nobody is around, then leads my friends and me to the back door. He opens it, hands me his watch, and says, "Have fun. Be back in an hour."

I buckle the watch's big leather strap around my arm. Outside, I look up at the dark sky and gulp deep breaths of the warm, sweet night air and I feel light enough to fly. For a whole hour, there won't be anyone telling me what to do or what not to do or what's wrong with me. That, in my opinion, is the perfect life. I skip across the empty parking lot and down a path that winds between trees. Dot and Maureen puff along after me. Soon the lights of Haven House are far behind us, and we laugh. Dot and Maureen dance under the moon that shines through the clouds. The feeling of being on an adventure is wonderful. I'd like to be an explorer someday, to see the whole world. But I'll be lucky to go to college and take a junior year abroad in Europe like my sisters did. If I get to Europe, maybe I'll take off for Egypt or Siam or Madagascar before anybody can stop me.

Dot asks, "Do you think we'll see the ghosts tonight?"

Maureen says, "Sure."

I don't believe in ghosts, but I'm glad Dot and Maureen do. Ghost hunting makes them willing to sneak out and risk getting caught and sent to lockdown, or worse. This place is spooky at night, even without ghosts. I act brave, but I really don't like to be out here alone.

"Let's go to the orchard. I want to look for Dr. Cutler," Dot says.

He's the doctor who supposedly shot himself. The apple trees look like crooked monsters, their leaves silver and black in the moonlight.

"There he is!" Dot cries, pointing. "Hello, Dr. Cutler."

"Ooh, half his face is gone," Maureen says, "and there's blood all over his clothes."

Maybe the ghosts are all in their heads, but the way they describe them and talk to them, I can almost see them too. I shiver. Dot and Maureen also claim to have ESP. They spend hours trying to guess each other's thoughts. Usually it just turns into a big giggle fest, but sometimes they scare me by guessing mine.

I look at Fred's watch. We have forty-five minutes left. "Come on." I hurry them out to the road.

A car comes toward us. The night guard is making his rounds. Before we're caught in the headlights, I drag the girls into the bushes. The car stops by the library and a woman in a white coat gets out.

"It's Dr. Kendall," Maureen whispers.

"Yeah," I whisper. "I met her when I was trying to run away. She came to see me while I was in the cold pack."

"She sat with Maureen and me at lunch. What do you think of her?" Dot forgets to keep her voice low.

I touch my finger to my lips. "She's just like all the rest. They pretend they want to help you, then they do you dirty."

We watch Dr. Kendall walk toward the library. Dot mutters, "Maureen almost told her that we see the ghosts outside. I had to stop her before she blabbed that we sneak out at night."

"Tattletale." Maureen shoves Dot.

Dot stumbles backward and jostles the bushes. Dr. Kendall's head snaps around. She heard. Maureen giggles. I shush her. Dr. Kendall runs to the library, drops the keys as she tries to unlock the door. Then she's inside. The basement windows light up.

Mother always said I'm too curious for my own good. I was maybe six years old when I realized I'm not like my sisters. I preferred to dress like a boy and play with boys and boys' toys. One day I led the housekeeper's two sons on a hunt for buried treasure, and we dug up the rose garden. They got spankings, and Mother made me embroider a sampler that said, "What are little girls made of? Sugar and spice and everything nice." I may never explore Siam, but I can try to find out what Dr. Kendall is doing. I urge Dot and Maureen to the nearest basement window. We kneel and look inside.

Dr. Kendall is sitting at a table, looking at an open file folder. We wait. Maureen parts the bushes outside the window to get a better view, and the branches scrape the glass. Dr. Kendall looks up, as frightened as if she's seen a ghost.

"Let's get out of here," I say.

I don't want to get caught, and we only have half an hour left. We circle the campus along a path through the woods to a clearing. There's a pointy-roofed house with an arched doorway and a big chimney in front. It looks like the witch's cottage in "Hansel and Gretel," but it's made of brick and wood and plaster instead of gingerbread. Yellow light glows in the front window, which is made of glass, not sugar candy.

This is one of three private cottages at RKH. They're called cottages even though they're big enough for a whole family. Each is for a patient who lives by himself with his own private nurses and servants instead of in the wards with the other lunatics. Faith Cottage and Charity Cottage are empty. Hope Cottage, where we are now, is the only one occupied. I got interested in it when I heard the nurses say that nobody knows who he is. They think he might be a rich criminal hiding from the law. Or the president's illegitimate, insane son. Or foreign royalty. Well, I made up my mind to find out who he is. I like knowing things that other people don't. Maybe I should be a detective someday. Are there any women detectives? I could be the first, if I ever get out of here. So when we started sneaking outside, I made Dot and Maureen come to Hope Cottage with me and spy on it. I might be a good spy, too. I could work for the FBI. You would know everything that's happened at Hope Cottage since then, if you'd read my letters.

It's a good thing the nurses didn't read my letters before they tore them up. If they knew what I've been up to, I'd be in lockdown now for sure.

Maureen nudges me and whispers, "He's coming."

We watch the door open and light spill out. The dark shape of the man who lives in Hope Cottage beckons to us. We move toward the cottage, drawn to it like Hansel and Gretel to the gingerbread house.

Stay tuned for my next episode.

Love,

Rory

CHAPTER

9

Safe in my room, I drop the file folders on the desk, kick off my shoes, and lie on the bed, panting from exertion. It took me an hour to find my way back to the mansion. My shirt is soaked with perspiration, my mouth is dry, and my heart still pounds with residual fear. Out on the dark, deserted campus, the ghosts of RKH seemed all too real. I lie there until I feel steadier, then I go to the bathroom and drink a glass of water. At my desk, I take my file from the stack and open it to the first page in the folder.

It's a form with RKH's insignia at the top, dated July 25, 1941. Typewritten words fill in the blanks. Patient name: *Caroline Marguerite Lennox*. Age: *14*. Date of birth: *October 22, 1927*. Occupation: *Student*. Address: *502 Chestnut Lane, Great Neck, New York*. Reason for admission: *Nervous breakdown*. Father: *Dr. William Lennox, M.D., surgeon*; Mother: *Mrs. Mildred Lennox, housewife*. Siblings: *1 brother, Brian Charles Lennox, age 16, student*.

Those basic facts about me were laid out on the form, but not the world behind them. Bringing that world into view was the object of my first psychoanalytical sessions with Dr. Koffka. Under her questioning, a portrait of my family emerged. It showed my father as a wealthy, respected pillar of the town, my mother as a glamorous socialite, my brother as the golden son who would follow in his father's footsteps, and myself as the dutiful daughter destined to go to finishing school and marry well. Dr. Koffka fleshed out the bare bones of the story according to Freudian interpretation. To her, I was a classic example of the Electra complex—I was in love with my father and wanted to replace my mother as his mate. She saw my brother and me locked in sibling rivalry. When I said that her interpretation was different from what I remembered, she invited me to try free association—to talk about my family without censoring myself or thinking too deliberately about what I was saying. She said it would help me uncover repressed thoughts, emotions, and memories.

I described a scene that repeated itself many times, with variations, throughout my childhood. On this particular occasion, it was Christmas Eve—seven months before I was admitted to RKH. My parents hosted a party for some dozen friends. They had many friends and hosted parties all year round. As a shy child, I dreaded those parties. In addition to too much drinking, raucous chatter, and feverish gaiety, there were plentiful opportunities to embarrass myself. I preferred to hide in my room with a book, but my father wanted his children on display. Dressed in my red velvet Christmas frock, I sat at the dining room table where he presided at one end and my mother looked beautiful at the other. As I picked at my roast beef, I thought I might come through this ordeal unscathed.

My father gestured to Brian and announced proudly, "Brian is a junior at Hotchkiss."

My brother grinned, blond and handsome and comfortable in the sudden limelight. He gracefully accepted praise from the guests and answered their questions about his classes and sports. He was on the football and basketball teams and belonged to the popular crowd at school. Basking in his reflected glow, I forgot myself.

Unfortunately, my father didn't forget me. "Caroline is a straight-A student at Knox School."

One of the women guests asked, "What's your favorite subject, dear?"

Panic-stricken, I couldn't remember what subjects I was taking, let alone my favorite. I had to clear my throat twice before I blurted, "Music."

I knew it was the wrong answer the moment I spoke, but any answer would have been disastrous. My father said, "Sing a song for us, Caroline. How about 'Joy to the World'?"

When I opened my mouth, tuneless croaks came out. My father regarded me with disgust, then laughed and said, "Maybe I should move her to a cheaper school. The sky-high tuition I'm paying is wasted on her." The guests laughed too.

I certainly wasn't in love with my father. I feared him because of these humiliating situations he always seemed to put me in. I think I would have been happy to never see him again.

My mother said, "Caroline, your hair is a mess." Her voice was slurred; she always drank too much at parties. "Go fix yourself up."

I didn't understand why she always added to the humiliation he caused. I ran upstairs to my room, lay on my bed, and sobbed.

A minute later, Brian came in. He sat beside me and said, "Cary, I'm sorry. I hate it when they do that to you."

He was the only one in my family who was ever kind to me. He was also the only person to call me Cary, an affectionate nickname that made me feel cherished and special.

"Why do they?" I cried.

He frowned, puzzled and worried. "Beats me."

"They don't love me," I said, and the truth hurt me even more than the humiliation.

"Yes, they do." Brian's voice lacked conviction. "They just have an odd way of showing it, I guess."

"Maybe they were treated that way when they were children. Maybe they don't know any better." I was making excuses for them, but also, I think, already finding my way toward a profession in which I could analyze and understand people's behavior.

"Maybe so," Brian said, "but it wouldn't let them off the hook." I was so thankful to have him on my side. "I hate how they treat me like something special and you like you don't matter."

"I guess I don't." My voice wobbled.

"You matter to me, Cary." He grasped my hand and smiled. "You're my favorite sister."

"I'm your *only* sister." I laughed, heartened by the joke we'd shared for as long as I could remember.

He stood up and tugged my hand. "Come on."

I shrank from him. "I don't want to go back to the party."

"That's not where we're going."

Minutes later, we were bundled in our winter coats and mittens and boots, sledding together down the snow-covered hill behind the house. I sat in front between his legs, secure with his arms around me. The night sky was filled with stars, and the wind was cold and fresh. I laughed for sheer joy.

By the time I finished telling this story, my face was drenched with tears. I last saw Brian before I went away to RKH. I don't even recall the occasion; it's another vanished memory. When I came back, he was gone. I still miss him every day.

"So you see, he wasn't my rival," I told Dr. Koffka. "He was my hero."

She regarded me with the same expression as when she'd sensed that I'd lied during the Rorschach test. After a weighty pause, she said, "It's possible for a girl to have both an Electra complex and a sister complex."

Meaning, I had an obsessive, unhealthy love for my brother as well as my father. I gave up arguing with her Freudian logic. I also didn't tell her about the tunnel nightmare or those lost months. Now I wonder what she would have made of them. Could she have helped me recover my memory, perhaps through hypnosis? There's a nineteenth century case in which a French neurologist, Dr. Hippolyte Bernheim, hypnotized a patient and told her that she had witnessed a violent rape. He fabricated the story about the rape, fed her the details, and when she awakened, she repeated them verbatim and insisted that she had indeed witnessed the crime. I want the truth, not a hypnotically induced fantasy.

When I told Dr. Koffka I'd made up my mind to do my residency at RKH and asked for a letter of recommendation, she said, "Very well. I hope you find whatever it is you are seeking."

She must have suspected that I had depths which Freudian analysis had failed to plumb. If I'd told her what I was really seeking at

RKH, might she have used her professional contacts to help me find out what had happened to me while I was a patient? I can't ask her. Mere days after I finished my training and she wrote my letter of recommendation, she died of a massive coronary. Too late, I wish I could confide in her and unburden myself. Now I'm alone with my secrets.

I belatedly notice that my file is much thinner than the others I took; it contains only two more pages. I turn to the next page, a continuation of my admission form. Commitment: *Involuntary.* Preliminary diagnosis: *Hysteria. Prior to her commitment, the patient experienced severe anxiety and agitation and hallucinations. Deemed a danger to herself, she was under sedation when she arrived at RKH.*

The sedation explains my drowsy, confused state. The preliminary diagnosis leaves me as mystified as ever. "Hysteria" was originally associated with disorders of the female organs. Freud extended it to cover psychosomatic illness—organic symptoms with psychological origins. He theorized that hysteria was caused by phenomena ranging from penis envy and past trauma to moral conflicts. Dr. Koffka said the diagnosis had fallen out of favor and called it an old-fashioned, catchall diagnosis for any female patient exhibiting any form of socially unacceptable behavior that lacks a clear reason.

My form offers no clear reason for my "anxiety and agitation" and fails to describe the "hallucinations." It looks as though my midnight expedition to the library was a disappointing waste of time. Without much hope, I turn to the last page in the file.

It's a photostat—white text on a black background. In the top left corner is the seal of the town of Resurrection, New York. The heading, in Gothic calligraphy, reads, "Certificate of Death." Someone must have put another patient's document in my file by mistake. Then I see the line beneath the heading. In the blank for "Name of Deceased" are the hand-printed words *Caroline Marguerite Lennox.* "My Cause of Death" was *Natural.* I frown in bewilderment.

According to the town's official record, I am dead.

Perhaps another patient had the same name as mine, unlikely though it seems. But the date of birth and place of residence are my own, and my parents are listed as the decedent's next of kin. An eerie chill washes through me as I read the place and date of death: Resurrection Kill Hospital, December 14, 1941.

I was discharged from RKH in December 1941, but this certificate says I died here.

How can that be?

My hands pat my arms in a frantic, instinctive attempt to convince myself that I'm solid flesh and bone. Common sense helps me regain control of my thoughts. I'm here, now, living and breathing, twelve years after my discharge. The death certificate seems more like a deliberate falsification than an honest mistake. But who was responsible?

The person who certified my death was *Dr. Isaac Franz.* The name is unfamiliar. Was Dr. Franz on the RKH staff while I was a patient? Is he still here? I don't see how he could have faked my death on his own. He must have had the cooperation of his superiors—including Superintendent Van Pelt. My mind reels with confusion, disbelief, and more questions. Why would they fake my death? What possible benefit could they have gained?

One thing is horrifyingly certain: My parents were a party to the deception. It explains so much that happened after my discharge from RKH.

When I arrived at home on Long Island, I found the house in a state of upheaval—furniture covered in tarps and wound with rope, pictures taken off the walls, and everywhere, open boxes filled with our possessions. "We are moving," my father said.

A few days after we arrived in Grosse Pointe, Michigan, and settled into our new house, my father told me that he and my mother were divorcing. My mother and I were to live by ourselves. I'd known they didn't get along, and I supposed that, with Brian gone, they had nothing to hold them together anymore. They wouldn't feel obligated to stay together for my sake; I knew how little I meant to them. Before my father left, he took my mother and me to a lawyer, and she and I signed the papers required to legally change our names. Caroline Marguerite Lennox became Claire Marie Kendall. I don't know where

"Kendall" came from, and of the choices of first names offered to me, I picked "Claire" because it sounded like "Cary," my brother's special nickname for me.

"You'll have a fresh start," my father said. "Your mental hospital record won't ruin your future."

At the time, I accepted whatever I was told, without question. Everything was so jarring and confusing, there seemed no other choice. The big changes in my life coincided with big changes in the world. The Japanese had bombed Pearl Harbor a week before I came home from the hospital, and America was at war. My past as a mental patient was lost in the general commotion. In our new hometown—an affluent suburb of Detroit—strangers gathered on the corners of the unfamiliar streets, discussing the war. News from Europe and Asia blared from radios in the unfamiliar shops. At my new private school, students collected money for the soldiers, air raid drills interrupted classes, and the talk was all about relatives and friends in the army. No one paid much attention to me, the shy, quiet new girl. My mother said my father was working as a surgeon at a military hospital. If she said where he was going to live after the war ended, I don't remember. I never visited him. During the years since, I've believed that, by changing my name, he'd protected my future.

Now my new name seems part and parcel of an attempt to maintain the pretense that I was dead. Relocating my mother and me to Michigan made it unlikely that we would run into someone from our past, and after the move, we lost touch with our relatives. Was the estrangement deliberate, to keep them in the dark about our affairs? Installing me in RKH for five months had gotten me out of the way while my parents reorganized our lives. A birth certificate, school records, and other documents with my new name were obtained somehow. But why go to such lengths to engineer the fraud? Why the conspiracy between my parents and RKH?

I can't ask my mother, who died in 1942 of a head injury sustained when she fell down the stairs while drunk. I can't ask my father; I haven't seen or spoken to him in years, and I don't even know where he is. I'm too stunned to think how to find out the answers.

Suddenly I remember Maureen and Dot's ghost stories. I don't believe them, but at least one dead former patient has come back to Resurrection Kill Hospital—I'm the ghost of Caroline Lennox.

CHAPTER 10

Every day, Superintendent Van Pelt leads morning rounds for the residents. We tour different houses, where he introduces us to patients whose cases he considers salient. They respond eagerly to his attention, and I think each feels better afterward. He has an effect on them that seems almost magical—a talent that can't be learned or imitated. I can only hope that I possess that talent and it will develop during the course of my career.

Once a week, we have afternoon clinical training sessions. This is Wednesday, and we're riding in the tram to our first training session since we started work at RKH on Monday. Superintendent Van Pelt is deep in conversation with Dr. Mandel while I sit with Daniel Tanaka and the Nortons. The roof shades us from the sun that glares down on the campus, but my white coat is uncomfortably warm. A heat wave is pushing temperatures into the nineties.

"Man, in three days, I've met more certified lunatics than most people meet in their entire lives," Ronald Norton says.

Daniel Tanaka and I laugh in spite of ourselves. Ronald is earning a reputation as the most obnoxious resident, and his comment wasn't particularly funny, but we understand that humor is necessary for keeping one's own sanity.

"We mustn't call them lunatics," his wife says, gently reproachful.

"One of them called me a chicken-hearted commie bastard to my face," Ronald says. "I can call them anything I want behind their backs."

Judy Abbott calls me every vulgar name when I come to insert her feeding tube, but I feel compelled to defend the patients. After all, I was once one of them—a certified lunatic at age fourteen. "They're helpless and frustrated. We shouldn't blame them for lashing out."

Daniel and Jean nod, but Ronald shrugs and says, "I actually like some of my lunatics. They're smarter and more fun than some normal guys I know."

Perhaps I judged him prematurely. I've been so busy with paperwork and emergencies that I've had no chance to get to know my patients. I've barely seen Rory, Dot, and Maureen.

Ronald Norton looks at his watch. "These rounds and training sessions are going to take up a lot of time. I'll have to work late to catch up."

So will the rest of us, but I welcome the rounds. Being in the strange position of investigating my own death, I need to find patients or staff members who were at RKH with Caroline Lennox, who might know what happened to her here. Visiting different houses gives me a chance to look for them. Nobody I've met so far seems familiar. Above all, I need to find Dr. Isaac Franz, who signed my death certificate. He's not on the list of current personnel.

The tram stops outside Shelter House, a two-story brick mansion with white trim and columns and a circular driveway. It's the lockdown house. Inside, the reception room is bare of vases, figurines, or other decorations that could be broken or thrown. An iron grille surrounds the staircase we climb to the second floor, where the hall is empty of patients and safety glass encloses the nurse's station. The walls and linoleum floor are drab gray, and the ammonia odor of urine stings my eyes. It's another scene from insane asylums of old—grimly depressing.

"We put patients in lockdown when they're especially dangerous to themselves or others," Superintendent Van Pelt says.

We peer through the small, wire-gridded window in each steel door along the hall. The rooms are small with padded walls and no furniture except beds bolted to the floors. I wonder if I was ever in lockdown. The patients in the beds look more comatose than dangerous.

"They're sedated with Thorazine," Superintendent Van Pelt says, "also known as the chemical straitjacket."

While he describes Thorazine as a humane alternative to physical restraints, a breakthrough in the treatment of schizophrenia, mania, and other disorders, I'm wondering what part he might have played in my "death." Would he commit or abet such a fraud and risk the reputation of his hospital? I feel an increased urgency to find out what happened to me that summer. It must be connected to something far more serious than I can imagine. Why else would anyone fake a fourteen-year-old girl's death? At the same time, I'm aware that if I ask questions, people will wonder what I'm up to, and I'll risk exposing my past as a former RKH patient named Caroline Lennox.

Two orderlies pushing a stretcher join us as Superintendent Van Pelt unlocks the door to a room. Inside, we gather around the woman in the bed. A sheet covers her stout body. Her short, tousled hair is too red to be a natural color. Her eyes are sunken, and deep lines carve parentheses from her nose to her slack mouth.

"This is Mrs. Alice Dunne, a forty-three-year-old schizophrenic," Superintendent Van Pelt says. "She was admitted last year after exhibiting severe paranoia. She thought her neighbors were conspiring to kill her. The crisis came when she tried to strangle her young son because she thought he was in on the conspiracy. Her symptoms have been resistant to medication. The next phase of her treatment is electroshock therapy. That's the subject of today's training session."

I sense that my fellow residents share my curiosity. I think we've all heard of electroshock therapy but never observed it. The orderlies transfer Mrs. Dunne to the stretcher. She groans but doesn't wake up.

"She's sedated with phenobarbital," the superintendent explains. "It minimize's the discomfort from electroshock. She's also been given succinyl choline to relax her muscles and prevent spinal fractures during the convulsions."

These pharmaceutical details go right over my head because we're taking the stairs to the basement. We meet the orderlies, who've brought the patient down in the elevator. The dank chill arouses my claustrophobia even before Superintendent Van Pelt opens the door marked "Tunnels." A chilly draft that smells of detergent and mildew wafts from the doorway. Fear paralyzes me. I can't go in there. But I have to or I'll disgrace myself. Step by reluctant step, I follow the other residents into the tunnel. It's a dim corridor with white tiled walls that seems to go on forever. As the orderlies push the stretcher ahead of us, the echo of its wheels rattling mingles with distant voices. Nausea washes through me; sweat beads on my face. The reality of my footsteps on the floor fades away. I'm riding on my back on a stretcher, looking up at the pipes attached to the low ceiling, shuddering with terror as an unseen person pushes me.

This is the scene of my recurring nightmare.

As my heart thuds in my ears, I hear Superintendent Van Pelt's voice, faint and disembodied. "The uneducated public thinks electroshock is a modern technique, but it's as old as the hills. Ever since electricity was discovered, doctors have been shocking patients, trying to cure ailments when they didn't have any remedies. In the eighteenth century, it was used to treat hysterical fits, then for other mental disorders during the nineteenth century. Nowadays, electroshock is prescribed mainly for schizophrenia and manic depression. But we don't know exactly how it works. The brain is the dark frontier of science."

Weak and unsteady, I trip on a rough patch of floor. Daniel Tanaka catches my arm. His support restores me to my present-day self, walking with my fellow residents, led by Superintendent Van Pelt, the orderlies, and the stretcher. The tunnels are a labyrinth, our destination a windowless room furnished with a desk, magazines on a table, and a row of empty chairs. The room is as cold as the tunnels; the dark-haired nurse at the desk wears a white cardigan sweater over her uniform. It's a normal scene transplanted to a cave, surreal and disorienting. Claustrophobia squeezes my lungs; I struggle for air. The orderlies wheel the patient through the office, down a short hallway, and through one of four numbered doors. The nurse accompanies our group into the room. The orderlies lift the patient onto a hospital bed. Along the walls are a sink, glass-fronted cabinets, and a counter with jars, paper towels, and medical paraphernalia. Superintendent Van Pelt points to a wheeled cart near the bed. The cart's top shelf holds a machine the size and shape of a breadbox. Meters, switches, and dials stud the front of the machine's beige-enameled metal case. A black cable hangs from its back to the lower shelf, ending in an instrument that looks like headphones with black-rimmed metal discs instead of earpieces.

"Ladies and gentlemen, meet the newest version of the electric convulsion apparatus," Superintendent Van Pelt says proudly.

I have no memory of the apparatus or this room, but I'm certain that when I rode on the stretcher through the tunnels, I was bound for electroshock therapy. It's the cause of the terror I feel in my nightmare.

The orderlies cover the patient with a sheet and buckle straps around her body. The nurse swabs her temples with a greasy substance, then puts the headband on her, positioning the metal discs on her temples and securing a chinstrap. She gently opens the patient's mouth. The patient mewls, not entirely unconscious. The nurse inserts a pink rubber bite stick between her teeth.

"I need a volunteer," Superintendent Van Pelt says.

The other residents step forward eagerly. I hang back, assailed by the bizarre sensation of being two people at the same time. One the psychiatrist standing in her white coat, the other Caroline Lennox, my fourteen-year-old self, strapped down with electrodes on my head.

"Dr. Jean Norton, step right up," the superintendent says.

She smiles, pleased to be chosen, then casts an anxious glance at her husband. He and the other men look disappointed. Thank God it wasn't me.

Superintendent Van Pelt chuckles. "Don't worry—you'll all have your chance eventually." He instructs Jean how to use the electric convulsion apparatus. "Turn on the main switch." When she obeys, a red light on the machine goes on. "Turn the timer dial to one second and the voltage dial to seventy volts. Good. Now throw the voltage switch."

My breath catches as the needles on the meters jump. A mechanical hum emanates from the device. My mind is like a movie projector that shows me different images alternating in rapid succession. I see Mrs. Dunne's body convulse and her back arch. I see Caroline Lennox grimace, her eyes squeezed shut and her teeth clamped down on the bite stick. The white explosion from my nightmare obliterates both images. A sizzling sensation tightens my muscles and clenches my jaws as I relive a moment when the electricity shot through my head twelve years ago. Freudian dream interpretation be damned—my nightmare wasn't about sex.

The timer clicks off. Mrs. Dunne falls back on the bed. The sizzling sensation fades, and I'm trembling, clammy with cold sweat. Fortunately, everyone else's attention is on the patient.

"Turn the voltage up to a hundred," Superintendent Van Pelt orders Jean. "The seizure needs to last two minutes."

Jean twists the dial. The device hums louder. A memory blazes in my mind like fireworks in the night sky. Prone on the bed, my eyelids stretched wide open, my whole body vibrating from the current, my teeth locked on the bite stick, I stare up at a doctor and nurse who loom over me. They calmly observe my agony. The doctor is a younger Superintendent Van Pelt, his hair gray instead of white. The nurse is the same one who's standing with the other residents now.

Nurse Janice Peters, I suddenly remember.

She was my favorite nurse, the youngest, kindest one.

The last time I saw her, she was waving goodbye to me from a doorway decorated with Christmas lights.

The hum from the device rises to a shrill, ear-splitting pitch. I can't bear to watch the patient and relive the ordeal through her. The other residents' expressions are somber, controlled—the masks that doctors wear when confronted with gory medical spectacles. The bed rattles, and involuntary grunts issue from Mrs. Dunne.

Superintendent Van Pelt raises his voice over the hum. "Turn off the voltage switch."

Jean obeys. Mrs. Dunne collapses with a loud thump. Relief shows on the other residents' faces. Sweat trickles from my forehead into my eyes. I surreptitiously wipe it away with the sleeve of my white coat. Mrs. Dunne's raspy breathing is loud in the sudden silence. Her eyelids flutter open. Her gaze is foggy, confused. Nurse Janice removes the bite stick and the electrodes, then takes her pulse and blood pressure.

"Welcome back, Mrs. Dunne." Superintendent Van Pelt bends over the bed. "How are you feeling?"

He seems unaffected, cheerful even, while Nurse Janice, the orderlies, and my fellow residents are somber. A new emotion ignites in me. It's anger, directed at this man who prescribes electroshock therapy and probably never experienced it himself.

Mrs. Dunne strains to focus her gaze on the superintendent. "Where am I?" Her voice is hoarse. "What happened?"

"You're in the electroshock therapy clinic," Superintendent Van Pelt says. "You just had your treatment."

She frowns. "I don't remember."

He pats her shoulder. "It's all right."

"My head hurts."

"We'll give you something for that. You're going back to your room now, to rest." As the orderlies unstrap Mrs. Dunne, transfer her to the gurney, and wheel her out the door, he says, "Headaches, nausea, and muscle weakness are side effects of electroshock. So is amnesia."

Foreboding trickles through me like ice water in my veins.

"Amnesia is rather a blessing," Superintendent Van Pelt says. "If patients can't remember their previous treatment, they won't fear the next one."

My lips part in protest. Electroshock was so terrifying that I remember it even though I forgot so much else.

The superintendent asks if there are any questions about the procedure. I say, "How much does the patient forget?" I'm surprised at how normal and businesslike I sound.

"Usually just the treatment itself. Some patients may be unable to retain information learned shortly afterward. Some experience short-term memory loss months later."

"Do patients ever forget things that happened before their electroshock therapy started?"

"In rare cases, after extended courses of treatment. There was one woman whose daughter got married a month before she came here.

She completely forgot the wedding. The whole big day was erased from her memory."

The other residents shake their heads, sympathizing with the poor woman. Revelation stuns me. Electroshock treatment erased virtually the whole summer of 1941 from my mind.

"It's called retrograde memory loss," Superintendent Van Pelt says. "Sometimes the memories come back. Sometimes not."

I now know how I lost my memory. It's a start toward unburying my past, but my brief spate of euphoria gives way to indignation.

"In the case of the woman who forgot her daughter's wedding, the benefits of electroshock greatly outweighed the disadvantages," Superintendent Van Pelt says. "She had such severe paranoid schizophrenia that she had hit people on the street and been arrested twice. After her therapy, she was tranquil and happy."

What benefits were there for *me*? I don't believe I was mentally ill before I was committed to RKH, and if I were to diagnose myself now, I would say that the nightmares and panic attacks I've experienced *since* my treatment constitute mental illness. What happened to me at RKH *made* me sick, and whoever was in on the conspiracy not only erased my memory, they erased Caroline Lennox. It was a form of murder. She's virtually as dead as her fake death certificate proclaims.

"That's it for today, doctors," Superintendent Van Pelt says. "Back to your posts."

The other residents thank him, but good manners desert me. Was he responsible for my "death" as well as my amnesia? What did he have to gain? I'm growing certain that my erased memory wasn't just an unfortunate side effect of shock treatment but part of a deliberate cover-up . . . but of what?

As my colleagues and I traipse out of the clinic, I glance over my shoulder at Nurse Janice. She smiles at me, a pleasant, impersonal smile. She doesn't recognize me. But we'll get reacquainted soon, when I ask her a few questions.

CHAPTER 11

BY THE TIME I get back to Haven House, it's two o'clock. The wards are quiet in the oppressive heat. The radio is tuned to classical music. In the living room, two girls are styling Lulu Shelton's long blonde hair, as if she's a big doll. I've learned that Lulu is the daughter of an old-money family in Philadelphia, mentally retarded due to oxygen deprivation at birth. Her intellectual and emotional development stalled at approximately age ten. Prone to tantrums, she was sent to a series of special schools, all of which expelled her for hitting her classmates. At fourteen, she sneaked out of her home at night to meet boys. Her parents, fearing pregnancy and scandal, committed her to RKH, where she was given a lobotomy to "calm her down." It left her incontinent, unable to speak intelligibly, walk normally, or feed, dress, or wash herself. She lives in Haven House with the most disturbed patients because she still has violent tantrums.

Seated in my tiny office behind the nurse's station, I bow my head over the charts I'm reviewing and ponder my new dilemma. I'm at RKH to complete my psychiatric training and serve my patients, yet I also came here to pursue a private agenda. Can I do both without violating my professional or moral code of conduct? Investigating my past is already putting my own mental health at risk. If I continue, will I be in any shape to treat my patients?

Dr. Koffka once said, "A doctor need not have her own life in perfect order before she can help other people." Although I doubt I can help Lulu or the chronic, seriously ill patients who haven't improved despite years of care from experienced doctors, I believe I have a chance with Rory, Dot, Maureen, and others. I don't want to leave before I've done my best for them . . . or before I've solved my personal mystery. And there's one additional reason to stay at RKH. Has whoever erased my memory with shock treatments and faked my death done the same, or worse, to other patients? Is it still happening now?

I listen to the sounds of the ward, the muted voices, Mozart on the radio and occasional howls from patients in isolation cells. Outside the window, a cloud casts a shadow over the campus. I could report my experience to the authorities, but which ones? Not the RKH board of directors, who might be complicit in the fraud. The police? I haven't any evidence except my death certificate, and the fact that I'm a former mental patient would deeply undermine my credibility. Besides, if my story becomes public, RKH will fire me, no other hospital will want me, and I'll never practice psychiatry or any other kind of medicine. But I can't let matters lie. I have to find out whether current RKH patients are in danger. If they are, then I'll risk my career to protect them, come what may. But I need proof that such danger exists, and the only way to get it is to stay at RKH and keep digging. Digging my own grave, perhaps.

But Caroline Lennox is already in my grave, and I feel as if I'm exhuming her corpse.

It's three o'clock, time for shift change, when Nurse Norris gives an oral report to the nurses who will begin their afternoon shift in half an hour. I've been listening in on this daily report and the one at seven AM when the night staff hands the ward over to the morning staff. It's a way to keep up with things that happen while I'm away from Haven House.

"Word just came down from Dr. Mara," Nurse Norris says. "Dorine Fletcher, Martha Anderson, and Nancy Warren are scheduled for discharge on Monday."

"Why?" I ask. "Their charts show that they haven't made any improvement."

Nurse Norris answers slowly and carefully, as though I'm a child. "That's why they're being discharged. Because they aren't getting better, and they won't get better. We need their beds for patients who *can* get better. Dr. Mara is cutting out the dead wood."

Crudely put, but I can see the point. Private mental hospitals are overfilled with chronic incurables while the demand for beds is always rising.

"Besides, they can't afford to stay. RKH just raised the rates," Nurse Norris says.

Clearly I'm not the only one with an agenda besides patient care. RKH is balancing patient care versus its own financial interests. "Where will they go?" I ask.

"The state hospital, if their families don't want them at home."

State hospitals are overfilled too. The number of mental patients in the country has increased dramatically during the twentieth century. The reasons are debatable. Perhaps the complexity of modern life has exacerbated mental illness; perhaps fewer families are willing to tolerate their disturbed relatives at home when it's possible to send them away.

"We're stuck with patients like Leonora Hirschfeld," Nurse Norris says. "She's been here since 1932—first, at Haven House, then she moved to Solace House a few years ago. RKH is her permanent home, courtesy of her big trust fund."

Leonora Hirschfeld was at Haven House while I was a patient. I must speak with her, but I don't have time now. After the report is finished, I make my rounds of the wards. I find Dot and Maureen in Maureen's room, sprawled on the bed, eating chocolates. When they see me, Dot shoves the box under the bedspread. They swallow their last bites and sit up. They aren't supposed to eat between meals because they're overweight.

Maureen licks her lips. Dot says, "Oh, hi."

I greet them and say, "I came to talk about your treatment program."

They glance at the upholstered rattan armchair, just as they did at the empty place at the table when we had lunch together. "Okay," they say cautiously.

I take the chair at the desk instead of sharing the armchair with whatever figment of their joint hallucination is seated there. "Have you ever been in group psychotherapy?"

It's part of the special program I want to start at Haven House. I thought the girls might have participated in it elsewhere, but they shake their heads. From reading their files I know they've both been in other hospitals. Dot is manic-depressive with obsessive neurosis, Maureen schizophrenic. Yesterday I asked Dr. Bullard for permission to try group psychotherapy, and he said, "Sure, whatever you think might help."

"In group psychotherapy, a small number of people meet together with a psychiatrist," I explain. "They share their experiences and problems and help each other."

Modern group psychotherapy originated in 1905, when Dr. Joseph Pratt experimented with tuberculosis patients in Boston. In the 1930s, its use expanded to prison inmates and psychiatric patients; then, after the war, to emotionally disturbed soldiers and victims. Group psychotherapy enables understaffed hospitals to treat multiple patients simultaneously. Here at RKH, it could solve my problem of not having enough time with each patient every week.

Dot and Maureen look mildly curious. Encouraged, I say, "I'd like to start a group psychotherapy program here at Haven House, and I think the two of you are excellent candidates." They're alert and coherent, unlike some other patients. "Are you interested?"

For best results, participation should be voluntary. Maureen and Dot glance at the armchair, then at each other, then say, "Sure."

They probably think they can't afford not to cooperate. As their psychiatrist, I have a say in important decisions such as whether they get electroshock treatment or when they'll be discharged. Still, they perk up, either flattered to be chosen or eager to score points with me.

"Do we start right now?" Dot asks.

"We can. If it goes well, I'll bring other patients into the group."

"How does it work?" Maureen asks.

I'm wading into uncharted waters. I've only experienced group psychotherapy via acting as the psychiatrist with classmates at the Manhattan Psychoanalytic Academy. It's a free-flowing process that requires the psychiatrist to improvise based on what the participants say and lead the conversation into productive channels. "I'll start by asking how you're feeling right now."

The girls look at each other, then chorus, "I'm okay."

I grope for questions to break the ice. "Has anything happened that you'd like to talk about?"

Maureen says, "The other night we saw—"

"My mother came to visit me yesterday," Dot interrupts loudly.

I wonder what Maureen meant to say before Dot cut her off. Rather than risk more talk of ghosts, I ask Dot, "What happened during your mother's visit?"

"She brought me a birthday present. It was a bathrobe." Tears roll down Dot's plump cheeks.

Surprised by the strong emotion unleashed so early in our session, I say, "Why did that upset you?"

"She knew I wanted new sheet music. But she thinks a bathrobe is the only kind of thing I need because I'm never getting out of here." Dot says between sobs, "I threw the bathrobe in the trash. She was all perky and sweet. She said she understood I was having a bad day, then she left."

Maybe Dot's mother put on a cheerful front because her own anguish might further upset Dot. But my duty is to support Dot, not make excuses for her mother. "I'm sorry to hear that."

"Sometimes she smothers me with love and milk and cookies and 'put on your sweater, it's cold outside,' and 'if anything happened to you, I would die,'" Dot says. "And sometimes she acts like she doesn't care. She's the one who's crazy, not me."

There's a psychological phenomenon known as the "schizophrenogenic mother"—a mother whose neglect or overprotectiveness causes her child's mental illness. Perhaps Dot's mother is one.

"I can see why it's difficult for you," I tell Dot. "We can explore ways for you to cope with your mother."

Dot gives me a tremulous, grateful smile. I'm glad to think I've begun to establish a therapeutic bond with her. She says, "I want to go back to Vassar. I'm majoring in music and drama. I write songs, and I pitch them to the music publishers on Broadway. Someday I'll sell a song, and it will get recorded and be a hit. Someday I'll act in movies and be famous."

Her dreams are so big. My heart aches for her because mental illness makes even small dreams hard to achieve.

"It's not so bad here," Maureen says. "We have fun, don't we?" She seems anxious to convince Dot, afraid that Dot will leave her behind. "We're friends."

"We'll still be friends after we get out," Dot reassures her.

"I'm never getting out." Maureen's eyes fill.

With her violent episodes, she's much sicker than Dot, and she's sane enough to know it. I'm about to suggest exploring ways to cope with her schizophrenia—which is all I can offer—when Rory appears at the door.

"Can anyone join the party?" Rory wears a pale blue dotted-Swiss dress with a full skirt and puffy sleeves, her dark hair curled and adorned with a blue bow.

"Hi, Rory!" Dot says.

"Come on in," Maureen says.

Rory saunters over to the armchair. Having read her file, I know that as part of the program to cure her of lesbianism, she's supposed to dress in feminine style and take comportment lessons. Despite her delicate white sandals, she walks like a boy. Her curls are disheveled, her bow crooked. At first glance she looks charmingly pretty, at second, unhappily wrong. She sits down in the chair with her legs apart. As Maureen and Dot beam at her, I understand their glances at the empty chair. It and the vacant seat at the lunch table belong to Rory. The three of them are a clique, and Rory is the leader. The other girls look to her for guidance even when she's absent.

"What are you doing here?" Rory asks me.

"I'm starting a psychotherapy group," I say. "Would you like to participate?" She's the patient I most want to include.

"What are you going to do to me if I don't?"

"Nothing. It's completely voluntary."

"Yeah, right."

"We're going to talk about our problems and work on them together," Dot says.

"Come on, Rory, it'll be better with you here," Maureen urges.

Rory's expression darkens. "She's trying to trick you into telling her things she can use against you."

Her friendship with the other girls must be one of the few bright spots in her existence, and I think she's afraid their loyalty could shift from her to me. A disadvantage of group therapy is that a hostile, resistant person can disrupt it. I still want to include Rory, but breaking through her defensive shell will be even more difficult if she sees me as a rival.

"Nothing that's said in the group will be used against anyone," I say. "I'm here to help you help each another cope with your challenges."

The other girls look at me, then at Rory, their expressions worried. I sense they want to believe that group psychotherapy can turn their troubled lives around, but they're used to accepting her leadership.

"This is a prison, and she's just another jailer who's paid to keep us locked up so that RKH can rake in more money," Rory says.

Her insolence goads me to defend myself. "I'm not here to keep you locked up," I snap. "I want you to be able to leave." I immediately realize my mistake. I reacted not only to her insult, but to my fear that I'm doing to these girls what was done to me when I was fourteen. I've let my own issues undermine my professional detachment.

"Oh? Then why don't you let us out?" Rory demands. "Sign the paper that says we're not crazy anymore?"

Flustered because she's gotten under my skin, I say what psychotherapists say to validate a patient's feelings and defuse an argument. "I'm hearing that you're angry. Shall we talk about it?"

She tilts her head, giving me a look that combines scorn with pity. She's been a patient longer than I've been a psychiatrist, and she's probably seen every therapeutic ploy. "I don't think you're a bad person. So I'm going to warn you: Some pretty shady stuff has happened at RKH. If you don't want to be mixed up in it, you'd better get out."

Dot and Maureen nod. Rory smiles; she's got them back under her thumb. I flounder in a sea of new dilemmas. Rory is obviously trying to scare me away, but I already know that "shady stuff" has happened here, I'm already mixed up in it, and they may be in more danger than I am. I want to know how much she knows, but gossiping with patients is unprofessional.

"The focus of group psychotherapy is you, not me," I tell the girls. "Dot, you were talking about your mother—"

Dot flaps her hand, as if shooing away a mosquito. "There were three mysterious deaths."

Vexed because Rory has succeeded in derailing the session, I attempt to get it back on track. "You've already told me the legend about the patients who died in 1885. So let's—"

"Those weren't the only ones," Maureen says. "There were three more. In the summer of 1941."

The summer when I was a patient at RKH. The breath goes out of me as if all the oxygen has been sucked from the room.

A mischievous smile lifts the corner of Rory's mouth: She saw that the news of the more recent deaths struck a nerve. "I suppose you're not interested to know who those patients were or how they died."

She's baiting me, even though she doesn't know why I'm interested. Another new dilemma arises: I want information about any unusual events at RKH that coincided with my stay, but a psychiatrist mustn't use her patients to fulfill her own needs. To question them as part of my investigation into my past is unethical. My mind scuttles frantically, then pounces on a compromise.

"Let's make a bargain," I say. "We can talk about the legend for five minutes if you agree to continue our group therapy right afterward."

Dot and Maureen smile hopefully at Rory.

Rory pauses, considering, then says, "Okay." She must realize that if she keeps too tight a rein on her friends, they'll rebel.

"The first patient was Peter Kramer," Maureen says. "He was a businessman who lived at Mercy House."

"The second was Adeline Peck," Dot says. "She was a widow at Serenity House."

Rory says, "The third was a girl here at Haven House. Her name was Caroline Lennox."

I'm so blindsided by shock that I gape at Rory before I can control myself. My own faked death is one in a second series of fatalities at RKH? My mind teems with chaotic thoughts. Were the other two real or faked? Coincidences or connected to mine?

"How do you know this?" I blurt.

"People talk." Rory narrows her eyes, wondering why I reacted so strongly. "We listen."

"Which people?" My voice is harsh and too loud. Dot and Maureen sit back in surprise.

"Why do you care? It's just a 'legend.'" Rory mimics me in a prissy voice.

I strive for an authoritative manner. "If someone is spreading rumors that could disturb the other patients, you should tell me who it is."

"Why?" Dot's expression turns hostile. "So you can report them and get them in trouble?"

Maureen crosses her plump arms over her full bosom. "We're not tattletales."

Rory smirks: she's got the upper hand. "Wouldn't you rather hear how those patients died?"

I'm desperate to know how *I* supposedly died. Rory's sly manner suggests that the deaths resulted from something more sinister than natural causes. Having already crossed a line, I take another step in the wrong direction.

"Tell me." I speak through the breath caught in my throat.

Dot opens her mouth to answer, but Rory says, "Wait." She holds up her finger, then points it at me. "If we tell you, what are you going to do for us?"

The damned girl is using her knowledge to extort favors! Outrage boils up inside me, but I can't help admiring Rory. She's smart and bold; the world hasn't been kind to her, but she's not taking its cruelty lying down. She also has a force of personality that bends others to her will, and not just her peers.

The loudspeaker in the hall plays a recording of a bell ringing. Maureen says, “Dinnertime. Yay!” She and Dot scramble off the bed and out the door.

As Rory follows them, she grins at me over her shoulder. Even though I’m not at all sure whether anything she’ll tell me is true, I have to think of something to offer her in exchange for information that could be a key to the secrets of my past.

CHAPTER

12

AFTER DINNER, I walk across the campus. The brick buildings glow deep red in the mellow golden sunlight, birdsong fills the trees, and the warm air is sweet with the scent of night-blooming flowers. It's hard to believe that such peace outdoors can coexist with such troubled minds indoors.

"Hello," Daniel Tanaka says, catching up with me. "Where are you headed?"

"Oh, just for a walk. For some fresh air." I don't want him to know what I'm really up to. "Where are you going?"

"Back to the dorm. I have to write up my reports."

"I have to write up mine too."

Our duties include writing a weekly report on each of our patients. The reports are due on Thursday, tomorrow morning.

"That was an interesting training session today," Daniel says.

I recognize a psychotherapeutic technique: He's not going to ask outright why I was disturbed; he's opening the door for me to talk if I choose to. I turn the tables on him, a strategy used when a patient asks personal questions of the psychiatrist.

"Yes, it was interesting. What did you think of it?"

His smile indicates that he knows what I'm doing, but he respects my privacy. "I think shock is risky because we can't predict its long-term effects."

I avoid his gaze. Is he wondering if I've had shock? I become aware of the warmth of his voice, like a fire in a hearth on a winter's day, an invitation to pour my heart out in a safe place where I can receive sympathy and not fear judgment. His concern seems genuine; he's not after gossip to spread, he really wants to help. I can't help liking him. I think he likes me. He's going to be an excellent psychiatrist. If I want to keep my secrets, I need to be careful around him. He's dangerous.

To change the subject, I say, "Philadelphia is a long way from California. How did you end up at Temple University?"

"I wanted to go to Stanford, but Japanese students were banned from California colleges during the war."

"Oh." Our conversational terrain is strewn with landmines, and not just because of my own past. My fending off his attention made Daniel reveal painful personal information about himself. "I'm sorry."

He shrugs as if to say he's taken no offense. "The National Japanese-American Student Relocation Council helped us find places in out-of-state colleges. A representative came to the camp and interviewed me and other kids to make sure we were loyal to the United States. I was lucky that Temple accepted me. There weren't many schools that could. They had to be far from California and not near major defense installations and not engaged in military research or training. The council raised money to pay for our tuition and transportation. I boarded the train to Philadelphia with one suitcase and twenty dollars."

I picture him, scarcely more than a child, traveling three thousand miles alone to an uncertain welcome in a strange, cold city. I think of how I was left on my own after my father left and my mother died.

"Your family . . . ?" I hesitantly ask.

"My parents, siblings, and relatives are still in California. They stayed there after they were released from the camp. I've seen them twice since I left—once after I graduated from college, once after I graduated from medical school. It's too far to go often. I'm saving up money to visit next summer."

"That must be difficult for you, and for them." Envy colors my sympathy. At least he still has his family.

"At least I still have my family," Daniel says.

There are times when one can perceive another person's thoughts as clearly as if they'd been spoken aloud. It only happened to me with Brian. I knew what mischievous act he was contemplating the instant before he stole the cookie off my plate or threw a snowball at the neighbor. I've never been as close to anyone since, and I'm surprised Daniel Tanaka seemed to know my thoughts.

He looks into the distance. I follow his gaze and see Dr. Joseph Mandel walking rapidly across the campus, a dark figure in the bright summer landscape. Now I can tell what Daniel is thinking: Joseph wasn't as fortunate; his family died in the Nazi concentration camps. Joseph must have confided in Daniel, yielding to the same temptation that I struggle to resist. I'm shaken by the sense of connection I feel with Daniel in this moment, even more so when he turns to me and his eyebrows lift. He feels it too; he knows that I know what he was thinking about Joseph Mandel. Our gazes hold for an uncomfortable moment before we look away from each other.

I hurry to keep the focus of the conversation on him and away from myself. "I'm sorry you had to go through that," I say.

"It's over," he says easily. "I've put it behind me."

I hear the eerie echo of my father's voice. I can't begin to imagine everything that Daniel Tanaka and Joseph Mandel experienced. New questions occur to me: Is it easier to put things behind you when you're conscious of them or when you can't remember them? Is a mystery about the past harder to jettison than even the most terrible memories?

We're nearing the men's and women's staff dormitories—identical plain, three-story brick buildings separated by tennis courts. Players swing rackets, and I hear the pop and bounce of balls. People lounge on benches. Heads turn in our direction, and I notice speculative gazes. If I'm not careful, I'll feature in gossip about a romance between two new doctors. The gossip could be particularly vicious because it involves a woman who's white and a man who's not. I glance at Daniel Tanaka. The same awareness sharpens his eyes.

"Well." His expression conveys more concern for me than himself. "Good night. I'll see you tomorrow."

"Good night." As I pause to watch him go inside the men's dorm, I can't deny that I'm drawn to him. I'm both glad and sorry about our tacit agreement to avoid each other in the future. The less attention paid to me while I dig for information about events at RKH during the summer of 1941, the better. But I feel lonelier having lost Daniel's company. This is another in a long series of occasions when my past has put a distance between me and other people. To make close friends is impossible without confiding personal facts. It's as if I'm in a glass bubble, isolated from the world. I can't shatter the glass without revealing my secrets.

On the tennis courts, I see Nurse Janice playing, dressed in yellow shorts and T-shirt instead of her uniform, with her dark hair in a ponytail. This spares me having to look for her at the dorm. I sit on a bench to wait until her game is finished. The popping of tennis balls, the fragrance of grass and flowers, and the golden evening light are quintessentially summer. My thoughts drift back to the summer of 1941.

I always looked forward to June, July, and August, which my family always spent at our house in Arden Spring, New York, in the Hudson Valley. Since Brian was away at school except for holidays, summers were our only chance for much time together. But that year, things were different. Brian had grown three inches and gained twenty pounds of lean, strong muscle during the fall and winter. At age seventeen, he seemed no longer a boy but a young man, much older than my fourteen years. And there was tension between our parents. As we drove into town in the Cadillac, my father scolded my mother about her drinking; she berated him for too many trips away from home. I tried not to listen.

We always stopped at the town drugstore for Brian's and my ritual first ice cream cones of the summer. When we got out of the car, my father greeted the locals as if he were a visiting dignitary. They happily welcomed our family back; we were good customers at their stores, restaurants, and other businesses. My mother stayed in the car and sulked. Instead of going into the drugstore with me, Brian joined some teenagers who were standing on the corner. One was a pretty blonde girl named Donna Wright, dressed in denim shorts and a ruffled halter top, the local belle and daughter of the mayor. She and her friends were all a year older than Brian, and he'd never hung out with them before, but now they accepted him as if he'd always been part of their group. For the first time, I ate my ice cream cone alone.

Our house was in the wooded hills outside town. After we settled in, I asked Brian if he wanted to go to the waterfall. We always visited the waterfall and other favorite spots on our first day, another ritual. But Brian said, "Maybe later. I think I'll walk back to town."

We never did visit the waterfall or the cave, or swim in the pond, or play Monopoly and toast marshmallows together that summer. I have only fragmented memories of what I did. I sat by the pool at the country club and watched Brian, Donna, and other teenagers talking and laughing by the lifeguard stand. I read by the fireplace at the house while rain poured down. I was awakened late every night by the sound of the back door closing when Brian came home. It seems that one minute I was at the summer house, then arriving at RKH with my father; and then, leaving RKH with my father. I saw him only twice after my mother died. The first time, he dropped me off at the boarding school where I would stay, except for summers at camp, until I started college. The second time was at my graduation from Radcliffe. He told me that he'd remarried and had two sons. I was like the skin shed by a snake that had outgrown it. He didn't bring his new family with him, and I never met them. He took me out to dinner—the last meal we ever ate together, filet mignon and baked Alaska. He said he would pay for Columbia Medical School, just as he'd paid for Radcliffe.

"I'm proud of you for carrying on the tradition of a doctor in the family," he said.

It was the first nice thing he'd ever said to me. I was so happy; I didn't want to spoil the occasion by questioning him about that summer. He'd told me to put it behind me, and my obedience was the price of his goodwill.

Now someone joins me on the bench by the tennis courts. It's Dr. Jean Norton. She sets a stack of file folders between us and peruses the top one while writing in a notebook.

"I hope I'm not bothering you," she says. "There wasn't room on the other benches."

So she doesn't want my company. "I thought you lived in town."

"I'm waiting for my husband. He's playing tennis with some of his patients."

On the court is Ronald Norton, dressed in tennis whites, playing doubles with three men. His opponents cheer as they score a point. Ronald laughs good-naturedly. It occurs to me that he's doing more for them than I did for Rory, Dot, and Maureen during my attempt at group therapy. Dr. Koffka once said, "Sometimes, simple positive attention from a doctor is the best medicine for his patients." Ronald Norton, for all his faults, may be a better psychiatrist than I am.

"I saw you with Dr. Tanaka," Jean says. "What were you two talking about?"

Great, I think. *She'll spread the word, and it won't be long before everyone believes Daniel and I are romantically involved and I'm the kind of female doctor who sleeps around.*

"College," I say. "What are you writing?"

"My reports."

The heading on the top page of her open file reads, "Mercy House." She works in Grace House. She's writing her husband's reports, not her own.

She notices me looking, quickly closes the file, and speaks as if she's anxious to make me forget what I saw. "So you went to med school at Columbia. I was accepted there."

She must have been waiting for a chance to tell me that she's not as academically inferior to me as I might think. "Why didn't you go?"

"Ronald and I wanted to go to the same place."

Meaning, Ronald *hadn't* been accepted at Columbia. I wonder if he'd have made it through med school at all without her help. "Why did the two of you choose psychiatry?"

Jean's expression turns wistful. "I wanted to be an obstetrician, but Ronald's father is a psychiatrist."

I feel sorry for her and the many women who sacrifice their opportunities and waste their talents for a man.

"A career isn't everything. Freud said, '*Love* and work are the cornerstones of our humanness.'" Jean smiles triumphantly. She's the woman who has both her career and a husband; I'm the lonely old maid.

After watching my parents fight constantly, I have no desire to marry. It's only late at night, after a long, hard day at work, that I think it would be nice to go home to someone who loves me. Eager to end the one-upmanship contest with Jean, I'm glad to see Janice walk off the tennis court. "Excuse me," I say, "there's someone I need to talk to."

I intercept Janice on the path to the dorm. "Janice Peters?" She turns to me with a friendly smile. "I'm Dr. Kendall. From the electroshock training session this morning."

"Oh, yes, I remember you." Janice's brown eyes are as kind as when I was her young, frightened patient. She must be in her mid-thirties now, but her round, pretty face is still youthful, her skin glowing with health.

"Do you have a minute to talk?"

"Sure, but let's go inside. I'm dying of thirst."

She leads me into the dorm, to a lounge where women are playing bridge or watching television. Janice sets down her tennis racket and buys us Cokes from a machine, and we sit in the armchairs by the fireplace. I recite the speech I prepared.

"I'm doing research for an article about past and current treatments for young girls at psychiatric hospitals. Someone mentioned you once worked in Haven House."

"Oh, I've worked all over RKH. They send me wherever patients need to be calmed down." Janice smiles. "I seem to have a knack for it."

I glance at her neatly manicured left hand. There's no wedding ring. She lives at the hospital. Is this her whole world, or does she have a life outside? But her personal affairs aren't my main interest.

"I looked up the records of some former Haven House patients," I say. "My plan is to compare the therapy they received to the therapy that's used nowadays, and to determine whether the results are different."

"That sounds interesting." Janice swigs her Coke. Unlike Nurse Norris, she doesn't seem suspicious of me. "What can I do for you?"

"I need some background information on the patients. Your memories of them would help me round out the picture. So if I may ask you some questions . . . ?"

"Fire away."

"Thank you." I name one of the patients whose files I took from the archives. "Do you remember Eleanor Cox?"

"Oh, yes." Janice's expression combines fond nostalgia with sympathy. "She was a scholarship student at Sarah Lawrence. She had a nervous breakdown and was admitted to RKH after she tried to commit suicide with sleeping pills." Janice describes Eleanor as a pretty blonde honor student with dates every weekend and a hectic life as class president, newspaper editor, and a member of many organizations. "It was too much. We get a lot of girls like her, unfortunately."

According to her file, Eleanor received insulin and shock therapy. "Do you know what became of her?" I ask.

"She got better and was discharged. She graduated and went to work as an editor in the city. She still sends me a Christmas letter every year. She's married now, with two children."

I'm glad to hear that someone who came out of RKH fared well. I ask about Marjorie Whitman and Joyce Buell, whom I selected because they too were teenage patients at Haven House within a few years of my own hospitalization. Janice happily talks about them. Marjorie, a debutante diagnosed with anorexia nervosa, was treated with shock therapy and force-feeding during several stays at RKH; never married, she now serves on the boards of various charities. Joyce, a schizophrenic, has a sadder history as a chronic patient at other hospitals. They both correspond faithfully with Janice.

Maybe this is why Janice stays at RKH: She maintains her connections with patients and has the satisfaction of knowing they appreciated her kindness. I ask, "What can you tell me about Caroline Lennox?"

Alarm wipes the smile off Janice's face. "I . . . don't remember a patient by that name."

A hot topic at the Manhattan Psychoanalytic Academy was how to tell whether a client is lying. Janice is so obviously lying that I don't need psychological tricks. "Caroline Lennox lived in Haven House while you worked there."

Janice sets her empty Coke bottle on the floor. "There've been so many patients. I can't remember them all." Her voice is flat, unfriendly.

"She was diagnosed with hysteria," I prompt.

"Doesn't ring a bell." Janice looks me in the eye, as if she thinks it will convince me she's telling the truth.

"She died here." How strange, talking about my own death.

"Lots of patients have died here. It's an old hospital." The fear in Janice's eyes belies her nonchalant tone.

"Patients including Adeline Peck at Grace House and Peter Kramer at Mercy House?" I say, recalling Rory, Dot, and Maureen's tale.

Janice's gaze skitters away from me. "I—don't remember them either."

Surely she would remember a series of three deaths that occurred during the same summer. I ask, "Why does it bother you to talk about those particular patients?"

"It doesn't bother me. Look, it's been nice talking to you, but I have to go." Janice hurries out of the lounge and disappears through the door to the stairwell.

Instead of answers, I'm left with the tennis racket she forgot and many, many more questions.

CHAPTER 13

THE NEXT MORNING, I drop off my report, which I stayed up late writing, in Dr. Bullard's mailbox in the mansion. Then I walk toward Haven House. The sky is a hazy pale blue, the already warm air alive with butterflies and dandelion fluff. It's a fresh new day, but my mind is stale with thoughts left over from last night. Why did Janice lie? Is she in on a cover-up of what happened to me? But what exactly is RKH covering up? And how could it have involved me, a fourteen-year-old girl?

One thing is unfortunately certain: Janice knows about my interest in Caroline Lennox. Who might she tell?

At Haven House, I join the day and night shift staff at the nurse's station on the first floor. The night charge nurse gives the report. Lulu Shelton had a tantrum for no apparent reason. The doctor on duty gave her a sedative injection and ordered hydrotherapy for her. Haven House will be shorthanded today because one nurse has to "special" another patient, who's coming back from lockdown, where she was sent after she punched an aide. "Special" nursing means one-on-one care, an extra burden for RKH's already strained workforce. After the night shift leaves, the day nurses count pills into plastic cups, and the aides wake the patients up, calling, "Rise and shine!"

Groggy, disheveled young women line up in the hall while an aide brings out the scale; patients are weighed every Thursday. Rory,

Dot, and Maureen stand together. Other patients give them a wide berth. The three are like a schoolyard gang that commands fearful respect. After weighing, the patients go to the dining room, and Judy Abbott needs her feeding tube. After a prolonged tussle, I wash her spit off my face and hands, then check on Lulu Shelton.

The hydrotherapy room is in the basement. Three white bathtubs stand in a row beneath faucets and temperature gauges on the tiled wall. The facilities look dingy enough to date from when RKH was built. Two tubs are empty. In the third lies Lulu, imprisoned by a canvas sheet with straps on its sides buckled around the bottom of the tub, only her head visible. She wears a white plastic shower cap. The air is dankly warm. Hydrotherapy is the modern name for the ancient technique of soaking agitated persons in hot water to relax them. Lulu certainly appears relaxed, her eyes closed, her mouth slack. I recall Rory, Dot, and Maureen's story about Jennie Washburn, who drowned in a bathtub in 1885. A cold, shivery sensation worsens my discomfort with basements. A soft whimper startles me. I gasp, looking around, afraid to see Jennie's ghost.

It's only Lulu, whimpering in her sleep.

When I go back upstairs, I look over the day's schedule. Two patients are going out with relatives, and three others have dental appointments in town. Visiting hours are from ten AM to four PM. Patients authorized to leave Haven House, chaperoned or by themselves, can stroll the campus or go to the gymnasium. All of this activity benefits the patients, but it limits the time for psychotherapy. Chatter fills the hall as the patients return from breakfast. I head toward Rory, Maureen, and Dot, intending to ask them about the three patients, including myself, who supposedly died in 1941.

The girls see me and scatter in different directions. Dot runs toward the lounge; Maureen ducks into the utility room; Rory hurries up the stairs. I go after Rory. On the second floor, the hall is empty. My steps slow as I walk up to the third floor, which I've been avoiding. My avoidance tells me it's where I lived when I was a patient. My gut remembers even though my mind forgot. The door to Rory's room is ajar but not enough for me to see inside. My chest tightens; the coffee and toast I had for breakfast turns sour in my stomach.

That room was once mine.

Is Rory lying in wait for me? Are memories from my time as a patient? I feel the vertigo that signals a flashback coming on. I need to talk to Rory, and I need whatever memories the room can evoke, but I'm not ready to go in there. Not yet. Panic constricts my trachea. I can't breathe. The edges of my vision darken. I stumble along the hall and down the stairs.

Outside Haven House, I turn my face to the sun and gratefully take in the fresh air. I've so much to do—seeing patients before their dental appointments and visiting hours, writing notes on their charts, attempting psychotherapy with as many as possible—but I'm too shaky to return to work. I spot Dr. Bullard hurrying across campus, listening to his walkie-talkie. When I approach him, he stops reluctantly.

"Ah, Dr. Kendall." His round face is all cheery smiles, but he holds up the walkie-talkie as if he's expecting another call. "How are things going?"

"Fine," I lie. "I wanted to talk to you about one of my patients. Rory Kirkpatrick."

Dr. Bullard nods. "She's a tough nut to crack."

I dislike the idea of Rory as an object that needs breaking. "I haven't been trained in homosexual conversion therapy, and I'd like to learn what it involves." Once I understand what Rory is going through, perhaps I can form a therapeutic bond with her. "May I sit in on her treatments?"

"You may. In fact, the next one is a training session for the residents." He consults his datebook. "On July twenty-seventh. Now if you'll excuse me . . ."

* * *

RKH has two gymnasiums for the patients—one for men, one for women. They're Tudor-style buildings with half-timbered walls, brick chimneys, and slate roofs, separated by a half acre of ground divided down the middle by a row of evergreen trees. Walking past the men's grounds, I see a baseball game in progress. On the women's, badminton players send a shuttlecock flying back and forth over the net. It's been half an hour since I left Haven House, and I feel like a child playing hooky from school—or a fugitive escaped prisoner.

The entrance hall of the women's gymnasium reminds me of the lodge at the camp where I spent my summers after my mother died until I started medical school. Rattan chairs stand on the scuffed wood floor and shelves contain magazines and paperback books. The girls lying on the hearth rug in front of the rustic stone fireplace, weaving leather string into bracelets, even look like campers. It all provokes an ache of nostalgia. Camp was the closest thing I had to a home in those days. It was owned by a middle-aged couple, Mr. and Mrs. Ryan. They were like parents to me and the other girls, many of whom were orphans or had parents who couldn't or didn't want to take care of them. That I managed to finish my education and live on my own is due in no small part to the kindness and support I received from the Ryans. They welcomed me back every year as if I were a favorite daughter. After I turned eighteen, they hired me as a counselor, my first job. I lived in a cabin with a group of little girls, supervising their activities, comforting them when they were homesick. I did it every summer during college, and there I began to think that, by ministering to other girls, maybe I could heal my own childhood wounds.

I smile wryly at my youthful naivete. Here I am, in over my head at RKH, where I've met my match in Rory Kirkpatrick.

Upstairs, one room is a kitchen where women in frilly aprons are baking cookies. In another, patients work at sewing machines. These aren't just pastimes but a form of therapy. They prepare the women to resume their roles as homemakers when they're discharged. The idea that their recovery is measured by how well they perform domestic duties doesn't sit right with me. There's more to mental health than that.

I find Leonora Hirschfeld alone in a painting studio that smells of turpentine and oil. Here's one female patient who's avoiding domestic re-indoctrination. Art can help the mentally ill express themselves. They may find it easier to describe their thoughts, feelings, and hallucinations via drawing or painting than with words. Using clay, paints, or charcoal can also relieve their suffering, and unlike electroshock and drugs, it doesn't have dangerous side effects. From the doorway I watch Leonora swirl her paintbrush, mixing colors on her palette. In her early forties, she's homely, with short iron-gray hair cut in bangs straight across her broad forehead, black-framed glasses, and full, sensuous lips. Her thick figure is clothed in a paint-stained white smock over faded blue dungarees and fuzzy yellow bedroom slippers. I can't summon up a memory of her. Does she remember me from twelve years ago, when I was a fellow patient?

A ripple of fear puzzles me for a moment before I remember Freud's doppelganger concept. Leonora is the darkest reflection in the dark mirror—an image of myself if I'd never left RKH, if I had stayed on as a patient until I was her age.

"Don't just stand there, come in," she says without looking at me.

As I approach Leonora, I notice empty easels and stools around her facing a table that holds fruit, a vase of flowers, and a violin. She ignores the still life, glancing at small pictures spread on a taboret beside her as she paints. Her easel holds a large canvas that's angled away from me so I can't see what's on it.

"I'm Dr. Kendall," I say, "one of the new residents. May I have a word with you?"

Before coming here, I went to Solace House. The charge nurse told me where to find Leonora and let me read her file. Leonora is from a family that owns a famous luxury hotel in Manhattan. Her symptoms of schizophrenia first appeared when she was twenty and studying at the Art Students League. They include mania, paranoia, suicide attempts, seizures, and catatonic states. At age nineteen, she eloped with her art teacher, a handsome but penniless man. Her symptoms worsened, and eventually she was committed to RKH after she was arrested for stabbing a bus driver with a pencil. She claimed he'd tried to rape her. The other passengers said she attacked him for no apparent reason. Her family paid off the bus driver and persuaded the police to hush up the incident. Leonora has been here ever since. Her symptoms ebb and resurge; she has periods when she's lucid, calm, and sane. Last month, during a bad episode, she claimed that nurses performed satanic rituals on her. She hit them and spent a week in lockdown. She's been treated with shock, insulin coma, and Thorazine. Now, fortunately for me as well as her, Leonora is in one of her sane periods.

She turns an appraising stare at me. Her hazel eyes are keen and intelligent, magnified by her thick glasses. "Whose side are you on?"

Confused, I say, "I beg your pardon?"

"My husband and my family are suing each other for legal control over me. My family thinks I should be moved to a different hospital. My husband thinks I'm fine here. So does Superintendent Van Pelt." Leonora adds wryly, "They all want my money."

I have no idea whether it's true. In the short time I've worked at Haven House, I've heard all manner of stories. My patient Marcia Boothby claims she was abducted by spacemen.

"So." Leonora points her brush at me. "Whose side are you on?"

"I'm on your side," I say. "What do *you* want?"

Leonora shrugs instead of answering but seems satisfied with my response. "I sense that *you* want to talk about something other than penis envy, so would you cut to the chase? I need to finish this painting for a show at the National Arts Club in the city."

I move beside her to study the canvas on her easel. It depicts a portion of the RKH campus in colorful, primitive style and meticulous detail, Haven House and the mansion and other buildings instantly recognizable. But the scene is lush with tropical flora and populated with naked women who have butterfly wings. The pictures on the taboret are pages from the RKH brochure and clippings from magazines. The brochure pages show the hospital buildings; the magazine clippings are of naked women, perhaps from *Playboy*, and of the sorts of animals and plants shown in *National Geographic*. Leonora has collaged the images together. Anecdotal evidence suggests a link between mental illness and artistic talent; whether one causes the other is debatable, but Vincent van Gogh, Edvard Munch, Francisco Goya, and other afflicted artists have produced some of the world's greatest works of art. According to Freud, the creative process is a defense mechanism against neurosis, a socially acceptable outlet for expressing unconscious conflicts and desires.

"Your work is beautiful," I say. It's also surrealistic and disturbing. "You're very talented."

She smiles smugly.

"I'm doing research for an article about young girls at psychiatric hospitals," I say. "I looked up the records of some former patients. My plan is to follow up on them and see how they're doing now. If you can tell me your impressions of them, it would be very helpful."

"Okay, as long as you don't mind if I work while we talk."

I name Joyce Buell, Marjorie Whitman, and Eleanor Cox. Blending turquoise paint into the sky on her canvas, Leonora says, "Sorry, I don't remember them."

"They lived at Haven House with you."

Leonora chuckles. "Queen Elizabeth could have lived at Haven House with me, and I wouldn't have noticed while I was catatonic."

So I'm not the only one whose recollection of that summer is incomplete. "What about Caroline Lennox?"

Leonora shakes her head, then holds her paintbrush upright. "Wait—I do remember her. She's that kid we all talked about."

My heart jumps. Here's the first eyewitness account of my younger self at RKH.

"She looked like a sleepwalker when the nurses brought her in," Leonora says. "They took her straight to her room, and she stayed there. I only saw her when they brought her out for shock treatments, which was three, four times a week—more than anybody else. They must have given her big jolts, because she always came back on a stretcher, either unconscious or raving mad. We had all kinds of ideas about who she was. A juvenile delinquent? A murderer?"

I feel the dreadful sensation of a door opening inside my mind that I didn't want opened. I'd believed that I was committed to RKH because of a nervous breakdown, but is it possible that I did something terrible that summer and I was put here as punishment as well as to erase my memory of it?

"Caroline Lennox had a special nurse." Eyes focused on her painting while she works, Leonora doesn't notice my distress. "The nurse was Janice Peters. She stayed in the room with Caroline day and night. You might want to talk to her. She works in the shock room now."

Well. Not only did Janice lie, but she's probably the person at RKH who spent the most time with me. What does she know that she refused to tell?

"After a couple of months, they stopped Caroline's shock treatments," Leonora says. "Janice started bringing her to the lounge and dining room. She seemed dazed and confused and afraid. We asked her questions, like where she came from and why she'd been sent here, but she wouldn't, or couldn't, speak. Then suddenly one day—" Leonora wields her paintbrush like a magic wand. "She was gone. We never got any answers. Janice was transferred to a different house, and the other nurses were as much in the dark as we were."

Another talk with Janice is in order. Can I press her to tell the truth without revealing why I want information about Caroline Lennox?

"I seem to remember hearing Caroline had committed suicide," Leonora says.

Did I try, and fail, to kill myself at RKH? Had I done something awful, for which I thought I deserved to die? "Committed suicide, how?" I ask, even though I shouldn't be discussing the suicide of one patient with another, especially when the other patient has a history of suicide attempts.

"She drowned herself in the bath, or she cut her wrists with a broken glass, or managed to get hold of extra pills," Leonora says. "All rumors, no facts. Hey, if you find out who she was and what became of her, let me know."

"I will." I don't mention that Caroline Lennox is alive and standing right next to her. That would lay my secrets wide open to Leonora and anybody she chose to tell.

"That would be one of RKH's mysteries solved," Leonora says.

"Are there others?" I think of the three deaths that Rory, Dot, and Maureen mentioned.

"Oh, yeah. Two other patients disappeared. A woman named Adeline Peck from Grace House and a man named Peter Kramer from Mercy House. Around the same time as Caroline Lennox, same kind of rumors, no real explanation. But I've always wondered if whatever happened to Caroline Lennox happened to the others."

Were the girls lying when they claimed the other two patients had died? Or do they have information that Leonora and her fellow inmates didn't?

A nurse pokes her head in the door. "Dr. Kendall?" she says. "Nurse Norris called. She said to tell you that you're needed at Haven House."

I feel a queasy blend of suspicion, alarm, and fear. How did Nurse Norris know where I am? Who told her? Does the staff keep watch and report on all new employees or only me?

Paranoia is contagious too.

How long was that nurse standing outside the door? What did she overhear, and to whom might she talk about it? I'll have to be more careful.

"It was nice to meet you," I say to Leonora.

"Likewise." She's absorbed in her work before I'm out of the studio.

What might I have done to warrant my commitment to a mental hospital and shock treatments that erased my memory? I leave the gymnasium more mystified than ever, and more afraid of what I'll eventually find out.

CHAPTER

14

Dear Celia,

I'm in the wardrobe room at the RKH theater with Dot and Maureen. Dot is trying on a man's gray Victorian-looking suit with long coattails and black stripes down the sides of the pants.

"It's too tight," she says. The buttons and holes on the coat won't meet across her fat stomach. The pants are too short, and the fly gapes open.

"People were so small back then," Maureen says. She's sitting at the dressing table, wearing a long pale green dress with puffed sleeves and a lace collar. A blonde wig makes her look like the picture of Marie Antoinette in my history book.

RKH has a "Cultural Program." That means arts and crafts, literature, theater, and music, which are supposed to have a healing, uplifting effect on us lunatics. They bring in artists and authors to give lectures and classes. There are concerts and plays by local orchestras and theater troupes. RKH also has a tradition of patients performing in musical recitals and producing plays they've written themselves. I don't care about art. That's my least favorite subject at school. I prefer sports and playing football with my boy cousins. Dad coached me. Whenever I was tackled and got back up again, he yelled, "That's the spirit, Rosie!"

He's the only person I don't mind calling me "Rosie." It sounds little-girlish when anyone else says it. He said I was the kid who was the most like him, full of "piss and vinegar."

I miss him most of all.

They don't let girls play football at RKH. They don't let me play anything because it might worsen my "combative behavior." Instead, they sent me to a writing class. They thought it would be good therapy for me to write about my thoughts and feelings, so I would see the error of my ways, I guess. Well, I wrote a composition where I said I'm not crazy and described how I'm being tortured here. The teacher was a local poet named Anne Walden. She was about forty years old and dressed like a gypsy in long skirts and embroidered blouses and colorful beads. She smoked all the time and smelled like booze and told wild stories about famous writers she knew. She believed what I wrote. One day she hid me in her car and smuggled me out of RKH. The police caught me at the train station. Mrs. Walden's class was canceled, and I'm not allowed to have contact with outsiders. But I am allowed to participate in supervised activities with other patients. So when Dot said she wanted to put on a play for the talent show, I decided to try writing one. I have a story that needs to be told. Our play will go down in the history of the RKH "Cultural Program," for sure.

Maybe I'll be an author someday.

Maureen says to me, "Your costume fits perfectly."

I look at myself in the mirror, and a young man from an old gangster movie looks back at me. I tug the wide lapels of my gray suit coat, touch the brim of the black fedora that I've hidden my long hair under, and grin.

"Ooh, you're so handsome," Dot says.

Celia, I hope you would think so too if you saw me. The play will be the first time I don't have to wear a goddamned dress at RKH. Dot and Maureen are happy to take the female roles. I'm having the most fun I've had here. It reminds me of the skit that you and I put on at our school talent show.

Do you remember?

We called it "Holy Redeemer High-Jinks." We kept the story a secret and hid in a closet in the auditorium so nobody would see us in our costumes until we went on stage. I don't need to tell you this because you were there, but I like thinking about it. When the curtain went up, I was sitting at a desk, dressed in black pants and shirt and white collar. I impersonated Father Bernard, the principal, giving his morning address over the loudspeaker. The girls in the audience laughed so hard, they practically rolled in the aisles. Even Father Bernard smiled. Then I pulled a whisky bottle out of the desk and pretended to take a swig, and the girls kept laughing, but he wasn't smiling anymore.

Then you walked onstage dressed in a nun's habit. I said, "Ah, Sister Theresa. Would you like to feel the holy spirit enter you?"

The laughter turned to uneasy mutters, and when "Father Bernard" and "Sister Theresa" started kissing, there was a big gasp of shock, then the curtain slammed down. The next thing we knew, we were in Father Bernard's office, and he was bawling us out. He called us juvenile delinquents and scolded us for slandering servants of God. You started crying. I tried to explain that it's not slander if it's true. That's what Dad says. And everybody knows Father Bernard and Sister Theresa fool around. I've seen them kissing, and I bet they go even further in private. But Father Bernard only got angrier. He said, "Both of you are suspended!"

We were sent home. When Dad heard about it, he burst out laughing. "Exposing the sins of the high and sanctimonious," he said. "That's my Rosie!"

But Mother was furious. So were your parents. We were both grounded for two weeks before the school let us come back on probation. The first night, I climbed out of my bedroom window, sneaked over to your house, and climbed up the trellis to your window. We lay in your bed together. I said, "I'm sorry for getting you in trouble." You said, "I don't mind getting in trouble as long as it's with you." That was the first time we made love. We were shy and awkward, not knowing how to do it, but we figured it out, and we did it again every night afterward. That was the best time of my life.

I try not to think about how it ended, because it makes me too sad.

We wanted each other so badly, we got careless. We made love in your car behind the school or on the side of the road. The danger was part of the thrill. But then came that party at the country club. The punch was spiked, and we got pretty drunk. We stumbled out of the clubhouse to the pool and went inside a cabana. We tore off our dresses, and I was kissing you down there when a bunch of people found us and started yelling. I didn't see who they were. I guess it doesn't matter. Everyone had heard about us by the next day.

This time, Dad didn't laugh. He slapped me across the face and called me a pervert and a sinner and a disgrace to the family. That wasn't what hurt me the worst. The worst was when he said, "A child of mine should know better than to get caught."

I turn away from Dot and Maureen so they won't see me wipe my eyes, and I paw through the racks of clothes. We need more costumes because we're each playing multiple characters. Other girls at Haven House begged to be in our play, but we can't let them, for reasons that will become obvious later.

"Where did they get all these clothes?" I say, finding ball gowns and tuxedos, shorts and blouses, pajamas and housedresses, winter coats and bathing suits.

"I heard that some were donated by people in town or bought at sales," Maureen says. "Others are from former patients who left them behind."

Dot looks down at her costume in horror. "This could have belonged to a crazy person. Or to somebody who got sick and died." She starts tearing off the jacket and pants. "I have to take a shower."

Dot has phobias. She's afraid of dirt and germs, and she thinks insanity is a kind of germ that can infect her just like measles. She doesn't mind being around Maureen and me—I guess she thinks we have all the same germs—but she doesn't like anyone else to touch her. She washes her hands a lot.

"These clothes have been washed a hundred times," I say, even though my jacket smells faintly of stale B.O. "You're okay, Dot."

Dot is breathing hard, scratching red hives that have broken out on her neck. "Really?"

"Yeah," I say.

She sighs with relief, and her hives disappear. Thank God she listens to me. Otherwise, we'd never get through this play. I'm glad Maureen and I don't have germ-o-phobia. Dad cured me of any inclination I might have had. He taught me to shoot and started to take me hunting when I was twelve. My first time out, I shot a deer. He made me cut it open and take out the insides myself. "You kill it, you dress it," he said. I like walking in the woods and shooting, but I hate killing animals. The deer was so beautiful. But it's what our family does, and after you've touched blood and guts, anything else doesn't seem so bad.

Dad was so proud of me that day. He's not proud of me now.

Since that scolding, he's never spoken to me. Mother locked me in my room and brought my meals on a tray. My sisters and brothers didn't come to see me. I don't know if it was their choice or if they were ordered to stay away. The window was nailed shut, and I couldn't call you because I wasn't allowed to use the phone. Every night I prayed that Dad would forgive me and I could see you again. After three days, Mother told me that we were taking a trip, just her and me. When I asked where we were going, she said I would find out when we got there. I thought that if I didn't fuss, everything would be okay. The chauffeur drove us to RKH. It wasn't until we went inside that I realized it was a mental hospital and Mother was leaving me there. I screamed and ran after the car and kicked the orderlies who caught me. A doctor gave me a shot that knocked me out, and I woke up in a cold pack. But the worst thing was, Dad must have known where Mother was taking me. He'd washed his hands of me, just like Dot washes the germs off her hands.

Stop thinking about that, *I tell myself.* It's just making you more miserable. *I say to Maureen and Dot, "Time to rehearse." I'm the director as well as the playwright.*

Maureen says, "Where's my script?" She searches through the junk on the dressing table.

"Don't you know your lines yet?" I say. "The talent show is less than a month away, and we've still got lots of stuff to work out."

"Do you really think we'll be able to put on the play?" Dot says, suddenly wistful.

"Sure," I say with more confidence than I feel.

"We don't have permission yet," Maureen says. Every act in the talent show needs to be approved by Superintendent Van Pelt or Dr. Mara.

"Who's going to ask?" Dot says.

We look at each other and shrug helplessly. When Dot was supposed to play the piano at a recital, she got so nervous that she had to be sedated. Maureen had a bad spell during a concert. The music set her off, and she thought someone was attacking her. She spent four days in lockdown. As for me, I don't think Superintendent Van Pelt and Dr. Mara have forgotten the writing class, and after I stole the truck . . . well, none of us is likely to get permission.

But I say, "I can talk them into it."

Dot and Maureen brighten up. Dot says, "I'll be fine as long as I'm not onstage alone."

"I'm better now," Maureen says. "I won't flip out."

I have my doubts, but I'm glad to give them hope. They certainly aren't getting it from anyone else. "Okay," I say. We go next door to the little room that's used for theater classes. "Let's take it from the top."

CHAPTER

15

ON MY WAY from the gymnasium, reluctant to return to Haven House, I pause by the square brick building that houses the theater. Letters carved into a marble frieze read "Van Pelt Hall." The double doors are open, releasing the dissonant sound of an orchestra tuning up. Beyond the lobby, I enter the auditorium, a dim, hot, musty-smelling space with seats for several hundred people. The ornately carved white plaster ceiling is cracked, the burgundy velvet upholstery on the seats is worn thin, and the matching carpet is threadbare. On stage, a male conductor gestures while a group of men and women begin playing classical music I don't recognize. I walk down a side aisle, through a door at the back. The sound of voices draws me along a hallway.

"Just put yourself in my hands, my dear. I promise you all will be well." It's Dot.

"Make your voice deeper. You're supposed to be a man." It's Rory.

"Will I be able to travel, and play the piano, and go to dances?" The girlish voice belongs to Maureen.

"Most certainly. You can do whatever your little heart desires," Dot says in a deep, gruff voice. She giggles.

"Don't laugh," Rory says. "This is serious."

Aha, I've got them cornered; they can't run away this time. Peeking through the open door, I see a room with rows of chairs set before a dais. On the dais, instead of my girls from Haven House, stand three strangers—a fat man and a slim one in old-fashioned suits, and a fat blonde woman in a long, voluminous green dress. Surprise halts me at the threshold.

The woman clasps her hands, looks heavenward, and sighs. "O, brave new world, that has such miracles in it!"

"Try to sound more excited," the slim man says.

Moving closer to the dais, I now recognize the fat man as Dot, the slim one as Rory. The woman is Maureen wearing a blonde wig. They notice me, and their eyes widen. They stand stiff and silent, like squirrels I've come upon in a forest, paralyzed for the instant before they scamper away.

Rory recovers first. "Hi, Dr. Kendall," she says with the blend of contempt and wariness she usually displays toward me.

"Hello, girls." I speak in my doctor voice, calm and friendly and professional. "What are you doing?"

"We're rehearsing a play," Rory says. "For the talent show."

I recall that the RKH brochure mentioned amateur theatricals as part of the therapy program. "What's your play about?"

Dot and Maureen cast panicky glances at Rory. The three of them must be up to something they shouldn't be.

"It's a fairy tale," Rory says. "I wrote it, and I'm directing it as well as acting in it." She sounds proud of herself—for the play, or for thinking fast on her feet? "It's about a poor girl in Victorian England." Rory points at Maureen, who giggles nervously. "She has two men wanting to marry her. One is a wealthy prince." She points at Dot, who tugs at her too-small coat, trying to close it. "If she chooses him, she'll live in a castle and have everything money can buy. The other man is the king of the fairies." Rory points her finger at her own chest. "If she marries him, she'll become a fairy queen and be able to fly and cast magic spells. The story is about which man she chooses and what happens."

Dot and Maureen avoid my gaze. Rory keeps a straight face, and even as I suspect she's pulling the wool over my eyes, I have to admire her yet again. She's given a plausible explanation for the lines I overheard and the period costumes.

"Well," I say, "I'd like to watch your rehearsal."

Dot's and Maureen's eyes pop. Covering their mouths with their hands, they turn to Rory, who says, "Actually, we're finished for now. Come on, girls, let's change clothes. See you back at the house, Dr. Kendall."

Why would they not want me to watch? They step off the dais and head for the door, but I block their way. "Have you told anyone else about your play?"

Sudden uncertainty quenches the pride in Rory's eyes. "No."

"Then how did you get permission to be in the show?" I can't imagine Superintendent Van Pelt or Dr. Mara letting patients perform without first knowing what they intend to do while they're onstage.

"We didn't," Maureen admits.

Rory's expression turns crafty. "Hey, Dr. Kendall, I just thought of something you can do for us."

I compress my lips with irritation at myself for falling into a position where she can manipulate me again.

"Get us permission to put on our play," Rory says, "and we'll tell you all about those patients who died."

My need to find out what happened that year has increased in urgency since Nurse Janice proved uncooperative and Lenora Hirschfeld's recollection sparse. And the idea that my stay at RKH was punishment for something terrible I'd done festers in my mind. It seems odd that three teenagers would have information about Caroline Lennox; where would they have gotten it? But if Rory, Dot, and Maureen do have it, I must pry it out of them.

"Suppose I do get permission for you," I say. "Information about dead patients from 1941 isn't enough in exchange. I want more."

Rory's face shows the first glimmer of approval for me: She respects me for upping the ante. I feel a worrisome degree of pride. Dr. Koffka said that a psychiatrist should be secure in her own self-esteem; a craving for approval from patients motivates the psychiatrist to try to please them instead of focusing on the therapeutic process.

"Oh, yeah?" Challenge sparkles in Rory's eyes. "What do you want?"

I tell myself that if Rory respects me, it improves my chances of helping her, and what I mean to ask of her is in her best interest. "I want you to participate in individual psychotherapy sessions with me."

Surprise lifts Rory's dark eyebrows. Whatever she'd expected me to ask of her, that wasn't it. Maureen and Dot watch her, waiting to see what she's going to say. Her eyes flash with rebellious temper, as if she'd thought she had me where she wanted me and now I've tricked her and won our battle of wills.

Her expression turns cunning for the instant before she smiles brightly and says, "Okay."

My triumph quickly gives way to the suspicion that I've just made a deal with the devil.

CHAPTER

16

THE OPPORTUNITY TO ask Dr. Van Pelt to allow Rory, Dot, and Maureen to put on their play at the talent show came sooner than I expected. I thought I would have to wait until morning rounds, but I met with him just a few hours after I saw the girls.

I had just attempted psychotherapy with Andrea Bond, the young wife who writes constantly in a notebook, trying to record her every thought. It's a form of obsessive neurosis that has taken over her life. Her husband committed her to RKH because she was neglecting her children, household responsibilities, and personal hygiene. She was reading aloud to me from her notebook as she scribbled frantically, describing a childhood trip to the circus, when she dropped her pencil. I bent down and picked it up. She cried, "No! Don't take my pencil!"

She snatched it from my hand, then punched my face so hard that I fell off my chair. She screamed, "It's mine. Leave me alone!"

Nurses came running. They found me on the floor and Andrea standing over me, threatening to kill me. They held her down, she fought them, and I had to administer the sedative injection, my first time.

I was in the utility room, applying an ice pack to my cheek, when Nurse Norris came and said, "Superintendent Van Pelt wants to see you in his office."

Now, with my cheek sore and swelling, I hurry to the mansion. Have I accidentally broken some rule, violated some therapeutic protocol? Or am I about to face the consequences for my midnight trip to the archives, the files I stole, and the questions I've asked about Caroline Lennox? My blouse is wet under my arms as I walk into the mansion. Like a schoolgirl called to the principal's office, I cautiously step through the superintendent's open door into air-conditioned coolness—a luxury that's scarce at RKH. Superintendent Van Pelt occupies a high-backed leather chair behind the massive carved desk. His office is fit for a European aristocrat, with oil paintings on the paneled walls and leatherbound books on the shelves. A glass-fronted case contains antique microscopes and other medical instruments. He hangs up the telephone when he sees me.

"Ah, Dr. Kendall," he says with a friendly smile. He gestures toward a chair in front of his desk. "Please."

I perch on the edge of the chair, then slide back into it in an attempt to look relaxed.

"I like to have impromptu chats with the new residents to find out how they're doing," Superintendent Van Pelt says. "They tend to answer more frankly when they haven't had time to prepare a speech."

I'm only a little relieved that he didn't call me in to reprimand me. He takes a closer look at me, and I stifle a flinch. This is my first one-on-one time with him. Will he realize he's seen me before my first day as a resident?

"What happened to your face?" He touches the spot on his cheek where the bruise must be turning purple on mine.

I'm afraid it's only a matter of time before he recognizes me as Caroline Lennox. I try to appear calm and businesslike while I explain about Andrea Bond.

Superintendent Van Pelt shakes his head with little concern or sympathy. "Your first battle scar. Welcome to the club."

"Thank you." I'm not offended that he's taking my injury so lightly; I'm glad he doesn't think I'm a delicate flower of womanhood who has no business on a psychiatric ward.

"So, Dr. Kendall, aside from taking one for the team, how are you doing?"

I can't tell him how overwhelmed, lost at sea, and doubtful about my own competence I feel. That would be admitting weakness, a feminine flaw. "Fine. I'm adapting to the routine at Haven House and getting to know my patients."

"Good, good." Either he believes me or he doesn't want to know—or doesn't care—if I'm not fine. Making his residents happy would require big changes—fewer patients, shorter hours, and more guidance as well as higher pay. "And what are your impressions of RKH?"

I could say that I don't have enough time for psychotherapy, the patients spend most of their time sitting around or wandering the halls, and Dr. Bullard is a useless, absentee supervisor. But I won't. One of my fellow interns at Mount Sinai complained about the conditions there. It didn't change anything, and he got a reputation as a whiner, universally disliked.

"The campus is beautiful," I say. "The patients are lucky to be here."

"It's my pride and joy," Superintendent Van Pelt says complacently. "I'm glad you appreciate it. I'm also glad you've managed to find some free time in your schedule."

"Free time?" I say, confused because I'm working twelve hours every day.

"For your research project on historic and contemporary psychiatric treatment of girls."

"Oh." I'm so disconcerted that I lose my speech. Who told him about my research? Was it Nurse Janice, Leonora Hirschfeld, or someone they told? Whoever is watching and reporting on me, Superintendent Van Pelt probably knows I've looked in the archives, where Nurse Norris told me the records for former patients are kept. I wouldn't be surprised to learn she's his spy. Does he also know I've been asking about Caroline Lennox?

"I should have told you about my project," I say. "I didn't think you would mind."

"I don't mind. Far from it. I'm glad to have the tradition of research at RKH revived."

This interview isn't just a how-are-you-doing chat. He's letting me know that he misses little of what happens at RKH, and he's warning me that I won't get away with poking my nose where it doesn't belong.

"What progress have you made so far?" he asks.

He speaks casually, but I wonder if he's worried that I've discovered something dangerous to him. I feel sure that he was involved in erasing my memory and faking my death. But I still can't imagine his motive.

"Not much," I say. "I've only begun interviewing longtime patients and staff members about their recollections of RKH in the past." Afraid of accidentally letting on that the research project is a cover for a personal investigation that could be detrimental to RKH, I change the subject. "I have learned that recreational and cultural activities are important features of both past and present therapy at RKH."

Superintendent Van Pelt regards me quizzically. "Yes, they're among our cherished traditions." Does he wonder what else I've learned that I'm not telling?

I wave my hands, as if to stir up mud in a clear river and hide what's on the bottom. "The talent show seems particularly beneficial." This remark, pulled off the top of my head, leads conveniently into the subject I wanted to broach with Superintendent Van Pelt. "Rosemary Kirkpatrick has written a play that she and Dot Powell and Maureen Murray want to put on at the talent show. I told them I would ask you for permission."

He raises his thick white eyebrows: for the first time, I've said something he finds surprising or original. "Rosemary Kirkpatrick." He frowns and drums his fingers on his desk. "Did she put you up to it?"

Not wanting to appear that I've been manipulated by her, I say, "I happened upon the girls' rehearsal. They're very enthusiastic about the talent show, and I think it would be good for them to feel a part of the community."

"I should warn you about our Rosemary. She's very clever and very good at getting what she wants from people." His gaze seems to see right through me as if I'm transparent glass.

I try not to squirm. "I know. Still, I'd like to give her a chance to enjoy a positive experience here. It might make her more amenable to therapy."

His scrutiny of me only intensifies. "Rosemary is a beautiful girl and very charming when she wants to be. Of course you're aware that she's a lesbian."

I nod. Where is he going with this?

"She knows how to make herself attractive to members of her own sex."

He's implying that I have homosexual inclinations, and Rory is taking advantage of my desire for her! A blush heats my face. "There's nothing of the sort going on between me and Rosemary."

"I'm glad to hear that, Dr. Kendall," Superintendent Van Pelt says somberly. "For a psychiatrist to engage in sexual relations with a patient is inappropriate, unethical, and grounds for expulsion from RKH."

He doesn't quite believe me. He's warning me to behave properly. My blush deepens as I feel the hint of professional misconduct clinging to me like a dirty film.

"Furthermore, homosexuality is a mental disorder that disqualifies lesbians from entering the psychiatric profession," he says.

That sounds like more than a hint of a threat. I don't want to offend him, but he's the man who was in charge of RKH when my memory was erased, whether or not he was directly involved. "For one to make assumptions when one knows nothing of the matter in question is irresponsible, unwise, and not a hallmark of a good psychiatrist," I snap.

The new expression on his face is oddly familiar. It's the same as Rory wore when I upped the ante in our bargain: he respects me for showing some spine. Then anger edges his smile: he doesn't like backtalk. He shakes his finger at me.

"I could say the same to you, *Dr.* Kendall." He gives my title the indulgent tone he would use with a child playing doctor. "You're inexperienced with mental patients. You haven't learned what they're capable of. Young, novice doctors are prime targets for someone like Rosemary. Especially doctors who are vulnerable because of their own issues."

Issues such as amnesia, a stay in this very hospital, and long-term aftereffects. *Does he know about me?* Was the purpose of this "impromptu chat" to let me know that he knows? Thanks to four years of medical school, I've had abundant practice in coping with innuendos and outright personal attacks from male doctors.

"Thank you, Superintendent. I'll keep that in mind," I say in the same cool, normal tone as when I recited the names of the muscles in the corpse I was dissecting while my anatomy professor squeezed my bottom. I wanted to grab his hand, slam it onto the table, and impale it there with my scalpel, but I couldn't afford a failing grade in the course. If I want to keep my residency, I can't afford to make an enemy of the superintendent.

"You do that, Dr. Kendall." He lets his words sink into the uncomfortable silence that makes the room too small and too hot. "What is Rosemary's play about?"

The sudden change of subject tips me off balance. I feel caught between two expert manipulators—my patient and my superior. I'm also having second thoughts about letting Rory, Dot, and Maureen stage their play at the talent show. But I give Superintendent Van Pelt the description that Rory gave me.

Steepling his hands under his chin, he ponders a moment, then shrugs. "Sounds harmless enough. I'll tell Dr. Mara to put the girls in the lineup." He stands; our chat is over.

I stand, glad that my lab coat hides the damp patches on my blouse. "Thank you."

Superintendent Van Pelt points his finger at me. "I'll rely on you to keep the girls on their best behavior." The twinkle in his eyes isn't quite friendly. "Back to the trenches, Dr. Kendall."

On my way back to Haven House, I don't give any visible sign that all is not well. But inside, I'm tense with fear that I've set things in motion that I'll wish I could stop when it's too late. Now that Superintendent Van Pelt knows about my "research," he'll be watching me even more carefully. The risk of my true purpose coming to light is greater than ever.

* * *

I work until eight o'clock, making up for the time I spent with Leonora Hirschfeld, Rory and her friends, and Superintendent Van Pelt. When

I go to dinner, nobody is in the mansion's dining room except maids cleaning up. They bring me iced tea and a plate of leftovers, which I carry outside to the terrace. I eat at a wrought-iron table, thankful for the solitude and quiet as the sky changes from rose gold to lavender.

"May I join you?" Dr. Mara approaches, carrying a plate of food and a coffee cup. Dressed in a pale gray tailored suit, with every hair of her blonde chignon in place, she looks as fresh as if it's morning instead of the day's end.

"Please do." I'm rumpled and grubby, and I don't want to talk to anyone, but I can't rudely spurn her company. Still on edge after my talk with Superintendent Van Pelt, I especially don't want to talk to his wife. Does she know about our meeting?

Does she know what happened to Caroline Lennox?

She sits down, and we eat in silence for a moment. Her chef's salad looks fresh and crisp. "Difficult day?"

"Yes." My chicken, potatoes, and peas are dried out, unappetizing.

She regards me sympathetically. "It'll get easier."

"I'm glad to hear that." All I can see in my future is an endless string of fraught days like this. "By the way, three of the girls at Haven House want to perform at the talent show. Did Superintendent Van Pelt ask you to put their play on the program?"

"Yes, and I did."

I feel both satisfaction and anxiety, having advanced my cause but perhaps in the wrong direction. "Thank you. I'll tell the girls tomorrow."

"I'm glad you've taken an interest in Rosemary, Dot, and Maureen," Dr. Mara says. "It sounds like you're making more progress with them than anyone else has, especially with Rosemary."

This is the first compliment I've received from anyone on the staff since I started working at RKH. Elated, I say, "I hope I can help her."

"If you can win her trust, it will help Dot and Maureen too. If she cooperates with our therapy program, so will they. She's a natural leader, despite her problems."

"I've noticed." I'm afraid I've become another baton twirler in Rory's little parade.

"But enough talking shop. The workday is over." Dr. Mara sighs with relief and lays her fork across her empty plate. "What do you like to do in your spare time?"

"What spare time?" I ask wryly.

Dr. Mara laughs. "I know." A shared memory of nonstop toil during medical school and internship warms the atmosphere between us. "Let me rephrase that: What would you do with your spare time if you had any?"

I find myself enjoying Dr. Mara's friendly conversation, and I'm relaxed enough to answer spontaneously. "I like exploring new places." When I'm under stress, it's soothing to go somewhere I've never been, where nobody knows me and I have no responsibilities. Best of all, there are no flashbacks. I can temporarily put the past behind me. "It's fun to visit museums, restaurants, and historic sites, even tourist traps."

"A woman after my own heart," Dr. Mara says. "May I call you Claire? You can call me Mara."

"Yes. Thank you, Mara." Now that our conversation has taken a personal turn, I feel comfortable enough to venture a question. "Where do you go to explore?"

"I take a cruise every winter by myself. My next one is to the Caribbean."

I picture her elegantly clad in a sundress and straw hat, strolling the deck of a ship. "Your husband doesn't go with you?"

"He prefers hunting in Africa or Alaska."

What does it say about their marriage that they vacation separately? I don't dare probe for intimate information. Maybe they just need time on their own. Despite my history with RKH and my antipathy toward Superintendent Van Pelt, I experience a moment of envying Dr. Mara and wishing myself in her shoes. The idea of married psychiatrists running a hospital, together yet independent, affluent enough to travel abroad, is deeply appealing to me—and far out of my reach.

"You have a day off soon," Dr. Mara says. "You can use it to go exploring."

"I need to stay and catch up on work."

"Time off is essential. We can't help our patients when we're mentally and physically drained ourselves. And you'll be starting nights on call soon. You need to build up a reserve of energy. Take your days off, Claire. That's an order." Dr. Mara smiles to soften the words.

I'm reluctant to leave; my days off are my chance to visit the different houses and question people who were at RKH when I was a patient. The possibility that I committed some sin or crime that I can't remember gnaws at me like termites on fragile wood. I'm growing desperate to exterminate it.

But I obediently say, "All right. Thank you."

I'll just have to pursue my inquiries during moments stolen from workdays. And if I can't figure out how to ask Dr. Mara about Caroline Lennox and the three deaths without arousing her suspicion, I'll have to find another path to the truth.

CHAPTER

17

At breakfast time in Haven House the next morning, I go to the patients' dining room. It's another hot summer day, the windows open to let in sunlight, air, and the drone of lawn mowers. The scent of freshly cut grass blends with the odors of coffee, toast, and fried eggs. Two teenage girls roam around, snatching food off other people's plates. They're among the patients who constantly wander the halls because their nervous disorders won't let them sit still. Rory, Dot, and Maureen are at their usual table by themselves. The sight of Rory in a pink, ruffled dress and pink ballet flats gives me a little shock, as if I'm seeing someone costumed for Halloween in July. Yesterday, dressed in a man's suit, she looked more normal.

"Hi, Dr. Kendall," Dot and Maureen say. Rory regards me with frowning suspicion.

"I have good news for you," I say. "Superintendent Van Pelt has given you permission to put on your play at the talent show."

Dot and Maureen cheer and clap their hands. Rory says, "Really?"

"Yes, really," I say.

Delight transforms Rory's face. She looks like a different person, younger and innocent. Dr. Koffka said these moments are like stepping stones that can lead a troubled soul out of darkness. I put aside the memory of my difficult conversation with Superintendent Van Pelt and my suspicion that Rory lied to me about the plot of her play.

"So it's time to begin your psychotherapy." Mornings are busy, and I really can't afford to spend an hour with one patient, but I have to pin Rory down before she can wriggle away.

"Oh, all right." She looks chagrined; she probably thought she need never fulfill her part of our bargain.

I'll have to conduct our session in her room; there's no place else in Haven House to talk privately. My heart pounds in accelerating alarm as we climb the stairs to the third floor. Many other patients must have lived in that room after I did, and it must have been cleaned hundreds of times; there can't be anything left of me. But my stomach tightens and I hear the rush of blood in my ears as I follow Rory through her door. It's as though I've stepped into the past. The slanted ceiling and bay window, the plank floor and braided rug, the smells of old wood, paint, and plaster, are instantly, dreadfully familiar. The air shimmers, my vision blurs, and I feel dizzy and nauseated. Through a black haze that pulsates in rapid rhythm with my heartbeat, I see Rory kick off her shoes, plop herself on the bed, and lean against the headboard, her legs outstretched on the rumpled white chenille spread. As I force myself to sit down, I experience a sensation of splitting into two different people—Dr. Claire Kendall in the armchair and Caroline Lennox on the bed where Rory is sitting. I glance up at the ceiling and see a jagged crack that resembles a mountain range, painted over but still visible. I used to stare at that crack and imagine myself flying over the mountains. On the other side was the waterfall near my family's summer place. I hoped that if I imagined hard enough, Brian and I would be together at the waterfall again. I look through Caroline's eyes toward the armchair. In it sits Nurse Janice, keeping watch over me. I'm lying in the bed while Superintendent Van Pelt looms over me, staring into my face.

We're the image I saw during my Rorschach test—the small figure threatened by a large one.

"Are you going to say something or are you just going to sit there?" Rory asks.

My vision of Superintendent Van Pelt and Nurse Janice fades, but I can feel the presence of my younger self. RKH is haunted by Caroline Lennox's ghost. And I brought her here. The only way to exorcise her is to find out what happened to her and make peace with it. In the meantime, I have a patient to treat. Shaken and breathless, I somehow manage to regain my professional composure.

"I want to help you, but I'm at a disadvantage because I'm new here," I tell Rory. "So it would be good if you could fill me in on what's been going on with you."

"Okay." Rory looks wary, on her guard.

"Why do you think you're here?" I say.

"I like girls?" Her inflection asks me if the obvious answer is the one I want. "I got caught?" Scorn tinges her voice; she thinks I already know what brought her to RKH.

Which I do. According to her file, she had a lesbian relationship with a girl identified as "X" to preserve her anonymity, and the two had been observed in the midst of a sexual act during a party. The incident had caused a scandal in their high-society circle.

"How did you feel about getting caught?" I say.

Rory rolls her eyes. "Not good?"

"I'm sorry you had to go through that." It must have been terribly humiliating for Rory and her friend. I hope my sympathy will melt her resistance.

She shrugs. I ask, "How did it lead to your being here?"

"They wanted to fix me." Her flat voice doesn't quite mask her hurt and resentment.

"Who are 'they'?" I say in my best quiet, nonjudgmental tone.

"My family." Rory's voice trembles, and for the first time I see a crack in her armor.

"Can you tell me about them?"

"Well, there's my dad and my mother," Rory sounds both reluctant and eager to speak. "And four brothers and three sisters."

Dr. Koffka said most clients are willing to discuss their relatives, even if only to complain about them. "Which family member is the most important in your life?"

"My dad," Rory says promptly. "He's a lawyer and a state senator. And he's running for Congress."

"Can you describe your relationship with him?" I don't have an Electra complex, but the diagnosis may be accurate for Rory.

"He takes me places he never took my sisters, like football games and boxing matches and hunting and deep-sea fishing. He says I'm smarter and braver than my brothers, always ready to try anything, no matter how scary or hard or dangerous." Rory's eyes are bright with love and pride.

Apparently, her father encouraged her tomboyish behavior, one trait that her therapy is designed to change. "How did he react to your situation?"

Rory squirms as if recoiling from the memory. "He blew his top." Pain extinguishes the light in her eyes.

"I'm sorry to hear that." I've never met her father, but I'm angry at him on her behalf. "How are things between you and your father now?"

She snorts. The sound is more mournful than derisive.

Brokering a reconciliation between Rory and her family would be a positive thing I could do for her. "How about if I talk to your parents?" Dr. Koffka advised involving the family in the patient's psychotherapy.

"Good luck. They never come here. They haven't even called me or written."

"That must be difficult for you. I'm sorry." My sympathy goes far deeper than is safe. Rory's father did essentially the same as my own father—washed his hands of his daughter. But it must be worse to be abandoned by a father who previously adored you than by one to whom you were nothing. I'm verging on dangerous territory, identifying too closely with a patient. "Who brought you to RKH?"

"My mother and the chauffeur." Bitterness tinges Rory's voice. "She dumped me here and left."

What happened to Rory is too much like what happened to me after my discharge from RKH: my father passed the buck to my mother.

"That's terrible," I blurt, my professional detachment gone.

"Yeah." Rory brightens, as if she sees that my sympathy is genuine and it's some comfort to her. Then she hastens to say, "But I know that what I did was bad. There's something wrong with my mind. I need to be fixed."

I've been taught that in cases where a patient has been involuntarily committed to a mental hospital, the therapist should help him embrace the decision to receive treatment as his own and cooperate with it for his own good. But last night I reread my notes on Freud's view of homosexuality. He saw it as a biological variation, not a disorder or illness: "Many highly respectable individuals of ancient and modern times have been homosexuals, several of the greatest men among them." "It is a great injustice to persecute homosexuality as a crime." "To undertake to convert a fully developed homosexual into a heterosexual does not offer much more prospect of success than the reverse." I think Freud was right even if he was wrong about other things. So which should I do—convince Rory that her family was correct to hospitalize her and she should cooperate in fixing her problem? Or tell her that her nature is set in stone and she's in good company with Sappho and Michelangelo? *The Diagnostic and Statistical Manual of Mental Disorders* categorizes homosexuality as a sociopathic personality disorder. I'm a novice disagreeing with the establishment and with the law that says homosexuality is a crime.

"It's my fault I'm here." Rory hangs her head. "I brought disgrace upon my family. I committed a sin against God. I deserve to be punished."

How terrible for a young girl to think she's evil! I know how it feels, the self-hatred, the misery. During my first year at boarding school after my mother died, I blamed myself for her death. If I'd watched over her, she wouldn't have fallen down the stairs. If I'd been a prettier, more accomplished and poised daughter, my father wouldn't have left. Brian's death became my fault too, even though I couldn't have prevented him from getting tuberculosis. Losing him wasn't enough punishment. Those thoughts sent me into such a deep, self-lacerating depression that I slit my wrists. I was saved by the school doctor, who came to my room to check on me after I didn't show up for class. His sympathy opened the barriers of my reserve. I told him about my family history, although not my stay in a mental hospital, which I was still trying to put behind me. He told me that my situation wasn't my fault, and eventually I managed to believe him. Unfortunately, I didn't have his wise, compassionate counsel during college. Plagued by the flashbacks of tunnels and electroshock treatments, I thought I was going insane and took an overdose of sleeping pills. After I vomited them up and survived, I somehow pulled myself together. I decided to become a psychiatrist so I could understand mental aberrations and help other troubled girls. Now I fear for Rory, seemingly headed down the same dark path that almost claimed my life.

"None of this is your fault," I tell her, passionate in my anger at the people who made her think so. "You're not a bad person." The school doctor saved me; I have to save Rory. Now I understand that her life is at stake, and I feel responsibility for her resting on my shoulders. "You don't deserve to be punished."

Ever present in my mind is the question of what transgression Caroline Lennox might have committed to deserve punishment by shock treatment at RKH.

Rory stares at me in surprise. She leans toward me, and I think she wants to believe I'm on her side. I reach my hand toward her. She lifts hers, then lets it fall. Of course she doesn't dare trust someone whose words run counter to everything she's heard from everyone else.

"I'm sorry for fighting everybody here who's tried to help me. I'm sorry I tried to run away. And I've done some serious thinking." Somber and earnest, Rory says, "I realize that I need to change or my life will be ruined. So I've given up tomboy clothes and games and I've learned how to set my hair and dress like a lady." She smooths her long curls and pink frock. "I'm going to date boys, and I want to get married and have babies someday. I'm ready to show my parents that I'm a normal girl now, so they'll let me come home."

Filled with rage and sorrow, I don't know what to say. RKH changed me from a normal teenager into a confused, haunted soul with amnesia, nightmares, and flashbacks. I hate the very idea that I'm part of RKH's effort to change bright, spirited Rory into a sad imitation of a conventional woman.

"So . . . could you discharge me from RKH?" Rory says.

I would like nothing better than to release Rory from this place that's holding her against her will, obliterating her true nature. Dr. Koffka said that patients shouldn't be forced into a mold, made to conform to society's standards; for some, if they can stay out of trouble and be content, that should be enough. In Rory's case, I agree.

Rory smiles, as innocent and winsome as a child asking for a pet dog. Sudden suspicion undercuts my sympathy for her. I thought she was opening up to me, genuinely engaging in psychotherapy, but was it all a ploy? Did she say the things she said just because she thought they would convince me to let her out?

I stall. "I'm afraid it's not that simple. Residents don't have sole authority over patients. Whether you can be discharged is up to Superintendent Van Pelt."

"But you could put in a good word for me, couldn't you?" Desperation shows through Rory's earnest appeal.

Is she tugging my heartstrings, trying to use me as a passport to freedom? Since I'm already on shaky terms with the superintendent, pushing him to discharge Rory could worsen my position even more.

"It would be irresponsible for me to recommend discharging a patient I've known for only a few days," I say.

"Just tell him I've done everything I'm supposed to and I'm ready to leave," Rory wheedles.

"Dr. Bullard would be asked for his opinion," I say, "and it would be given more weight than mine." His notes in her file are sparse, but they say she's fought every single treatment. He deems her "hostile and violently noncompliant."

Rory's manner abruptly changes from winsome to angry. "You say you want to help me, but you won't even try to get me out. What good are you?"

I've fallen into what I call the "transference trap." Transference is when the patient transfers his early experiences and relationships onto the therapist. He responds toward the therapist with the same emotions he felt during interactions with significant people in his life. The upside of transference is that the patient and therapist can analyze the patient's past traumas and relationships, work through repressed feelings, resolve old conflicts, and break negative behavior patterns. The downside is that when the patient harbors feelings of distrust, disappointment, or hostility toward those significant people, his feelings can turn on the therapist. Rory sees in me the parents who committed her to RKH.

"I'm sorry." I hurry to make excuses even as I feel like a hypocrite. "But now is not the time for me to recommend discharging anyone. I'm just a junior member of the staff." I mustn't promise Rory something I can't deliver, but I want to give her some hope as well as shore up the bond I thought we were beginning to build. "What I can do is work with you so that you'll be ready to leave eventually."

My conscience revolts against colluding in Rory's mistreatment, but I have no choice.

Rory folds her arms across her chest and glares at me, hurt and disappointed. "Yeah, right."

I'm ashamed because my sympathy has been proven useless; I'm just another adult who's let Rory down. She fumes as if she wants to tell me to go to hell but is restraining herself because every black mark on her chart will only lengthen her stay at RKH. I reluctantly stand up. No matter what else I say, her psychotherapy with me is over.

I've lost the right to ask Rory to fulfill her half of a bargain I never should have made, but nevertheless I say, "Tell me about those three deaths."

Her expression shifts from rancor to cunning to exaggerated bewilderment. "What deaths?"

CHAPTER

18

I STALK ACROSS THE campus, ignoring the people I pass. The atmosphere is close, humid, as though the world is holding its breath. That Rory reneged on our deal, pretending that our conversation about the three deaths never happened, is no more than I deserve, but I feel duped, thwarted, and furious. I need someone to talk to. I think of Dr. Koffka, whose German-accented voice speaks words of wisdom in my mind, as though she's a benign ghost that haunts me. But she's silent now.

Distant thunder rumbles. Moist wind cools the sweat on my skin. The fragrance of earth fills the air as the world exhales. Sprinkles of rain pelt me. Lightning veins the darkening sky above the pointed gables and barred windows of Mercy House. Taking shelter inside, I ask the nurse at the desk where I can find Dr. Tanaka. She says, "Second floor, east ward."

I climb the staircase enclosed by its iron grille. Shouts blend with gunfire from a television show. As soon as I step through the door that the orderly unlocked for me, I understand why new female residents aren't allowed to work in the maximum-security ward for the most disturbed male patients. Wolf whistles erupt from men pacing the corridor. Young and old, some dressed only in boxer shorts, they barrage me with calls of "Hey, baby!" and "You here to see me?" A fellow makes a vulgar gesture even though his hands are strapped to his wheelchair. Nurses, all women over forty, watch me from inside the cage around their station. The air has a sweaty, feral odor. Someone grabs my sleeve. I pull free, quicken my steps, and peer into rooms, searching for Daniel Tanaka. Some patients glare at me from their beds; one presses his angry face against the wire-gridded window in his door and yells obscenities. The gunfire grows louder as I enter the lounge. There, men are sitting on a beat-up sofa in front of the television that's enclosed in a metal cage. The show is a war movie, soldiers shooting from a trench. Daniel Tanaka accompanies a nurse who carries a tray of paper cups to a burly man in shorts and an undershirt. The man shakes his head, refusing to take his cup.

Daniel lifts the cup from the tray. "Alfred, you need your medication."

Alfred slaps the cup out of Daniel's hand. Pills go flying. "Dirty Jap!" he yells. "Get away from me!"

I'm shocked even though I've heard derogatory language against the Japanese before—on television, in movies, from people on the streets; I've read it newspapers and magazines and war posters. But I've never heard it flung at someone I know and like; I've never known a Japanese person before.

"I'm going to kill you!" Alfred lunges at Daniel.

Daniel grasps the man's thick shoulders. "Calm down, Alfred. We're here to help you."

Alfred howls and throws punches. There's a brutal tornado of wrestling, thrashing, hitting, and kicking as Alfred screams and Daniel struggles to subdue him. Spectators gather around them, yelling, "Fight! Fight!"

They stamp their feet, pump their fists. The nurse runs to the door, calling the orderlies. It all happens so suddenly that I'm too stricken to do anything but stand there. Daniel grabs Alfred in a headlock. He's at least four inches shorter and twenty pounds lighter than Alfred but stronger than he looks. Orderlies rush in and drag Alfred away. He shouts, "Yellow peril! Kamikaze bastard!" all the way down the hall.

The spectators resume watching television. Daniel puffs out his breath, runs a hand over his hair, and notices me.

"Claire. What are you doing here?"

Shaken by the violence I just witnessed, I can't admit that I need someone to talk to and chose him. He has his own troubles. "Dr. Bullard said to visit other houses, so I dropped by."

Daniel laughs with rueful humor. "You picked a good time." He touches his cheekbone, then winces at the blood on his fingertips.

The bruise under the makeup on my own cheek aches in sympathy. I'm inexplicably, embarrassingly moved by the sight of his wound. Resorting to brisk, businesslike doctor mode, I say, "Let me patch that up for you."

He hesitates. "Sure. Thanks."

We go to the utility room. Laying out sterile gauze pads, a bottle of alcohol, and adhesive bandages, I feel awkward because of what I just overheard. I don't know whether he would want me to say anything about it, but to sweep it under the rug feels wrong. "I'm sorry he said those things to you," I say.

Daniel shrugs as though he's heard those slurs so often that he's inured to them. "I don't hold it against him. He's a war veteran with combat fatigue, like some of the other men in Mercy House. He was stationed at Pearl Harbor, and he sustained a head injury during the attack. When he sees me, he sees the enemy who killed over two thousand of his comrades."

"I admire you for being so understanding." I'm shy because I spoke so frankly and nervous because we're having another personal discussion. I soak a gauze pad with alcohol and say the doctor's standard line: "This will only hurt a little."

We laugh, easing the tension. But when I daub the blood off his cheek, my fingers graze his skin. It's warm and smooth, and my uneasiness returns. Aside from two men I dated briefly during college, Daniel Tanaka is the first man whose face I've touched who wasn't a hospital patient. The realization makes me feel lacking and inferior, an abnormal woman. My two relationships were both consummated, awkwardly and with little pleasure on either side. Both ended soon after those encounters. Now the intimacy that's arisen between Daniel and me makes my heartbeat quicken with the need for more. He and I are the same height. There's an unexpected attraction in standing eye to eye with a man I admire. My hand trembles, and I hold my breath to steady it. Daniel is holding his breath too. I don't dare try to read his expression. I quickly apply the bandage and step back.

"Thanks." His voice isn't quite calm, but I can't tell what he's thinking or feeling.

Turning away from him, I wash my hands at the sink. "We both have battle scars. I got hit by a patient yesterday." I describe the incident with Andrea Bond. "But she's not my main problem."

"Who is?" Daniel asks.

"Rosemary Kirkpatrick." Now that we're on an impersonal topic, I can look at him again. I wanted to break out of the bubble of my isolation, but I'm sequestered inside it, my hands and nose pressed against the cold glass. "The girl who stole the truck."

"Is she in trouble again?"

He shows no sign of attraction to me; we're just colleagues discussing a case. I can't help feeling disappointed. I remember that I must censor what I tell him about Rory. To him, the deal I made with her would sound like a mistake, if not professional malfeasance. Besides, I don't want him to ask me why I want information about three deaths in 1941.

"The trouble is that I don't think Rory is being treated properly," I say. "I have doubts about whether homosexual conversion therapy really works, and I don't believe it's good to lock a seventeen-year-old girl up in a mental institution with seriously disturbed patients for an indefinite period of time."

Daniel nods. "Mm."

I recognize a standard therapeutic ploy: make "listening noises," let silence fall, and the client will talk just to fill it. Uncomfortable because I think Daniel suspects there's something I'm not telling him, I keep quiet.

He breaks the silence, as a therapist eventually has to if his patient won't talk. "I have the same doubts about some of my patients. I think the drugs and the shock treatments may be doing them more harm than good."

I recognize another ploy—share a common experience to create rapport and invite confidences. But I don't think Daniel is merely practicing his therapeutic skills on me, nor do I think he's just nosy. I think he really does have doubts and questions about whether RKH's treatment protocols are effective or safe. I feel better just knowing I'm not alone.

"The only apparent criteria for whether Rory is 'cured' is how good a job she does acting 'normal,'" I say.

Daniel chuckles. "'Acting normal' is one definition of sanity. Patients at RKH who were involuntarily committed have to pass an interview with Superintendent Van Pelt before they're discharged. I heard two of my patients trading tips on how to 'act normal' during the interview. They know they won't get out if they 'act crazy.'"

We laugh. *Humor is a valuable tool for creating bonds between people,* Dr. Koffka says in my mind.

"Stealing the truck moved Rory backward on the spectrum of 'normal' behavior," I say regretfully.

"But it wasn't a sign of insanity. The only patients who don't want to leave are the ones who've been at RKH for so long that it's home. They're not examples of perfect mental health."

It's such a relief to talk to someone who shares my views, I hadn't realized how much I needed it and how much my isolation pains me. "What should I do?" I think I can rely on Daniel's judgment.

He takes his time answering, as if my problem is as important to him as it is to me. "You could discuss your concerns with Dr. Bullard."

If Superintendent Van Pelt has told Dr. Bullard about our conversation regarding Rory, then Dr. Bullard will be more inclined to think Rory is manipulating me than to take my concerns seriously. "I'm afraid now is not a good time."

Before I can explain, we notice faces in the safety-glass window of the utility room door. Two patients are ogling us. An orderly removes the patients. A nurse peers in and smiles slyly before she walks away. We look at each other and wince: We've just given more fodder to the RKH rumor mill.

"I'd better get back to Haven House," I say.

"I saw the residents' schedule," Daniel says. "Don't you have the day off tomorrow?"

"Yes."

"How are you going to spend it?"

"I thought I'd go for a drive." I feel guilty about walking freely out of RKH while Rory and my other patients are stuck here, but an order from Dr. Mara is an order.

"Before you decide on any action about Rory, why not give yourself the day not to worry about it? And then come back with a fresh mind?"

"That's a good idea," I say, glad for a reprieve and his wisdom. "Thank you, Daniel."

I never imagined that one day could change things so drastically.

CHAPTER

19

A WARM BREEZE BLOWS through my open car windows as I drive through the Pocantico Hills, a gently rolling terrain of green pastures and white fences, woodlands and occasional houses. On the roadside, blue chicory, yellow dandelions, and white Queen Anne's lace bloom. Reeds border ponds that reflect the blue sky and majestic white clouds. I left RKH this Sunday morning with no destination in mind and nothing but a New York State map as a guide. Blissfully free of the ward routine, putting aside the fear of what unwelcome facts my investigation might uncover, I turn on the radio. The news broadcast is a mixture of good and bad, entertaining and serious: the Miss Universe pageant in California, the record-breaking heat wave in New York City, Senator Joseph McCarthy's crusade against communism. It's a reminder that there's a whole world outside RKH.

About twenty miles from the hospital, I see a sign for U.S. Highway 202. My hands involuntarily signal that I'm taking the detour and turn the steering wheel. I recognize the route my family took every June to our summer place in Arden Spring when I was a child.

Freud said that the mind has three levels: the conscious, the preconscious, and the unconscious. The conscious encompasses thoughts and perceptions that we're aware of. The preconscious is the repository of accessible memories and stored knowledge. The unconscious is a hidden cauldron of visceral desires and memories, of primitive urges and irrational impulses. The conscious is like the visible tip of an iceberg; the preconscious floats just below the surface; and the unconscious is the vast, submerged, invisible portion. The unconscious contains material that's repressed because it's too disturbing, unacceptable, or painful for the rational self to acknowledge. But the influence of the unconscious is mightily strong. It asserts itself in dreams and Freudian slips—errors in speech or actions. My unconscious mind has taken control of my car.

I've never been back to Arden Spring. The summer place was the scene of my happiest childhood memories, which I wanted to keep sealed as if in amber, inviolate. I suppose I've known all along that I eventually must go back. What better place to seek clues about what happened in the summer of 1941?

A cold weight of dread settles in my stomach, and the steering wheel grows slippery with sweat from my hands.

I'm not ready.

On the east, to my right, wooded cliffs studded with bare rock loom above the highway. On the west, scenic lookouts offer views of the sunlit Hudson River. On the pavement ahead of me, a heat mirage forms, and in the shimmery illusion I see my father's car, a blue Cadillac convertible with the top down. Chasing the illusion, I see my parents in the front seat, him wearing a straw boater, her in a flowered headscarf, both in sunglasses. Brian and I sit in the back, our blond hair windblown. Suddenly I'm split into two people again—the adult driving my own car and the eight-year-old riding in the convertible with my family. Brian is ten. We're playing our usual game, vying to be first to call out the landmarks we pass.

"There's Bear Mountain Bridge!" I cry.

I round a curve, and the steel bridge that spans the Hudson River comes into view.

Brian shouts, "Castle Rock!"

I see the stone castle high on a hilltop, a railroad tycoon's summer estate.

We laugh, excited because we're almost there. Our parents turn to each other and smile.

They were happy together then. But at some point their quarrels became the background noise of my life, like static on the radio, the volume gradually going up as the years passed. Their most vicious arguments were about other women. But that summer, all was well. Or was I just too young to detect the faults beneath the surface?

Crossing a bridge over the spring, I glimpse smokestacks.

"The old foundry! I win!"

Arden Spring is a village of some twelve hundred people, about seventy miles north of New York City, bordered by the river on the west and the Hudson Highlands on the other sides. I automatically turn left on Main Street and drive toward the river. The town is familiar yet strange, like a movie set instead of the actual place. The businesses that were open during my childhood are still there—the restaurant, general store, bar, tailor's, barber shop, movie theater, post office, and taxidermist's—but they're spruced up with fresh paint and colorful awnings. Other buildings, once vacant, now contain art galleries, an ice cream parlor, and stores that sell clothing, books, and jewelry. The town is crowded, with a different sort of people. Instead of the few locals driving old cars and trucks or loitering outside the bar, fashionably dressed couples browse the new stores, and suntanned teenagers cruise in convertibles. By the river, families stroll around a bandstand in a park that has replaced grim warehouses. Arden Spring, downtrodden by the closure of the foundry and the Depression, is enjoying a renaissance. Prosperous folk from the city, looking for a summer getaway, have discovered the town.

I feel like a ghost from its past, insubstantial and out of place. Arden Spring isn't a time capsule like RKH, virtually unchanged since 1941. Here, the new covers the old like a thick layer of spackle. What traces of my fourteenth summer could I possibly find?

The parking spaces along Main Street are filled with the tourists' shiny late-model cars, so I turn onto a side street, take the first empty space I find, and climb out of my car. In front of me is the library, a tan brick building. Arched windows flank a front door with a fanlight. It's the only building I've seen today that looks exactly as it did during my childhood. Inside, I find that the reading room has the same high white ceilings and dark wood floor, bookshelves and furniture I remember. The cool, quiet atmosphere breathes the familiar syrupy smell of old books. In the children's section at the back, I remember the last time I was here.

It was during that strange summer of 1941, a hot, still August day. I was restless, bored, and lonely. My father was at work in the city; my mother was by the pool, drinking. Although Brian was usually out with his friends, he was in his room. I knocked on his door and asked him to walk to the library with me. He wouldn't come out. He said, "Get Sam to take you." Sam was our chauffeur and handyman; his wife Rita was our cook and housekeeper. That day, Sam drove me to the library.

Now, twelve years later, I remember wondering why Brian was behaving so strangely and wishing we could play together like we used to do. There, my memory fizzles out. I look around the library. Beside the librarian's desk, an easel holds a poster. A memory flickers in my mind. I walk over to the easel. The poster is an announcement for the county fair. The one I saw the last time I was here had an enlarged black-and-white photograph of a person, but the image in my mind is fuzzy. I ask the librarian about the poster that was displayed in August 1941. She says she doesn't know; she only moved to Arden Spring last year.

When I head back to Main Street, it's as if visiting the library has peeled back the scrim of modernity that overlays the scene. In the windows of the bar, the tailor's, and the movie theater box office, I picture the blurry white rectangle of the poster. I recall people clustered by the posters, in hushed, anxious conversation.

Something bad happened here, but try as I might, I can't remember what it was.

The clock over the bank reads one-thirty. It's lunchtime, and I'm hungry. I walk into the restaurant. My parents used to bring Brian and me here. The shabby interior has been redone with fresh paint and new steel-and-Formica tables in sunny yellow and turquoise, but the smell of coffee and fried food is the same. In the past, there were never more than a few other customers, but now the place is full and noisy. I take the empty stool at the counter, between an old man and a teenage girl. As the counterman takes my order for iced tea, an egg salad sandwich, and blueberry pie, I think he's the same person who served my family, older, gray-haired, and stouter now.

"Were you working here in 1941?" I ask him.

"Yes, miss." He looks quizzical, as if wondering whether we've met before.

"I passed through town with my family that summer, and we ate here," I say.

He gives me a friendly smile. "Welcome back."

"I remember seeing copies of a poster all along Main Street," I say. "It had a photograph of someone. What was it about?"

"Ah." His expression turns grave. "That was the summer when Donna Wright went missing."

I'm startled to hear the name. Donna Wright was Brian's pretty blonde girlfriend. I remember Brian walking over to join her and the other local teenagers outside the general store.

"The posters had a photograph of Donna and a message asking for anyone with information about her whereabouts to report it to the police," the counterman says.

The news is upsetting. So is the fact that I can't remember Donna going missing, another piece of information lost to amnesia. "Was she ever found?"

The old man sitting next to me looks up from his club sandwich. "Yes, but unfortunately not alive." His thin figure is clothed in a blue-and-white-striped shirt, black suspenders, and gray trousers. White hairs fringe his bald head. Gold-rimmed glasses circle blue eyes that are still sharp and clear. "Her body was found in the woods. She had been raped and murdered."

I stare at him in horror. The counterman turns away to serve another customer, and the old man says, "I'm Edward Humphrey. I was the editor of the *Arden Spring Chronicle* before I retired. I ran the story about Donna Wright."

"Claire Kendall." I'm still trying to absorb the terrible story I've just heard, of which I have absolutely no recollection.

"Nice to meet you." Mr. Humphrey says, "We never had much crime here in Arden Spring. Still don't. Petty theft, bar brawls, and such. The Donna Wright case was big news. Her parents reported her missing after she didn't come home from a party the night of July twenty-third. The police organized a search. People from town came out to help. They brought dogs."

To my astonishment, I begin to remember. From the porch of our house in the Highlands, I had watched lights flashing and heard voices shouting and dogs barking in the woods.

Mr. Humphrey doesn't seem to wonder why a stranger would be interested in an old local crime; he must be glad to have a new audience for the biggest story of his career. "Three days later, the dogs found her in the woods."

My food comes, and I eat without tasting it, my mind busy collating the events of that summer. There were three deaths—Donna's, Brian's, and my own faked one. Or five, counting the other two at RKH—Peter Kramer and Adeline Peck. Are they pieces of the same puzzle? Or am I seeking a connection between them when there is none?

"The autopsy showed a fractured skull and a broken neck," Mr. Humphrey says. "She'd been hit on the head, but the cause of death was strangulation."

How could her murder be connected to a death from tuberculosis and three at a hospital forty miles away? The timing must be a coincidence. But my gut feeling says it's not.

"Did they ever find out who did it?" I ask.

"No. The case is still open."

A reason for Brian's abnormal behavior becomes clear: His girlfriend had disappeared and been raped and strangled. It must have happened shortly before he was diagnosed with TB. He would have been upset, grieving.

"There was a suspect, though," Mr. Humphrey says. "One of the summer people, a boy named Brian Lennox."

The bite of sandwich I was chewing goes down the wrong way. *Brian was a suspect in Donna's murder?* Choking and coughing, I gulp my iced tea. I manage to swallow the morsel, but the cold, sweet tea can't wash away my horror.

"Brian was at the party with Donna," Mr. Humphrey says. "Friends who were there said they went off alone together, and that's the last they ever saw of Donna."

My brother was the last to see her alive. My ears start to ring. Maybe grief wasn't the only reason he wouldn't come out of his room. Was it guilt? But Brian was good and kind and had never been in trouble; he would never have hurt anyone. He couldn't have done it! Dizziness washes over me. A memory starts to surface, dark and thick and foul, but my mind tamps it down like an iron lid on a manhole. *What happened that night?* All I know for sure is that there was far more to that lost summer than I thought, and it might be far worse than I could have imagined. The story I'm trying to piece together is no longer just about my lost memory or suspicious deaths and possible malpractice at RKH. It includes an actual murder case involving a girl I knew and the person I loved more than anyone else in the world.

"What happened to . . . ?" My voice is raspy from fear as well as from choking. I can't bear to say my brother's name.

"Brian Lennox was questioned by the police. He stated that he didn't rape or kill Donna. His attorney instructed him not to say anything more."

The iron lid on my memory remains closed tight. Did I forget all of this, or did Brian and my parents keep me in the dark while it was happening?

"The police were still looking for evidence against him when it turned out that he had tuberculosis. His parents sent him to the state sanatorium in Ray Brook. He developed pneumonia and died there."

The tuberculosis, the sanatorium, and the death from complications jibe with the story that my parents told me, but that brings me no relief. Brian went through a terrible ordeal, and I was oblivious to his suffering. My guilt about his death resurfaces, sharp and corrosive. What I now know of that summer is too little too late.

"The police thought he was guilty," Mr. Humphrey says. "So did most folks in Arden Spring." His nod says he thinks so too.

"Donna's father was the mayor. He pushed hard for Brian to be arrested and put on trial. A jury probably would have convicted him. There was so much bad feeling toward the Lennox family. None of the local businesses would serve them. They had to leave town."

So that's why we never came back. I'd thought it was only because of Brian's death and my parents' divorce.

"They still own their property in the Highlands, though."

I'd assumed it had been sold long ago. My father kept it, but why?

"The caretaker and his wife live there."

Sam and Rita. I picture Sam, a husky dark man mowing the lawn; Rita, plump and motherly, smiles from behind a tureen of soup. Even as I realize that they're two people who might be able to fill me in on the events of that summer, the egg salad I ate pushes up into my throat, acrid and sulfurous. I need to hear whatever else Mr. Humphrey can tell me about my family, but if I listen any longer, I'm going to be sick.

Looking at my watch, I say, "Goodness, it's late. It was nice talking to you." I take some bills out of my wallet, throw them on the counter, then rush out the door.

* * *

Our summer house is a mile or so east of Arden Spring, on twenty wooded acres in the Hudson Highlands. It blends in with the forest, invisible from the road. There wasn't another house within sight or earshot. The only manmade noises from outside were the infrequent cars on the road below us, the rumble of distant trains, and the drone of airplanes overhead. By night, owls hooted and crickets chirped in such darkness that a million stars were visible in the sky. As a child, I eagerly looked forward to going to our summer place each June, reluctantly left it on Labor Day, and pined for it during the cold winter months. It's a lost paradise that I thought I would never see again.

Until today.

My purpose has metastasized beyond its original shape and limits. Now it's not only about myself and RKH and discovering what happened to me there that summer. Now I need to exonerate my brother. Even though Brian is dead, I can't bear the idea that people think he was a murderer. And what if Donna's murder and my amnesia are part of a larger picture? Casting light on one part might illuminate the other.

I drive along the road that winds up into the Highlands, between tall trees whose cool shadows dapple the pavement. My heart starts to race. Despite encroaching dizziness, I bear down on the gas pedal. The summer place is the scene of the events preceding my commitment to RKH. If I see it, maybe I'll remember that I knew something that will clear Brian's name, perhaps the identity of the actual murderer.

The road is narrow with tight curves and blind spots. Slowing down at a driveway flanked by two pillars made of piled stones, I signal a right turn. Gravel on the long, curving, uphill driveway crunches beneath my tires. Grass grows between wheel ruts. I yearn and dread to see the house again. Has it changed? What will I say to Sam and Rita? If I stop to think, I'll lose my courage. I round the final, ascending curve and slam on the brakes just in time to avoid crashing into a chain-link fence that wasn't here the last time I came. Some ten feet high, it blocks the driveway and extends into the woods on either side. A sign on it reads, "No Trespassing." A heavy lock secures the gate. Maybe the house needed protection because of the bad feeling toward my family after Donna Wright was murdered. I turn off the engine, get out of the car, and walk up to the gate. There's an intercom mounted on the fence, but I can't bring myself to use it. All I can see of the house is dark green rooftops half hidden by trees. All is quiet. I can't tell if anyone is at the house. The wind that stirs the forest smells of pine and earth. Squirrels chatter in the foliage. Then I hear faint music.

I spin around, unable to tell where it's coming from. The music is tinny, as if from a radio. My vision shimmers, and the music grows louder through the ringing in my ears. The song is "My Sister and I," by the Jimmy Dorsey orchestra, played everywhere in the summer of 1941. The song is about two children during the war, sent away from their ravaged homeland in Europe to begin a new life abroad. As they make the best of their exile, they wistfully recall their friends and tulip garden, the Dutch mill and the fishing boats. A tenor whose name I've forgotten begins to sing:

The warm and lovely world we knew
Has been struck by a bitter frost . . .

Vertigo whirls me into a flashback. It's night, and I'm fourteen years old, standing on the balcony outside my room at the summer house. The distant music accompanies boisterous shouts and laughter. The air smells of smoke from a campfire. I hear a door open and close. Peering down, I see Brian emerge from the house, onto the patio. Dimly visible in the moonlight reflected in the swimming pool, he glances over his shoulder, then tiptoes to the trail that leads into the woods. He has a flashlight. Its beam flickers through the trees as he moves down the trail. Brian isn't supposed to go out. My father grounded him because he'd been staying out all night with kids from town, and yesterday he hit a tree while driving drunk and broke a headlight. And my father doesn't like Brian dating Donna; he calls her a cheap little gold digger.

I hurry down the stairs from the balcony. I never made friends here, because in previous years I never needed any; I always had Brian. This summer I've been so lonely, and I want to see the fun I'm missing. I follow Brian along the trail, which leads down a ravine and then up into the hills. The trail narrows; the trees grow closer together amid thick underbrush and vines. After the terrain levels out, Brian hurries toward orange light and pungent smoke, the sounds of music and laughter. I hang back as he joins the teenagers sitting around a campfire in a clearing. Donna smiles up at Brian. Her blonde hair gleams in the firelight. He sits beside her, and they share a bottle of beer. Hidden behind the trees, I watch them. Brian tosses aside the empty bottle and pulls Donna to her feet. They slow-dance, her cheek against his shoulder. The others hoot and whistle. My heart fills with a new, painful emotion—jealousy.

I don't like Donna. I want Brian to be my companion again. But I'm all alone outside the circle of firelight.

The song ends. Brian and Donna look deep into each other's eyes and smile. Arm around her waist, he leads her into the woods amid calls of "Attaboy!" and "Have fun!" from their friends.

Propelled by curiosity, I follow them along a trail to a smaller clearing. I hear the murmur and ripple of the waterfall that Brian and I used to visit together. It's dark except for moonlight that filters through the trees. The two shadowy figures merge into one. Sick with shame, I watch Brian and Donna kiss and caress. Donna giggles. Clothing rustles. Brian groans. They sink to the ground together. A dark, hot excitement burgeons in me.

The scene brightens jaggedly around the edges like a photograph lit by a match. The brightness spreads until I'm standing at the fence in broad daylight, abruptly returned to the present. The song on the radio echoes in my mind.

. . . my sister and I recall with a sigh
The world we knew and loved and lost.

What did I just remember? Was it the night Donna went missing? What else did I see when I spied on her and Brian? Shuddering, I fall to my knees. Did I witness my brother raping and killing Donna Wright?

The terrible suspicion rises up in me. I slam down the iron manhole lid, but the influence of the unconscious mind is hard to repress. Noxious thoughts seep around my mental barrier like sewer gas. They're not just doubts about Brian, the last person to see Donna alive. Someone else was in the woods with them; someone who disliked Donna; someone the newspaper editor doesn't know about and apparently never came to the police's attention.

The memory of my jealousy sickens my stomach.

I imagine sneaking up behind Donna after she and Brian part company. I imagine a large, rough rock in my hands, the deep breath

I draw before I bring it down on her head. I can almost feel her smooth, warm neck as I squeeze the life out of her. The sensations are frighteningly real.

Oh, God, no.

Sour bile pushes up into my throat. I lean over and vomit.

CHAPTER

20

IN MY REARVIEW mirror, the evening sky wears a faint red rim near the horizon, but the highway is dark, lit only by my headlights and the roadside reflectors. So much for my refreshing day off. I'm exhausted, reluctant to go back to RKH, dreading the duties and ordeals I'll face there. But I need a cool bath, Pepto-Bismol for my stomach, aspirin for my aching head, and sleep. Tomorrow I'll be able to think clearly about what happened today and what to do next.

I'm afraid that if I keep digging into my past, dredging up buried memories, I'll find out that either Brian murdered Donna Wright after raping her and I was a witness, or I killed her myself. Should I fight to tear through the veil of my amnesia or let sleeping dogs lie? The decision is mine to make . . . tomorrow.

At the hospital's Victorian gatehouse, a guard raises his hand. I stop, roll down my window, and hear shrieks from patients in the houses. The hospital sounds are clearer at night when there's no traffic noise to drown them out. The guard leans in the window.

"Dr. Kendall," he says. "Dr. Mara wants to see you in her office."

"What for?" I don't want to talk to anyone. I'm busy trying to argue myself out of the notion that I killed Donna. I wasn't capable of bashing her on the head and strangling her; as a child, I'd never even slapped anybody. *But the unconscious mind is a cauldron of primitive urges, and jealousy can drive the tamest souls to violence.* I wasn't strong enough to kill a girl who was three years older and bigger than I was. *But Donna had been drinking, and I could have caught her by surprise.*

The guard gestures in the direction of the mansion. "Right now."

I drive through the dark campus, park in the lot behind the mansion, and enter through the back door. Brian was never violent either, but if his primitive urges caused him to rape Donna, he could have gone one fatal step further. The last thing I need now is another problem. Has something bad happened during my absence? Did I do something wrong? Perhaps Dr. Mara has learned my identity and she's going to expel me because I failed to disclose my history as a former RKH patient. If only I had time to rest before facing the music.

The mansion is deserted; the only light comes from the open door of Dr. Mara's office and the sconces on the stairway landing. My footsteps ring loudly on the marble floor. I find Dr. Mara seated behind her desk and Dr. Bullard in one of the two chairs in front of it. They regard me with somber, opaque gazes.

"Dr. Kendall. Please sit down," Dr. Mara says.

She's been so friendly, but her manner is cold and formal now. The fluorescent lighting doesn't flatter her or Dr. Bullard; it gives their skin and her blonde hair a greenish-gray cast. I must look like death warmed over. I sit, clenching my hands in my lap, bracing myself for the end of my career. Four years of medical school, a year of internship, and a year at the Manhattan Psychoanalytic Academy, for nothing. And Brian and myself implicated in a murder. I should never have come here. My headache throbs. I really should have left the past behind me.

"I have bad news," Dr. Mara says. "Leonora Hirschfeld committed suicide."

My reaction hits me like a series of thunderbolts. First comes shock: the news is terrible but so far from what I expected to hear. Next is relief: my secret is safe. Then a double blow of horror and shame: a patient I know has taken her own life, and I was selfish enough to think of my own career.

"She hanged herself in her bathroom, with a stocking tied to the shower curtain rod," Dr. Bullard says. He and Dr. Mara watch me closely for my reaction.

"But I just saw her on Thursday." What a stupid thing to say; my having seen her doesn't negate the fact of her death.

"That's why we called you in," Dr. Mara says. "Any death at RKH requires an investigation. We need to determine all the circumstances of the death, which means interviewing everyone who had contact with the deceased. I know that you talked to Leonora."

Even while my mind reels with the shock of Leonora's suicide, I wonder how Dr. Mara knows I talked to Leonora. I recall a nurse interrupting our conversation. Nurse Norris somehow knew where I was. Did she tell Dr. Mara? Is the whole staff watching and reporting on the activity of all the residents, or just me? Am I becoming as paranoid as I fear?

"What did you and Leonora talk about?" Dr. Bullard asks.

My mind scrambles to figure out what it's safe to tell, what better to omit. "She told me that her husband and family are suing each other for control over her." I speak slowly, giving myself time to think. "We talked about her painting. I told her about my research for an article about girls at psychiatric hospitals, past and present. I wanted to interview her because she's a long-term patient." Here is where I edit my recollection. "I asked for her impressions of what RKH was like when she first came here." Now I lie: "She said it was all a blur."

I hate putting words in a dead woman's mouth—or taking them out—and I feel guilty because I'm hindering the investigation into her suicide, but I can't mention Caroline Lennox and provoke questions about why I'm interested in her death.

"Is that all?" Dr. Mara asks.

Again I wonder what the nurse who interrupted us might have overheard, and if Leonora discussed our conversation with anyone. "Leonora said she needed to finish her painting for a show at the National Arts Club. I'm surprised that she would commit suicide when she was looking forward to the show."

"Leonora was mentally unstable," Dr. Bullard says. "Her moods could turn on a dime."

"That's why we need to know what you said to her," Dr. Mara says.

Horror fills me: they think I said something that drove Leonora to suicide. My guilt burgeons because perhaps I did. By encouraging her to talk about the deaths of other patients, had I unwittingly nudged her toward taking her own life?

"That's all," I say.

Dr. Mara and Dr. Bullard exchange a glance I can't read. Dr. Bullard says, "Leonora wasn't your patient. You shouldn't have interviewed her on your own, especially since you're completely inexperienced with complex cases like hers."

Fighting tears, I bow my head, unable to bear the thought that I could be responsible for Leonora's death. I became a psychiatrist because I want to help mentally ill people; now, after only a week on the job, one is dead, possibly because of me.

"Your research project is over," Dr. Mara says. "You showed poor judgment by conducting it without permission and supervision. From now on, you will concentrate solely on your duties as a resident. Do I make myself clear?"

Well aware that I deserve the rebuke, I answer humbly. "Yes, Dr. Mara."

"All residents make mistakes." Dr. Mara's smile expresses tolerance without warmth. "Learn from yours, Dr. Kendall."

* * *

I walk up the stairs in as dignified a style as I can muster. It's all I can do not to flee the mansion like a jail-breaking convict. The airless heat suffocates me as the bleak reality of my situation sinks in. The selfish part of me is relieved that I wasn't fired, but I no longer have an excuse to question patients or staff about Caroline Lennox and the deaths in 1941. If I carry on with my "research project," Dr. Mara will surely hear of it. And why should I carry on? My inquiries have brought nothing but trouble—possibly Leonora's suicide as well as my discovery that Brian was a suspect in a murder and that I myself might be the killer. Still, I can't believe that quitting is the best option. If Brian is innocent, then clearing his name matters, even at my own expense.

My love for Brian is meaningless if I killed Donna and let him take the blame. If I am indeed guilty, I should be the one to suffer the notoriety, the punishment.

And if RKH is currently engaging in malpractice, it needs to be exposed and the patients protected.

The only certain thing is that if I want to keep my residency at RKH, I'll be walking on eggshells from now on.

In the second-floor corridor, I run toward my room. A male voice halts me. "Hello, Dr. Kendall." The man walks toward me from the far end of the corridor. It's Ronald Norton, an unpleasant surprise.

"What are you doing here?" I ask.

"I wanted to say I'm sorry you got in trouble about Leonora Hirschfeld." Ronald oozes sympathy.

"How did you know?" It feels like he's been lying in wait for me.

"It's all over campus."

That's not what I wanted to hear, and I desperately need to be alone to rest and collect myself before I face tomorrow. "Well, good night." I start toward my door.

Ronald falls into step beside me. "I don't think you did anything wrong."

"Thanks." I can't tell if he really means it.

"They're just looking for someone other than themselves to blame. You're the scapegoat."

That doesn't make me feel any better. If Leonora's family sues RKH, Dr. Mara and Superintendent Van Pelt will throw me to the wolves rather than risk losing their shirts.

At my door, I say, "See you tomorrow."

"Why don't you invite me in for a drink?" Ronald pulls a silver flask out of his pocket and grins. His teeth are white, perfect, and sharp. "I bet you could use one."

Anger flares in me. Ronald isn't just the womanizer I thought he might be, he's seeking to take advantage of me when I'm upset and vulnerable.

"No, thanks. I'm going to call it a night."

"Don't you want a shoulder to cry on?" Lowering his voice to a husky whisper, he backs me against the door and puts his hands on it, so I'm trapped between his arms. His breath smells like alcohol.

My heart beats wildly as I remember an incident at Mount Sinai Hospital. I was asleep in the room where the interns and residents nap during overnight shifts, and I woke up to find the senior resident lying on the cot beside me, fondling my breasts. As I screamed and thrashed, my elbow hit his face. He recoiled from me, and I ran out of the room. When I saw him the next day, he was missing a front tooth. I never reported him; it would have been my word against his. I overheard him telling people that he'd been in a fight at a bar. I suppose he was ashamed to admit that a woman had knocked his tooth out. So we were even, I guess.

I duck under Ronald's arm.

He grabs my waist, nuzzles my neck. "Be nice, Claire."

Furious, I say, "No! Stop it!"

"You know you want it as much as I do." The hardness in his groin presses against me.

I fight him, never mind the consequences. There's nobody around to protect me, and I'm damned if I'll meekly let him have his way.

"Ronald?" a woman calls. "Are you up there?"

He freezes, still gripping my shoulders. Footsteps ascend the stairs, and his wife enters the hallway. "Dr. Bullard said he saw you come in—" Jean stops in her tracks and stares at her husband and me, her eyes and mouth open wide.

"Jean." Flustered, Ronald steps away from me. "Dr. Kendall and I were just . . . discussing a problem with one of her patients."

Jean glares at me. Her expression when she turns to her husband is a mixture of anger, humiliation, and resignation. "I want to go home." Her voice wobbles on the brink of tears.

I seize the opportunity to unlock my door, slip into my room, and lock myself inside.

CHAPTER

21

"THEY ALL KNOW," Nurse Norris says, "even when they're not conscious. They can feel it."

Staff members at RKH say that the insane have a sixth sense, and from what I observe after Leonora Hirschfeld's suicide, there's truth to the theory. The patients in Haven House are restless. Their paranoia, mania, depression, and compulsive behaviors worsen. Every isolation room is occupied. Lulu Shelton has a temper tantrum. She screams, tears her hair out, and pounds her fists against herself and the orderlies who finally restrain her. After I give her a sedative shot, the janitor mops blood off the floor. And all three of our catatonic patients began having seizures. Maybe they understand conversations even though they seem oblivious to the world. Maybe they really do have a sixth sense. RKH's protocol for times like this is to keep the patients busy. Any who aren't catatonic, in isolation, or unruly are taken on walks or to the gymnasium for sports or occupational therapy.

Three of my patients seem impervious to the turmoil. Rory, Dot, and Maureen constantly rehearse their play. I see them in Dot's room gesturing and emoting as they whisper their lines. I still don't know what their play is about, and I don't have time for psychotherapy with them. Several nurses and aides have called in sick, which I hear is not uncommon after a suicide at the hospital. I pitch in to help dole out pills, administer cold packs and hydrotherapy, and I learn a technique for calming patients down. I gather them in front of the television. We watch a program and discuss it during the commercials. The patients seem to enjoy this, and they reveal information about their thoughts, feelings, and experiences. During the newscasts we learn that the Korean War has ended and Jackie Robinson hit his hundredth home run—historic events that we celebrate together. I'm forming bonds with the patients that I haven't had time to develop via formal psychotherapy sessions.

I don't tell anyone that Ronald Norton made a pass at me. Probably Dr. Mara and Dr. Bullard would decide it was my fault, another result of my own poor judgment. They would think even worse of me than they already do.

* * *

RKH holds a memorial service for Leonora. Her body was sent home to her family in New York City for the funeral and burial, but staff members and patients who knew her gather in the small stone chapel on the campus. I slip into a back pew. Sapphire, ruby, and emerald light from the stained-glass windows shines on the assembly. A painting of the resurrection of Christ hangs above the altar. The hospital chaplain speaks in a somber voice.

"We are gathered here to remember our dear friend Leonora Hirschfeld. She was a talented artist and an intelligent woman with a keen sense of humor. Life posed serious challenges for her, but she embraced it during the good times and bravely fought her demons during the bad times."

What a terrible disease schizophrenia is. The delusions, hallucinations, and paranoia rob the afflicted of the chance for a happy, productive life. For them, there's little promise of resurrection into mental health.

"In a moment of despair, Leonora departed from us," the chaplain says.

What was the final challenge she couldn't overcome? What demon made her life unbearable? I envision the ghosts of RKH telling patients to kill themselves. But it seems more likely that Leonora faced the grim reality of lifelong insanity and confinement in a mental institution.

"Let us have compassion for Leonora instead of sitting in judgment," the chaplain says. "All people are made in God's image, even those who suffer, whether from physical or mental ailments."

It's a good attitude to preach in a place where mental suffering is so abundant.

"Neither death nor life, neither thought nor deed, neither mistakes nor failings can separate us from God's love."

It's better than fire and brimstone and the traditional religious concept that suicide is a sin which deserves punishment rather than mercy.

"Let us pray for Leonora."

We in the congregation bow our heads.

"God have mercy on her soul and help her family and friends heal from this deep wound and sorrow. God help us to live with grief, anger, loss, and guilt." The chaplain's gaze meets mine for a moment.

I look away, disconcerted at the thought that he's speaking directly to me. Were Dr. Mara and Dr. Bullard correct when they implied that I drove Leonora to suicide?

"Let us learn patience and forgiveness and show love and kindness to those who are suffering."

If my words or actions contributed to Leonora's death, there's no forgiveness for me. I think of Donna Wright. If I killed her, I should go to prison.

"The sun that sets also rises. May the pain we carry grow lighter. May we find purpose in the darkness and courage in our togetherness. May the radiance and beauty of Leonora's life be undiminished by her death. Amen."

The congregation echoes, "Amen." I'm speechless with distress, thinking of Brian. I've never visited his grave, which is in the cemetery at the tuberculosis sanatorium; I couldn't bear it. Does his soul rest in peace or suffer the burden of guilt?

"Now we'll have a performance of Leonora's favorite song," the chaplain says.

A woman rises from the audience. She's dressed in a black suit and veiled hat, maybe a patient or an off-duty nurse. At the piano beside the altar, she plays "Blues in the Night."

The bittersweet, melancholy, yet vibrant notes seem a perfect expression of Leonora's unconventional spirit. Tears sting my eyes. My sense of loss is out of proportion to my brief acquaintance with Leonora. I'm grieving anew for Brian.

After the Lord's Prayer, the service is over. As people move down the aisle, I look for Nurse Janice. Since she worked at Haven House while Leonora lived there, I thought she would come to the memorial service. I need to know why Janice claimed she didn't remember Caroline Lennox. But Janice isn't here. After exiting the chapel, I walk across campus. Ahead of me are two nurses who were at the service. Snatches of their conversation drift back to me.

". . . can't believe Janice left."

"Yeah, me either. This place was her whole life."

I stay a few steps behind them so they won't notice me eavesdropping.

"So sudden too. Why did she quit?"

"I heard she got a job offer from a hospital in California, and the pay was too good to turn down. They wanted her to start right away."

What a coincidence it is that both people I asked about Caroline Lennox are gone. But is it really a coincidence? Did Janice leave voluntarily, or was she sent away because Superintendent Van Pelt didn't want her talking to me? Perhaps he used his contacts at other hospitals to find her a new, higher-paying job. I pursue this train of disturbing thoughts: Did Leonora really commit suicide? Or did someone stage her death to make it look as if she killed herself? Was she murdered to guarantee her silence? Other people would surely find the idea absurd. RKH is a reputable hospital, though not top-flight; surely no employee would deliberately kill a patient. This is real life, not a detective novel. But I can't dismiss the possibility that I'm to blame for the murder of an innocent person.

* * *

The questions weigh upon my mind, but I don't have time to do anything about them because on the day after the memorial service, I go on night call, my first time at RKH. From six PM to six AM, three nights in a row, myself and a senior resident are in charge of the entire hospital. The senior resident on call with me is a pale, gangly man with wire-rimmed glasses, who never looks me directly in the eye.

"Our job is to put out fires and keep everybody alive until morning," he tells me when we meet in the overnight room. "If nobody dies, that's a good shift."

The overnight room contains a cot, desk, and telephone. I brought a bag packed with toiletries, food, extra clothes, and a book, the way I did during my internship days when I didn't have time to go home on breaks. It turns out that I don't need any of those items because I'm constantly on the run until morning. I carry a walkie-talkie that sends me to one ward after another. Three hundred patients is a huge caseload for two residents. Many patients with mental illness also have physical ailments. I examine patients with colds, asthma, diarrhea, and fevers. I prescribe antibiotics, aspirin, and laxatives. One patient falls, and I send him to the infirmary for X-rays. Oddly, I feel most useful on night shift. The patients are so thankful for my attention and their relief. One man called me his angel of mercy. It's an unexpected gift. But I'm so busy with paperwork that I don't get back to the mansion until after eight in the morning. Half starved, I eat breakfast before showering and falling into bed to sleep until it's time to get up for the next shift.

Sleep eludes me while my mind goes over and over my conversation with Leonora Hirschfeld. The notion that someone at RKH murdered her to keep her quiet about Caroline Lennox clings to my brain like a poisonous barnacle. In late afternoon, when I finally fall asleep, I dream that I'm in the tunnels under the hospital, strangling Donna Wright while the naked, butterfly-winged women from Leonora's paintings watch.

The next two nights bring added excitement. An elderly patient has chest pains, and I send him to the general hospital in Tarrytown because RKH lacks facilities for advanced cardiac care. A female patient threatens to commit suicide by cutting her throat with a knife that she got from God knows where. I talk her out of it, then sedate her. Nobody dies. With three good shifts under my belt, I'm so exhausted, I can't think straight. I slog through morning rounds. Afterward, there's a training session for the residents.

The session takes place in a room at the research laboratory. Shades are pulled over the windows. There's a movie screen mounted on one wall and a chair in front of the screen. Behind the chair, a table holds an electrocardiogram machine and a slide projector. Behind the table is another chair by an electronic apparatus—a big gray metal box with knobs, dials, switches, and gauges on its front panel. Cables snake from the equipment, some to the table and others to the chair that faces the movie screen. The chair has straps attached to its arms and legs.

I sit with the other residents in a row of chairs placed on the side of the room. My head lolls as I doze off. Daniel Tanaka, beside me, nudges my arm, and I snap awake. It's not until Dr. Bullard brings Rory in that I recall him telling me that this was the day the residents would observe homosexual conversion therapy.

Now I'm fully alert.

Rory, wearing a lacy white dress, is strapped into a wheelchair, pushed by two orderlies. Her face twists with fear, defiance, and rage. Her long dark hair is disheveled, her skirt torn, and she's minus one white ballet flat—signs of a struggle. She sees me and the other residents and demands, "What are they doing here?"

Dr. Bullard, calm in his white lab coat, says, "They're here to watch your therapy."

"Fuck you," Rory says. The orderlies transfer her from the wheelchair to the chair in front of the movie screen. She fights as they buckle the straps around her wrists and ankles. "Fuck you all!"

Her glare includes me, and I flinch. It's apparent that when she claimed she's been cooperating with her treatment, she was lying, but I'm less upset by her attempt to manipulate me than confused about the nature of the treatment. What could be so bad that she resists even though resisting will only lengthen her stay at RKH? Why does she need to be strapped down?

"Our patient today is Rosemary Kirkpatrick, age seventeen, a lesbian." Dr. Bullard unbuttons the front of Rory's dress. She curses and spits at him as he attaches electrodes from the EKG machine to her chest. He wipes his face, then picks up electrical cables from the floor near her chair and holds them up. The cables in his right hand have small rubber caps on the ends; those in his left hand, flat metal discs.

"These connect the subject to the aversion apparatus," he says.

As he puts the rubber caps on the index fingers and thumbs of Rory's hands, she snarls. He pulls her skirt up and her underpants down. I gasp with alarm. So does Jean Norton. The male residents stir uneasily. Rory struggles in vain while Dr. Bullard tapes the electrodes to her pubis.

"Bastard!" she cries. "I'm going to kill you!"

Dr. Bullard ignores her. "Aversion therapy uses negative reinforcement to weaken the patient's attraction to members of his or her own sex." He sits in the chair behind the table and turns on the EKG machine. The mechanical pen jumps rhythmically, printing spikes on graph paper. "The procedure is to show the patient photographs that provoke a sexual response." He turns on the slide projector. A bright white rectangle appears on the movie screen. He presses a button, and an image of a pretty blonde in a bikini appears.

So this is what Rory meant when she asked me if I was going to make her *look at pictures*. She squeezes her eyes shut. Dr. Bullard says without changing his calm, detached tone, "Open your eyes, Rosemary, or the orderlies will open them for you."

She reluctantly obeys. While she stares at the picture, the pen on the EKG machine draws higher spikes at narrower intervals as her heartbeat accelerates.

"The patient is aroused," Dr. Bullard says. "Now we deliver the negative stimulus."

He flicks a switch on the electronic apparatus. The needle on the gauge jumps. Rory screams as the electric shock stiffens her hands and legs. I'm flabbergasted, horror-stricken. Jean Norton's mouth drops. Ronald Norton, Daniel Tanaka, and Joseph Mandel can't quite hide their dismay. The orderlies stand by, looking bored; they've seen this before.

Dr. Bullard turns off the current. "It's classic Pavlovian conditioning. The patient learns to associate homosexual arousal with pain."

Rory's body goes limp. She inhales and exhales harsh, ragged breaths. The electrocardiogram machine prints out jagged, irregularly spaced spikes. Dr. Bullard seems completely indifferent to her pain. I'd thought him to be pleasant and kind, but he's showing a different side of himself, Dr. Jekyll turning into Mr. Hyde, treating Rory like a rat in an experiment. He clicks to the next slide. It shows the same woman, reclining nude on a sofa. Rory yells and strains violently against her bindings; her chair doesn't move, it's bolted to the floor. Dr. Bullard flicks the switch again.

"We gradually increase the intensity of the stimulus and the sexual content of the pictures," he says.

Rory screams louder, her rigid limbs vibrating with the current. Dr. Bullard raises his voice to be heard. "In other sessions, we give her an emetic instead of shocks. It makes her vomit when she sees the photographs. Eventually, she'll avoid lesbian sex because it triggers nausea and disgust. I don't conduct those sessions before lunch. It'll ruin your appetite." He chuckles.

I feel such hatred for Dr. Bullard and distress at Rory's suffering that I can't sit passively watching any longer. I rise from my chair. Daniel rises to stop me; I ignore him. I lurch toward Rory on legs sore from running around during my night shifts. In a brief, searing flashback, I'm strapped down on the bed in the electroshock room while the current sizzles through my body and the white explosion blanks out my mind. I grab the cables that connect Rory to the shock apparatus.

"Dr. Kendall, what are you doing?" Dr. Bullard says.

I yank the electrodes off Rory. She gazes up at me in astonishment. Then Dr. Bullard is beside me, grabbing my arm, dragging me out of the room.

CHAPTER 22

HALF AN HOUR later, I'm facing Superintendent Van Pelt across his desk in his office. He says, "Dr. Bullard isn't pleased with you." His manner is as cold as the air blasting from the air conditioner.

"I know," I say.

Dr. Bullard reprimanded me in the hall outside the aversion therapy room. He left the door open so that everyone inside could hear every loud, angry word. Then he sent me to the superintendent's office. During the time it took me to get here, he must have telephoned the superintendent to tell him what had happened.

"Explain why you interrupted the training session," Superintendent Van Pelt says.

Still shaken, I struggled to defend myself. "It was cruel and painful."

Superintendent Van Pelt narrows his eyes at me. "Have you ever seen someone reset a dislocated shoulder?"

Confused by this seemingly irrelevant question, I say, "Yes." It was during my internship at Mount Sinai, my rotation in the ER. The patient, a high school football player, had howled in agony when the doctor wrenched his shoulder back into place.

"It's certainly painful," Superintendent Van Pelt says. "The patient probably thinks it's cruel. But what's the alternative? Leave him crippled for the rest of his life? It's the same with mental illness.

Leave that girl untreated, and there'll be no limit to the trouble she'll get herself into and the pain she'll suffer."

I can't deny that life can be difficult for homosexuals. At age seventeen, Rory has already been shunned by her family and committed to a mental institution. She faces a future of conflict between acting on her own desires and fitting into society. But I don't think the superintendent's analogy is accurate.

"Homosexuality isn't a dislocated piece of brain that can be reset with electric shocks," I say.

"And you know this how?"

"Freud said that trying to convert a homosexual into a heterosexual is about as likely to work as trying to convert a heterosexual into a homosexual."

Superintendent Van Pelt flicks his hand at me. "Freud was a great man. His theories are fine for psychiatrists in private practice with clients who lie on the couch and talk about their mothers. But he isn't running this hospital. Aversion therapy is a standard, accepted modern technique."

I persist even though I'm digging my grave deeper. "Aversion therapy isn't changing Rory's basic nature." Three days with virtually no sleep have eroded my inhibitions. "It's only teaching her to hate this hospital and everyone here who's making her suffer."

After a pause filled with mutual animosity, Superintendent Van Pelt says, "You're a graduate of Radcliffe and Columbia. You interned at Mount Sinai. We were glad to have someone with such impressive credentials, but now I see they've made you arrogant. You think you know better than psychiatrists with many years of practical experience. That's a serious fault, Dr. Kendall. You won't learn anything as long as you think nobody has anything to teach you."

The criticism stings because it's not entirely unjust. I'm proud of my credentials, and although I'm a novice, I do take issue with RKH's treatment of patients. But I'm convinced that aversion therapy is terrible abuse of Rory, and a lifetime of experience won't change my mind.

"Have you watched Dr. Bullard conducting aversion therapy on Rosemary Kirkpatrick? If you have, how can you think it's not doing her more harm than good?"

He ignores my questions. "Speaking of Freud, could it be that you're experiencing countertransference with Rosemary?"

Countertransference occurs when the therapist experiences feelings toward the patient that go beyond the desire to help him. Sometimes it's sexual desire, which Superintendent Van Pelt had wrongly insinuated that I feel for Rory. This time he's accusing me of another major fault—wanting to rescue or redeem Rory, styling myself as her savior. I'm angry at him because he's not wrong.

Before I can defend myself, he says, "The fact that you're challenging me instead of accepting criticism proves my point about you, Dr. Kendall. And this isn't the first time you've displayed poor judgment. There was the issue of Leonora Hirschfeld. I'm beginning to think we made a serious mistake by accepting you as a resident."

He's a close-minded old man who refuses to consider another point of view. His hospital perpetuated the abuse that robbed me of half a year of my life and damaged my mind. Now he's condoning the abuse of a current patient. Fear permeates the hot, bitter stew of my emotions. He's going to throw me out. My career is over. I'm going to lose my chance to find out the truth about my past as well as Leonora's death. I won't be able to help Rory or save other patients who might be in danger.

"But here at RKH, we believe that people can change," Superintendent Van Pelt says. "It's one of our guiding philosophies. We understand that residents are bound to make mistakes and should be allowed to learn from them." His eyes twinkle as he smiles at me. "Let this be an opportunity for you to learn and change, Dr. Kendall."

I bristle at his patronizing tone; I bite my tongue. Relieved that he's not firing me, I ought to accept defeat gracefully. "Thank you, sir."

"Mistakes have consequences, however," he says. "That's crucial for learning from them. You will have no further contact with Rosemary Kirkpatrick. Effective immediately, Dr. Jean Norton will take your place at Haven House, and you will transfer to Grace House."

Although I know I'm getting off lightly, I'm appalled. "But I was supposed to restart the special program for girls."

"Either Dr. Jean Norton will do it, or it will have to wait until I hire a permanent staff doctor for Haven House." Superintendent Van

Pelt adds, "Don't push your luck, Dr. Kendall. You've already got two strikes against you."

* * *

As I hurry down the front steps of the mansion, my eyes flood with stinging tears. I'm angry at Dr. Bullard and Superintendent Van Pelt, but also at myself. How could I let this happen? Only two weeks into my residency, I've been transferred out of the house where I want to work, and by trying to rescue Rory today, I lost the chance to help her, Dot, and Maureen. And by investigating the mystery of my past, I may have driven Leonora Hirschfeld to take her own life—or compelled someone to murder her and disguise her death as suicide.

It's lunchtime, and I'm weak from hunger, but I can't face the dining room. I don't want to run into Dr. Bullard, who never misses a meal, or the other residents, who heard him scolding me. I can't bear to start work at Grace House or to hide in my room like child who's been spanked. The sky is blue, the sun bright on the panorama of architecture, woodlands, gardens, and orchards. Everything around me, all that I can see, is Resurrection Kill Hospital. The natural beauty and rose-scented air are camouflage for misery. For five months when I was fourteen, I was trapped here. Now I feel trapped again, at the scene of my mistakes and failure. But this time I don't have to stay here. I walk around the mansion to the parking lot, hurry to my car—and remember that my keys are in my room.

I'm about to burst into sobs when I see Daniel Tanaka. He walks briskly down the row of cars, stops at his, and takes his keys out of his pocket. I don't want to talk to anyone, but he's seen me; it's too late to run away.

"Claire."

He looks surprised to see me, and unhappy. Then he notices my expression, and concern alters his. "Let's get out of here." He opens the passenger door of his car for me.

Desperate to escape the hospital, I forget that I need to avoid him, and I don't care who sees us together. I get in the car, a rusty, beat-up blue Ford. He drives us through the campus. Gazing straight ahead, we ride in silence for a mile down the road, as though lightning will strike us if we look backward or speak before we're safely away from RKH.

Daniel says, "If it hadn't been you, it would have been me."

"What?" I say, confused.

"I was going to stop the aversion therapy. You beat me to it."

I turn to him in surprise, remembering that he'd stood up when I did and I'd thought he meant to restrain me. "You hated it too?"

"'Hated' is putting it mildly. I thought it was horrible abuse of that poor girl. Sheer psychiatric malpractice."

"Thank God I'm not the only one," I say fervently.

"We're not the only two. After Dr. Bullard dragged you out of the room, Joseph Mandel threw up in the wastebasket. Jean Norton looked as if she wanted to be sick." Daniel smiles wryly. "Ronald Norton couldn't think of anything obnoxious to say."

His humor lightens my misery a little. "I'm glad to hear that."

I feel less alone, glad to be riding with Daniel in the safe, private space of his car. I find myself happy that I'm the one in trouble instead of him, like a soldier who took a bullet for his comrade. The sunlight gilds the tops of the trees we pass, and yellow dandelions bloom amid the grasses on the roadside. I roll down the window. Beyond the confines of RKH, the summer air smells cleaner and sweeter.

"Dr. Bullard postponed the aversion therapy session. He said, 'The disruption made the patient less amenable to treatment.'" Daniel exaggerates Dr. Bullard's detached, robot-like tone.

I have to laugh, but my amusement turns bitter. "Postponed but not canceled, I suppose."

Daniel sighs. We fall silent again, riding through the outskirts of the town of Resurrection. Small, modest houses appear along the road that descends toward the town's center. Beyond the distant buildings is the Hudson River, sparkling against the hills on the New Jersey side. Daniel steers the car onto a driveway that ends at a gas station with a small restaurant. A yellow milk truck stands by the red gas pumps. The driver cheerfully greets the attendant who comes out of the station. The scene embodies pleasant, ordinary life.

"This is where I go when I need to get away from the hospital but I don't have time to go very far." Daniel parks by the restaurant.

Inside, the cook is flipping hamburgers on the grill. An older woman in a pink uniform and white apron pours coffee for two men in denim overalls who sit at the counter by the glass case of pies and cakes. Recalling the patient who assaulted Daniel, I have a sudden fear that the restaurant employees are prejudiced against Japanese and might refuse to serve us. Having never gone anywhere with a man who wasn't Caucasian, I don't know what to expect.

The cook nods at Daniel, and the waitress calls, "Hello, Dr. Tanaka."

I'm relieved that they accept him as a regular customer. As we sit in a booth by the window, they look curiously at me, and I intuit that he's never brought anyone with him before. I'm suddenly shy. Perhaps he is too. This feels like a first date, not what either of us intended. We study the menus as carefully as if they're patients' charts. After we order, we sit in awkward silence until the waitress brings our Cokes. We take our time peeling the paper off our straws, glad for something to occupy ourselves. I hadn't realized that I was parched with thirst. The icy, sweet, fizzy cola gives me a jolt of energy that overcomes my natural reticence. I tell Daniel about my conversation with Superintendent Van Pelt.

"I'm sorry, Claire. It should have been me. You were not only quicker than I was. You were braver." Daniel says with a self-deprecating grimace, "He who hesitated is a coward."

"She who didn't hesitate is in the doghouse," I say.

We laugh. Even though my situation isn't as humorous as my quip, I feel better, and the awkwardness is gone. The waitress brings our food—giant hamburgers with piles of French fries. We devour it all, savoring the grilled beef, the crunch of lettuce, tomatoes and pickles, the sweet ketchup and hot, crispy fries, wiping our greasy hands on the thin paper napkins. With the edge off my appetite, I give in to my urge to confide. I tell Daniel that I've been banned from further contact with Rory and transferred to Grace House.

"I couldn't persuade Superintendent Van Pelt that aversion therapy is hurting Rory," I say. "He's not going to put a stop to it. Dr. Bullard will go on torturing Rory and God knows how many other patients. I don't know what to do."

"I should talk to him," Daniel says.

Although I'm glad to have an ally, I say, "It wouldn't do any good. You're just a resident like I am. Why should he listen to you?"

"I have a good record at RKH."

He's too tactful to mention that he's heard I was called onto the carpet after Leonora Hirschfeld's death, or that our superiors will give him more credence because he's not suspected of any involvement in it.

"Superintendent Van Pelt's mind is closed, and nothing you can say will open it." I warn Daniel, "You'll only ruin your good record."

He considers for a moment, his handsome face somber. "Someone outside the hospital might listen."

"Who?"

"The New York State Department of Health. It regulates hospitals. I'm going to register a complaint against RKH."

The magnitude of what he's suggesting takes my breath away. "Criticizing RKH within RKH has already gotten me in trouble," I say. "To take our concerns to a higher authority?" I shake my head. "That's a dangerous step."

"I know. But when I think of that poor girl, I can't just do nothing."

I feel the same way, but I say, "If aversion therapy really is a standard practice, why would the health department do anything?"

"They would have to investigate my complaint," Daniel says. "If they come to RKH and watch aversion therapy with their own eyes, they can't help but put an end to it."

"How can you be sure?" I ask, admiring him for the courage of his convictions but doubtful myself. "The people at the health department might agree with Superintendent Van Pelt. And he could fire you for going over his head."

"That's a chance I'll have to take."

I picture the boy with one suitcase and twenty dollars, traveling alone on a train from the Japanese internment camp in California to Temple University in Philadelphia. "I can't let you do it. You've gone through so much to be a doctor."

He smiles at my vehemence but shakes his head. "What kind of doctor am I if I don't act in the interest of the patient?"

"But your family . . ." I think of the parents, siblings, and other relatives he's seen only twice in the last eight years, who must be so proud of him. And for a Japanese man, it would be difficult if not impossible to get another residency if he were fired from RKH.

"My family would want me to do what's right," he says simply.

"I'm already in trouble," I say. "I'll register the complaint with the health department."

I omit to mention that when I go to the health department, aversion therapy won't be the only subject of my complaint. I'll report what happened to me at RKH when I was a patient. Maybe their investigation will uncover the truth. I feel guilty for hiding things from Daniel, sad that my secrets are a wall between us. I'm afraid of what he would think if he knew I was a former patient, working at RKH under a different name. Or if he knew that the small part of my memory I've recovered may have implicated me in the murder of my brother's girlfriend.

"No." Daniel pushes his plate away and leans across the table. "I won't let you."

"It's all right. I don't have anybody to care what happens to me."

The minute I say it, I'm crushed by such misery that my chest caves in and tears fill my eyes. I've known it for years—ever since Brian died—but I've never spoken it aloud, never acknowledged the sad fact. I turn away from Daniel, fighting to control my emotions.

"Claire. It's not true." His warm, gentle voice compels me to meet his gaze. "You have me. I care."

When I look into his eyes, I can tell he means it. He's not just saying it to make me feel better or because he's a man who can't stand seeing a woman cry. I feel the expression on my face shifting with my emotions. I'm happy because I've found what I've needed for so long—a friend and comrade. I'm relieved because I'm not as alone in the world as I thought, but I'm overwhelmed with fear. Fear of losing Daniel the way I lost Brian. If he reports RKH to the health department, he'll be fired and I'll probably never see him again. Fear of my dawning realization that I want more from Daniel than friendship; fear that he doesn't want more than friendship from me.

I can't say any of this; it would scare him away. So I say, "Thanks. I appreciate it." I try to convey that I'm moved but not how embarrassingly much. I manage only to sound flippant.

Regret colors his gaze, as if he thinks he spoke too freely from his heart. Now my fear is that he does share my feelings and interpreted my response as a rejection. The awkwardness between us returns.

Daniel speaks in a neutral tone. "So we agree on something: each of us doesn't want the other to report RKH to the health department."

Sorry that the intimacy between us has vanished but not knowing how to restore it, I say, "Maybe that means it's not a good idea." Coming here with him wasn't a good idea. Now I'm afraid I've hurt him, and I ache for the loss of what might have been if I'd behaved differently.

"I still think it needs to be done," Daniel says, "but not on the spur of the moment. Let's take some time to think it over, shall we? And then talk again later?"

I nod, relieved because he's not going to sacrifice his career, and I won't have to sacrifice mine either. At least not yet.

Daniel signals the waitress to bring our check. He pays at the cash register, waving away my offer to pay for my meal. As we drive back to RKH, I don't dread my return as much as I thought I would. Whatever happens when we get there, at least I have another talk with Daniel Tanaka to look forward to, and perhaps another chance for friendship, or something more.

CHAPTER

23

THE AUGUST AFTERNOON is warm and still. Bees buzz around the poppies, black-eyed Susans, and delphiniums in the flower border around Grace House. It's teatime, a daily ritual conducted on the veranda in good weather. Patients sit at little tables while maids in black uniforms and ruffled white caps and aprons pour tea into porcelain cups for them and serve little sandwiches and cakes from tiered stands on a trolley. Not one of the patients is under sixty. The women are dressed in picture hats and long, full-skirted tea gowns, the men in formal summer suits. It's a scene from a Gilded Age garden party.

I sit with two of the women. Clad in my white lab coat, I'm an anachronism. So are the uniformed aides who are wiping faces and cleaning up spills. Most Grace House patients have dementia, commonly known as senility. Some have underlying mental disorders; others are longtime alcoholics. A few men have brain damage from syphilis they contracted decades before penicillin came into use for treating that particular venereal disease. But they all enjoy the pleasant routine, except for those whose minds are too far gone and are fed in their rooms.

"What is your name, dear?" the white-haired woman in a lilac gown beside me asks.

"Dr. Kendall," I say.

"It's lovely to meet you, dear. I'm Mrs. Arthur Newton. Please call me Maude."

Maude, aged eighty-five, has been my patient for the two weeks that I've been the resident psychiatrist at Grace House. Several times a day she asks me what my name is and introduces herself.

Our companion, Phyllis Biddle, is plump and rosy, dressed in sherbet-orange silk. She talks to the large blonde doll in her lap. "Finish your lunch, Alice, or you can't have any cake." She presses a cucumber sandwich to the doll's lips. She thinks the doll is her granddaughter Alice, who's now an adult and visits her on Sundays.

At the next table, Colonel Dwight Fraser regales two women with stories of his military service during the Great War. The women are silent, nibbling their scones, trembling constantly. They both have Parkinson's disease, which impairs their speech as well as their muscle control.

"What is your name, dear?" Maude asks me again.

This is how most of my conversations with my patients go: they forget everything that's said as soon as it's said. Except for a few combative ones and an old man who grabs at my breasts, they're docile. I mainly tend to their physical ailments—arthritis, high blood pressure, gout, heart conditions. Psychotherapy is useless. I take some pleasure in my affection for my patients. All my grandparents died when I was very young; I never really knew them. I imagine that if they'd lived longer, they might have become like these gentle souls. So might I, in my old age. I treat my patients with kindness, which is really all I can do for them. Their undemanding company and the humdrum routine at Grace House are soothing.

For two weeks, I've concentrated on my work. During morning rounds, I speak only when Superintendent Van Pelt calls on me, which is seldom. Dr. Bullard ignores me during training sessions. Dr. Mara's cool, impersonal friendliness warns me not to step over the line again. At meals with the other residents, Jean Norton looks pleased that she's taken my place in Haven House. Ronald Norton once bluntly asked me what happened after I disrupted the aversion therapy session. Daniel Tanaka cut him off and changed the subject. I haven't seen Daniel alone since our lunch at the restaurant. I'm disappointed because he hasn't sought me out. I often wonder how Rory,

Dot, and Maureen are. I miss all my Haven House patients, even Lulu Shelton and her tantrums. I bide my time.

This stasis can't last indefinitely. There's too much hanging fire. My need to regain my lost memory, put a stop to any bad business that's going on at RKH, and protect the patients has only intensified. So has my determination to exonerate Brian. My fear that *I* may have killed Donna Wright is a shadow that darkens my days and keeps me awake at night. My nerves vibrate as if I'm standing on railroad tracks while a train that's a pinpoint on the horizon approaches. Something has to happen.

Chatter and laughter accompany the sound of footsteps on the path beyond the lawn that slopes gently down from Grace House. A dozen young women appear, walking singly or in clusters, led by a nurse. Rory, Dot, and Maureen lag at the end of the little parade. They see me and hesitate. Rory motions Dot and Maureen to follow their group, holds her finger to her lips, and runs up the lawn toward the house. I hurry over to the veranda railing.

"Hi, Dr. Kendall." Rory has on a pink dress that's streaked with green, as if she's been tumbling on the grass.

"Hello, Rory." I smile, glad to see her but grieved by the memory of the last time we met. "How are you?"

"I'm okay." *In spite of everything*, says the defiance that twists her smile.

I admire her spirit, her determination not to be crushed by the conversion therapy. Although I could be fired for talking to her, it's worth the risk.

"I wanted to say thanks," Rory says. For the first time, there's no scorn in her manner. Her earnest gratitude is heartbreaking.

"I'm sorry." Unable to force more words past the tears that clog my throat, I can't say, *Sorry I couldn't stop it, sorry I let you down*.

Rory nods as if she understands. "At least you tried. It's the thought that counts."

I see in her eyes the trust that I wanted so much from her. I've earned it too late.

The group walking on the path halts. The nurse calls, "Rory! Get back here."

"My dad says always return a favor. So I need to warn you," Rory says. "This isn't a good place. You should leave." She's said as much before, but she sounds more urgent now.

"Rory!" the nurse calls. "Come now, or no more grounds privileges."

"Are you coming to our play at the talent show tomorrow?" Rory asks me.

I'd forgotten about the show. "I'll come."

"Good. Then you'll see what I mean." Rory turns and runs to join her group.

* * *

The next day, I tell the charge nurse at Grace House that I'm taking some patients to the talent show. It takes ages to get the eleven patients ready. They're excited and confused about the special outing. Phyllis Biddle wets herself and needs to change clothes. Colonel Fraser loses his cane, and I spend half an hour looking for it until I find it under a sofa in the lounge. Finally, two nurses and I get everyone out of Grace House and into the tram. We arrive inside the theater forty minutes after the show started.

On stage, a young man plays Beethoven's "Moonlight Sonata" on the piano. It takes another ten minutes to get my patients seated in a row at the back. The audience is restless; nurses shush chattering patients. The pianist finishes his performance and bows to a smattering of applause. I'm afraid I've missed Rory's play.

A woman comes onstage and speaks into a microphone. She has on a glittery black evening gown, as if this is the Metropolitan Opera and not an amateur production in a mental hospital. "Next, we have an original play: *Resurrection Kills,* written and directed by Rosemary Kirkpatrick, and acted by Rosemary, Dot Powell, and Maureen Murray from Haven House."

I note that she mistakenly pluralized the word "Kill." The curtain opens. On the stage, a table holds a large box with sides and top made of transparent screens. At one end of the box, long white gloves dangle from a round porthole. On the other end is another round hole, covered by a rubber seal with flaps. I recognize the apparatus from college biology experiments: it's a cage for insects. Dot and Maureen walk onto the stage. The audience claps. Dot wears the man's old-fashioned suit that I saw her in during the rehearsal I interrupted. Maureen is dressed as a nurse. A high, buzzing whine comes from backstage—sound effects from Rory.

Dot places her hands on the cage and speaks in a mannish voice with a vaguely European accent. "Behold my lovely mosquitoes. They've fed on the blood of malaria patients at the Army Hospital." She inserts her hands in the gloves and thrusts them into the box. The whine from backstage grows louder. "See them swarm. My little beauties are hungry. They're looking for human flesh." She throws back her head and bellows with maniacal laughter.

The audience titters. I thought the play was going to explain why Rory warned me to leave RKH, but it seems like a bad amateur horror movie.

"Now my experiment can begin," Dot intones. "Are my guinea pigs ready?"

"Yes, Doctor." Maureen clasps her hands and gazes at Dot in exaggerated admiration. "Soon you'll be famous for discovering a cure for insanity!"

The curtain closes, and I hear the sounds of furniture scraping on the stage floor. When the curtain opens a few minutes later, the set consists of three office chairs lined up in a row. The two chairs on the left are occupied by Rory and Maureen, wearing the costumes I saw at the rehearsal—Rory, the gangster suit; Maureen, the long, old-fashioned green dress and blonde wig. The third chair is empty. Dot enters, wearing a white lab coat over her suit and carrying papers on a clipboard. She walks over to Rory, who grins and tips her derby hat.

"Mr. Peter Kramer," Dot says, consulting her clipboard. "A businessman who has schizophrenia and thinks he's Al Capone."

Rory wisecracks, "When I sell liquor, they call it bootlegging. When my customers serve it on silver trays, they call it hospitality."

The audience laughs. Rory hurries offstage. Dot moves on to Maureen. "Mrs. Adeline Peck, a widow who thinks she's the reincarnation of Marie Antoinette."

Maureen regally waves her hand and exclaims in a bad French accent, "Let them eat cake!"

Adeline Peck. Peter Kramer. They're the patients who died in 1941, the year I was a patient.

Dot paces the stage, proclaiming, "My new treatment will cure these poor souls of their delusions and restore their sanity. They will be able to live normal lives outside the prison of this asylum."

Rory returns, clad in one of her own feminine dresses and sits in the third chair. I pay little attention to the girls' ingenuity, filling multiple roles instead of recruiting other patients to be in their play. I'm stricken with astonishment because I know who the third patient is before Dot says, "Miss Caroline Lennox, age fourteen. She had a nervous breakdown accompanied by delusions."

According to Rory, *I* was a guinea pig in the experiment. My breath is knocked out of me in a puff of incredulity. Is *this* what I was brainwashed to forget?

"Just put yourself in my hands, my dear," Dot says to Rory. "I promise you all will be well."

"Oh, Doctor." Breathless with hope, Rory says, "Will I be able to travel and have dates with boys and go to college someday?"

"Most certainly," Dot says. "You can do whatever your little heart desires."

The play isn't the fairy-tale romance that Rory described. It's a true-life science fiction/horror show. She couldn't possibly know that I'm one of the stars. Does anybody else know? I search the audience for doctors and nurses, but it's too dark to see. The curtain closes, hiding noisy movements onstage. When it reopens, the chairs are gone, replaced by a hospital bed. Rory as Caroline Lennox sits up in it. Dot comes onstage, pushing a cart with the insect cage on top while Maureen, backstage, imitates mosquitoes whining.

"Are you ready, my dear?" Dot asks.

"Yes, Doctor," says Rory/Caroline.

"Please put your hand through the hole with the rubber flaps," Dot says.

"Will it hurt?" Rory/Caroline asks as she nervously obeys.

"Perhaps just a little," Dot says.

The mosquitoes whine louder. Rory/Caroline wriggles her fingers and says, "Oh, they're biting me."

"That is good," Dot says. "The mosquitoes will infect you with malaria. The fever from the malaria will burn out the diseased tissue in the brain that's causing your mental illness."

I stare, appalled. I've heard no scientifically valid theory that says fever cures mental illness. Having studied malaria at medical school, I know it's a dangerous disease that kills thousands of people every year. Was this experiment really conducted at RKH?

"That should be a sufficient number of bites," Dot says, pulling Rory/Caroline's arm out of the cage. "Now sleep, my dear."

"Thank you, Doctor," Rory/Caroline says.

Exit Dot with mosquito cage. The whining backstage fades. Rory/Caroline scratches her arm. She lies down, snuggles under the covers, and pretends to fall asleep. The stage lights dim and brighten, dim and brighten to indicate the passage of days. She starts to writhe and moan. The audience grows more restless. Somebody whimpers. A woman hurries up the aisle, out the door. It's Nurse Norris. I wonder now if electroshock treatment was the only reason for my amnesia. Did malaria contribute to it? Or did Rory make up the whole revolting scenario?

Dot comes on stage, sticks a thermometer in Rory/Caroline's mouth, and says, "Her fever is a hundred and four degrees. That should be sufficient to destroy the diseased brain tissue."

Maureen, in her nurse's uniform, rushes over, crying, "Peter Kramer and Adeline Peck just died!"

Rory/Caroline stiffens, her back arching up from the bed. She shrieks in agony as she feigns violent convulsions. Dot pretends to inject her with a hypodermic syringe while Maureen holds her down. Then Rory/Caroline goes limp and still. The whole audience, including me, inhales a deep, suspenseful breath. People murmur anxiously as Dot feels Rory/Caroline's pulse.

Dot looks up at Maureen and announces somberly, "She's dead."

The audience exhales. For a moment the only sound is the hiss of air. I'm frantic with revulsion and bewilderment. I've just witnessed a reenactment of my own death . . . but of course I didn't die. What really happened?

"Oh, no!" Maureen cries with dramatic alarm.

Her exclamation sends the audience into a turmoil. Women begin sobbing. A man yells, "Murderer!" Patients chant, "Kill the doctor! Kill the doctor!" They rise from their seats as nurses try to calm them. It's as if the play has released their pent-up misery and anger—and mine. If the story of the experiment is true, and I actually was a guinea pig, then I suffered terribly, and two other patients did die.

Dot raises her masculine, European-accented voice over the noise. "Nobody must know what has happened. We will say that Peter Kramer, Adeline Peck, and Caroline Lennox died of natural causes."

"Yes, Doctor," Maureen says.

The curtain closes, but it reopens minutes later. On the stage are three hospital beds that contain pillows arranged to look like bodies, covered by sheets. The three actresses glide out from the wings. Transparent veils cover them from head to toe. Dot now wears Peter Kramer's derby; Maureen is in Adeline Peck's green frock and Rory in Caroline's clothes.

"Nobody knows except us, the ghosts of RKH," they intone in funereal voices. "We tell the patients." They lean over and pretend to whisper in the ears of the slumbering figures. "Nobody else hears us. And when they tell our story to other people, nobody believes them. Because they're INSANE!" Rory, Dot, and Maureen shriek. They howl and dance, waving their arms, tossing their hair, and leaping around, like maenads at a Dionysian revel.

Superintendent Van Pelt rushes in, followed by Nurse Norris, who apparently fetched him. He shouts, "Stop the play!"

But the wild frenzy infects the patients. They jump from their seats, wave their arms, stamp their feet in thunderous rhythm, and yell. My elderly patients clamor in fearful confusion. Maude Newton clings to me. Colonel Fraser aims his cane at the stage as if it's a rifle and we're in a trench, under attack.

Superintendent Van Pelt shouts from below the stage, gesturing angrily at Dot, Maureen, and Rory. The girls stand immobile, grinning with delight at the havoc they've wrought.

CHAPTER 24

"That was some play at the talent show," Ronald Norton says at dinner. He chuckles. "Those three girls were more fun than a barrel of monkeys."

"You were there?" I'd hoped none of my fellow residents had seen the play.

Ronald doesn't look at me when he answers, "Yep." Since I spurned his advances, he avoids me or ignores me whenever he can. When he can't, he pretends nothing happened.

Jean, sitting beside him, nods to say that she was at the play too. Although the Nortons live off campus, they usually stay for dinner. Tonight it's baked ham with pineapple, sweet potatoes, and fresh garden salads—better than what Jean could whip up after a hard day's work. I doubt Ronald ever cooks.

"So was I," Joseph Mandel says.

Daniel Tanaka gives me a rueful smile; he too witnessed the fiasco. But of course everyone at RKH probably knows about it by now, whether they attended the play or not. The grapevine must have been going strong all day.

"Three of my patients played in a jazz band during the show, and I brought some others along," Joseph Mandel says. "I wish I had not. I had to sedate them when we got back to Mercy House."

"Same with my patients," Ronald Norton says.

And mine. I gave pills or shots to the eleven patients I'd brought to the show. I feel guilty for upsetting them so badly.

"Whose idea was it to let them put on that awful play?" Jean asks.

Joseph Mandel shrugs and shakes his head.

"Superintendent Van Pelt had the final say," Ronald answers. "He must not have known what those girls were up to. Mosquitoes and fever and death, oh, my!" He guffaws.

Daniel Tanaka gives me a quizzical look. He knows Rory was my patient, and he must be wondering if I had anything to do with the play. Word of my involvement must not have gotten out yet, but I suppose it will eventually.

"How are Rory, Dot, and Maureen?" I ask Jean.

She prisses up her mouth. She's been hostile ever since she saw her husband make a pass at me, as if she blames me instead of him. "I shouldn't talk to you about them. They're not your patients anymore."

She's right, but I can't stop caring about the girls. I'm desperate to know what's happening to them, and I have to talk to Rory.

* * *

I wait until nine o'clock, then go to Haven House. Fewer employees are on duty now than during the early shift, which means less chance that one will see me and report me to Superintendent Van Pelt. I'm afraid that tomorrow he'll call me on the carpet to blame me for the play and fire me. This could be my last chance to see Rory. I use the back door and stairs to avoid the nurse at the reception desk. At Rory's door, I knock softly. Nobody answers. I cautiously open the door and peek into the room. It's empty. I feel the dizziness and shimmer of a flashback coming on, so I hurry down the stairs to the second floor. Tiptoeing along the hall, I hear music and laughter from a radio, but the coast is clear. I enter Dot's room without knocking. Maureen is flopped on the bed. When she sees me, she sits up. Dot barely glances at me as she paces back and forth across the floor, counting her steps. "Two hundred thirty, two hundred thirty-one," she mutters.

The girls wear short-sleeved, short-legged pajamas. Dot has pink, swollen bumps all over her arms, legs, face, and neck. The healed scars on her wrists are painfully visible. I'm dismayed to see that anxiety has driven her to compulsive behavior and caused her to break out in hives, and it's surely because of the play.

The play that I talked Superintendent Van Pelt and Dr. Mara into letting them perform, that caused such an upheaval.

"Hi, Dr. Kendall." Maureen's face twitches, and her eyes look inward.

I've seen those symptoms in patients on the verge of psychotic episodes. "Dot," I say, "why don't you sit down and we'll talk?"

"I can't stop," she says, her breath puffing. "I have to do five hundred steps before bed. Two hundred forty . . ."

"They're coming." Maureen cowers on the bed.

"Who's coming?" I ask.

"The ghosts of Peter Kramer, Adeline Peck, and Caroline Lennox."

She believes she's haunted by the ghosts. I can't tell her that even if they did exist, Caroline Lennox wouldn't be one of them because she's still alive, right here now, resurrected as Dr. Claire Kendall.

"They can't hurt you," I say.

"Yes, they can." Her eyes move wildly, scanning the perilous terrain of her own mind.

"Why would they want to?" I ask, even though I know that logic is powerless against schizophrenic paranoia.

"Because they're angry," Dot says, panting as she paces. "Because nobody who's not crazy can hear them. They're jealous of everyone who's not dead. Oh, darn, I lost count! Now I have to start over. One, two, three . . ."

The girls need help, and I can't even call in the night doctors without confessing that I've been at Haven House, where I don't belong.

I glance at my watch. It's twenty minutes to ten. At ten, the nurses will come around to make sure the patients are in bed. "Where is Rory?"

"In isolation," Dot says. "Seventeen, eighteen, nineteen . . ."

"With a special nurse," Maureen says.

I flash back to myself at age fourteen, lying in bed while Nurse Janice sits beside me like a watchdog. I won't be able to talk to Rory. My only hope is that Maureen and Dot have the information I need.

"Where did Rory get the idea for the play?" I ask.

Maureen's face crumples. "She swore us to secrecy. We weren't supposed to tell."

"But Dr. Mara made us," Dot says, pacing and counting. "She wouldn't let us have anything to eat until we told her."

"We were so hungry," Maureen wails.

I'm furious with Dr. Mara for extorting information from the girls, using their hunger as a weapon. "Tell me what you told Dr. Mara."

"We've been sneaking out late at night." Dot counts under her breath. "We visit the patient in the private cottage."

"*What*?" I'm shocked because the doors to the wards are locked and the night staff does bed checks to make sure all the patients are safe and sound.

"Yeah," Maureen says.

If they're telling the truth, security at Haven House has broken down. "How do you get into the private cottage?"

"He lets us in," Maureen says. "He likes having people to talk to. Nobody else ever visits him. He told us about the mosquito experiment. His name is Dr. Isaac Franz."

Where have I heard that name?

"He's the mad scientist that I played." Dot paces and counts faster. "After his guinea pigs died, he had a nervous breakdown and committed himself to RKH."

"He's been in that cottage ever since," Maureen says.

It's three minutes to ten. "I have to go," I say. "Good night."

As soon as I'm outside Haven House, I remember why Isaac Franz's name sounded familiar. He's the doctor who signed Caroline Lennox's death certificate.

* * *

Walking around campus, through the warm night that vibrates with the hum of cicadas, I try to sort out fact from fiction. Did Rory make up the whole story, putting the blame for three deaths on a man who has nothing to do with the events in the play? Is the patient in the private cottage really Dr. Isaac Franz? If he's not, then where did Rory get his name? Is it a mere coincidence that his signature is on my faked death certificate? Does he have a real connection to the other patients who supposedly died in 1941? Are they still alive too? Rory has lied to me before; why should I believe her or Dot or Maureen? The mosquito experiment seems preposterous. Rory is in isolation with a special nurse, apparently as a punishment for the play and the trouble it caused. What did she expect to gain from putting RKH in such a bad light?

It's almost eleven o'clock, and I need to get up early for morning rounds, but I'm too agitated to sleep. I decide to check on my patients at Grace House.

"How are they?" I ask the nurse at the station.

"Colonel Fraser had a nightmare. He thought he was fighting on the Western Front again. Dr. Mandel gave him a sleeping pill. Everyone else is as quiet as a mouse."

Joseph Mandel is on night call. He's the resident I've had the least contact with; he keeps to himself and often avoids the dining room. "Is Dr. Mandel still here?"

"Yes. He's upstairs."

It occurs to me that Joseph Mandel is just as alone at RKH as I am. Our only friend is Daniel Tanaka. We could both use another. If tonight is like the nights I was on duty, Joseph's walkie-talkie is running him ragged. I'll offer to take his next call for him so he can have a break.

On the second floor, the nurse's station is vacant. The hall is decorated like a fancy old-fashioned hotel, but the royal blue carpet with gold fleurs-de-lis smells of urine from patients' accidents. Doors are decorated with family photographs and other memorabilia so the patients with dementia can remember which room is theirs. Colonel Fraser's door has an old photograph of him in army uniform, impossibly, touchingly young. Fluorescent light shines through the window of the closed door to the utility room. I look through the glass and see Joseph Mandel take two bottles from the cabinet, place one on the counter, and unscrew the lid of the other. He shakes small white pills into his hand. Closing his fingers around the pills, he starts to put them in the pocket of his lab coat and glances at the window as if to make sure no one is watching. When he sees me, he startles violently. The pills go flying. He drops the bottle, which falls onto the floor but doesn't break. Pills from it scatter. I enter the room.

"What are you doing?" I ask.

"I—I was—" His panicky gaze avoids me as he scrambles for an excuse. "Counting the pills. To make sure there were enough."

"No." The truth is obvious. "You were stealing them." I pick up the fallen bottle. The label on it reads Luminal. The pills are barbiturates—sedatives.

Joseph Mandel's face falls; he realizes I'm not buying his lie. "I have trouble sleeping. I need a little help." The bottle he set on the counter contains Benzedrine—amphetamine, a stimulant. He follows my gaze and says, "It is so hard to stay alert during night call."

I exhale, distressed by the familiar scenario. At Mount Sinai, drug use among interns and residents wasn't uncommon. We were working long hours, overwhelmed by responsibility, and terrified of making fatal errors. Anxiety plus constant switching between day and night shifts equaled insomnia during the few hours we had for rest. Barbiturates provide easy sleep; amphetamines can wake up even the most exhausted, groggy intern; and drugs are so accessible in hospitals. I used them myself when aspirin, warm milk, coffee, and Coke didn't suffice. I never stole them, and I'm fortunate that I didn't become dependent on them, as Joseph Mandel apparently is.

What he endured during the war, and the terrible experiences that he can't put behind him, must be contributing to his stress and insomnia, but I can't ignore his attempted theft. "You know this is illegal, don't you?"

He hangs his head. "Yes."

"Why don't you write yourself a prescription and fill it at a drugstore?"

"I do not want anyone to know I am taking so many pills."

Crouching, I gather up the pills from the floor and put them back in the bottle.

“Please. Let me have them.” Joseph holds out a trembling hand. “I need them.”

I’m angry at him even though I feel sorry for him. He’s stealing from houses where he’s not the resident in charge so if anyone notices pills missing, he won’t be blamed. His thefts could land not only me but the nurses and the other residents in trouble. I put both pill bottles back in the cabinet, close the door, and turn the key that he left in the lock. Removing the key, I say, “I’ll return this to the nurse’s station.”

“Please don’t report me!” His voice shakes; his eyes well.

If I report him, he could be fired and lose his medical license or even go to jail. Still, I can’t pretend nothing happened. A drug-addicted doctor is a danger to himself as well as his patients. I know of an intern at another hospital who overdosed and died.

“I’ll have to,” I say, “unless you turn yourself in.”

“All right. I will,” he says, too readily. “Just give me a little time.”

I reluctantly nod. His walkie-talkie chatters, summoning him to Mercy House. I don’t offer to take the call for him. “Let’s go.” I’m not leaving him at Grace House to steal the pills the moment I’m gone.

We walk downstairs. I drop the keys off at the nurse’s station and escort Joseph outside. He hurries off into the night as if the law is already after him. I walk down the steps and stand with my back to the dark bulk of Grace House, gazing up at the star-flecked black sky above the vast, sparsely lit campus. I’m just as compromised as Joseph Mandel. Neither of us should be working here, but I’m the one who’s been reprimanded twice and may be responsible for the death of a patient. It seems that either I resign or get fired. Whichever happens, my days at RKH are numbered.

If I want to discover the truth about my past, and RKH, I’ll have to act as fast as I can, as soon as I can. Which means now.

CHAPTER 25

AFTER A MONTH of strolling the RKH campus during my few leisure hours, I know my way around, even in the dark. Following the main road, I smell smoke in the air and picture bonfires in back yards and local parks near town. I remember summer nights when Brian and I toasted marshmallows and scared each other with ghost stories. There are happy memories from my childhood, but my learning of Donna Wright's murder casts a cold shadow over them. Now I can't think of the summer place without wondering who was guilty—Brian or me? How can I exonerate one of us without incriminating the other?

I reach the lane that leads to the private cottages. This may be my only chance to ask Dr. Isaac Franz whether the events in Rory's play have any basis in fact. I also want to confront him about my "death." Why was it faked? Who else at RKH was involved?

The lane is just wide enough for one car to pass. Dense woods flank each side. Moonlight filtering through the tree canopy shows asphalt pavement that curves toward Hope Cottage. I emerge from the woods into a clearing. Beyond a small parking area and lawn stands a Tudor-style house with pointed roofs, an arched doorway, and a tall front chimney. A lantern glows over the door. The brick walls are half covered by ivy. The smoke smell is stronger; I see haze in the air. I hurry around the house. The flagstone patio and overgrown back garden are dark. Orange light flickers in one window.

Hope Cottage is on fire.

I push through the shrubs below the window, stand on tiptoe, and peer inside. The window is open; heat from the fire wafts through the screen. A shade pulled halfway down and some potted plants block my view. All I can see in the room is the light of the crackling flames.

"Hey!" I yell, pounding on the screen. "Your house is on fire. You have to get out!"

Nobody answers. I run back to the front of the cottage and try the door. It's not locked. I burst inside. Groping my way through dark halls and rooms, I bump into furniture. Smoke fills my lungs and stings my eyes. I cough as I call, "Is anybody here?"

The patient in Hope Cottage has private nurses and servants, but there's no sign of them. I find the room that's on fire. Heat blasts from the open door. I reel backward, coughing in the smoke that engulfs me. I smell gasoline. Covering my nose and mouth with my sleeve, I peer inside the room. The striped curtains and braided rug are burning. So is the white canopy on a four-poster bed where a man lies flat on his back, motionless, his body a narrow ridge under the patchwork quilt. His eyes are closed, his mouth open. His thin face is all sharp angles, beaky nose and pointed chin, but Dr. Isaac Franz is younger than I expected, perhaps in his late forties. His close-cropped hair is dark, he has all his teeth, and his complexion is unwrinkled. The flames shimmer, and the familiar dizziness whirls my head.

I'm lying in bed, looking up at Dr. Franz. He lays his hand on my forehead. I shrink away from his cold touch.

Dr. Franz was my psychiatrist when I was a patient at RKH.

I call his name. He doesn't answer, doesn't move. The flames from the rug are climbing up the dust ruffle on his bed, licking at the quilt. When I take a step into the room, the fire roars, heat sears my face, and I jump backward, coughing. I run back through the house. Smoke clouds the hallway. I stumble out the door and down the steps. Gasping and wheezing, I call, "Fire! Help!"

The night absorbs my voice, which is hoarse and faint from the smoke. I falter along the lane. On the main road, the twin white circles of a car's headlights zoom toward me. I stand in the middle of the road, wave my arms, and yell, "Stop!"

Brakes squeal. The car halts; my hands thump the hood. I run around to the driver's side. The car is an RKH security patrol vehicle. The guard puts his head out the window.

"Fire!" I point toward the cottage.

He guns his car down the lane. I run after it. When I get to the cottage, the windows are bright with orange light; the fire has spread to the other rooms. The guard sits in his parked car, talking on the radio.

"There's a man inside," I say, panting. "We have to bring him out."

"It's too dangerous," the guard says. "I told the night switchboard operator to call the fire department."

Minutes later, I hear sirens. Their wails grow louder, closer. A black Cadillac pulls up to us, and Superintendent Van Pelt jumps out. The guard must have alerted him too. It's the first time I've seen him wearing casual clothes—khaki trousers and a white polo shirt, like a golfer. When he sees me, the concern on his face gives way to displeasure.

"Dr. Kendall. What are you doing here?"

My throat is clogged with smoke; all I can do is cough. The guard says, "She discovered the fire."

The arrival of a fire engine and an ambulance spares me the necessity of explaining myself. Superintendent Van Pelt goes over to meet the commander. The firemen spray water on the cottage until the fire is extinguished, the cottage is dark, and the air smells of wet, scorched wood. They wheel a stretcher into the house and bring out a body wrapped in a black rubber bag.

Dr. Isaac Franz is dead.

My eyes flood and I clasp my arms across the ache of grief and helplessness in my chest. It's the same emotion I felt when I was an intern at the Mount Sinai emergency room, my most difficult rotation. The paramedics had brought in a man they'd rescued from a burning building. We worked frantically to save him, but we failed. I understood then that being a doctor to seriously injured or ill patients meant experiencing the same failure, loss, and emotions over and over. Now it takes me a moment to realize that whatever Dr. Isaac Franz knew about Caroline Lennox and the events of 1941, he can never tell.

The paramedics load the stretcher into the ambulance. Superintendent Van Pelt glances at me and orders the security guard, "Take her to my house."

* * *

Superintendent Van Pelt and Dr. Mara live on the south part of the campus, in a brown brick Tudor mansion. It's like a lord-of-the-manor estate, distant from the other hospital buildings. The drawing room where the guard leaves me with Dr. Mara is the first modern room I've seen at RKH. White walls and lampshades set off simple furniture upholstered with tangerine, lemon, and lime-green linen. The rug on the dark hardwood floor has a geometric pattern in gray and beige. The painting over the white brick fireplace is a semi-abstract scene of blue ocean and sky, golden sand, and terra-cotta houses. Having lived in school dormitories, summer camp cabins, and temporary apartments for so many years, I feel a wistful envy of people with proper homes. If and when I ever have one, this is how I would like it to look—clean, colorful, uncluttered.

"I wanted a change from the Victorian décor in the rest of the hospital," Dr. Mara says, putting a tray laden with a stainless-steel coffee pot and pale blue stoneware mugs, sugar bowl, and creamer on the coffee table in front of the lime-green sofa where I sit. "Modern style is elegant but refreshing, don't you think?"

"Yes," I say.

Dr. Mara is no less elegant despite the fact that it's three o'clock in the morning. Her blonde hair is loose around her shoulders, and her only makeup is a touch of powder and rose lipstick. She wears a pale blue linen caftan and gold sandals, fashionable enough for an afternoon summer party. She sits beside me, and I gladly accept the cup of coffee that she pours for me.

"Thank you." I hold the mug in both hands because they're trembling so hard that the hot liquid sloshes. "And thank you for having me here."

Although I'm far from being friends with the Van Pelts, I don't want to be alone. I think of Daniel Tanaka and wonder if he was awakened by the sirens.

"You're welcome. I'm sorry you had such a terrible experience." Dr. Mara's manner is solicitous but cool.

"I'm sorry I couldn't save the man in the cottage. Who was he, by the way?" I want to know if he really was Dr. Isaac Franz.

"I'm afraid that's confidential. You don't need to know."

I'm not surprised by Dr. Mara's evasion. Does it have to do with more than just RKH's policy regarding the private cottages? "I need to know who I risked my life trying to rescue."

"Is that what you were doing there?" Dr. Mara scrutinizes me intently.

"Excuse me?" What other business does she think I had at the cottage? How could she know that Dot and Maureen told me about Dr. Franz?

With a smile that doesn't reach her eyes, she says, "Let's not discuss this until the superintendent gets here."

A car pulls up outside. A moment later, Superintendent Van Pelt comes into the room with another man. The man bears a resemblance to the superintendent even though he's dark-haired and some dozen years younger. The resemblance owes to his air of authority. He wears a navy sports coat over khaki pants and polo shirt that look less expensive than Superintendent Van Pelt's. He's what the superintendent might be without the advantage of inherited wealth.

"Hello, Bill." Dr. Mara greets him with a warm, genuine smile.

"Hello, Mara," he says. "I came as soon as I could after Adrian phoned me."

Superintendent Van Pelt introduces him to me. "This is Bill Jansen. He's the police chief of Resurrection."

Learning that he called in the police does nothing to relieve my anxiety. Chief Jansen says to Dr. Mara, "I called the mayor and told him about the fire. He said that if there's anything he can do, just let him know."

The Van Pelts are not only on cozy first-name terms with the police chief; they seem to have the mayor, and perhaps the whole town government, in their pocket. That could explain how RKH managed to fake my death.

"Chief Jansen has some questions for you, Dr. Kendall," Superintendent Van Pelt says.

He and the chief pull armchairs up to the opposite side of the coffee table and sit down, too close to me for comfort. His having me brought to his house wasn't an act of kindness. He was positioning me for a police interrogation.

"I understand that you were the first person at the scene of the fire." The chief's formal manner, tone, and wording are ominous. "Is that true?"

"Yes." I imagine myself in a small, windowless cell with a bare light bulb hanging over my head and wonder if it would be possible to get up and leave.

Three pairs of unfriendly eyes fixed on me pin me to my seat. The chief asks, "What were you doing out there at two o'clock in the morning?"

My heart is pounding. It's one thing to lie to my superiors, riskier to lie to the police. Are the Van Pelts using their friend the chief as a lever to pry the truth out of me? I have a split second to decide which is more dangerous—a lie or the truth.

"I was taking a walk."

"Do you often take a walk in the middle of the night?" Chief Jansen makes the mere act of walking at night seem like a crime.

"Sometimes." I breathe easier; the truth is the safer ground, however temporarily.

"Why?"

"To relax." If I really am under surveillance, then Dr. Mara and Superintendent Van Pelt already know I take solitary night walks.

"All right, you were out walking at two AM in order to 'relax.'" The chief's tone implies that my claim is a flimsy cover for guilty behavior. "How did you discover the fire?"

"I smelled smoke. I followed it to the cottage."

"What did you do then?"

"I tried to warn whoever was in the cottage." I'm so tired and jittery that I can't think ahead, anticipate his next questions, or prepare my responses. "I called out while I ran around the cottage, but nobody answered. So I went inside."

"And what did you see?"

I swallow hard. "A man." Dr. Isaac Franz, my former psychiatrist. "Lying in bed." Asleep, unconscious, or dead. "In the room that was on fire." The flames climbing up from the carpet, onto the bedclothes, burning toward his body.

"What did you do?"

"I called to him, but he didn't move. I couldn't reach him." Ashamed of my own helplessness, I say, "The fire was too hot."

"Then what?"

"I ran for help. I stopped a security guard in his car. He called the fire department." I feel relieved that I've safely reached the end of my story.

Chief Jansen and the Van Pelts exchange glances that I can't read. The chief says, "You smell like gasoline, Dr. Kendall. Care to explain why?"

The abrupt change of subject feels like the drop in the atmospheric pressure before a rainstorm. The vacuum sucks the air from my lungs. I pause, my mouth opening and my brow knitting, before I can frame a reply. "The house smelled like gasoline. My clothes must have absorbed the fumes."

A likely story, the chief's expression says. "So the house was on fire when you went in. Is that correct?"

I hesitate, confused about where he's going with this. "Yes."

He raises his eyebrow; my hesitation has made him doubt my word. "Did you see anyone in or near the cottage?"

"No."

"So the only person there, other than the deceased, was you." He points his finger at me, triumphantly, as if he's scored a point.

Alarm bells clang in my ears. "I guess so." Nobody has spoken the deceased's name; it can't be an accident. Does that mean they're not aware that I know he was Dr. Isaac Franz? Or are they aware, and they want me to slip up and reveal that I know? What does confidentiality matter to a dead man?

"The presence of gasoline suggests arson," the chief says. "Which means the deceased's cause of death was murder."

I have to think hard about what he said, and the accusing tone in which he said it, before I can believe I heard him correctly. "You think *I* set the fire?"

"What should I think, Dr. Kendall?" His puzzlement is obviously, theatrically feigned. "Two people were in the cottage. You were the only one who came out alive."

I sputter in indignation. "No! Someone may have set the fire, but it wasn't me!"

I look to Superintendent Van Pelt and Dr. Mara. They eye me dubiously. Of course they wouldn't lift a finger to defend me. They already hold me responsible for Leonora Hirschfeld's suicide. If they need a scapegoat to blame for arson and murder at RKH, why not me?

"Then who was it?" the chief asks.

"I don't know."

"Sometimes the first person on the scene of a crime is the perpetrator himself." An insinuating grin lifts one side of the chief's mouth. "Or herself."

"Not this time." Anger combines with exhaustion and stress, loosening my hold on my temper. "You've been watching too many detective shows on television."

The sudden rise in the emotional temperature of the room tells me I've made a mistake. The Van Pelts shake their heads in disgust. Hostility broadens Chief Jansen's grin, showing his uneven, discolored teeth.

"Dr. Kendall, if you think this is a game that you can smart-talk your way out of, then you're the one who's confusing fiction with reality." He switches subjects again. "Did you know the man you allegedly tried to rescue?"

"No." I'm on dangerous territory, the thin line between the truth and a lie. Just because he was my psychiatrist twelve years ago doesn't mean I ever really knew him, and I barely remember him. I don't dare look at the Van Pelts, lest they sense my dishonesty. Instinct warns me to say as little as possible, but I add, "Which means I had no reason to kill him."

Chief Jansen laughs with condescending amusement. "If I took your word for it, Dr. Kendall, I wouldn't be doing my job."

His repetition of my name lends an insulting note to his accusations. Perhaps he resents me because he thinks I'm a wealthy, privileged, overeducated female and he feels outclassed. And whatever Superintendent Van Pelt told him about me couldn't have been complimentary.

"The cottage was on fire before I got there," I say. "Someone else set it. Maybe someone who sneaked onto the grounds from outside the hospital."

"Ah, yes—the mysterious drifter that every criminal tries to pin his own crimes on. Maybe *you're* the one who's watched too many detective shows, Dr. Kendall."

So he thinks the arsonist is a member of the RKH community. I'm alarmed because I have cause to agree. If I weren't so exhausted and panic-stricken, I would have realized earlier that this is the second death in three weeks connected to the time when I was a patient here. Dr. Franz was my psychiatrist, and Leonora Hirschfeld lived at Haven House then. I can't believe it's a coincidence that they both died after I started asking questions for my "research project." It makes frightening sense that they were murdered to silence them—Leonora because she'd talked to me; Dr. Franz because he'd told Rory, Dot, and Maureen about his fatal experiment after apparently keeping mum about it for twelve years. Until now, neither posed a threat that necessitated their removal. But I don't know what they might have revealed that someone wanted to stay a secret.

Someone within RKH.

Not an outsider.

If my theory is correct, then I'm responsible for both deaths even though I didn't tie the stocking around Leonora's neck or set the cottage on fire.

I can't tell Chief Jansen any of this without exposing my past.

Instead, I say, "I don't watch much television, but I have read a few Perry Mason novels." The library at camp had a whole shelf of them. "And I think I should get a lawyer before I answer any more questions."

The antipathy in the chief's eyes deepens. Superintendent Van Pelt and Dr. Mara give me a look that combines irritation and respect.

"That's your right," Chief Jansen says. "In the meantime, I'll be conducting an official investigation of the fire."

"You'll have our full cooperation," Superintendent Van Pelt says. Dr. Mara nods.

"In case we need to speak with you again," Chief Jansen says to me, "don't leave the hospital."

"We'll see that she doesn't," Dr. Mara says.

My panic skyrockets to a whole new level as I see the three of them ranged against me. I'm as trapped here as I was at age fourteen, and it's too much to hope the police will find evidence that incriminates the actual culprit. Probably they'll focus on building a case against me. Invoking my right to a lawyer only made me look even guiltier, and I'm afraid my history as a former patient will come out. My history will suggest a grudge against Dr. Franz, a motive for murder. The fact that I concealed my identity will surely convince Chief Jansen that he need look no further for the arsonist. Getting fired and losing my career pales in comparison with the threat that I'm up against now: I could be sent to prison, if not executed, for Dr. Franz's murder.

"My officers will be interviewing other people at RKH, Dr. Kendall," Chief Jansen adds. "We'll see what they have to say."

The possibility that the police will find other suspects is more dismaying than comforting. Suddenly, my concern is no longer only for myself—because I know of three other people who knew Dr. Franz, who sneaked around the campus at night making clandestine visits to his cottage.

Rory, Dot, and Maureen.

CHAPTER 26

Mornings at Grace House proceed in slow motion. By the time my elderly patients are out of bed, dressed, and breakfasted, it's almost time for lunch. I occupy myself with tending to their physical ailments, thankful that the work is relatively easy. I didn't get to bed until four AM, and I was too upset to sleep. The atmosphere at Grace House is soothing, like the blankets in the chilly basement where we went for air raid drills at school. But the warm blankets couldn't shield us from the terrible fact of the war, and news about the fire soon filters into Grace House.

The patient in the private cottage died of smoke asphyxia. His name is apparently still a secret. His private nurse had the night off, the substitute didn't show up, and the housekeeper had gone out of town for a funeral. It sounds highly suspicious. Did the killer know Dr. Franz would be alone? Superintendent Van Pelt and Dr. Mara would be in a position to know. His private staff aren't coming back to RKH; they're no longer needed now that he's dead. Were they sent away to prevent them from talking too much? I recall Nurse Janice's swift departure.

The charge nurse calls me to the phone. As I take the receiver, I'm afraid the police are summoning me for another interview . . . or to arrest me. "Hello?"

"Claire, this is Daniel Tanaka." A strained note inflects his warm voice. I hear chatter and noise in the background. "Can you come and meet me?"

I'm as relieved as if I'm drowning and he's a life preserver. I feel the thrill of a teenage girl getting her first call from a boy she likes. "Where?" I ask.

"The swimming pool."

As I hurry across the campus, the clouds darken, the wind gusts, and the air smells of rain. I see signs that the police investigation has begun—a squad car parked by the administration building, strange men talking on radios. I hunch my shoulders to shrink myself and avoid their attention. Other men must be at the cottage, searching the ruins for clues.

Jean Norton comes walking toward me. When she sees me, she hesitates.

"Jean," I call.

She backs away. "What?"

"How are Rory Kirkpatrick, Dot Powell, and Maureen Murray?" I'm not only worried that the girls will reveal that they told me about Dr. Franz; I'm afraid for their safety. They may have learned more from Dr. Franz than they put in their play, and they may be the next targets of whoever wanted him and Leonora Hirschfeld silenced.

"All I have to say to you is this." Jean jabs her finger at me. "Stay away from my husband!"

That business seems so petty compared to arson and murder. "Jean, he was the one who made a pass at me."

"He told me you would say that." Disgust twists Jean's mouth. "He tried to console you when you were in trouble. You mistook it to mean he was interested in you, and you threw yourself at him."

"Jean, he's lying," I say, furious at the husband's deceit, exasperated by the wife's blindness. "When you caught him with me, I was fighting him off."

"You're just like all the others. You can't get a man of your own, so you try to steal mine!"

So Ronald has cheated on Jean multiple times, no surprise. "Open your eyes, Jean. Your husband is a womanizer and a liar. You're a fool to write his reports for him."

"Shut up! Leave us alone. Or I'll—" Jean stammers as if she can't think of a threat that's serious enough. She steps around me and runs away.

Any hope I had of straightening things out with her is gone. But she's the least of my problems.

* * *

The long, rectangular swimming pool looks like an ancient Roman spa. The men's and women's changing rooms are in miniature classical-style temples at each end. Raindrops dimple the water in the pool, and the wind ripples the black Greek key pattern that borders the blue bottom. No one is in sight except Daniel Tanaka, standing under the colonnade that fronts the men's changing room. In this weather, no one will come to swim; no one will see or overhear us. I gasp with relief as I run to Daniel. A frown creases his brow, but he smiles as he holds out his hand to me. Resisting the urge to hurl myself into his arms, I stop several paces short of him. He's wearing gray trousers, a white shirt with the sleeves rolled up, and a blue tie. His stethoscope hangs around his neck, the end tucked in his shirt pocket. His hair is disheveled by the wind. No one ever looked so good to me.

"Claire. I just heard about the fire," he says. "Are you all right?"

I was asked so many questions after the fire but never that one. Neither the Van Pelts nor the police chief had cared about my well-being. Daniel's concern brings tears to my eyes.

"Yes. I feel better now." The rain is coming down in sheets, the columns of the colonnade are cracked, and the marble dolphins that flank the building are green with algae, but this place and his presence are a shelter from the rest of the world.

"Your voice sounds hoarse," Daniel says. "Have you been examined for smoke inhalation?"

I shake my head. In the confusion of last night, it hadn't occurred to me that someone should have examined me.

"May I?" He puts the ear tips of his stethoscope in his ears.

I nod, glad to feel taken care of. It's a rare, warm feeling. Daniel gently presses the diaphragm of the stethoscope against the front of my blouse and listens. He's careful not to touch me with his hands. I'm his colleague, not his patient.

"Your lungs are clear," he says, removing the ear tips and replacing the end of the stethoscope in his pocket. "Your heartbeat is strong."

"Thank you." My voice is unsteady with emotion.

"How come you're working today? You should rest."

I didn't think to ask for the day off, and Superintendent Van Pelt and Dr. Mara didn't offer it. Do they think I'm safe to be around the patients until I'm proven guilty of arson and murder? Or does RKH just not have anyone else to cover Grace House? Chilled by their indifference, all I can do is shrug. "How did you know I was in the cottage during the fire?"

"One of the nurses at Mercy House mentioned it."

Besides the security guard, the only people at RKH who knew I was there are Dr. Mara and Superintendent Van Pelt. The guard probably briefed his day shift counterpart, and the police chief or the firemen could have told acquaintances who work at the hospital, but it's easy to picture the Van Pelts passing the word. My heart drops because I think they want people to jump to conclusions about why I was at the cottage. When the police interview the staff, they'll find plenty of witnesses who are prejudiced against me. That's bad, but it's not the worst thing about the situation.

"I tried to save him. I failed." I can't hold back the tears.

Daniel gives me his handkerchief. "You did your best."

I mop my eyes. "The chief of police interrogated me last night. He thinks I set the fire."

"That's ridiculous," Daniel says flatly. "Of course you didn't."

His faith in me is such a relief that I sob. "How do you know I didn't?"

"I know you, Claire. You're not capable of murder."

I feel worse again because he doesn't really know me. He doesn't know about the murder of Donna Wright. If he were aware of the things I've concealed, he might change his mind. I wish I didn't have to keep secrets from him, but the habit of distrust is hard to break.

"Superintendent Van Pelt and Dr. Mara think I did it," I say.

"They can't possibly," Daniel protests. "They're intelligent, sensible people. If they gave that impression, it must have been because they were upset."

In spite of how the world has treated him, he thinks the best of people because he's a good person himself. I'm sorry I can't set him straight about the bad things that have happened at RKH and why I think the Van Pelts were involved. The rain is letting up, and the sun glints through the clouds. We have to get back to work. If the police look for me at Grace House and I'm not there, I'll seem even guiltier.

"Daniel," I say, "I need to ask you for a big favor."

He spreads his arms. "Just name it."

He's the nicest person I've met at RKH, but I hesitate to trust him because he seems too good to be true. Still, I don't have anyone else to ask. "It's about Rory Kirkpatrick, Dot Powell, and Maureen Murray. My former patients at Haven House."

"Uh. About Rory." Daniel inhales and exhales deeply. "I went to the health department and lodged a complaint about Dr. Bullard's aversion therapy."

"*What*?" Shocked, I say, "When?"

"The day after we talked."

"Why didn't you tell me?"

"I didn't want you to stop me. Or beat me to it."

"Oh, God." I'm horrified that he risked his career. It should have been me.

"The health department is going to send an inspector," Daniel says.

I'm in awe of his courage, and I hope the inspector observes the aversion therapy and shuts it down for good. "But the superintendent will find out that the complaint came from you!"

"The official at the health department promised to keep my identity confidential."

I'm far from sure that it won't come out. Daniel says, "I'm sorry I dumped this on you right after what you've been through. I was afraid we might not have another chance to talk. What's the favor you need from me?"

"I need to know if Rory, Dot, and Maureen are all right. Would you check on them and tell me how they are? And help them if need be?"

"Of course."

I sigh with relief. "Thank you."

Daniel's perceptive gaze studies me. "Is there something you're not telling me?"

Oh, so much. "I'll tell you if you promise not to repeat it to anyone."

"I promise."

Again I have to decide what and what not to reveal. This time I'll be lying by omission to my only friend. "After the play at the talent show, I spoke with Dot and Maureen. They said Rory based the play on a story that the man in Hope Cottage told them about fever therapy experiments at RKH. The girls have been sneaking outside at night and visiting him. His name is Isaac Franz. He's the doctor in the play."

"Whoa," Daniel says, clearly awed by the revelations and the girls' antics.

"I went to the cottage to ask him if the story is true." I don't explain why it matters personally to me. "That's why I was there." I swallow hard at the memory of Dr. Franz in the burning bed. "But I never got a chance."

". . . Okay." Daniel looks more mystified than enlightened.

"If the girls are questioned by the police, they might break down and confess." I'm so upset, I'm talking fast, my words jumbling. "And I'm afraid the police will suspect them of setting the fire."

Dr. Mara already forced the girls to spill their story. If she can't pin the arson on me, will she try them next? I'm astonished to realize that this crime is like the Donna Wright murder all over again. In both cases I'm a suspect, and the alternative suspects are people whom I least want to see incriminated—Brian for Donna's murder; Rory, Dot, and Maureen for Dr. Franz's. Freud described a phenomenon that he called repetition compulsion—the unconscious tendency to repeat traumatic events or circumstances. It can take the form of putting oneself in a situation where the event is likely to recur. By investigating my past, I unwittingly sowed the seeds for the past to repeat itself.

Daniel shakes his head somberly. "This is serious."

I'm glad he agrees, even though I'd hoped he would assure me that my concerns are unfounded. Then he says, "Are you afraid they did it?"

"No!" I blurt.

"The irresistible impulse to start fires is associated with some mental illnesses, including schizophrenia," Daniel says. "Also with self-harm and suicide attempts."

I'm aware of the pathology, but I say, "I really don't think the girls are capable of it." I have my doubts about Freud's theory that fire-setting is a form of masturbation provoked by unconscious sexual drives. But Maureen is schizophrenic, and I saw the scars on Dot's arms.

"Disturbed children and adolescents are the most at risk for pyromania. Two of my younger patients were committed after setting fire to their family's homes." Seeing the dismay on my face, Daniel says, "But I don't know those girls, so I won't make a case against them. Tell me what else I can do besides checking on them."

I'm thankful that he wants to help, but I say, "There's nothing."

I can't bring myself to ask him to ask the girls if they sneaked out of Haven House last night after I talked to Dot and Maureen. I'm afraid to know the answer.

"I know how much you care about the girls, but what about yourself?" Daniel says. "You're the one who's under suspicion. We should be trying to exonerate you."

My fear for myself is a black, clawing force that threatens to reduce me to helpless shreds. Things were dire enough when my flashback suggested to me that I had killed Donna Wright. But the police investigating her case overlooked me as a potential suspect. This time, I'm the prime suspect in Dr. Franz's murder, and my mission has grown exponentially more difficult. It's no longer just Brian and myself that I need to clear, but Rory, Dot, and Maureen.

"If there's any chance that the girls are guilty—" Daniel begins.

I interrupt him. "I won't put the girls on the hook to get myself off it." Or let whoever set the fire go after them next. Or let the blame for Donna Wright's murder rest on my brother if he's innocent. "I'll figure something out."

I only wish I knew how.

C H A P T E R

27

In the wake of the fire, I hear of fights breaking out among the male patients and an epidemic of quarrels, panic attacks, and self-mutilation at the women's houses. The emergency siren blares from loudspeakers all over campus. RKH goes on lockdown. Visiting hours, grounds privileges, and trips off campus are canceled. Patients are confined to their rooms, and all treatments except those which are medically necessary are postponed. Staff members check on each patient every half hour. My ladies and gentlemen at Grace House complain about missing their afternoon tea party. That's tame compared to incidents that the other residents describe over our dinner of broiled chicken, wild rice, Jell-O salad, and pineapple upside-down cake that night.

"At Mercy House, the patients have been beating on their doors with their shoes and chanting, 'Let us out! Let us out!'" Daniel Tanaka says.

"Yeah," Ronald Norton says, "it's like a scene from a prison movie."

"Some of the girls at Haven House are so upset that they've regressed." Jean Norton's narrow-eyed glance dares me to ask about Rory, Maureen, and Dot just so she can have the pleasure of refusing to answer.

Joseph Mandel isn't with us. I haven't seen him since I caught him stealing pills. I only came to dinner because I need to eat and I'm not supposed to leave the campus. Superintendent Van Pelt, Dr. Mara, and Dr. Bullard usually dine later, so I excuse myself before they come. I can't risk antagonizing them again. As it is, I'm afraid my days at RKH are numbered.

"Good night, Claire." Daniel Tanaka's gaze signals his concern.

The Nortons don't acknowledge me. It's as if I'm already gone.

* * *

There's a scene that I saw again and again, heartbreakingly often, while I was an intern at Mount Sinai. The families of terminally ill patients who didn't have long to live held vigils in the lounges. They passed the hours with conversation, telephone calls, and newspapers; trips to the restroom and cafeteria; cigarettes and cups of coffee. Life went on even while they waited for the inevitable. It's been two weeks since the fire, and it has felt like a similar vigil to me. Every day I work at Grace House. I talk to patients and staff; I perform examinations and give medications; I write reports. Life goes on. My career is the terminally ill patient, and I'm waiting for its inevitable, premature end.

I'm not the only one who believes I'm not long for RKH. The nurses, aides, and orderlies are polite, but they don't talk to me about anything that's not related to work. If I'll be gone soon, why bother getting to know me? Dr. Mara keeps her distance, and I only see Superintendent Van Pelt and Dr. Bullard at rounds and training sessions, where they and Joseph Mandel and the Nortons pretend I'm not there. I think they're ostracizing me so that I'll quit, which would spare RKH the unpleasantness of firing me. Only Daniel Tanaka treats me as a colleague and a friend—or he did, until I put stop to it.

Several days after our talk by the pool, he caught up with me as I was walking toward Grace House and said, "I went to Haven House and talked to your girls. I told Jean that I was visiting the different houses to learn what's going on there. Dot and Maureen are feeling better. Rory has been taken out of isolation. They're all behaving themselves."

"Thank you," I said, relieved. The lockdown has been lifted, and the hospital is calm. There've been no other deaths. "Do you know if they were questioned by the police?"

"I asked them, and they said no." Daniel added, "All the patients were accounted for the night of the fire. They were all in their rooms during every bed check."

That didn't relieve my fear that they might be suspected of setting the fire. They could have sneaked out of Haven House somehow; they'd done it before. Someone might have seen them near the cottage, someone yet to be interviewed by the police. And knowing Rory's propensity for trouble, I don't think she can keep up her good behavior for very long.

"I feel like getting away from here for a while, don't you?" Daniel said. "Would you like to have dinner in town with me tonight?"

His expression told me more than his casual words: he was concerned about me, but he also liked me, and he'd worked up his courage to ask me out. I was delighted by his interest as well as grateful for his kindness.

But I said, "I don't think I should." It wasn't just because the police chief told me not to leave the hospital.

"Oh." Daniel made an obvious attempt to hide his hurt behind nonchalance.

Lest he think I was rejecting him because society disapproves of interracial dating, I hurried to explain. "It's not a good idea for you to associate with me."

He looked relieved but puzzled. "Why not?"

"Because I'm an arson and murder suspect."

"I don't believe it. If you were, the police would have arrested you by now. Their investigation seems to be over."

It's true that the police hadn't been seen at RKH lately, and they'd left me alone since the interview at the superintendent's house, but I don't think their investigation is over or that they're finished with me. And that's not the only reason I warned Daniel to keep his distance.

"A bad reputation is contagious," I said. "Stay away from me. Protect yourself."

Concern that bordered on tenderness vied with shock in his eyes. "Claire—" His hand reached toward me.

I desperately wanted him to say that we were friends and he wouldn't drop me just because public opinion had turned against me.

But he's worked so hard to become a psychiatrist, and his future mustn't be a casualty of my problems. I swallowed the sob in my throat.

"Stay away," I repeated, then turned and ran from him.

Soon afterward, I fell into a depression as deep as those I experienced at boarding school after the deaths of Brian and my mother and my abandonment by my father. Just as then, my own mind became my enemy.

I blame myself for Leonora's suicide and Dr. Franz's murder. If I hadn't tried to excavate the past, they would still be alive.

I chose psychiatry with such idealistic hopes of helping other troubled girls, but I've ruined my chance to help Rory, Dot, Maureen, and the other patients at Haven House. I've been relegated to custodial care of patients for whom there's no hope of resurrection from mental decline. And if something is wrong at RKH, I'm powerless to change it.

I can't even focus on recovering my lost memory, because further efforts in that direction might not only cause more deaths but also reveal that Brian or I killed Donna Wright. Exonerating one of us can only incriminate the other.

My purpose in life is gone.

I find myself dwelling on my two suicide attempts, the glint of the razor blade as I drew it across my wrist, the round white pills that I swallowed with a glass of cold chocolate milk. The memories have a seductive allure.

Then the nightmares begin. They're always a variation of the same scenario: I'm walking in the woods near my family's summer house. It's dark, and I'm following a flashlight beam that flickers through the trees. I don't know who I'm following or why. I'm terrified but I don't know of what or who. The danger seems to be everywhere—in the shadows, the hoot of an owl, the crack of twigs underfoot and the rustling leaves. Sometimes the dream segues into my old nightmare of the tunnels under RKH. I always wake up in shuddering, heart-pounding dread of whatever horrible thing I was about to experience.

Meanwhile, I go through the motions of life and work. I can't shake the sensation that I'm broadcasting doom, silent and invisible as radio waves. It's as though I'm one of the RKH ghosts, unseen and unheard by everyone except some of my more sensitive patients, who become agitated in my presence. I can't go on like this. My own disturbed mind makes me a danger to the patients. A mistake made during a lapse in concentration could be fatal.

Since Superintendent Van Pelt apparently isn't going to fire me, I must resign. I have to do it before my next night call, when I'll be responsible for all the patients for three twelve-hour night shifts in a row beginning on August twenty-fifth. I won't give advance notice. Superintendent Van Pelt and Dr. Mara can't stop me from walking out as soon as I tell them I'm leaving. Probably they'll be glad to be rid of me. It seems like the best deal for all involved. I'll stop prying into RKH's secrets, go away, and keep my mouth shut. They'll call off the police.

Where I'll go or what I'll do after I leave, I wish I knew. I can't see any farther into the future beyond driving my car out the gate.

CHAPTER

28

In the same building as the laboratory, RKH has an operating room for minor procedures such as suturing wounds and pumping stomachs. On August twenty-fourth, the day before I plan to resign, there's a training session in the operating room. The other residents are already seated there when I arrive ten minutes late, having almost forgotten about the session. My mind is focused on tomorrow, constantly rehearsing the moment when I'll walk into Superintendent Van Pelt's office and tell him I quit. Daniel Tanaka is the only resident who greets me. His manner is reserved. We haven't seen or spoken to each other since I told him to stay away from me. The Nortons and Dr. Mandel give me the cold shoulder. Two other people are present—a nurse standing beside a patient strapped into a hospital bed. The patient is a woman, her head covered by a white surgical cap and immobilized by a brace. Her eyes slowly open and close, as if she's on the verge of sleep.

"Dr. Bullard shouldn't keep us waiting," Ronald Norton says. "We have work to do."

"I'm sure he'll be here soon," Jean says.

Joseph Mandel fidgets. He looks pale, sweaty, and thinner. I suspect he's still taking pills, although he hasn't stolen any from Grace House; I've checked.

Superintendent Van Pelt comes into the room with another man. The man is slender, lanky, in his fifties, clad in a white lab coat and carrying a black leather medical bag. Sharp-featured, he has a gray goatee and wears gold-rimmed glasses.

"Where is Dr. Bullard?" Superintendent Van Pelt asks. When nobody seems to know, he grimaces in annoyance. "We'll have to carry on without him. This is Dr. Bradley Buscher. He's going to demonstrate a lobotomy."

"Good morning," Dr. Buscher says, bright-eyed and chipper.

I see that the other residents are as stunned as I am; the schedule didn't say what the training session was about. Now we're going to witness the most drastic intervention that psychiatry offers mental patients.

"Dr. Buscher is a neurosurgeon and a graduate of Yale Medical School," Superintendent Van Pelt says. "He's performed over five hundred lobotomies. RKH doesn't employ a full-time lobotomist because lobotomy isn't as common as it once was, now that there are drugs for all but the most serious, recalcitrant symptoms. Dr. Buscher works on call at hospitals and clinics all over the country."

While Dr. Buscher unpacks his bag, the superintendent reads from the patient's chart. "This is Mrs. Paula Scott, age twenty-nine, housewife. She suffers from severe depression and has attempted suicide multiple times. Mrs. Scott, can you say hello to the doctors?"

"Hello," she mumbles groggily.

I remember Lulu Shelton at Haven House, unable to speak clearly since her lobotomy ten years ago.

Superintendent Van Pelt smiles, says, "Take it away, Dr. Buscher," and sits down beside Ronald Norton.

"Lobotomy was invented by a Portuguese neurologist, Dr. Antonio Egas Moniz." Dr. Buscher sets instruments on the tray table beside Mrs. Scott's bed. "He won the 1949 Nobel Prize for pioneering the use of lobotomy to treat psychoses."

The fact that lobotomy received science's highest accolade doesn't quell my uneasiness about it. Drug treatment and psychotherapy can be discontinued at any time, but the results of brain surgery are permanent.

"More than twenty thousand lobotomies are performed every year in the United States alone. It's proven very effective in cases of schizophrenia, manic-depression, and other disorders that don't respond to other therapies."

Mrs. Scott appears oblivious to what's about to happen to her. I picture my fourteen-year-old self in her place, another double in the dark mirror.

"Psychosis results from obsessive self-reflection, destructive thoughts that circle around and around nonstop," Dr. Buscher says. "Lobotomy breaks the circle by severing the connections to and from the prefrontal cortex."

In other words, brute force is the last-ditch resort after all else fails.

Dr. Buscher dons a surgical cap, mask, and latex gloves. He says to Mrs. Scott, "Can you hear me, dear?"

"Yes," she mumbles, her eyes half closed.

"Very good, dear."

I figure he's performed so many lobotomies that he doesn't remember the patients' names and he's already forgotten Paula Scott's.

"Bombs away!" Dr. Buscher says brightly, removing Mrs. Scott's cap.

The top of her head has been shaved. The nurse swabs her bare scalp with a gauze pad dipped in alcohol and applies local anesthetic. Dr. Friedman picks up an instrument from the tray. It's a cranial drill with a white plastic handle and a fine, sharp bit. He plugs it into the wall socket, turns it on, and speaks over the high-pitched whine.

"I make two holes." He drills one after the other on the top of her skull near the front.

Superintendent Van Pelt and the nurse watch with no visible reaction, as if they've seen this many times before. The other residents and I wince, although we all must have opened skulls in anatomy class if not assisted with brain surgery at other hospitals. But I've never seen holes drilled in the head of a conscious person.

Dr. Buscher sets down the drill and holds up a steel instrument that resembles a hypodermic syringe, with a plunger on one end and a narrow shaft at the other. "This is a leukotome. When the plunger is depressed, a wire loop comes out of the shaft." He demonstrates, then pulls back the plunger, retracting the loop. "I insert the leukotome about five centimeters deep."

As the shaft slides into the hole on the right side of her skull, Mrs. Scott doesn't even blink; the brain has no pain sensors. My own skull throbs. For the first time I truly appreciate that I'm among RKH's luckier former patients.

Dr. Buscher depresses the plunger. My throat constricts as I imagine the loop poking into the soft brain tissue like a spoon into Jell-O. He says to Mrs. Scott, "Dear, can you sing 'The Star-Spangled Banner'?"

Her lips barely move. "Oh, say can you see . . . by the dawn's early light . . ." Her slow voice is hoarse, tuneless.

"I rotate the leukotome." Dr. Buscher suits action to words. "This cuts a cylindrical core in the brain tissue."

". . . What so proudly we hailed . . . at the twilight's last gleaming . . ."

"When she stops singing or becomes incoherent, the connections to and from the prefrontal cortex are severed," Dr. Buscher says, "and I stop rotating."

"Whose broad stripes . . . and buh, bright stars . . . thuh, thuh, through the p-p-p—" Mrs. Scott's singing dwindles into gibberish.

Dr. Buscher retracts the plunger and withdraws the leukotome from her head. Superintendent Van Pelt nods in approval. I see my horror in the other residents' expressions. None of us will ever hear the national anthem again without recalling the sound of Mrs. Scott garbling the lyrics.

"Now, the other side," Dr. Buscher says.

I can't watch anymore. I look above Dr. Buscher's hands inserting and manipulating the leukotome. I try to tune out his cheery commentary.

"Lobotomy surgically returns patients to a state of childhood. They gradually mature and develop a personality that's more acceptable to society."

Ten years postlobotomy, Lulu Shelton still acts like a two-year-old and wears diapers. That she's a permanent patient at RKH would hardly indicate that she's more acceptable to society than she previously was. My amnesia seems almost trivial compared to her fate and Mrs. Scott's.

"Finito!" Beaming, Dr. Buscher holds the leukotome aloft.

The shaft is wet with bloody slime. Mrs. Scott gurgles. The nurse swabs the holes in her head and applies adhesive bandages.

"By the way, there's a simplified lobotomy procedure," Dr. Buscher says. "A portable electroshock machine renders the patient unconscious, and a sharp instrument called an orbitoclast is inserted in the eye socket and tapped with a mallet to drive it into the brain. The simplified lobotomy can be performed outside a hospital, in the comfort of the patient's own home, by someone with no surgical training."

That's great news. I wish I'd resigned yesterday. The lobotomy is one terrible incident at RKH that won't be erased from my memory. But I'll never have to see any psychiatric atrocities again. This is my last day. Tomorrow it will all be over.

Loud, shrill screams come from outside the room. Startled, everyone looks toward the door. A nurse rushes in, crying, "Superintendent! Come quick, it's Dr. Bullard, he—" She lapses into stammers and gasps.

Superintendent Van Pelt strides out the door after the nurse, motioning everyone else to stay. But we all follow them, Ronald Norton in the lead. We rush down the hall, a dingy corridor with a speckled gray terrazzo floor, gray walls, and dim Victorian-era lamps. Near the end, a maid wearing a gray uniform sits slumped in a chair, her head between her knees, her broom and dustpan beside her. The nurse points at the maid and says, "She found him. He's in there!" and points at the open door to the aversion therapy room.

Our group crowds inside. Superintendent Van Pelt and the other residents block my view. Jean Norton moans. They recoil toward the edges of the room. Now I see Dr. Bullard lying on his back, arms outflung, on the floor near the movie screen. A chair is overturned near him. His vacant eyes stare at the ceiling, and his mouth gapes open as if in surprise. A red splatter of blood surrounds his bald head. His white laboratory coat and white shirt are hiked above his waist, exposing his fat belly; his gray trousers and white boxer shorts are pulled down around his thick, hairy thighs. I gaze in astonishment.

The flat, round metal electrodes, connected by cables to the electric shock machine, are taped to Dr. Bullard's naked penis and testicles.

CHAPTER

29

Superintendent Van Pelt sends Dr. Buscher on his way, then tells the other residents and me, "Go back to work. Don't speak to anyone about this."

"This," meaning the apparent murder of Dr. Bullard.

At Grace House, I tend to my patients. The murder doesn't change my plans. It only solidifies my decision to resign tomorrow. Why stay at a hospital that's had two horrific crimes in less than two months? Whatever I could learn by staying isn't worth the potential harm to others or myself. Feeling better because I've made the decision, I begin to hope that there's still a chance for me to become a psychiatrist. I have a good record as an intern at Mount Sinai; maybe they'll let me come back for my residency. If they won't, and no other major institution will accept me, I can probably find a place in a small-town hospital that's desperate for doctors. I'll practice medicine even if it's not psychiatry. I'm young and strong; I can make a life for myself.

But I can't help feeling sorry that I wasn't able to help Rory, Dot, and Maureen, and I'll be leaving them behind in this place.

That night, I skip dinner in the mansion and eat crackers and peanut butter in my room. Then I pack my suitcases so I'll be ready to leave as soon as I've handed in my resignation first thing in the morning. I fold up my lab coat with my badge clipped to the pocket. I'll give it back to Superintendent Van Pelt. I'm thinking, *good riddance*, when there's a knock at the door. I don't answer. Everyone and everything in RKH are already part of the past that I'm putting behind me.

The knocking continues. "Claire, are you there?" Daniel Tanaka calls.

My heart thumps.

"Claire. I have to talk to you." He knocks louder.

"You shouldn't be here," I call. "Go away."

The fact that associating with me could hurt his reputation isn't the only reason. Seeing Daniel will make it hard for me to leave.

"It's important. Don't make me shout it through the door."

Whatever he has to say is probably not something I want broadcasted to everyone within earshot. I reluctantly open the door. The very least that I owe him is to tell him I'm leaving and say goodbye. When Daniel steps into the room, I savor the warmth and concern in his dark eyes. My heart is sore with the knowledge that this is the last time we'll see each other.

"Rory Kirkpatrick was just arrested for the murder of Dr. Bullard," Daniel says.

My breath gusts from my mouth. I'm stunned speechless as Daniel explains, "The police say he was hit on his head with the chair, knocked unconscious, then electrocuted with his shock machine. They found out that Rory is the last person known to have seen him alive, during her aversion therapy session."

Horror releases my voice. "Oh, God."

This is far worse than when I'd feared that Rory, Dot, and Maureen had set fire to Dr. Franz's cottage. Rory is officially a murder suspect, in police custody. And she hated Dr. Bullard for torturing her. The police must have heard that she threatened to kill him, in front of all the residents and Superintendent Van Pelt.

"I'm sorry, Claire," Daniel says. "I know you care about Rory. I thought I should tell you in case nobody else had."

"But she couldn't have done it!" Now I'm awash in disbelief. "She's a troublemaker but not a murderer!" I stifle the notion that giving Dr. Bullard a taste of his own medicine is exactly what an angry, vengeful, and clever girl might have done.

Daniel regards me with sympathy. "I agree, but since I don't really know her, my opinion doesn't count for much."

Neither would mine, I realize. Rory was my patient for a mere two weeks, and my name is mud at RKH. I think of how frightened she must be, alone in jail, her parents far away.

"I have to see her." Who else is there to stand up for her except me? I pick up my purse. "I'm going to the jail."

"She's not in the jail," Daniel says. "It doesn't have facilities for mental patients. The police are holding her here, in the lockdown house."

"Oh." I'm glad Rory isn't at the mercy of the police, but the lockdown house is the terror of all the patients, and I've seen for myself how grim it is. "Well, I'll talk to her over there."

"You can't. Nobody is allowed except her special nurse." Daniel looks around the room, notices my open suitcases on my bed, and says in surprise, "Are you leaving?"

"I was going to leave, but now I guess I'm not."

Rory's arrest changes everything. I mustn't let her be blamed for a crime she didn't commit. Maybe there's nothing I can do to save her, but I have to try. I won't be another adult who abandoned her the way my father abandoned me. I feel as if I've been sealed in a dark vacuum chamber with my own miserable thoughts, and now it's cracked open, letting in air and light.

It seems I've found a new reason to stay at RKH, and a new purpose in life.

* * *

Dear Celia,

I thought it was bad when they sent me here, but this is the worst. And now I don't even have the comfort of thinking about you and looking forward to seeing you again someday.

This is the last letter I'll ever "write" to you.

The day before yesterday, I was eating dinner with Maureen and Dot as usual. The girls at the next table were having the same conversation that probably happens at every mental ward in the world: "When I Get Out of Here."

"When I get out of here," Sheila Stewart says, "I'll go to the movies every night and eat strawberry ice cream sundaes afterward."

I don't like Sheila because she's mean to Lulu Shelton. She pinches Lulu when the nurses aren't looking, and when Lulu has a tantrum, they don't understand why. I say to her, "When I get out of here, I won't have to listen to your idiotic blabber anymore."

Sheila glares at me as if she wants to say, "Shut up and die, bitch." But she doesn't say it because she's afraid of me. Maureen and Dot and I smile innocently at her and go on eating. Just a normal night at the loony bin.

Suddenly, the chatter in the dining room quiets down as two cops walk in. Superintendent Van Pelt is right behind them. They all come straight to me.

"Rosemary Kirkpatrick," one of the cops says, "you're under arrest."

The whole room gasps. Nothing like this has happened in Haven House since I've been here, maybe never.

"Why?" I'm so flabbergasted, I can't move.

"For the murder of Dr. Robert Bullard."

"What?" I can't believe I heard right. Dr. Bullard's not dead; I just saw him this morning. The other girls are chattering, all excited.

The cops grab my arms and pull me out of my chair. "Come with us."

I remember Dad saying, "It's not the size of the dog in the fight, it's the size of the fight in the dog." There are two cops and they're bigger than me, but I have enough fight in me for ten people. And I don't want to go to jail.

I lash out with my fists, punching one of them in the jaw, the other in his stomach. I scream, "Get away from me!"

They say, "Shit!" and step back. They obviously didn't expect me to resist. Superintendent Van Pelt should have warned them. When they grab me again, they hold on tighter. I kick their legs.

"Let me go!"

"Let her go!" Dot and Maureen cry.

Other girls start chanting, "Let her go! Let her go!"

They're the girls who like me. Sheila and the others who don't like me yell, "Take her away! Take her away!"

The cops pull me toward the door. I'm kicking and jerking and snapping at them like a wild animal. A blob of something wet and cold hits my cheek. I look around and see Sheila holding her bowl of green Jell-O, giggling as she throws handfuls at me. Suddenly, food is flying from all directions, bread rolls and mashed potatoes and chicken bones, hitting me and the cops. Nurses rush around, shouting at the girls to stop throwing food. The girls keep chanting, "Let her go!" and "Take her away!" The cops should have waited until after dinner to arrest me. I guess they don't have any experience with crazy girls. They haul me out of the dining room. It's just the cops and me and Superintendent Van Pelt in the hall. I kick and fight harder.

Superintendent Van Pelt says, "Rosemary, be a good girl and come along peacefully, or I'll have to give you a shot."

A shot will knock me out, and I'll be totally helpless while the cops do whatever they want to me. I stop fighting, and the superintendent gives me that twinkly-eyed smile of his. He looks like somebody's nice grandfather. I hate him. He's in on everything that's been done to me here. The cops handcuff me and put me in their car. I'm plotting to escape once we're away from RKH. I can jump out of the car and run into the woods, and if I can figure out how to get the damned handcuffs off, I can hitchhike to the city and hide there. But instead of driving out the gate, the cops take me to the lockdown house.

The lockdown house, where they turn you into a zombie and then you'll be a mental patient in a loony bin forever.

The cops take off the handcuffs and turn me over to the nurses, who lock me in a cell. There's only one good thing about being arrested for murder: Now Dad and Mother will have to come. They were on vacation in Ireland, a nurse just told me. She said Superintendent Van Pelt called them and they flew back to the U.S. I'm practically bouncing off the padded walls of my cell while I wait for them, I'm so happy. Then the door opens and there's Dad, tall and strong and handsome. I start crying like a baby. I jump up from the bed, and I'm about to throw myself into his arms when he holds up his hand. The look on his face stops me. It's cold and angry, as if I'm a stranger who crashed into his car.

"Rosemary," he says, "I've hired a lawyer for you. He'll be here to see you tomorrow."

"Here?" I say. "Aren't you taking me home?"

"Just do as he says. And don't talk to anyone else." He turns to walk out the door.

"Dad! Please don't go!" I beg him. He's rich and important, and he knows people in high places. He should be able to pull some strings, call in some favors, or bribe the police to let me out, but he isn't going to. He's abandoning me. Again.

But I guess I shouldn't be surprised. Once I was Rosie, his favorite child, but now that I'm a lesbian under arrest for murder, he's not going to waste any more attention or love on me.

"Your mother wants a word with you," he calls over his shoulder.

He's gone and she comes in, dressed in a black jacket and skirt and heels, her hair pinned up under a little black hat with a black veil, like she's going to a funeral.

"Mother, please, get me out of here," I beg her. "I want to go home."

She's as calm and dignified as ever, but she's changed since she brought me to RKH. She looks older, frailer. Her thick makeup doesn't hide her red eyes or the dark circles under them. She must be worried about me, but she shakes her head.

"I'm sorry, Rosemary," she says quietly.

I think she really is. I think she loves me in spite of me not being a proper girl. But I know that even if she could rescue me, she won't go against Dad.

"There's something I need to tell you," she says.

What could be worse than the police thinking I killed Dr. Bullard? Then Mother says, "Celia is married."

I feel dizzy, and my head is filled with a ringing noise as if I've been punched in the ear. "She can't be."

Celia, you told me I'm the only one you'll ever love.

Mother reaches in her purse, pulls out a newspaper clipping, and hands it to me. There's the awful truth, in black and white: Celia Katherine Wentworth and James Hugh Donnelly III, Esq., married August 8, 1953. *My heart feels like it's shattered into a million pieces. I crumple the clipping and throw it on the floor. I sink onto the bed, doubled over in pain, moaning. James must be over forty, and everybody knows he's an ugly, mean jackass who gropes young girls. Your parents must have forced you to marry him because they wanted you to be normal.*

"Mr. Donnelly will be managing the Hong Kong branch of his family's law firm," Mother says. "He and Celia have already moved there."

And they wanted to get you far away from me. Hong Kong might as well be on Mars.

Tears are running down my face. We'll never be together. I'll never see you again.

If they send me to the electric chair for killing Dr. Bullard, I don't care. In fact, it would be a blessing because I don't have any reason to live anymore.

I know you can't hear me, you never could, but I'll say this anyway: I love you I love you I love you.

Rory

CHAPTER

30

A PURPOSE IS A more effective tonic than any drug. My depression clears like the stale air in a house when a tornado blows the roof off. Today was the day I'd planned to resign, but instead, I'm still working at Grace House. A rainstorm starts midafternoon. Tea won't be served on the veranda. At three o'clock, the elderly patients are gathering in the parlor, the maids bringing the carts laden with the tea urn and sandwiches and cakes, when a nurse says brightly, "Ladies and gentlemen, we have a surprise for you!"

Enter Dot and Maureen, wearing pastel flowered dresses. Dot carries a thin stack of sheet music. As they smile at the patients, they spot me where I'm seated on the sofa beside Colonel Fraser. Behind the nurse's back, they gesture and make faces at me, silently communicating that they need a word.

"Here are Dorothy Powell and Maureen Murphy from Haven House," the nurse says. "They're going to entertain you with some music today."

Some patients chatter excitedly. Others look blank. Dot sits down on the piano bench; Maureen stands beside her. I get up and refill my teacup at the urn near them. While Dot arranges her music on the rack, Maureen whispers to me.

"We told Dr. Norton we wanted to make up for causing a ruckus at the talent show, and we volunteered to perform for the old people. She let us come."

Dot plays "Barbara Allen." She and Maureen sing together. "In Scarlet Town, where I was born, there was a fair maid dwelling . . ." Dot has a lovely soprano voice. Maureen warbles off key. They finish to enthusiastic applause from the patients who are mentally competent enough to listen.

"We're worried about Rory," Maureen whispers. Despite their pretty clothes and their smiles, the girls look unwell, with purplish shadows under their eyes, and Dot's face is red with hives. "Have you heard anything?"

I pretend to drink my tea. "No," I murmur. The grapevine has been busy with rumors in the absence of facts.

"Everybody thinks she killed Dr. Bullard." Tears leak from Maureen's eyes. "They say she's going to be tried and convicted."

"But she's innocent," Dot hisses, playing the introduction to "Greensleeves."

"Please help her, Dr. Kendall," Maureen says. "You're the only one we could think to ask."

"I'll try."

They smile, relieved. I can't promise more, but I'm glad they came to me. While Dot sings, I whisper, "I don't understand why the police arrested Rory. When I watched one of her aversion therapy sessions, the orderlies brought her into the room and stayed the whole time. She wouldn't have been alone with Dr. Bullard. She couldn't have killed him."

Dot shakes her head. Maureen says, "She said that sometimes the orderlies would leave her in the room with Dr. Bullard and return later to bring her back to Haven House. On those days, Rory was always sleepy and cross when she came back. She would curl up on her bed and not talk to anyone."

My heart begins a slow, grinding descent. "Did that happen on the day Dr. Bullard was murdered?"

"Yeah," Maureen says.

I picture orderlies strapping Rory into the chair in the aversion therapy room, then leaving. After the session, Dr. Bullard unbuckles the straps. Rory jumps up, lifts one of the chairs that the residents had sat in during the training session, bashes his head, and watches him fall down unconscious. While blood oozes from his head, she pulls his pants down, attaches the electrodes, and turns on the aversion machine. Dr. Bullard convulses as electricity sizzles through his body. Rory gleefully watches him die. When the orderlies knock on the door, she slips out of the room, closes the door on the grisly sight of Dr. Bullard's corpse, and goes back to Haven House as if nothing had happened. That must be what the police believe.

"But Rory was alone with Dr. Bullard plenty of other times," Maureen says. "She didn't kill him then."

"Alas, my love, you do me wrong, to cast me off discourteously." Dot pauses between lyrics to say, "She was framed."

I want so much to believe Rory is innocent, but doubt is like an infected sore in my mind. Robert Bullard isn't the only RKH doctor associated with Rory who ended up murdered. I force myself to ask, "Did you girls and Rory sneak out of Haven House on the night of the fire?"

Dot's hands fumble on the keys, producing a dissonant note. She and Maureen exchange frightened, guilty glances. Maureen says, "Please don't tell!"

Oh, no. "Were you at Dr. Franz's cottage?"

"We were back in Haven House before the fire started," Dot whispers, forgetting to sing while she continues to play the piano. "Dr. Franz was okay when we left him. I swear!"

"We didn't know about the fire until the next morning," Maureen says.

I believe them. I can't picture them pouring gasoline around the sleeping Dr. Franz and lighting it, but I'm sure the police could if they learned the girls had been there. Maureen, Dot, and Rory are reckless teenagers with mental illnesses, at risk for pyromania.

"We liked Dr. Franz," Dot says.

"He gave us milk and cookies," Maureen says, "and he treated us like normal people."

"He said that even though things are hard for us now, we shouldn't give up hope that they'll get easier," Dot says.

I begin to understand why the girls risked sneaking out at night to visit a recluse in a forbidden place. Dr. Franz had been kind and respectful to them, and he'd made them believe that a better life was possible. He sounds like someone I too might have liked, if not for what he'd done to Caroline Lennox and his other guinea pigs.

"His experiments killed people," I remind Dot and Maureen.

"He was only trying to help them," Maureen protests. "He felt so guilty about it that he tried to kill himself a bunch of times."

"We felt sorry for Dr. Franz," Dot says.

I can see another reason for the attraction he held for them and Rory. They knew what it was like to feel guilty for things they'd done, and Dot and Maureen have been through multiple suicide attempts. They formed a bond with the rare adult who understood and sympathized with them instead of judging or punishing them. But the police would see them as three troublemakers who'd amused themselves by killing a vulnerable man. And if they can pin Dr. Franz's murder as well as Dr. Bullard's on Rory, they'll close two cases at once.

"Somebody else killed him," Dot says, and Maureen nods.

"Who, then?" I ask.

They shake their heads. Maureen says, "All we know is, it wasn't us."

A choice looms in front of me like a tunnel cut into a cliff face that I'd thought was solid rock. By repeating Dot and Maureen's story to the police, I could avoid being charged with Dr. Franz's murder. But I still consider them my patients although they're officially not, and I'm duty-bound to serve their best interests, honor-bound to keep what they tell me confidential.

The elderly patients are getting restless, wandering around or talking over the music. When Dot and Maureen finish "Greensleeves," the nurse says, "That was lovely, girls. Time to go back to Haven House."

As they exit the room, the girls cast pleading looks over their shoulders at me. I've learned much from our stolen conversation—too much. But I still don't know whether Dr. Franz told the girls anything more about Caroline Lennox than what they put in their play. Did he know what memories he erased from Caroline Lennox's mind?

I have a sense, based on nothing but my own intuition, that my lost memories are connected to both murders, which are part of a larger picture that I've yet to glimpse. It's high time to hear Rory's version of events.

* * *

I've been dreading night call, another trifecta of twelve-hour shifts when I and a senior resident will be responsible for the entire hospital. But night call will give me a chance to talk to Rory with minimal chance of getting caught.

During my first night shift, it's as if patients all over RKH have conspired to have emergencies. I spend the time coping with chest pains, stomach upsets, panic attacks, and violent outbursts. It's not until my second shift at three in the morning that I have a break. At Shelter House, I tell the guard that Dr. Tanaka asked me to check on a patient he sent to lockdown. I hope Daniel never learns that I roped him into my lie. The guard lets me into the second-floor ward, which is quiet, the nurse's station fortuitously unoccupied. I peer through windows in the steel doors along the hall. In the last cell, a nurse I don't recognize dozes in an armchair beside the bed in which Rory's dark hair spreads across the pillow.

My vision wavers, and for a split second I'm in the bed and Nurse Janice is guarding me.

I knock gently on the door, startling the nurse awake. "I'm here to check on Rosemary Kirkpatrick. You can take a break."

She's young, inexperienced, and probably new to RKH; new nurses are usually stuck with night shifts. She leaves without questioning my authority. As I step into the room and close the door, a call comes over my walkie-talkie. I haven't got much time. I gently shake Rory's shoulder. She stirs, rolling over onto her back. I've seen her fight ferociously as the guards pulled her out of the truck she stole; I've seen her surly and defiant in a frilly dress; I've seen her handsome and triumphant on stage in a man's suit. She's none of those things now. Her green eyes are bloodshot, underscored by purplish shadows, her lips chapped, her hair matted. Dressed in a wrinkled pale blue hospital gown, she looks smaller, diminished. She squints up at me as if she's at the bottom of a deep hole and I'm so far above her that she doesn't recognize me.

"Rory, it's Dr. Kendall," I say, more worried about her than ever.

"What do you want?" Her voice is hoarse, dull.

"I want to help you." I realize that her transformation isn't just physical. The animating spirit that burned so brightly in her is gone.

"Nobody can help me." Rory turns her head toward the padded wall. "I'm a goner."

The time to ask the difficult question is here, and first I swallow hard, then clear my throat. "Did you kill Dr. Bullard?

"No." Rory sounds impatient, as though she's tired of the subject.

My relief feels like unbuckling a belt that's too tight. Although Rory has lied to me before, I don't think she's lying now.

"But I'm glad he's dead."

"Don't say that!" I glance toward the door, hoping nobody's eavesdropping. "People will think you killed him."

"Everybody does already," she says with a doleful sigh. "Even my dad."

"*I* don't think so." I experience a daunting realization. "We have to prove you didn't kill Dr. Bullard. The only way to do that is to find out who did."

Rory sighs again. "Go ahead and try if you want to. There's nothing I can do."

I'm afraid she's right, but I push forward. "Yes, there is."

Engaging her in my quest to clear her name might pull her out of her depression, which at this moment is more dangerous than the threat of her being convicted of murder. While I was interning at Mount Sinai, a patient in the locked psychiatric ward at a different hospital committed suicide by cutting his wrists with scissors stolen from a doctor.

"You can tell me what happened the day that Dr. Bullard was murdered." I'm improvising; I actually have no idea how to solve a murder or if anything Rory can say will help.

"If I tell you, will you leave me alone?"

My walkie-talkie chatters again. "All right."

Rory gazes up at the ceiling and speaks slowly, as if it takes an immense effort to drag the words out of herself. "I had my session with Dr. Bullard. At nine o'clock in the morning." Her voice is flat, drained of emotion. "The orderlies strapped me to the chair. Dr. Bullard made me look at pictures and gave me electric shocks." She pauses, and her eyelids droop.

I suppose she was sedated with Thorazine, the chemical strait-jacket. "And then . . . ?"

"Dr. Bullard told the orderlies to leave and come back in an hour."

My heart starts to gallop. I turn off my walkie-talkie so it won't interrupt Rory.

"He gave me a shot that made me sleepy. He undid the straps and laid me on the floor. Then he unbuttoned my blouse and pushed up my skirt and pulled down my bra and panties." She relates this appalling information in that same flat, slow voice. "He laid down beside me and started touching me. I tried to push him away, but I was too weak. He unzipped his pants and pulled out his thing. He put my hand around it and made me jerk him, and when he was ready, he pushed it in me. I said no, but he slapped my face and kept going. He told me to shut up and learn to act like a normal woman."

Dr. Bullard hadn't stopped at training Rory to associate pain with attraction to her own sex. He'd raped her, ostensibly as preparation for marriage but surely also to satisfy his own lust. He'd taken advantage of a captive, vulnerable patient. On my first day at RKH, I thought Dr. Bullard was a nice, friendly man, but he was a monster.

Rory turns her gaze toward me and sees the horror on my face. A faint smile twitches her lips. "So now you understand why I'm glad he's dead. Wouldn't you be, if it had been you?"

It's not just Dr. Bullard's behavior, or the possibility that I myself was raped by some doctor while I was a patient at RKH, that horrifies me. It's my realization that Rory had more reason to hate him—and to kill him—than I thought.

"Rory," I say, "have you told anyone about this?"

"No." She looks back up at the ceiling. "Why would I? They wouldn't have done anything."

She's probably right. After the resident at Mount Sinai attacked me, I kept silent for the same reason. Anger burns in me as I recall Superintendent Van Pelt insinuating that I was having sexual relations with Rory, calling it inappropriate, unethical, and grounds for expulsion. I'll bet that if Rory had reported Dr. Bullard to him, he either wouldn't have believed her or would have condoned the rape as part of her therapy.

"Don't tell anyone," I say. Now, at least, there's a good reason to keep quiet. "It'll make you look guilty."

Rory shrugs her thin shoulders. "I look guilty no matter what. The lawyer Dad sent says I'm going to be indicted pretty soon."

I gather that indictment is a step along the way to a trial. "What happened after Dr. Bullard raped you?"

"He zipped up his pants and dressed me. The orderlies took me back to Haven House."

Dot and Maureen said that Rory was cross and silent on that particular day. It wasn't because she killed Dr. Bullard; she was traumatized by the rape. "What did Dr. Bullard do?"

"He stayed in the room."

"Did you see anyone nearby?"

Rory shakes her head and closes her eyes, exhausted.

"Who else might have killed him?" I'm desperate for clues that point away from Rory.

"I don't know. But I bet I wasn't the only person he did those things to."

Now I'm facing the opposite problem: dozens of patients possibly abused by Dr. Bullard, countless potential suspects. I don't have enough time to identify let alone investigate them all. "Then why is there such a rush to pin the murder on you?"

"Because they want me out of the way," Rory mutters. "So they killed him and made it look like I did it."

I thought Rory might be in danger, and it seems I was right. "Who framed you?"

"Superintendent Van Pelt and Dr. Mara or somebody who's in on it with them."

"Why?" I'm not quite ready to believe that Rory is in the same boat that I am—a victim of malevolent schemes at RKH. Her family is wealthy; they must be paying a fortune for her to stay here. RKH is having financial difficulties, weeding out patients who can't afford to pay higher rates. Why would Superintendent Van Pelt jeopardize a cash cow like Rory?

"They think Dr. Franz told me things that they don't want getting out."

"What things?" My heart beats fast with hope of information about Caroline Lennox.

Rory shakes her head. "Do you know why I'm here instead of in jail?"

Confused by her abrupt change of subject, I repeat what Daniel Tanaka told me. "Because the jail doesn't have facilities for mental patients."

"No. Because they're going to kill me." Rory delivers this alarming statement in a resigned, indifferent tone. "And they can't do it at the jail. So they made the police let them keep me where they can get their hands on me."

Dr. Franz was murdered; I believe Leonora Hirschfeld was too; and I've witnessed Superintendent Van Pelt's camaraderie with the police chief. Rory might indeed be the next victim. But the idea that Dr. Bullard's murder was nothing but fallout from a scheme in which she was the target strains credulity. Dr. Bullard was a senior staff member, not a patient, and not connected to the events of summer 1941. Maybe the Van Pelts knew Dr. Bullard was "inappropriate and unethical" and needed to get rid of him before somebody more credible than a teenage lesbian troublemaker complained about him.

"I suppose it could be true," I say, still doubtful. Rory's father is an important, politically connected man. No one would murder his daughter with impunity. I begin to wonder if Rory is delusional—or if I am, for giving her story serious consideration.

"Think whatever you want." Rory sighs. "I've told you everything. I'm going back to sleep." She turns to face the wall and pulls the sheet over her head.

I gaze helplessly at her. Exonerating her will be far more complicated and difficult than I thought, and she doesn't even seem to want to help herself. But I see that I'm not going to get anything else from her, and I've already stayed too long. I turn on my walkie-talkie, which immediately starts blatting urgent calls for my attention. When I crack the door open to make sure no one is around, I find myself face to face with Jean Norton.

CHAPTER

31

It's Friday, August twenty-eighth, at 3:56 pm. I'm four minutes early, but the conference room in the mansion is full of people. For a moment they're a faceless mob except for Superintendent Van Pelt at the head of the long table. He motions me to the empty chair at the end. I sit, belatedly recognizing Joseph Mandel at my left and Ronald and Jean Norton at my right. Their faces are carefully expressionless, as if they're about to observe a gory surgical procedure. Joseph glances in my direction, then looks straight ahead. Ronald Norton runs his finger under his collar. Jean glares briefly at me, hateful and triumphant.

Four nights ago, when she caught me in Rory's room, I blurted in dismay, "Jean. What are you doing here?"

Astonished and furious, she pointed her finger at me. "The question is, what are *you* doing here?" Without giving me time to answer, she ordered, "Get out!"

I finished my night shift with a sense of impending doom. I almost wished that the sun would never rise, that I could go on running from ward to ward forever and the axe would never fall. I took my time writing reports, and it was nine-thirty by the time I trudged into the mansion.

The receptionist called, "Dr. Mara wants you in her office."

Jean hadn't dawdled about reporting me. With a sick heart and stomach, I entered the office. Dr. Mara was seated behind her desk, coolly beautiful in a pale blue suit and lacy white blouse. Her expression was hostile. She didn't invite me to sit down.

"You violated a direct order when you visited Rosemary Fitzpatrick," she said. "You're suspended from duty."

She didn't give me a chance to defend myself, and I didn't ask for it. I was suddenly so overwhelmed by emotion that I couldn't speak. Earlier, I was ready to leave RKH, resigned to starting a new life elsewhere. Then I focused on saving Rory, virtually forgot the threat of losing my job, and allowed myself to believe I was the captain of my own fate, able to leave or stay as I pleased. But Dr. Mara showed me that I was as deluded as my patients. She cut me down to size. The indignity, the humiliation, and the knowledge that there was no one to blame but my own hubris was too much to bear. All I wanted was to get away before the tears could fall.

"This Friday afternoon, a disciplinary hearing will be held in the conference room at four o'clock," Dr. Mara says. "Your attendance is mandatory."

I walked out of her office, went up to my room, and packed a suitcase. I couldn't bear to live at RKH during my suspension. I carried my suitcase to my car and drove twenty miles to a motel. There I waited out the four days, eating my meals in the restaurant, lying awake at night, resisting the urge to call Daniel Tanaka and tell him what happened. The grapevine would tell him soon enough.

Although the other residents are here in the conference room, Daniel is absent. Dr. Mara is sitting at Superintendent Van Pelt's right, beautiful and severe in an ivory suit and toque, opposite three other people I don't know—two men and a woman, all in dark business attire, all upwards of sixty years old. Superintendent Van Pelt introduces them as members of the RKH board of trustees. I immediately forget the men's names. The woman is Miss Agnes Van Pelt, maybe a relative of the superintendent. She has a square, bony face, and her short, silver-blonde hair is neatly coiffed under a pillbox hat. Her piercing blue gaze scrutinizes me too closely.

Superintendent Van Pelt announces in a grave, formal manner, "We are here to charge Dr. Claire Kendall with violations of the RKH code of professional conduct and administer the appropriate disciplinary action."

This seems less a hearing than a tribunal, and I'm certain it's rigged against me.

"The first charge is inappropriate relations with patients," Superintendent Van Pelt says.

I hoped that my disobeying orders to stay away from Rory Kirkpatrick was the only issue on the table. Now I gather that the scope of this hearing is bigger than that and my situation is more dire than I first realized when I was suspended. A hollow in my chest fills with dread as cold and sharp as icicles.

"I call the first witness," Superintendent Van Pelt says. "Dr. Ronald Norton."

I stare at Ronald Norton in confusion. What could he have witnessed that proves I committed any violation?

With a furtive glance at me, he says too loudly, "I saw Dr. Kendall having sexual relations with a patient at Mercy House."

I exclaim in shock. "That's not true! I never—"

"Silence, Dr. Kendall," Superintendent Van Pelt says. As I stammer in protest, he talks over me. "Dr. Joseph Mandel, please state your evidence."

Joseph Mandel speaks to the wall he's staring at. "I was with Dr. Norton when he observed Dr. Kendall and the patient together. I saw them too."

Now I'm so flabbergasted, I couldn't have spoken had I been allowed. Gripping the edge of the table, I frown at the men in open-mouthed bewilderment. *Why are they lying?*

"Dr. Jean Norton, what can you tell us?" Superintendent Van Pelt says.

Jean looks straight at me with a smug, dirty look in her eyes. "I saw Dr. Kendall with Rosemary Fitzpatrick at Shelter House."

I can't argue with that. She caught me red-handed.

"What was Dr. Kendall doing?" Superintendent Van Pelt asks.

"She was in bed with Rosemary and kissing her."

Thoroughly blindsided and astonished, I burst out, "Jean! You know that's a lie!"

"Be quiet, Dr. Kendall," Superintendent Van Pelt says.

"I'm not going to keep my mouth shut and listen to this." Because I understand why Jean, her husband, and Joseph Mandel are slandering me. "They want to discredit me for their own personal reasons!"

"Dr. Kendall." Superintendent Van Pelt's tone is harsh with warning.

Miss Van Pelt leans forward. "I'd like to hear what Dr. Kendall has to say."

I doubt she's interceding out of sympathy for me. Her intense gaze has turned predatory, as if she's hungry for a carcass to pick. But I'll jump at any opportunity to explain that Ronald Norton made pass at me, Jean saw, and they view me as a threat to their marriage; and Joseph lied so that if I report him for stealing drugs, nobody will believe me. When Superintendent Van Pelt invited them to the hearing, they must have rejoiced at the chance to get me booted out of RKH.

Superintendent Van Pelt turns to the two other board members. "Gentlemen?"

They shake their heads. The superintendent says, "You're overruled, Agnes."

Displeasure tightens her mouth. She sits back in her chair.

I'm going to be fired, it's obvious. But why stage this kangaroo court? RKH must have a rule that requires three board members to vote on firings.

"Now for the other charges," Superintendent Van Pelt says.

I exclaim in fresh confusion, "What other charges?"

Dr. Mara speaks for the first time. "You misrepresented yourself on your residency application." Her husky voice is somber with reproach. "You gave your name as Claire Kendall, when it is actually Caroline Lennox."

I experience a sensation of being shoved into cold, deep water and held underneath it while my lungs fill with water. Blood pulses in my ears, and I can't get enough air to argue that my legal name is Claire Kendall. The Nortons and Joseph Mandel gape at me. The board members regard me with new interest, as though they're scientists who initially thought I was a garden-variety insect and instead have discovered I'm a rare species. I watch the surprise in everyone's expressions turn to displeasure as they comprehend that they've been deceived. There's no use denying that I am Caroline Lennox. The truth is surely written all over my face.

"How did you know?" I whisper.

I thought my past was well hidden. Nobody I've met since I changed my name ever questioned my identity. At RKH, I never noticed any sign that anyone recognized me.

"How we know is immaterial," Dr. Mara says. "You also lied on the section of the application form that asks whether you have ever been treated for a mental illness, and if so, where and when. You wrote 'No.' You neglected to disclose the fact that you were a patient at this very hospital in 1941."

I feel like I've bobbed up through the surface of the water only to be shoved back under before I could draw a full breath. I sit in rigid horror, but in my mind, I'm kicking and flailing in an effort not to drown. Joseph Mandel and the Nortons draw back in revulsion from me, the impostor, the lunatic disguised by a false name and a white lab coat.

Superintendent Van Pelt says, "I recommend that Dr. Kendall's residency be immediately terminated." His voice sounds unnaturally deep, slow, and punctuated by gurgles, as if I really am submerged in water that's filling my ears. "Members of the board, do you concur?"

Regarding me in impassive silence, the two male board members nod. Miss Van Pelt's face tightens; she doesn't speak.

"The content of this hearing is to be kept confidential," Superintendent Van Pelt instructs the board members and the other residents.

"Pick up your last paycheck at the office," Dr. Mara tells me. "You have until six o'clock to pack your things and leave."

* * *

As I walk out of the conference room, all I want is to put distance between myself and the scene of my disgrace. All my attention and energy are directed toward moving one foot in front of the other across the floor, out the door—don't pause, don't trip, eyes trained straight ahead—down the hall. I'm like a wounded cat that needs to escape from whoever wounded it but doesn't know where it's going or whether any place is safe. Climbing the stairs, heading to my room to pack the belongings I left there before I went to the motel, I begin to realize that being fired isn't the worst that's happened. I've not only lost my residency, my income, and my living quarters, but the circumstances under which I lost them have destroyed my career for good. Along with the charges against me, the facts exposed at the hearing are bound to leak out. The medical profession is like a gossipy small town. My history as a mental patient and my attempt to hide it by changing my name will be raw meat for scandal. A male doctor might eventually recover from such a scandal; a woman, never. No other hospital will accept me as a resident, and if I can't complete a residency, I can never help girls suffering from mental illness, never practice medicine at all.

At the top of the stairs, anger surfaces through my despair. I'm angry at myself for digging into the past. My efforts to recover my lost memories have not only cost me my future, they've failed miserably. I still don't know what happened that summer or who benefited from my forgetting, or why seeing the summer house filled me with dread. I should have put the past behind me when I could. I've been a fool—an overconfident, self-destructive fool.

Voices echo from below me. Looking over the balustrade, I see Joseph Mandel hurry out the front door while Dr. Mara escorts the three board members toward the dining room, followed by the Nortons. My anger homes in on them like a torpedo fired at an enemy ship. Joseph can steal pills without fear of me. The Nortons smile at each other, obviously relieved that I'm a goner. Dr. Mara pretended to be my friend, then turned on me. The board members must be eager for their cocktails; they don't care that they helped ruin my life without even challenging the testimony against me. But my hottest anger focuses on Superintendent Van Pelt. He allowed the other residents to slander me and serve as both players and audience in the drama of my downfall. Why stage that farce at all when he could have fired me in private without smearing my personal as well as my professional reputation? Seething with fury, I march down the stairs and across the lobby to his office.

"You can't go in there," his secretary calls.

I stride through the open door. Superintendent Van Pelt rises from behind his desk and frowns in annoyance. "Dr. Kendall." He looks at his heavy gold wristwatch. "It's five o'clock. If you're going to be out of here by six, you'd better hurry."

"First I have something to tell you." I plant my feet on the floor in front of him, my hands on my hips. "I'm going to contest my firing."

I didn't know what I intended to say until I said it, but it makes sense. Why take his abuse lying down? Why not fight back? What have I to lose?

"Contest it to whom?" he says, vexed yet amused. "The board members voted to fire you, and they have the final say."

"The state health department." I mentally thank Daniel Tanaka. I wouldn't have thought of it if not for our conversation.

Superintendent Van Pelt chuckles. "The health department doesn't deal with personnel matters."

Is that uneasiness I detect behind his scorn, a tiny shift in the balance of power? I sense that he doesn't want outside authorities to get involved. "They will when I tell them what's been going on here."

"Oh, come now." His manner turns patronizing. "Do you really expect them to believe stories from a former mental patient?"

Suddenly I understand why he mixed my past into the mud he threw at me: he wants enough of the mud to stick so that, if I oppose him, I won't have a leg to stand on. But oddly, I'm relieved that I've been exposed as Caroline Lennox. I've got nothing to hide, no reason to tiptoe around this man for fear that he'll remember me. It's liberating and empowering to have everything out in the open.

"I'm ready to gamble that, when they hear my stories, they'll be compelled to investigate. Especially the story about what was done to me while I was under your care."

It's also recklessly exhilarating to make things up as I go along, like an actress in a play without a script. Or like a hunter who shoots into the woods without knowing whether he'll hit a bear or the bullet will ricochet and kill him.

Superintendent Van Pelt frowns, unpleasantly surprised that I'm using my past as my own bargaining chip. "The story is that you were a severely disturbed little girl when you came to RKH, and after treatment here, you recovered enough to live a normal life and eventually graduate from Columbia Medical School." He smiles with an air of turning the tables on me.

With an adroitness that I'm proud of, I turn them back on him. "Every story has two sides. Mine is that you gave me so many shock treatments that you erased six months of my memory."

He laughs, regaining his smug self-confidence. "Amnesia is mighty hard to prove, young lady. Especially after so much time has passed."

I enjoy the heady sensation of knowing what to say without having to think, as if I'm guided by an inner, clairvoyant spirit. "My amnesia isn't the only issue. Here's another." I bluff recklessly. "I came to RKH to try to recover my memories from those six months. And it worked."

Superintendent Van Pelt's face freezes; the twinkle in his eyes goes out like a snuffed candle. His left hand jerks toward the side of his desk. Then he relaxes back in his chair and gives me an indulgent, pitying smile. "What do you remember?"

But his voice is tight; I've shaken him. "That's for the health department to hear. You can ask them to share it with you when they come to RKH to investigate." I smile before adding, "I'll be sure to tell them to look into the deaths of Leonora Hirschfeld and Dr. Isaac Franz while they're here."

We stare at each other. My heartbeat is skittery, my hands cold, my muscles rigid with the effort of keeping my body still, my expression calm. I can almost see poker chips piled on the desk between us. Superintendent Van Pelt has an advantage—he knows what was done to me at RKH; perhaps he even knows the secrets the shock treatments were meant to obliterate. But he doesn't know how much I remember. His eyes are a cold blue, like thin ice on a lake. I will my gray ones to be as opaque as steel.

At Radcliffe, my psychology professor had a special interest in facial expressions. He lectured my class about their various nuances and interpretations. I recall him saying that flared nostrils convey disdainful superiority in a subtle, sophisticated fashion. I flare my nostrils at Superintendent Van Pelt.

He can't control the instinctive, surprised lift of his eyebrows and the frown that creases his forehead. He's as disconcerted as if he's realized I can smell his body odor—which I suddenly realize I can. It's sharp and sour beneath the scent of his cologne.

He looks away first.

I imagine raking the poker chips toward me.

Superintendent Van Pelt recovers his poise quickly and smoothly. "Suppose I write you a letter of recommendation."

My heart pounds a victory cadence. His offer is tantamount to an admission that he's eager to prevent the state authorities from investigating the deaths at RKH for fear of what they might discover or who they might incriminate when they start turning over stones. A letter of recommendation could salvage my career.

"Suppose you do?" I recognize his offer as a bribe, and bribes never come without strings attached.

"You would keep your memories, your allegations, and your complaints to yourself. And stop poking your nose in where it doesn't belong."

It's my career in exchange for my silence and obedience. His bargain reeks of a cover-up. He must perceive how little I like it, for he says, "A good reference from me would secure you a residency in any hospital on the eastern seaboard." He studies me for a moment, then adds, "Gift horses aren't like streetcars, young lady. You can't count on another one coming along."

I know that, but if he's willing to bribe me, he must have something to hide. I need to find out what it is, and I won't give him the satisfaction of thinking I'm so desperate to save my career that I'll kiss his shoe.

"I'll think about it," I say, then I turn and walk away.

At the door, instinct makes me look over my shoulder. Superintendent Van Pelt reaches for the telephone and dials a number. That's why his hand moved when I said I'd regained my memory: His impulse was to make a call. I wonder who he's calling, who would want to know about our talk. Or who he thinks will help him deal with the consequences.

CHAPTER

32

In my room, I telephone Mercy House and ask for Daniel Tanaka. I tap my foot, watch the clock, and listen to the noise from the ward while I wait eleven long minutes before he comes on the line.

"Claire. I heard you were suspended for talking to Rory Fitzpatrick." Daniel sounds worried but relieved to hear from me. "Where have you been?"

I'm glad he hasn't heard the latest. "I can't explain over the phone. Can you meet me behind Tranquility House?"

"Okay—"

I hang up.

Hurrying across campus, I greet people without looking closely at them. I don't want to know whether they've heard I was fired and see pity, curiosity, or glee on their faces. The weather has turned even hotter, and I'm drenched with sweat by the time I reach Tranquility House. It's one of the buildings that was closed during the Depression, due to a shortage of patients when even RKH's wealthy clientele suffered financial setbacks. Because the patient population never completely bounced back, Tranquility House remains closed. The lawn is mowed, but overgrown shrubs crowd the long three-story building, which is so covered with ivy that it's impossible to see any architectural features. The dingy sign that bears its name is still by the driveway that I follow to the parking lot behind it. Daniel is standing in the shade of an oak tree. I restrain myself from running to him. When we're face to face, he says, "Claire, what's happened?"

I wanted him to hear it from me instead of through the grapevine, which will distort the story, making it even worse than it actually is. I should have left without seeing him. I miss him so much already, my heart swells with the pain.

"I'll tell you in a minute." I blink, fighting tears. "First, I want to say—" I swallow the lump in my throat. "Your friendship is one of the best things that's ever happened to me." It's difficult to force the words out; I'm unaccustomed to baring my soul. "You mean more to me than anyone since . . ." *Since Brian died.* "I want you to know that. No matter what you hear about me."

"Claire, you're scaring me." Daniel does look scared. My speech must sound like the prelude to a deathbed confession. "What's going on?"

There's no time for beating around the bush. "I've been fired."

He shakes his head in astonished disbelief. "Talking to Rory can't be enough grounds for firing you."

"It wasn't the only grounds. There was a disciplinary hearing. Jean and Ronald Norton and Joseph Mandel testified that they'd seen me having sex with patients, including Rory."

Daniel exclaims, "That's bullshit!"

I'm startled because I've never heard him swear before. His outrage is gratifying. He believes I wouldn't do such despicable things . . . but I'm afraid he's about to change his mind.

"I didn't know about the hearing," he says. "If I had, I would have been there to testify on your behalf."

Superintendent Van Pelt and Dr. Mara must have kept the hearing a secret to prevent anyone except my enemies from testifying. If Daniel had been there, it would have been terrible to have him witness my exposure and humiliation, but it would have spared me from having to tell him about it now.

"I never had sex with a patient. But that wasn't the only charge against me." My voice wobbles. "Superintendent Van Pelt found out that I was a patient at RKH in 1941 and I applied for my residency under a different name." Seeing shock enter Daniel's expression, I have to swallow hard before I can force myself to go on. "My original name is Caroline Lennox."

Daniel frowns. "Caroline Lennox. Wasn't that the girl in Rory's play?"

"Yes. That girl was based on me. I legally changed my name to Claire Kendall after I was discharged from RKH."

"But—?"

He must be wondering why the girl in the play died and I'm alive, but there's no time to explain about my faked death or the circumstances under which I changed my name. I inhale and exhale a deep, shaky breath. "My memory of that whole summer was erased by the shock treatments I had here. I came back to RKH for my residency to try to recover my lost memory."

Now I see on his face the expression that I was afraid to see, the incredulity that changes to wariness. He steps back from me as if I'm a swan that turned into a snake. I've committed the one offense that could turn him against me—dishonesty. My chest feels sore and empty, as though someone clawed out my heart. This man who believes the best about people no longer believes the best about me.

Hoarse with tears, I say, "Daniel, I'm sorry." *Sorry I didn't trust you enough to tell you the truth before; sorry because I'm not the person you thought I was; sorry that I've shaken your faith in human goodness.* "I'm leaving now." I back away from him before he can say he's revolted by my deception and we're no longer friends. I can't bear the pain of another rejection or abandonment. "Goodbye."

I turn and run.

* * *

In my room, I try to concentrate on filling suitcases with the books, extra clothes, and other things I hadn't taken to the motel. But my mind keeps replaying the awful scene at the disciplinary hearing and my wrenching parting from Daniel Tanaka. I picture the Nortons congratulating themselves on getting rid of me and Joseph Mandel breathing easier as he gulps down stolen drugs. By now Superintendent Van Pelt will have told Dr. Mara about his bargain with me, and they must think I'll come to my senses and RKH will be safe from the state authorities. My bitterness toward all of them spills over onto Daniel. He judged me based solely on the fact that I deceived him about my identity and my motives. He didn't consider that my deceit was trivial compared to what was done to me while I was a patient at RKH. He was nothing but a fair-weather friend, a false source of hope. It would serve him right if the health department shut down RKH and he lost his residency. Good riddance to him along with Jean and Ronald Norton, Joseph Mandel and the Van Pelts.

But I can't sustain my high dudgeon forever. I slide down into despair as the finality of my dismissal from RKH sinks in. My rancor toward Daniel is just bravado, an attempt to stanch the bleeding from a fatally ruptured heart. I can't deny my grief over losing his friendship. I'll never see him again and I already miss him terribly. I'll never see Rory Kirkpatrick again either; I've permanently lost whatever chance I had to help her. Who would listen to me—a doctor who's been fired and exposed as a former mental patient? There's nothing to back up my claim that I was given shock treatments as part of a deliberate effort to erase my memory. I think of my falsified death certificate, which is in a locker that I rented at the train station on one of my days off. Superintendent Van Pelt could claim that I forged it, and a court would probably believe him. He's a high-ranking member of the psychiatric establishment; I'm just a onetime lunatic with a grudge.

I slump on the bed. Maybe my wisest course of action would be to accept Superintendent Van Pelt's recommendation letter and obtain another residency. That would save my career. But taking his bribe feels so wrong, and not only because it goes against my conscience. I would have to keep silent about my experience as a patient at RKH and my suspicions about things that have happened to other patients—Leonora Hirschfeld's suicide that may not have been a suicide; Dr. Franz's murder; and Rory being framed for the murder of Dr. Bullard. And it would be accepting that I've failed. Failed to recover my lost memories; failed to save Rory; failed in my effort to see that everyone at RKH who's responsible for crimes is held accountable. I can't live with such egregious failure, and I don't want to wear a permanent gag, but what other choice do I have?

Unless I can find evidence that justifies my suspicions and corroborates my claims.

A revived sense of purpose nudges me like a stick poking my back. I check my watch; it's five-thirty. I steal down the back stairs to the basement, which smells of roasting meat and onions. In the kitchen, cooks labor amid the clatter of pots and dishware. I hurry along the passage to the door labeled "Tunnels." As I open it and slip through, my thudding heart and quickening breaths herald a panic attack. The long, dim, white-tiled tunnel swallows me up. It's deserted and quiet, but my memory fills it with echoes of footsteps, rattling wheels, and distant voices. The whirring ventilation fans blow the stale odors of dampness and detergent at me. I swallow nausea. Sweat trickles down my face as I enter a netherworld between reality and nightmare. I'm walking along the stone floor, then riding on my back on a stretcher. The view before my eyes swings dizzily between the passage that narrows toward its vanishing point and the rusted pipes on the ceiling. Unbalanced, I clutch the walls for support. My clammy palms smear the cold tile. Fighting the urge to turn and run to air and light above ground, I propel myself forward with the memory of the file cabinet in the library archives that's filled with information about the research conducted at RKH. The research hadn't seemed important when I'd been searching for Caroline Lennox's file. If only the archives contain the records of Dr. Franz's fever therapy experiment and its consequences for Peter Kramer, Adeline Peck, and Caroline Lennox. When I go to the health department, those records could help me prove my allegations against RKH. They're my faint but only hope that I'll be taken seriously, that I can hold RKH accountable for its crimes.

I follow the signs that point the way to different buildings. My old nightmare merges with my new one. The tunnels darken and become trails through the forest near my family's summer house. Tiles on the walls are the rough bark of the trees that close in around me. Rattling wheels crunch over dried fallen leaves. The air from the ventilation fans smells of earth and woodsmoke. Footsteps coming from all directions crunch on twigs. In both dreams, I'm following or being followed by someone. Forest and tunnels are full of invisible watchers who whisper threats. Shivering, I manage to reach the door with the sign that reads "Library."

Someone behind me grabs my arms.

My heart seizes. I scream in terror. A hand that's smooth and rubbery, covered with a latex glove, claps over my mouth. I bite, kick, and writhe, but I'm pushed to the floor. Dark cloth that smells of detergent is pulled over my head, tight against my face. My inability to see the person makes the attack all the more terrifying, as though I'm in the grip of an invisible monster. Thoughts skitter through my mind as I fight helplessly.

This never happened in my nightmares.

Is it what I woke up afraid of the instant before it happened?

Struggling to breathe through the cloth, I feel the sting of a needle jabbed in my thigh.

There's a humming in my ears, then a floating sensation, then nothing.

CHAPTER

33

THE SUN IS a white ball floating in mist above me, too bright, painfully bright. The sound of the ocean is a muted roar. I close my eyes. The space behind my eyelids glows red, laced with darker red veins. I bring my hand up to cover my face, but there's something around both my wrists, holding them immobile. When I try to roll over from my back onto my side, I can't because my legs are restrained too.

Alarm snaps my eyes open. What I first thought was the sun is the round white dome of a light fixture; the misty sky is a white plaster ceiling; the sound of waves breaking on a beach is voices echoing in a hallway. My mouth is dry and sour, my brain clotted with confusion. When I try to figure out where I am and what happened to me, it's like swishing a net in a cloud of butterflies and catching only air. I lift my head from a hard pillow that smells of disinfectant. Pain throbs in my temples. Dizziness tilts the world. I look down at myself. I'm wearing a pale blue hospital gown that leaves my legs bare below the knees. Beige cloth straps tether my wrists and ankles to the metal rails of the bed in which I'm lying. Fear rises like a black planet on the horizon of my consciousness. I turn my head to the right and see a woman sitting in a chair near me. Dark-haired, she wears a nurse's cap and uniform.

Nurse Janice.

My slow, lethargic heartbeat accelerates to a thunderous gallop. I've traveled back in time to the summer when I was Caroline Lennox, imprisoned at RKH. I moan, jerking at my restraints. The bed rails rattle. The nurse stands up and looms over me. She's not Janice. She's Enid Norris, the charge nurse from Haven House.

"Welcome back, Dr. Kendall." Sardonic amusement laces her solicitous manner. She's not merely observing that I've regained consciousness; she's enjoying my dismay.

"Where am I?" I demand.

"In Shelter House."

Now I recognize the padded walls, the lack of furnishings, the steel door with the gridded windowpane. I'm in lockdown. Panic shrills through me, an internal siren. "Untie me."

"Sorry, no can do."

"You've got no right to keep me here." I disliked Enid Norris as a colleague; as her patient, I hate her, and anger fuels my hatred.

"Yes, we do. It's for your own safety."

"My safety?" All the more confused, I say, "What are you talking about?"

"You tried to commit suicide."

How could she know? And why am I in lockdown now, after years have passed since those attempts?

Nurse Norris shakes her head with pity at my bewilderment. "Last night you overdosed yourself on phenobarbital you stole from Grace House. Don't you remember?"

"No. I didn't do that." I stare in disbelief. Memory starts coming back in disjointed fragments, like clips from a movie shown out of sequence: packing my suitcases; Superintendent Van Pelt glaring at me across his desk; cooks working in the kitchen; Daniel Tanaka's shocked expression; the maze of tunnels. Nowhere in there do I see myself stealing or taking drugs.

Nurse Norris pulls up my gown, touches my left thigh. "Here's the needle mark."

The spot under her fingertip is sore. It's as if she's pressed a button that puts the fragments in order and fills the gaps between them. Last night I was going to the library to look for information about research experiments at RKH. I was chased through the tunnels.

"After dinner, Superintendent Van Pelt asked the guards at the gates if you'd left yet," Nurse Norris says. "They said they hadn't seen you. Dr. Mara went to your room and found you lying unconscious on your bed with the empty hypodermic syringe beside you. Fortunately, you didn't give yourself a big enough dose to be fatal."

"That's not what happened! I was attacked. In the tunnel, on my way to the library." It's all terrifyingly clear now—the struggle, the dark cloth over my head, the gloved hand over my mouth, the sting in my thigh. "Someone gave me a shot."

"Sure they did." Norris speaks in the tone she uses when humoring difficult patients.

I piece together what must have happened. Whoever attacked me faked my suicide attempt. I can guess why. Superintendent Van Pelt wanted me to accept his bribe and depart meekly. He must have had someone watching me, following me. When I went prowling around instead, they nabbed me and sedated me. There must be something stored in the archives or buried in my memory that he doesn't want made public, something detrimental to RKH. To stop me from exposing it, he cooked up a reason to put me in lockdown. But if he was so eager to silence me, why not kill me outright? Someone at RKH murdered Dr. Franz and, I'm more certain than ever, Leonora Hirschfeld. Why was I allowed to live? Why not have my "suicide attempt" succeed?

The answer is simple: They're not finished with me. When they are, they'll kill me. My life is the price I'll pay for rejecting Superintendent Van Pelt's bribe.

"I'll let the superintendent know you're awake." Nurse Norris opens the door.

"No!" I struggle wildly to break free. The straps dig into my wrists and ankles. The bed rails jangle loudly.

Nurse Norris walks out of the room, closes the door. The key clinks in the lock. That ordinary little sound is like a match to the fuse on a stick of dynamite. The hard fact that I'm a prisoner in lockdown is an explosion that shatters my knowledge of myself. My career and my lofty aim of helping troubled girls were the concern of my conscious mind, the tip of the Freudian iceberg. So was regaining my lost memory of what happened to me during the summer of 1941. Now my unconscious mind is laid bare to me: All I really wanted was a place in the world, a community where I'm accepted and valued. That was the dream of Caroline Lennox, the outcast in her own family, a virtual orphan after her mother died and her father abandoned her. I thought my worst fear was of losing my career. But Caroline's worst fear was of becoming a mental patient again. Changing my name raised a boundary wall between Caroline Lennox and Claire Kendall, but now the wall is crumbling.

She's no longer my doppelganger.

She and I are one. I never really managed to put her behind me.

Her dream of a place in the world is my dream too. Now our dream will never come true. And our worst fear is the same.

Devastation swells inside me, so big and fierce that my body can't contain it.

I scream, "Let me out!"

Up and down the halls of Shelter House, other voices join mine. Shrieks, howls, and the clang of bed rails issue from the cells where RKH's most disturbed patients are locked up.

I'm one of them now.

CHAPTER

34

FOR THE STAFF of a hospital, the ideal patient is polite, pleasant, and passive. I do my best to meet those criteria. I stop struggling against my restraints; I thank the aides when they bring my meals and change my bed linens. When they take me to the restroom, I don't try to run away. The idleness and boredom, with nothing to divert my mind from my fear of what's happening to me, is almost unbearable, but I sit in feigned placidity while Nurse Norris watches over me. I don't ask questions. *Polite, pleasant, passive.* I smile a lot.

My professor who studied facial expressions believed that a smile causes a physiological reaction in the brain of the person who sees the smile, so that the smiled-at tends to feel positively toward the smiler and not suspect that she's up to no good. The acting is exhausting, but on the second day, my restraints are removed, and I'm not given sedative injections. Nurse Norris goes back to Haven House, and different nurses take her place during the morning and afternoon shifts. Superintendent Van Pelt must have decided I don't warrant his top watchdog. No one stays with me on night shift. During a staff shortage, why waste round-the-clock coverage on a patient who's so docile? Today—September second, my third day in lockdown—the nurses even let me take a shower, change into a fresh hospital gown, comb my hair, and read books from the library. But my mental and physical condition is precarious.

Flashbacks constantly assail me. One moment I'm my adult self, in the present time; the next, I'm Caroline Lennox trapped in Haven house. I silently repeat *Dr. Claire Kendall, Dr. Claire Kendall*, like an incantation to break a magic spell. I worry about Rory. Is she still being held here in lockdown? If so, it's been ten long, surely miserable days for her. How ironic that once I was her doctor and now we're both patients, more or less equals. My head aches, and when I pinch the skin on the back of my hand, it doesn't flatten immediately—symptoms of dehydration. Nausea, dizziness, and shakiness indicate low blood sugar. I drink all the juice and water and eat all the food on my trays. Bed rest causes muscle atrophy after only a few days, so during night shift, I do push-ups, knee bends, and run in place. By the third day, I feel stronger, healthier. I will myself into the mental state that got me through my surgical rotation at Mount Sinai. There, I focused solely on each operation—the anesthesia; the instruments; the patients' vital signs; the intravenous fluids; the surgeon explaining the procedure while he cut, excised, and sutured. Nothing else mattered. Now I focus solely on the task of regaining my freedom. Nothing else matters.

I see no chance of escape, but I cling to the belief that it's possible.

I'm given no clues as to why I'm here. It's as if I'm in cold storage like a side of beef, waiting . . . for what?

* * *

Dear Dot and Maureen,

I'm "writing" to you because you're my only friends now. When you said you have ESP, I didn't really believe it, but maybe you can hear me. I'm curled up in bed, facing the wall with my eyes closed. My body feels too heavy to move. My brain is full of fog, gray and blank.

The door opens. I hear Dad say, "Is she conscious?"

So he came back. I don't care. Now that Celia is gone, nothing matters. I'm not even curious about why he's here. To rub salt in my wounds? Let him rub. I'm numb all over, like your foot when it's gone to sleep.

Another man's voice says, "No. Her last shot hasn't worn off yet."

It's Superintendent Van Pelt. I hear my mother quietly sobbing. So what if she's sad? It's nothing to me.

"You wanted to see her one last time before the operation, Josephine," Dad says. "Here's your chance."

Operation? I feel a glimmer of curiosity. What's he talking about?

Mother comes to stand beside me. I smell her perfume, lilac and baby powder. She says, "When is it scheduled?" Her voice is hoarse with tears.

"Tomorrow morning," Superintendent Van Pelt says. "Dr. Buscher will operate at nine o'clock."

Dr. Buscher. *The fog in my brain evaporates like frost on a window in the sunshine. Dr.* Brad *Buscher. The girls at Haven House call him "Dr. Brain-Butcher" because he does lobotomies. He sticks an icepick through your skull and pokes around and wrecks your brain. I feel a tingling, pins-and-needles vibrating sensation, like a foot waking up after it's been asleep.* Oh, God. *I'm getting a lobotomy! Tomorrow I'll be like Lulu Shelton—drooling, baby-talking, and wearing diapers. Or, if Dr. Brain-Butcher really goes hog-wild with his icepick, I'll be a vegetable. Now I'm wide awake, alert, and terrified. After a lobotomy, I can never be an explorer or a writer or a race car driver, which I realize I still want to be. I'll never be anything except a mental patient forever.*

"Will it hurt her?" Mother's voice is muffled; she's talking through her handkerchief.

"Not at all," Superintendent Van Pelt says. "She'll be given a sedative and a local anesthetic."

"How long will it take?" Dad asks.

"It'll be over in two shakes of a lamb's tail," Superintendent Van Pelt says cheerfully.

If I had Dr. Brain-Butcher's icepick, I would jab it right through his twinkly eye. Well, I guess there's still some fight left in the dog.

Mother cries harder, little hiccups and gasps. Dad says, "Can you give us a moment, Doctor?" The door opens and closes as Superintendent Van Pelt leaves. Dad tells Mother, "It's for the best. She'll be declared incompetent. She won't have to stand trial for murder. There won't be a scandal." He adds in a lower voice, "With the election coming up, I can't afford a scandal."

Now that I can feel things again, I hurt all over, like your foot does when the blood starts flowing through it again. I once thought Dad was the best man in the world, but he's going to let Dr. Brain-Butcher give me a lobotomy just so I won't ruin his chance of becoming a congressman.

"Isn't there some other way?" Mother says, but her voice is weak.

"This is the best for everybody," Dad says. "She won't cause any more trouble. She won't suffer."

Best for him, he means. He doesn't care about my suffering. I didn't realize he was so selfish until now.

"Let's go. We need to get to the city," Dad says. "Cavanagh has the papers all drawn up." Mr. Cavanagh is our family lawyer. "We need to sign them so that we can take control of her trust fund as soon as she's had her operation."

It's like I've been sucking on a cherry lollipop that has rat poison in the center. That's how it tastes when love turns to hatred. He not only wants me turned into a baby or a vegetable, but he's taking my money! My money that Grandma left to me. *The money that I need to be free and independent and do whatever I want. I decide then and there that I'm not going to have a lobotomy, no way, no how. I'm getting out of here, come hell or high water.*

Mother leans over me, kisses my cheek, and whispers, "Goodbye, Rosemary. I'll pray for you."

It takes all my willpower not to hit her for being so weak, or throw my arms around her and beg her not to let them give me a lobotomy, or scream, "I don't need your goddamn prayers, I need you to protect me!" But if I do any of those things, they'll give me another shot, and I'll be even more helpless. And if I'm helpless, I won't be able to figure out how to escape before Dr. Brain-Butcher gets his hands on me.

Dad once told me a story about the time he went hunting alone and he fell on a sharp branch and it went right through his leg. When he pulled it out, blood started gushing from the hole. He took off his belt, tied it around his leg to make a tourniquet, walked back to his car, and drove himself to the hospital. He saved his own life. He said, "When the chips are down, Rosie, the only person you can count on is yourself."

I guess it's okay that Dad is leaving me high and dry. He's already taught me everything I need to know.

Rory

* * *

The afternoon of my third day in lockdown, the charge nurse comes in, announcing, "You have a visitor." I sit up in bed as the special nurse leaves my room and a man enters.

Dr. Koffka once said that a psychiatrist can glean a lot of information about a client before setting eyes on him. *Your visual sense is only one tool in your box. The other senses are also powerful diagnostic tools.* This man smells of expensive cologne with citrus and wood notes—he's rich. He's strong and confident—his steps sound firm, unhesitating. This impression is confirmed by the sight of him—his tallness and athletic physique, his neatly groomed silver-blond hair, the bright white shirt under a linen suit that's a shade lighter than his deep tan. My gaze fixes on his face, on familiar, handsome, masculine features to which twelve years have only added an aura of power.

A convulsive flinch stiffens my muscles, pressing my back against the headboard, stretching my eyes and mouth wide open. My hands claw the mattress, instinctively trying to dig a hole to hide in.

"Hello, Caroline," my father says.

His voice is hoarser than I remember, but it provokes the same fear as when I was a child. In shock, I grasp for my adult defenses. "It's Claire." My voice trembles.

"Oh, right," my father says, as if he forgot that changing my name had been his idea. "Forgive me if I still think of you as Caroline."

I doubt that he's genuinely sorry. I think he used my original name to put me back in my place as his cowed little girl. I feel myself shrinking, my accomplishments losing reality. *Dr. Claire Kendall, Dr. Claire Kendall.*

I sit up straight and say in my most authoritative doctor manner, "How did you know I was here?"

His smug smile asserts his superiority. "I've been keeping tabs on you."

"How?"

He shrugs off my right to know who's been spying on me and reporting back to him. "The news that you were a resident at RKH didn't reach me until after you'd been here a few weeks. I was cruising around the Mediterranean on a yacht."

That explains the tan. I remember he liked bragging about his expensive trips and possessions. His wedding ring is thick and gold, and a bulky, elaborate watch circles his wrist.

"As soon as I heard, I called Adrian and told him that you were working here under your new name," he says.

So that's how Superintendent Van Pelt found out who I was. "'Adrian?'"

"We're old friends from Harvard med school."

Well, that explains why I was committed to RKH instead of another mental institution.

"Adrian was second in our class." My father adds with a falsely modest smile, "I was first."

His bragging is odious to me, but I can understand why other people are attracted to him. Those who haven't fallen victim to his cruelty enjoy basking in the glow of such a handsome, wealthy, accomplished man.

"Adrian and Mara have been keeping me informed about you," he says.

I suppose he knows about everything that's happened to me during my residency. I remember the telephone call that Superintendent Van Pelt made the day he fired me. It must have been to my father. I taste the horrible gut certainty that he and Dr. Mara haven't been acting on their own; my father has been calling the shots from behind the scenes. I don't understand how he has power over them, but I'm convinced that they were doing his bidding.

"You're aware of the murders of Leonora Hirschfeld, Dr. Franz, and Dr. Bullard?" I say.

"Of course."

I purposely included Leonora's death among the murders even though its official cause was suicide. He's too smart not to spot the error, but he doesn't bother to correct me. Another devastating realization: he's behind all three murders, and he doesn't care if I know. He has a perfect alibi: he was on a yacht in the Mediterranean. Whoever hanged Leonora, set fire to Dr. Franz's cottage, and electrocuted Dr. Bullard, my father is technically, if not morally, innocent. And he doesn't care that I'm suspected of Dr. Franz's murder or that Rory Kirkpatrick is under arrest for Dr. Bullard's.

"Do you know that I'm in lockdown because after I was fired, I supposedly tried to kill myself?" I ask.

He nods. "What a little troublemaker you are."

I'm more incredulous about than hurt by his attitude. His daughter, his flesh and blood, means no more to him than Dr. Franz, Leonora Hirschfeld, Dr. Bullard, or Rory. He committed me to RKH, and he must have given the order for the shock treatments that erased my memory. Later, he jettisoned my mother and me as if we were cigarette butts tossed out his car window. And he seems to care just as little about Superintendent Van Pelt and Dr. Mara, who almost certainly engineered the murders on his behalf and put themselves at risk. His indifference is disturbing. I didn't understand it when I was a child. I think I understand now.

At the Manhattan Psychoanalytic Academy, I took Dr. Koffka's seminar on abnormal psychology. It covered various mental disorders, including psychopathy. According to Freud, a psychopath is an individual with a boundless ego and a lack of emotional appreciation of other humans. Psychopaths may seem sincere and charming, but that's a mask that conceals their true nature. In addition to intelligence and egocentricity, their personality traits include deceptiveness, antisocial behavior, manipulativeness, and lack of remorse. This description always struck a familiar chord, but I didn't know why. Now I see the truth that I didn't want to recognize then.

My father, Dr. William Lennox, M.D., successful surgeon, is a psychopath.

I'm elated because my professional training has solved a puzzle from my childhood, horrified because my father is a monster in disguise, and bewildered. "Why did you come?" I ask. After years without contact, he turns up like a bad penny.

My father spreads his hands, like Jesus offering a blessing. "I want to help you."

Against my will, I feel a rush of hope and gratitude. When I was a child, all I wanted was my father as my ally instead of my tormentor. But psychopaths don't change. They're incurable by any known therapy, and they don't even seek treatment because they don't think they have a problem; they believe they're saner than everybody else. My father is in his late fifties now. His nature will only have become more deeply entrenched. He's the same man from whom I never received kindness in the past. I should expect none now.

"How can you help me?" I'm stalling to give myself time to think, but also curious about his intentions.

"I can convince Adrian that you're no longer a danger to yourself, and he'll discharge you." My father sounds proud, confident of his authority.

To be released from lockdown, to walk out of Shelter House like a normal person! I hunger for freedom so badly that if I could gnaw through the walls with my teeth, I would. Then I remember Dr. Koffka's advice about psychopaths: *First and foremost, do not believe what they say. They lie.*

"That would be nice." I hide my emotions behind the calm, serious expression I wear while watching autopsies. Dr. Koffka's second most important piece of advice: *Don't show your emotions or weaknesses to a psychopath. He will use them against you.*

"But first, I need something from you," my father says.

Of course his help comes with strings attached. *Psychopaths serve only their own selfish purposes, and they will manipulate others toward that end,* Dr. Koffka's voice says in my memory. I picture her sitting in the chair by my bed, a ghostly ally.

"What is it you need from me?" I say cautiously.

"You told Adrian that you've remembered things that happened during the summer you were admitted to RKH. Tell me what they are."

Now I see his real reason for coming: to find out how much I know about the events of that summer. My remembering is somehow a threat to him. He had Superintendent Van Pelt erase my memory, and it worked as well as he could have hoped; I've got nothing to tell him. But my memories are the price of his help. There's nothing else he needs from me, and he seems to be my only hope of escape from lockdown.

He's waiting expectantly. I stall again. "How is telling you what I remember supposed to convince Superintendent Van Pelt that I should be discharged?"

"If you remember accurately, it'll prove you're sane."

"Who decides whether my memories are accurate?"

My father looks amused, but he glances at his expensive gold watch; he's impatient. "I do." He's the one person who knows what really happened that summer, the one person I can't ask for the information I want so badly. "I was there, Caroline."

Dr. Claire Kendall. Dr. Claire Kendall. It's not only psychopaths who wear a mask. My mask is the artificial calmness that hides my struggle to resist my father's attempt to turn me back into my frightened childhood self. It belies my anxiety as my mind races between two ways I can think of to play this. The easy, simplest way is to tell the truth: contrary to what I said to Superintendent Van Pelt, I really don't have any knowledge about that summer except fragmented flashbacks and what I learned during my visit to Arden Spring.

Do not share any personal information with a psychopath! Dr. Koffka warns me.

The truth is a kind of personal information, but I have to give my father something. So I choose the difficult, complicated way, as if I'm tossing a bone to placate a vicious dog.

"I remember Brian getting sick," I say. "He was coughing a lot, and he must have had a fever; his cheeks were red. He said his chest hurt."

Thanks to my class on infectious diseases, I know the symptoms of tuberculosis. I'm afraid to look directly at my father because he might discern that I'm lying, but avoiding his eyes would be just as much of a giveaway. I briefly look him in the eye, then focus my gaze on a distant point behind him as if I'm viewing the internal landscape of my memory.

"Brian could hardly eat. He lost weight. He was so weak, he stayed in bed. He couldn't stop coughing." I speak in a small, high voice, as if I've regressed to childhood. "When I brought him some ice cream, I saw blood on his pillow." I'm creating my story to agree with the official version that says my brother died of tuberculosis in the summer of 1941. I hope my father will think I've embraced it so absolutely that my unconscious mind invented the details and they're not deliberate fabrications.

He says nothing. He's completely still, watching me intently as he listens, expressionless. Whatever he's thinking is hidden behind his own mask.

"One day I heard Brian crying. I asked him what was wrong. He said he had tuberculosis and he was going away to a sanatorium. When he left, I couldn't kiss him goodbye because TB is contagious. That's the last time I ever saw him." Involuntary sobs heave my chest. "Every night, I prayed that he would be cured. But then Mother told me he had passed away." My story is false, but my grief for Brian is genuine.

"I was so upset that all I did was cry." Tears roll down my cheeks. "I didn't want to live without Brian. So one day I went to the kitchen and got a knife. I took it to the bathroom and cut my wrist."

Wiping my tears, I focus my eyes on my father. "That's why you committed me."

He contemplates me as if I'm a patient on his operating table, he's just cut me open, and he's seen an anomaly, perhaps a tumor, that he hadn't expected. I wait in dreadful suspense.

He shakes his head reproachfully. "You shouldn't have said that, Caroline."

I taste defeat, metallic and cold. He knows I lied. I've failed to make him believe that I believe my own story. If only I'd confessed that I really don't remember anything. I staked my all on my intuition, and it let me down.

"You're suffering from a psychotic breakdown with serious delusions." The look in his eyes is completely devoid of mercy.

A new revelation lands like a heavy rock on top of the others. His reaction amounts to an admission that the official version of that summer's events is false. But that's small satisfaction. Finding out the true version is the least of my concerns right now.

"I'll tell Adrian to keep you in lockdown while I petition the court for custodianship of you and commit you permanently to RKH," my father says.

I comprehend that he wouldn't have believed anything I said; he's a liar who assumes that other people are just as dishonest as he is. And he never intended to let me go while there was the slightest chance that I had information that posed a danger to him. Whatever I say, I'm damned. I lost the game before I started playing, and the stakes are even higher than freedom.

He engineered murders to cover up secrets from the past. Why would he let me live?

Psychopaths have no conscience, Dr. Koffka's voice says in my mind.

The only unanswered question is, why didn't he kill me, or have me killed, twelve years ago? My mask fails me. I can't keep my terror and despair off my face.

My father smiles with malicious pleasure. "Goodbye, Caroline."

CHAPTER

35

Dear Dot and Maureen,

Lockdown is quiet tonight. I must be the only patient awake. When the nurses look in on me, I lie still with my eyes closed so they think I don't need another shot. This is my last night before the lobotomy, and I don't want to waste it by sleeping.

But staying awake gives me time to think about the lobotomy. What will it feel like? The girls at Haven House said you get two black eyes and a terrible headache. Big deal. I've had black eyes from fighting with my cousins, and when I climbed a tree and fell, I got a concussion and ten stitches. The thing that worries me is the mental part. After Dr. Brain-Butcher jabs his icepick in my brain, will I remember how I used to be? Will I think of things I want to say, but nothing comes out of my mouth except goo-goo *and* blub-blub*? Or will my mind be totally blank? That might be better, because then I won't care about being an idiot. I won't be sad about all the things I wanted to do that I never will. But I'll forget everything from before the lobotomy. I won't remember hunting with Dad, or playing water polo with my brothers, or making love with Celia. The thought is so terrible that I put my pillow over my head so the night nurse* *won't hear me crying. My memories are the only thing in my life that's good. I can't bear to lose them, no matter how much it would hurt to remember and know that nothing will ever be that good again. I would rather die.*

Footsteps are coming down the hall. It's time for bed check. I hold my sobs, lie perfectly still, and wait for the nurse to look in the window at me and leave. But the key clinks in the lock and the door opens and shuts. A man's voice whispers, "Hi, baby."

It's Fred, my "boyfriend," the night orderly from Haven House. I roll over and see him standing by my bed.

In catechism class, we learned about the Annunciation. The angel told the Virgin Mary that she was going to give birth to Jesus. I wondered if Mary was scared, seeing this magical creature with wings. I wondered if she wished God had chosen someone else. But now, as I look at Fred, I think I understand at least part of what she felt: She was awed because everything had suddenly changed. Fred is a dark figure with the light from the hall making a halo around him. Yeah, it's blasphemous to compare us to the angel and the Virgin Mary, but that's how it feels. Everything has suddenly changed.

"My buddy's on duty here tonight," Fred says. "He let me in."

When Fred sits on the bed with me, I throw my arms around him and cry against his chest. "Shh, shh," he says, patting my back. "Glad to see me, huh?"

"I've never been so glad to see anybody." I force myself to calm down as I realize I need to play this carefully. I only get one chance.

"I can stay for an hour," Fred says. "Doris owes me a favor after all those nights I covered for her while she was with her boyfriend."

My mind races. I have to convince him to get me out of RKH, and I can't expect him to take such a big risk just for my sake. He's too selfish.

"I've missed you so much." I can't rely on his love for me. His love is only about sex.

"I've missed you too." His hand slides under my gown.

I sigh with pretend pleasure. "I wish we could be together always."

Fred presses my hand against his lap. "Yeah, that would be great."

I kiss him, putting my tongue in his mouth. He moans. "Let's run away together."

A jolt of surprise goes through Fred's body. "Huh?"

"Just think how wonderful it'll be," I say, stroking his crotch. "We can fool around any time we want."

"I don't know, baby." Fred is rock-hard, but he pulls away from me. "Letting a patient out of lockdown . . . I could lose my job."

"If you're with me, you won't need a job," I say. "When I turn eighteen in a couple months, I'll get my trust fund. We can get married. We'll be rich. You'll never have to work again."

Fred's jaw drops. "Really?*"*

"Yeah. And you can buy a motorboat." I know he wants one; he's said so often enough.

"But how would I get you away from RKH?"

"In your car." He lives in town with his parents and drives to and from the hospital.

Fred shakes his head. "I don't know."

Time is speeding by. "I love you. I want to be with you. Let me show you how much." I lie down on my back, pull up my gown, and spread my legs.

He groans and unzips his pants. As he lowers himself onto me, I put my hand against his chest to stop him. "Promise you'll take me out of here as soon as we're done?"

"Yeah, I promise."

While he does it to me, I close my eyes, grit my teeth, and think that pretty soon I'll be free. He gasps and shivers and moans. Thank God it's over.

"Was it good for you too, baby?" he says.

"Yeah. And it'll be even better next time." I scramble off the bed. "Let's go."

He zips up his pants as he looks out the door to see if anyone's in the hall. Luckily, no one is. We hurry along the hall, down the stairs, and through the back door. My feet are bare, I'm naked except for the hospital gown, and I'm dripping wet between my legs, but I don't care because I'm so happy to be outside. The night is warm and humid and smells like a swamp, but it's beautiful. So is the lightning that zigzags over the hills. I feel like dancing as we run across campus. His rusty old Chevy is parked behind Haven House. I lie on the dirty floor in the back. Fred gets in front and drives. He slows down at the gate, but the guard doesn't stop him, and he turns onto the road.

Goodbye, RKH! No lobotomy for me!

I wait until we're well away from the hospital, then climb over the front seat to sit beside Fred. "We did it!" I kiss him, the first time I've ever wanted to.

We laugh together. I'm free! Fred turns on the radio, and we sing along. Then we're on the highway, going seventy miles an hour, the wind blowing in the open windows. But soon I start getting nervous. I've got no clothes, no money, no plan. I can't see any further ahead than the next few minutes.

Fred turns off the radio and says, "I can't just go off without telling Ma and Pa. They'll be worried."

"Call them in the morning."

He eases up on the gas pedal, steering the car onto the exit ramp. "If I hurry, I can get you back to RKH before they notice you're gone."

Shit! *As he slows down around the curve of the ramp, I beg, "Please don't take me back! They're going to give me a lobotomy tomorrow!"*

"I'm sorry, baby." He pats my hand. "I just can't do this."

I take a deep breath for courage, open the door, and jump out of the car.

"Hey!" Fred yells.

Brakes squeal as I fly through the air. I land with a thump that rattles my bones. I roll down a slope, into tall grass. I lie there, breathing hard. I hear the car door open. I look up to see the car stopped alongside the ramp with the engine running and the lights on. Fred gets out. I burrow through the grass, away from him, as he calls my name. If he finds me, he'll drag me back to RKH.

He stops calling. A minute later, I hear the door slam and the car drive away. He must have figured that he doesn't have time to hunt me down; he needs to get himself back to Haven House. He's too stupid to think about what will happen when they find out I'm gone and he was the last person to see me. I lie in the darkness, gasping with relief.

Lightning flickers in the sky. Thunder rumbles. Oh, God. It's going to rain, and I'm all alone out here, with nowhere to go and nobody to turn to. Dot and Maureen, I almost wish I were back in Haven House with you.

Almost but not quite.

I push myself to my feet. I hurt all over, and my skin feels like it's been sandpapered, but I don't think anything's broken. I start walking back along the ramp to the highway.

Until we meet again someday, I hope,

Rory

* * *

After my disastrous reunion with my father, sleep falls upon me like the lead blankets used during X-rays. It's a common reaction after a shock. The nervous system releases adrenaline and other hormones during emotional or physical stress, triggering a "fight, flight, or freeze" response—an ancient survival mechanism. Once the stress is gone, the hormone levels drop. The body wants to shut down and recuperate, and if the mind tries to resist, it's like turning the key in the ignition of a car that's out of gas.

The door opens. I awaken with a start. My adrenaline immediately revs up again as an orderly says, "Rise and shine, Caroline."

My father must have ordered the staff to call me by my original name, surely to demoralize me. A man pushing a stretcher follows the orderly into my room. It's Daniel Tanaka.

Sitting up in bed, I exclaim, "Daniel!" I'm overjoyed to see him. He's on my side; he'll help me get out of lockdown, away from RKH.

His smile is impersonal, as if we've never met. He speaks in a cool, businesslike voice: "You're going to electroconvulsive therapy."

Hope turns to awful realization. The shock is intended to destroy my brain or kill me. And Daniel is now apparently in league with Superintendent Van Pelt and my father. They must have convinced him that I'm criminally insane, guilty of arson and murder, and he's doing their dirty work. As Daniel and the orderly drag me out of bed and onto the stretcher, I kick and twist, but the orderly holds me down while Daniel fastens the restraints around my wrists and ankles and the straps across my body. Daniel's betrayal of my trust is like acid poured into an open wound, searing, agonizing.

"Daniel, please don't do this," I cry as he wheels me along the hall.

The orderly doesn't question Daniel's authority or motives. He saunters off in the opposite direction.

"You're a good doctor," I tell Daniel. "Don't let them turn you into a monster!"

Without responding, he steers me into the elevator and pushes the button for the basement. We're going to the tunnels. When the elevator door opens, panic robs me of my ability to frame arguments that might change his mind. I scream, "Help! Let me go!"

I'm living my nightmare, riding backward on the stretcher as it rattles along the tunnel, seeing the rusted pipes on the ceiling, smelling the dampness and disinfectant, hearing the ventilation fans. Daniel is at the foot of the stretcher, pushing me faster and faster. It's as if a different person, a mindless tool of Superintendent Van Pelt and my father, has taken my friend's place. My heart batters inside my chest like the wings of a trapped bird. I scream louder while we turn corners in the maze of the tunnels.

There's no one around to hear me but this strange new Daniel, his expression as blank as a steel wall.

Suddenly we stop. Daniel opens a plain, unmarked wooden door. This isn't the shock room, but my panic only worsens. Why should they bother with shock treatments when it would be quicker and easier to kill me with an injection of air into a vein? Daniel pushes me into a small, dark room. I scream so hard that my throat feels raw. He turns on the light and shuts the door. We're in a janitor's closet that contains a sink, brooms, mops, other equipment, and cleaning supplies. When I pause for a breath, Daniel puts his face near mine.

"Claire," he says. "*Shut up.*"

His harsh voice is completely at odds with the tender anguish in his expression. Gone is his air of impersonal detachment. Surprise silences me.

"I'm getting you out of here," he says.

Astonished by this turnaround of events, I can only stammer.

"I came to lockdown to check on a patient," Daniel says, "and I overheard your father and Superintendent Van Pelt debating whether it would be better for you to have a lobotomy or a fatal accident."

The news comes as no surprise, but it's nonetheless devastating. A part of me clung to the stubborn hope that someday my father would care about me, would love me and protect me. The fact that he'll never change is painful to face. My eyes flood with tears.

"I'm not going to let either one of those things happen." Daniel reaches in a corner behind a floor-waxing machine and pulls out a brown paper grocery bag. He dumps the bag's contents onto the stretcher by my feet. They're clothes—a blue cotton shirt, blue baseball cap, black trousers, black socks, and white tennis shoes.

"Put these on," he says, unbuckling my restraints. "Hurry."

Now I'm crying tears of gratitude. Daniel is still my friend; he came to my rescue. I scramble off the stretcher, and he turns his back on me, giving me privacy while I take off my hospital gown and put on the clothes he brought. They're soft, worn-in—his own clothes. The shirt and pants are baggy, the shoes too big, but they'll do. That Daniel has justified my faith in his goodness fills me with optimism. *Everything is going to be all right.* We hurry out of the closet and run through the tunnels. It occurs to me what a huge risk Daniel is taking. My father and Superintendent Van Pelt could use their influence to prevent him from ever practicing medicine. They might even treat *him* to a fatal "accident." His family would never know what really happened to him. Superintendent Van Pelt's friend the police chief could easily sweep the death of a Japanese man under the rug.

"Daniel," I say, "if they find out that you helped me—"

He shushes me and pulls me through a door, into a basement under one of the hospital buildings. We climb a flight of stairs to an exit that leads to the parking lot behind the men's staff dormitory. It's night; I don't know what time it is, they confiscated my watch. Warm humidity coats my skin. Lightning flashes, white veins in the sky. The air smells of ozone. Daniel hurries me to his car, opens the passenger door, and says, "Get in."

I shy away from him. "I can't let you do this."

He stands there holding the door. "I'll drive you wherever you want."

"No." I push the door shut.

Even with my life at risk, I mustn't accept his sacrifice. We stand there, at an impasse. Any time now, someone will discover that Daniel didn't take me to the shock room.

Daniel hands me his car keys. "Then go alone. But for God's sake, go."

"I can't take your car," I protest.

"When you're finished with it, park it and mail me the keys with a letter that says where it is." He's taking money out of his wallet.

"Daniel, no!" I remember that he's saving money for a trip to California to see his family.

He grabs my hand, presses the folded bills into my palm. "Get out before they discover you're missing." He opens the driver's side door for me. His expression is intense with pleading. "Claire, I want you to be safe."

My will bends to the force of his. "Thank you," I say.

Words are so inadequate, time too short to express all that I'm feeling—my gratitude, my distress that I'll probably never see him again, my regret for what might have been. His expression is troubled and sympathetic as we gaze at each other for a moment. Then I climb into the driver's seat and start the car.

Daniel closes the door. "Good luck, Claire."

I drive away with his clothes on my back and his money in my pocket. The campus is so dark that I can't see him in the rearview mirror. At the gate, the guard barely glances in my direction; he must think I'm Daniel. Then I'm free, speeding down the road away from RKH.

I'm torn between my instinct to survive and my urge to run back to the only friend I have in the world.

CHAPTER 36

OUT ON THE highway, I drive seventy miles an hour, afraid to push Daniel's car any harder. I've more reason to be grateful to Daniel: although the Ford is old, it's well maintained. The lights and turn signals work, the gears shift easily, the steering and brakes respond without undue force. When the rain starts, the windshield wipers smoothly clear the drops from the clean windows. But the gas tank is only a quarter full. I won't get far before I have to stop.

Has Superintendent Van Pelt learned yet that I've escaped from RKH? I imagine police sirens and lights zooming toward me any minute.

Wind buffets the car. Thunder rumbles, and lightning exposes the trees by the highway in incandescent flashes. I'm driving with no destination in mind, no plan except to get far away from RKH quickly. But the rain comes down in sheets and blurs the beams of my headlights. I slow down for fear of skidding off the road. The adrenaline rush of escaping from lockdown trickles away. Panic yields to regrets. Was going back to RKH worth the consequences? What did I gain?

I've discovered the cause of my amnesia. I've become convinced that it was deliberately induced in order to cover up things I knew about that summer, and that at least two murders—of Leonora Hirschfeld and Dr. Isaac Franz—were part of the cover-up. And I've learned that my father, a psychopath, has been calling the shots from behind the scenes. But now that I've been exposed as a former mental patient who lied about her identity—and escaped a locked ward after supposedly trying to commit suicide—my prospects of practicing medicine are surely zero. When my father finds out I escaped, he'll use his money and influence to mount a widescale search for me. And I still don't know what happened in 1941 that was terrible enough to justify multiple murders as well as erasing a fourteen-year-old girl's memory.

I've failed at the mission that brought me back to RKH.

As for finding a place in the world with people who value me . . . a bitter smile twists my mouth. I've never been more rootless or alone than I am now.

My thoughts turn to Daniel Tanaka. The orderly at Shelter House knows he took me out of lockdown. Whatever happens to him is my fault, no matter that he acted of his own volition. My father will be furious, out for revenge. That I've jeopardized Daniel is my biggest regret of all.

A road sign informs me that I'm on the northbound highway. I should have headed south toward New York City, then west into New Jersey, Pennsylvania, and on to some distant city that's big enough to hide in while I figure out my next step. Instead, I'm driving upstate, retracing my route to Arden Spring. Freud was right: the impulses of the unconscious mind are hard to repress. I believe that if I see the summer house again, my memory will come back. Since I'll probably never return to this part of the country, tonight is my last chance. If my memory does come back, perhaps I'll have information that will help me put an end to the crimes and abuses at RKH and save not only Daniel Tanaka but Rory Kirkpatrick as well.

The summer house isn't just the key to unlocking my memory. It's also the last place my father and Superintendent Van Pelt would think to look for me. My father doesn't know that I've been back there and I know it wasn't sold long ago. Logically, he would I assume I would flee the region as fast as possible.

It's raining so hard that driving demands all my attention. I slow down to forty miles per hour. Luckily, there aren't many other cars out here. Great sprays of water splash up from the tires. The windshield wipers are turned up all the way, but it's like driving through a lake. As I veer around a curve, my headlights catch a pale human figure at the right. *How on earth can someone be walking in the dark in this weather?* The person lunges into the road, one arm extended with the thumb of its hand stuck out, the other hand waving frantically. My heart lurches as I swerve to avoid hitting the hitchhiker. I glimpse an open-mouthed face and wet, bedraggled hair. A strange intuition makes me pump the brakes and skid to a stop on the side of the road. Leaving the engine running, I get out of the car and run through the torrential rain toward the hitchhiker, a girl wearing a short, light-colored dress. Not a dress; a hospital gown. Her arms and feet are bare. Her hair is long and dark, her skin blanched.

"Please, I need a ride, can you please give me a ride?" she calls. Her voice trembles; she's shivering.

I recognize that voice, that face. Shock halts me in my waterlogged tracks. "*Rory*?"

Carl Jung, the Swiss psychiatrist and colleague of Freud, believed that coincidences weren't just random occurrences but *synchronicity*—manifestations of a secret order in the universe, an alignment between hidden forces. Jung's famous example of synchronicity is his story of a patient who described a dream about a golden scarab beetle. At that very moment, a real golden scarab beetle flew into his office. The universe has brought my former patient and me to the same rainy, deserted place at the same late-night time.

"Dr. Kendall?" Rory's expression alters from surprise to fear.

"What are you doing out here?" I thought she was in lockdown, and we're at least ten miles from RKH.

She backs away from me. "Did they send you to bring me back?"

"No." Whatever happened, this isn't the place for explanations. My mood suddenly brightens. At RKH I couldn't rescue Rory, but I can now. "Get in the car."

The rain lashes us. Rory hesitates, visibly wavering between two choices—trust me or stay out here alone, half naked, wet and cold. She hurries to the car. We climb in, and as I pull onto the highway, I turn on the heat full blast. The moisture evaporating off of us steams up the air. My drenched clothes cling uncomfortably to me. I wipe my face with my damp hand. Rory wrings water out of her hair. I drive for long minutes before she stops shivering.

"How did you get out?" I ask.

Rory shrugs. I gather she had help from someone on the staff, whom she doesn't want to get in trouble by naming.

"Why did you run away?"

"They were going to give me a lobotomy tomorrow."

"Oh." My mind replays Mrs. Scott garbling "The Star-Spangled Banner." Rory was in as much danger at RKH as I was.

"Where are we going?" she asks.

"To Arden Spring. My family's summer house."

"You're going there to stay for a vacation?" The eagerness in her voice says Rory hopes I'll let her stay with me.

"Well, no." I hate to disappoint her.

"Then why are you going?" Rory sounds suddenly distrustful, as if she realizes it's odd to drive through a storm in the middle of the night to a house where I'm not planning to stay.

I can't leave her to fend for herself. God only knows what the next person who sees her hitchhiking might do to her, and if Superintendent Van Pelt gets his hands on her, she'll be lobotomized. I've no choice except to take her with me, even though she's a fugitive murder suspect and if I'm caught with her, we'll both be arrested. A psychiatrist shouldn't reveal personal, sensitive information to a patient, but since Rory is my passenger, I owe her an explanation. I take a deep breath. Then I start talking.

* * *

An hour later, I'm driving up the road into the Highlands. Rory sits silently, gazing straight ahead, her fingers gripping the door handle. I can tell that she's dumbfounded by my story of that summer, my family, my amnesia, my theory that Dr. Franz and Leonora Hirschfeld were murdered, and how I came to be fired and put in lockdown. She must be afraid that I'm more insane than any of RKH's patients. I can hardly blame her if she's reluctant to join me on my quest to recover my lost memory and get to the bottom of the conspiracy and murders.

The rain has let up, but drops from the trees spatter the windshield, and the pavement is slick. I motor around the curves in low gear. Water splashes up from the ruts in the road. My heart skitters, and I feel lightheaded and shaky. I'm glad to have Rory with me but ashamed to need her for moral support. For a psychiatrist to use a patient to satisfy her own emotional needs is a violation of professional ethics. But of course we're not psychiatrist and patient anymore. We're now partners in my foolhardy venture.

I park in a clearing in the woods below the final, steepest curve of the road. Leaving the motor and lights on, I get out of the car. Rory follows suit, asking, "Why are we stopping here?"

I open the trunk. Inside, there's a jack and spare tire, a red toolbox, and a big silver metal flashlight. I pick up the flashlight and turn it on. When it lights up brightly, I wordlessly thank Daniel for being prepared for emergencies. I also find a pair of black galoshes and a blue denim jumpsuit stained with black grease, which he probably wears while working on the car. I give the galoshes and jumpsuit to Rory.

"Put these on," I say.

"Thanks." She pulls the jumpsuit up over her hospital gown, buttons it, then steps into the galoshes. She looks like a small, underaged gas station attendant.

I turn off the engine and lights. "Get back in the car."

"Hey! I'm coming with you."

Sick from fear, I desperately want company, but Rory shouldn't have to be a part of this. "Stay here." Armed with Daniel's flashlight, I start walking up the road.

The beam shines on the trees on either side and the puddles and fallen leaves on the ground. Over the pounding of my heart, I hear water dripping from the foliage and thunder in the distance. Then comes the faint, tinny music of an orchestra and a tenor singing:

The warm and lovely world we knew
Has been struck by a bitter frost . . .

It's from the memory I had when I came here last time. There's a howling in my ears, like the sound of a distant tornado coming. Up the road, Brian and Donna and their friends sit around a campfire. The hallucination is so real that I can smell the smoke and see the orange flames reflected in the bottle of beer that Brian passes to Donna.

. . . my sister and I recall with a sigh . . .

Gasping, I jerk the flashlight sideways. Its beam spotlights Brian and Donna dancing together. The dark forest around me echoes with hoots and whistles from their friends. I reel dizzily, and the beam of light pans from one brief scene to another: Brian leading Donna into the woods; the two of them kissing.

. . . the world we knew and loved and lost.

The past is everywhere around me. I feel the same jealousy, shame, and excitement as I did when I spied on Brian and Donna. I now recognize the excitement as sexual arousal. I cry out, whirling in a desperate attempt to escape it. Losing my balance, I stumble. The ground tilts, and I drop the flashlight. Hands grab me before I fall. I scream, trying to push them away.

"Dr. Kendall!" It's Rory. "What's the matter?"

Falling to my knees, I pant as the hallucinations fade. Rory picks up the flashlight and shines it on me. I raise my hand to ward off the glare.

"Did you remember something?" she asks.

I catch enough breath to whisper, "Nothing new." But a new emotion clings to the residue of the memory. It's dread that something terrible was about to happen. Was it the murder of Donna Wright, by Brian or me?

"Maybe you'll remember more if we go up to the house," Rory says. "Come on."

I should tell her to wait in the car, but I let her pull me to my feet. I'm not going to make it to the house without help from this girl I so desperately wanted to help. Rory holds the flashlight, and I lean on her as we walk up the road. She's smaller than I am but surprisingly strong. We reach the gate in the chain-link fence that blocks the driveway to the house. The tornado in my head howls louder. My thoughts scatter like flying debris, splintered boards and broken shingles from buildings lifted off their foundations. Rory fiddles with the lock on the gate, then reads the sign.

"No Trespassing? No problem." She gives me the flashlight and starts climbing the fence.

"Rory, don't!"

"How else are we supposed to get in?" She's already over the top of the fence, climbing down the other side. She lands gracefully and beckons me. "Come on, Dr. Kendall!"

If she's caught trespassing, the least I can do is be caught with her. I pass the flashlight through the fence to her then start climbing. The metal wires are cold and wet in my hands, slippery under the shoes Daniel loaned me. I awkwardly maneuver my legs over the other side. Halfway down, my hands slip. The fall twists my ankle. Supported by Rory, I limp up the curving driveway. In the beam of the flashlight she holds, the house materializes, two stories high, spreading over a grassy hilltop surrounded by woods. The original house, built almost a hundred years ago, has walls made of large, rounded rocks set in mortar. A slate roof shades a wide veranda. Additions with brown clapboard walls and green-shingled roofs branch off both sides of the original house and ramble down the far side of the hill. All the windows are dark.

"Neat place," Rory says. "Does anybody live here now?"

I can't speak. Again I have the sensation of being in two places at once—on the driveway with Rory and in my bedroom at the back of the house on the second floor of the newest wing. I simultaneously feel the cool, moist air from the forest and the rough wooden sill under my fingers as I peer out the window. I see Rory's face superimposed on the view of the pool and patio below my room. A wavering light shines from the trail that leads into the woods. It's my flashback about following Brian to the campfire.

"Do you remember something else?" Rory says.

Her eager voice sounds far away, as though we're separated by the twelve years between the present and the night I spied on Brian and

Donna. Then Brian emerges from the woods with his flashlight. I frown in surprise. It's not the same memory.

"What is it?" Rory says.

"He's not going into the woods. He's coming back."

"Who's coming back?"

"Brian."

"You mean your brother who died?"

"Yes." I once watched Dr. Koffka demonstrating hypnosis, guiding a classmate through his memory of a childhood experience. Rory and I have exchanged roles: she's the psychoanalyst; I'm the client.

"Wow!" Rory says. "You remembered! What's he doing?"

"He's crying." I hear Brian's jagged breaths between sobs. "He's coming into the house." Brian vanishes from sight. All I see is the vacant patio and the moonlit pool.

"What happens next?"

The memory repeats. The flashlight shines from the trail; Brian appears; he sobs as he vanishes into the house. Over and over. A mental block that's like the rewind button on a tape recorder prevents me from remembering more. Every time I reach the end of the scene, I shiver with inexplicable dread.

"What's the matter?" Rory says.

I hug myself to contain the tremors. "Something terrible is going to happen."

"What is it?"

"I don't know." *I don't want to know. I* need *to know.*

"Let's go closer to the house." Rory sounds excited. My problems must be a welcome distraction from her own. "That should help you remember more."

I don't want to go. Even as I shrink in fright, I let Rory take my arm and pull me along. *I* have *to go.* Brian's sobs echo in my memory. I quail before the gut knowledge that something terrible happened in the woods, and something even worse happened when Brian came home. We climb the wooden steps to the veranda. They're still dark green like the veranda floorboards and the trim on the house. The dark green front door has a small, four-paned window and a weathered brass handle and knocker. The window is dark. The silent house exudes menace like cold, poisonous fumes.

"Looks like nobody's home," Rory says. "Rats. I was hoping they'd give us something to eat. I'm starved." She tries the door handle.

My heart thuds so hard, I might have a coronary. The house was the stage for whatever drama led to my commitment to a mental hospital.

"It's locked," Rory says, disappointed.

My sensation of relief is like floating on a featherbed. Then Rory grabs the knocker. "No!" I cry, gripped by fear of waking sleeping dogs.

Rory bangs loudly on the door. The noise echoes and fades in the house's interior. She cocks her head, listening. "Did you hear that?"

Suspended between terror and doubt, I shake my head violently in stubborn denial, as if that could keep whatever is going to happen from happening. But I do hear it—footsteps and clanking sounds approaching us. The window in the door lights up. The lock rattles, and the door creaks open. I clutch my throat. I can't breathe. My heartbeats feel like explosions in my chest. If a coronary doesn't kill me, I'll suffocate to death. Rory flashes me a mischievous grin as the strip of light from the hallway broadens and illuminates us. I turn to flee, but she grabs my arm. We watch as the door opens wide enough for us to see the man standing at the threshold.

He's tall and heavyset, dressed in loose, pale blue trousers and shirt, his feet bare. His shaggy blond hair glows in the light from the ceiling fixture in the hall behind him. His face is in shadow, but I can tell he's not the caretaker, who must be in his fifties now; this man is much younger. Sam and his wife Rita don't live here alone. There's a stranger in my family's house. He scratches his head, puzzled to see two drenched, disheveled women who've appeared on his doorstep in the middle of the night.

"Who are you?" he says. "What do you want?"

His voice is hoarse with sleep, oddly familiar. It sends a wave of shock through me. Rory nudges me, expecting me to introduce us and explain our purpose. The man steps backward, as if my shock radiated outward and hit him like the blast from a bomb.

"Cary?" he says.

Only one person in the world has ever called me that.

The light from the hall shines on the man's face. His cheeks and neck are as fleshy as his body, with a hint of a double chin, and blond stubble roughens his jaws, but I recognize in him the boy that I last saw when he was sixteen. My heart leaps so violently, it feels like it's trying to fly out of my open, gasping mouth.

"*Brian*?"

CHAPTER

37

MY BROTHER IS alive.

How can it be?

The one thing I definitely know about that summer is that he died. But here he is, twelve years older, right in front of me.

We stare at each other, mirror images of amazement and disbelief, as if we're both seeing a ghost. I'm simultaneously in two places at once—facing Brian across the threshold of the summer house and standing apart from us watching my thin, awkward, fourteen-year-old self with her lithe, athletic, beloved older brother. My hand involuntarily reaches through the doorway toward Brian. He raises his hand to touch mine. We flinch at the contact between our fingers, mine damply cold, his warm.

He's real. So am I. This isn't a mutual hallucination.

Uttering a laugh that ends in a moan, I step into his embrace. He's solid in my arms; he smells muskier than I remember, but sweet with soap and fresh perspiration. I cry into the soft cotton of his pajama shirt.

"Don't cry, Cary," he says, hugging me, his cheek against my hair. He sniffles; he's crying too.

"Hey," Rory says.

Startled out of our embrace, Brian and I turn to her; we'd forgotten she was there. Seeing Rory and Brian together is a collision between my past and present. Rory points at Brian and says to me, "That's your brother? Didn't you say he was dead?"

"I thought he was." The simple logic of the situation astounds me: my death was faked, why not Brian's too? Another deception on top of all the others isn't so unbelievable.

"You thought I was dead?" Brian frowns. "I thought *you* were. Dad told me you died of tuberculosis."

"That's what he told me about you." Tears stream down my face. I'm overjoyed to see Brian, but so confused, so grieved that I spent twelve years missing him when we could have been together. And so angry at my father. What happened that could have justified his keeping Brian and me apart as well as committing me to a mental hospital and erasing my memory?

"Obviously, there's been a big misunderstanding," Rory says. "I'm glad it's cleared up." Although she sounds happy for us, her expression is wary.

"Who are you?" Brian asks her.

"Rory Kirkpatrick." She tilts her head at me. "I'm her patient. Or was."

Brian turns to me in surprise. "Your patient? Are you a doctor, Cary?"

"Yes," I say, "a psychiatrist. Or not quite."

"Well, it looks like you two have a lot of catching up to do," Rory says. "But first, I have a question for you, Brian. Why is there a chain on your ankle?" She points.

Disconcerted, I take a closer look at Brian's bare feet. A steel cuff circles his ankle. A long, heavy chain connected to the cuff extends down the hallway and through the door to the living room. I raise my shocked gaze to Brian.

He sighs. Shame and misery cloud his face. "We'd better sit down. Come in."

Rory and I follow him to the living room. The chain makes the clanking noise we heard before he opened the door. When he turns on the light, my first glimpse of the living room stuns me like a punch in the stomach. The worn floorboards; the dark beams on the ceiling; the copper chandelier fashioned to resemble a candelabra; the deer head mounted above the stone fireplace; and the brown leather sofa and armchairs are the same as I remember. I can picture my younger self lying on the bearskin rug by the hearth, reading a book, and playing checkers with Brian at the table by the window. I'm living in a flashback.

Brian sits in an armchair by the fireplace. His chain is connected to a metal ring bolted to the floor near him. I take the opposite armchair while Rory plops herself on the sofa. I realize now that everything isn't quite the same. The leather upholstery is more worn, and the coffee table holds a small ice chest and tins of potato chips and pretzels instead of my father's cigar box, lighter, and ashtray.

Rory eyes the food. Brian says, "Help yourself."

"Thanks." She takes a bottle of Coke from the ice chest and digs into the potato chips.

There are so many questions colliding in my mind. I ask the most obvious one. "Brian, why are you chained to the floor?"

"So that I can't leave."

Incredulous and dismayed, I say, "You're a prisoner? Who's keeping you here?"

"Sam and Rita. On Dad's orders."

Our father plotted to have me lobotomized or killed. He's keeping Brian chained up inside this house. There seems no limit to his evils. "But why?"

"It's a long story." Obviously reluctant to tell it, Brian says, "I've missed you, Cary. Now my little favorite sister is all grown up." He smiles sadly. "Tell me about yourself. Where did you go to med school?"

"Columbia University. Brian—"

"Columbia. That's great!" His face lights up with pride.

He was the only person in our family who was ever interested in me, who praised me for my achievements. My heart fills with the warm feeling he always gave me, but I can't let him sidetrack me. "Brian, where have you been all these years?"

Shaking his head, he sighs again. "When Dad told me you'd died, my only comfort was that you never knew about me."

Rory interrupts. "Quit beating around the bush." Munching potato chips, she eyes us eagerly, as if she's watching a movie. "Out with it!"

"All right," Brian says. "I guess you deserve to know."

Involving Rory in this is grossly inappropriate, but without her, I might never have reunited with Brian, never had a chance to hear his story. I suppose she deserves to hear it too.

"I was in a hospital in Switzerland for three years," Brian says. "Then it got too expensive, so Dad brought me back to the U.S. I've been here ever since."

Trying to make sense of this, I flounder in confusion. "If you didn't have TB, why were you in a hospital?" And he still hasn't explained why he's a prisoner at our summer house.

"It was a mental hospital."

I'd thought nothing could shock me anymore. "Our father put me in a mental hospital. He put you in one too?"

Regret saddens Brian's expression. "I'm sorry that happened to you. I had no idea."

I'm flabbergasted. "But why you? You weren't mentally ill."

"It was to protect me."

The story is getting more incomprehensible by the moment. "Protect you from what?"

Brian shifts uneasily, his chain clinks. "From the law."

"What? Why—?" My mind makes the horrible connection. "Donna Wright," I whisper. "Your girlfriend. She was murdered that summer. And you were a suspect."

Now I understand. Our father secreted Brian in a Swiss mental hospital and faked his death to prevent his being arrested for Donna's murder, to avoid the scandal of a trial and conviction and a sentence of life in prison or death.

"*Murder*?" Rory speaks through a mouthful of potato chips. "Dr. Kendall, you didn't say anything about murder." Eyeing Brian with alarm, she asks the question that I'm too afraid to ask. "Did you do it?"

The answer is written in the guilt, shame, and sorrow on Brian's face. "Cary, I didn't mean to."

I cover my mouth, fighting the urge to wail like Lulu Shelton during a tantrum. What I resisted believing is true: my brother killed Donna. Knowing that I didn't do it is no relief. The only member of my family that I thought was good, kind, and decent, the brother I adored because he loved me, who made up for my parents' cruelty, is a murderer. The song from that summer plays in my mind:

The warm and lovely world we knew
Has been struck by a bitter frost . . .

I see Brian emerge from the woods, crying as he stumbles toward the house. But this time the memory continues instead of repeating. I hurry out of my room, down the stairs. Brian is in the bathroom, retching into the toilet. His face is covered with raw scratches, his white T-shirt smeared red with blood. The flashback ends there, stopped by my horror. That night, when Brian came home, he'd just killed Donna.

"It was an accident, Cary," Brian says urgently. "I swear."

"Isn't that what they all say?" Rory moves to stand by the door, prepared to flee in case Brian attacks her. "Dr. Kendall, you've heard enough. Let's get out of here."

But I want to believe Brian. Old loyalty dies hard. I can't leave him—not after we've both been resurrected from the dead. And I've only begun to learn the facts about that summer, the truth I was seeking when I returned to RKH. Donna's murder must be at the heart of the cover-up, but there's still so much I don't understand. I have to know everything, no matter if it destroys my love for Brian, no matter how much it hurts.

"Tell me what happened, Brian," I say.

Rory is silent, watchful. Brian hesitates, then says slowly, "We were in the woods. We were, uh, fooling around."

Dr. Koffka once compared remembrance to a Möbius strip. Past and present are each on both sides of it, on a continuous, endless loop. My mind travels around the loop, from the here and now to my hiding place behind the trees in the woods twelve years ago. I watch Brian kiss Donna and fondle her breasts. He pulls her blouse off, and she tugs at the zipper of his jeans. My excitement fills me with longing and shame.

"We'd fooled around before, but this was the night we'd decided to go all the way." Brian says with a reminiscent smile, "The first time for both of us."

A needle of jealousy stabs me. Not that I'd felt sexual attraction to my brother, but Brian had been the object of my love, and Donna had become the object of his. It hurts, even after all these years.

"Things were wonderful until we were ready to do it," Brian says. "Then she changed her mind. She was afraid she would have a baby and her life would be ruined."

I don't remember that. Maybe I'd watched them not that night but during an earlier encounter. Brian says, "I told her everything would be all right. I said I loved her and I would marry her. But she said no."

It's an old story I've heard before, from girls in my college dormitory. The boys often wanted to go farther than the girls did. To get their way, they made all sorts of promises. It happened to me too. A blind date to a dance at Harvard ended with a wrestling match in the boy's car. As he tried to pull my dress up, he said he loved me, he'd never felt that way about any girl before, he wanted to marry me. I jumped out of the car. He was so angry, he drove away and left me. I walked two miles back to my dorm. But I was lucky. Some girls came home crying, with torn clothes, bleeding. One dropped out of school and went to live with relatives. We all knew she was pregnant and had been sent away until the baby was born.

"Donna told me to stop," Brian says, "but I thought she thought that if a girl gave in too easily, she was a slut. I thought she wanted to do it and was just pretending she didn't. And, well, I was too excited to stop." He rubs his hands down his face. "Cary, I'm so ashamed."

Rory makes a sound of disgust. I'm revolted to learn that my brother had been one of those selfish, reckless boys. Maybe he did love Donna, but he was only sixteen, and he must have known that our father never would have let him marry a "gold digger."

"Afterward, Donna was furious," Brian says. "She started yelling at me, she called me a bastard. She flew at me and hit me and scratched me."

"Serves you right," Rory says.

I circle back to that night; I see the red claw marks on his cheeks.

"I shoved her. She fell and hit her head on a rock. There was so much blood. I called her name and shook her and patted her face, but she didn't answer. She didn't move." Brian's voice sounds thick, as if with vomit. "I ran home."

My instinctive sympathy for him gives way to horror. "You killed her! And you just left her there!"

"You *are* a bastard," Rory says.

I feel sick too as I finally understand why my father faked Brian's death and why Brian is in hiding: my brother is a rapist and murderer. It's also clear why my father had my memory erased: I must have found out what Brian had done. If I'd told anyone, Brian would have gone to jail, and the scandal would have ruined our family name, which my father couldn't have tolerated. After my father faked my death, he relocated Mother and me to Michigan under new names and then left, to distance all of us from Arden Spring and Donna's murder. The truth is a letdown as well as a revelation. My amnesia, mental breakdowns, and suicide attempts were fallout from an ordinary teenage love affair gone badly wrong.

"It wasn't how it sounds." Brian's manner turns vehement with denial. "I didn't know she was dead. I thought she was just hurt. I went home to get Dad. So he could save her."

"I don't believe it." Contempt laces Rory's voice. "You wanted him to clean up your mess."

I think Brian is telling the truth. My father is a doctor; it's logical that Brian would ask for his help. Another spin around the Möbius strip takes me back to that night. I'm standing outside this very room, listening to Brian sob as he says, *Dad, something terrible's happened.* And Mother crying. And my father's voice loud with dismay and anger: *You did what? Where is she?* That was the critical moment in my past, when my family fell apart and the course of my life and Brian's took a disastrous turn.

. . . my sister and I recall with a sigh
The world we knew and loved and lost.

Just like the siblings in the song, my brother and I were cast out of our childhood, into troubled new worlds. My chest aches with sorrow for both of us. But there's one thing I still don't understand.

"Brian, why are you chained up?" I ask.

"Because I wanted to turn myself in to the police," he says. "I wanted to confess that I killed Donna. I couldn't change what I did, but I could try to make things right."

"Oh, Brian." I want to weep as my old admiration for him lessens my horror. He's still the brother I knew—honest and decent.

"But Dad didn't want me to," Brian says. "He said he wasn't going to let me ruin my life because of that little slut, which is what he called Donna. We argued. Dad finally told me to get some sleep and we would call the police in the morning. I said okay. Because I wasn't exactly looking forward to going to jail. He gave me a shot, and I went out like a light. The next thing I knew, I was strapped to a stretcher on an airplane going to Switzerland."

"Your dad sounds like what my dad would call a piece of work," Rory says.

I begin to see that, despite his pride in his golden son, my father didn't care any more about Brian than he did about me. Brian was just a reflection of himself—a Freudian double—and when Brian's behavior reflected badly on him, the golden son became a liability. My father had shipped Brian off to the mental hospital in Switzerland with the same cold lack of conscience as when he'd dumped me at Resurrection Kill Hospital. Perhaps his instinct for self-preservation was the only reason he didn't just kill us both. Perhaps he was too cautious to risk outright murder of his children, with his own hands, and that's why we're still alive.

"Even though I'm sorry you had to hear all this, I'm glad you came, Cary," Brian says. "You can go to the police. Tell them I want to confess. Bring them here so they can arrest me."

I'm stunned by the turn of events. After escaping a mental hospital, I find myself faced with this bizarre proposition from the brother I'd thought was dead. When we were young, I would have done anything for him. But now . . . and this . . .

"I can't," I say.

"Please. I can't reach the phone. I can't get out of the house." Brian moves his leg, rattling the chain on his ankle. "You're my only chance."

Rory chimes in. "Superintendent Van Pelt probably has the police looking for us. If we march into the police station, they'll put handcuffs on us and ship us right back to RKH."

I hadn't thought of that. Her head is clearer than mine. She's my passenger on this strange journey, she deserves a say in what I do, and she's right: for our own sake, we should steer clear of the police.

Brian turns his puzzled gaze on Rory. "What are you talking about?"

"Oh, right, we didn't tell you," Rory says. "We were in lockdown at the nuthouse, and we ran away. Just so you know, I'm a suspect in the murder of a doctor who tortured me. And your sister is suspected of setting a fire that burned a patient to death."

Frowning skeptically, Brian asks me, "Is that true?"

I have to say, "Yes."

Brian is momentarily dumbstruck as he struggles to make sense of the situation. Then he asks me, "Why did you come here?"

"My memories of that summer were erased by shock treatments, and I came here in a last-ditch attempt to recover them before I decide what to do next."

"We don't have time for this," Rory says. "We need to get back on the road."

Again, she's right, but I say, "I can't leave my brother. Not when I just found him."

"You two can catch up later." Rory jitters impatiently by the door.

"Just call the police before you go," Brian pleads. "The phone is upstairs."

"No." I grip the arms of my chair as though the two of them are physically forcing me in directions I don't want to go. Brian was the person I loved most in the entire world. He still is. The fact that he's a rapist and murderer hasn't changed my feelings.

Desperation raises Brian's voice. "Please, Cary."

"They'll put you in jail," I protest. Dr. Koffka was right: I do have a sister complex. I've never found a man to take Brian's place. My feeling for him is platonic, but it's stronger than any other attachment I've ever had. I can't turn Brian over to the law. "They could sentence you to death!"

The position I'm in is just as unexpected and shocking as discovering that Brian is alive. In all my thoughts of him, I never imagined that he would beg me to be the instrument of his destruction.

Brian's shoulders sag under the weight of misery. "I can't live like this anymore, Cary. I'd rather die."

I feel my resistance crumbling. When we were children, he never asked me for anything in exchange for the attention, encouragement, and love he gave me. How can I deny his wish? He protected me from our parents; I need to protect him from the law. But how can I refuse to help him atone for his crime?

The moment to make a decision that will determine the course of both our lives is upon me. My heart beats wildly as my emotions wage a tug-of-war. Brian leans toward me, his hands clasped, as if I'm a saint to whom he's praying for salvation.

Rory says, "I hear a car outside."

CHAPTER 38

"Sam and Rita must have decided to come home early," Brian says. "You remember them, don't you, Cary? They take care of me and the house. They give me shots when I get too upset."

Our family's caretakers have become his jailers.

"Dr. Kendall, we can't let anybody see us. We have to get out of here *now.*" Rory's voice is shrill with panic.

"They won't tell anyone you were here," Brian says. "It would get them in trouble with Dad. They're not supposed to let visitors in the house. They're not supposed to leave me alone."

"Yeah, well, I'm not taking any chances." Rory comes over to me and yanks my arm. "Let's go."

"Wait." I'm in the throes of mental agony, torn between opposing forces—go or stay; honor Brian's wish or my need to protect him; heed Rory or my own heart.

"Cary, hide in your old room until Sam and Rita are asleep," Brian says.

Rory grudgingly nods. I hurry her out to the foyer. Brian follows, his chain clanking. As I lead Rory up the stairs, the front door opens. I can't help pausing to look over my shoulder. It's not Sam and Rita coming into the house. It's my father, followed by Superintendent Van Pelt and Dr. Mara, all dressed in raincoats and hats, looking like enemy agents in a spy movie.

"Oh, shit," Rory whispers.

Synchronicity strikes again. Our wild flight from RKH has put us right in the path of the very people we were trying to escape. Rory tugs my arm. Stricken by a sense that defeat was inevitable, I don't move. Running around the Möbius strip does no good. The past will always catch up with the present.

My father beholds me with the same clinical curiosity as when I lied to him about my memories of that summer. Then he smiles with sardonic pleasure. "Well, hello, Caroline."

Superintendent Van Pelt and Dr. Mara gape in astonishment. "Rory," Dr. Mara says.

"How convenient." My father chuckles. "Our two birds, in the same bush."

I should have listened to Rory. Baffled, I say, "How did you know we were here?"

"I didn't. Nor did I know the girl was with you. This is a lucky accident."

Superintendent Van Pelt recovers his poise and chuckles. "An accident that spared us the time and expense of searching the country for those two."

Brian is watching in confusion. Probably he hasn't seen so many people in all the years he's been trapped in this house. "Who are they?" he asks my father, pointing to Superintendent Van Pelt and Dr. Mara.

"Colleagues. Where are Sam and Rita?"

"They went to a wedding in New Jersey."

Anger darkens my father's face. "They're going to regret it."

"If you're not here for Cary, then why did you come?" Brian says.

"For you," my father says. "You're coming with me."

The expression in Brian's eyes blends elation at the thought of leaving his prison with fear of the world outside. "I don't understand."

But I'm beginning to. My father suspected I'd lied when I told him that all I remembered about that summer was Brian dying of TB. He was afraid I remembered something different—something that, if I reported it to the police, would bring them to this house where they would find Brian, the suspect in Donna Wright's murder, who had purportedly been dead for twelve years. My father needs to hide Brian somewhere else.

My father beckons Rory and me. "You too."

All three of us are loose ends that he wants to tie up. I'm furious at him, and not only for that. His deception kept Brian and me apart for twelve years, each believing the other was dead. "I'm not going with you."

"Neither am I," Rory says.

My father and the Van Pelts, standing at the bottom of the stairs, are blocking our path to both the front and back doors. We can escape through my old room via the balcony and the stairs that lead to the patio and woods. But Rory doesn't know that, and before I can get her to follow me up the stairs, she barrels down them, charges at Dr. Mara, and gives her a hard shove. Dr. Mara topples backward against Superintendent Van Pelt. They stagger together as Rory opens the door. Superintendent Van Pelt lets his wife fall to the floor. He grabs Rory. She kicks, snarls, and punches as my father joins the battle. It's over in seconds, with each man holding one of her arms.

She writhes and screams, "Let me go!"

"Dad, what are you doing?" Brian says.

I'm standing frozen on the stairs. My father says, "Come down here, Caroline."

Every survival instinct tells me to save myself, but I can't leave Rory, or Brian. With every step down the stairs, my terror mounts. A sense of resignation keeps me moving. Dr. Mara gets to her feet and smiles triumphantly at me.

"Where are we going?" Brian asks my father. "What are you going to do to us?"

Rory screams, "They're taking us to the loony bin. They're going to give us all lobotomies. Or kill us!"

Brian stares, appalled. "If that's true, I'm not going."

"Bastards!" Rory yells, kicking at my father and Superintendent Van Pelt.

My father tells the superintendent, "We'll have to sedate them for the trip."

"I only brought one shot." Superintendent Van Pelt pants with the effort of restraining Rory. "I didn't know we'd have three passengers."

My father curses under his breath as Rory tries to bite his arm. "Give it to this one."

"It's in my pocket," Superintendent Van Pelt says.

Dr. Mara dips her right hand into his coat pocket and pulls out a glass vial and a hypodermic syringe. I lunge at her, grab her left arm, and twist it backwards, the way I once saw an orderly at Mount Sinai do to a combative drunk. I'm surprised that it works for me. Dr. Mara cries out; a spasm of pain stiffens her body. The syringe and vial go flying. The vial and the glass barrel of the syringe shatter on the floor.

Rory howls with wild laughter. Dr. Mara breaks free of my grip and shoves me. I fall backward, hitting my head on the stairs. Pain jars my skull with a bouncing, reverberating sensation. My vision goes hazy.

My father says, "There's medication somewhere in the house. Go look for it." His voice sounds muffled, as if I'm in an elevator that's suddenly plunged ten stories and my ears have popped. The word *concussion* swirls through the fog in my brain. I'm too dizzy to stand up. The people around me melt and distort. I hear men arguing and shrill, hysterical cries. My conscious mind knows it's Brian, my father, and Rory, but my unconscious mind denies reality. The dizziness and shimmering aren't only due to a concussion. I'm having another flashback, triggered by the blow to my head and my return to the scene of ancient trauma. Past and present merge. I'm Dr. Claire Kendall sitting by the stairs in my family's summer house; I'm Caroline Lennox peeking in the door to the living room after Brian came back to the house that night twelve years ago. Brian is kneeling by the hearth, blood on his shirt, his hands over his face. My parents are standing over him, scolding him. Their angry voices mingle with his sobs.

I told you that girl was trouble.
How could you do such a stupid thing?
I didn't mean to. I swear. I'm sorry.

My mother starts hitting Brian. He hunches over, sobbing as she rains blows and insults on him. My father pulls her away from Brian and lays her down onto the sofa. He opens the drawer of the side table and takes out a hypodermic syringe. He often gave her sedative shots. He injects her, and her wails subside into whimpers, then silence as she falls asleep.

Clean yourself up and stay in your room, my father tells Brian.

They exit the living room. Brian trudges upstairs; my father strides toward the back door. They don't notice me. Should I go to Brian and ask him what happened? A more daring impulse wins out. I follow my father. In the mudroom, he grabs one of the flashlights we keep there. I take another, but I don't turn it on. Once again I follow a flickering beam through the woods, along the same trail that Brian took that other night when I spied on him and Donna. My father lopes down the path that leads into the ravine and up to the hills on the other side. A safe distance behind him, I cross the flat, treeless spot where I saw Brian, Donna, and their friends having a party. Nobody's there. The night smells of smoke from the burned-out campfire. My father heads down the trail that Brian and Donna took when they went off together. His flashlight illuminates the clearing where I saw Brian with Donna. He cautiously steps into it. The waterfall murmurs like a warning whisper. A shrill cry stops me.

I dart off the trail, behind the trees that edge the clearing. I peer between them and see my father standing with his back to me, and beyond him, Donna. She's sitting on the ground, naked from the waist up, her blonde hair spilling over her breasts, her pink skirt bunched around her hips. Her skin and clothes are blood-splotched. She raises her arm to shield her puffy eyes from the glare of my father's flashlight. I'm two observers—Caroline Lennox and Claire Kendall. My younger self doesn't understand the full significance of what she's seeing. My adult self realizes that it negates what I thought I knew. I cry out: *She's alive!*

The flashback invades the present time. I'm simultaneously in the woods and in the house. The foyer is the clearing, surrounded by trees instead of walls. My father and Superintendent Van Pelt, Rory and Brian, turn to stare at me. They heard me; I spoke aloud. Just as plainly as I see their puzzled faces, I see the ghosts of Donna and my father, her sitting on the ground, him standing with his flashlight aimed at her. I say to Brian, "You didn't kill Donna."

Surprise and confusion pucker Brian's eyebrows. "What?"

"When she fell and hit her head, it must have knocked her unconscious," I say, "but she was alive when you left her."

Brian gapes. "How do you know?"

Turning to my father, I say, "I followed you into the woods that night, after Brian told you he'd killed Donna." I feel a surge of exhilaration, an intoxicating power. I've triumphed over my father's attempt to erase my memory, his abuse of me. "I remember."

Superintendent Van Pelt says, "What's she talking about?" Rory calms down, regarding me with avid interest.

My father gives me a pitying smile. "Ah, Caroline." He says to Superintendent Van Pelt, "She's having one of her hallucinations. She was a very sick girl, and I'm sorry to see she hasn't recovered."

But my new power boosts my perceptions. It's as if I can see beneath his urbane surface to the neurons firing wildly, the veins flooding with adrenaline, the thoughts like a swarm of spiders in his brain. He knows I'm telling the truth, and he's frantic to debunk me.

"I didn't kill her?" Brian's face lights up with his eagerness to believe me, but confusion quickly dims it. "Then how did she die?"

I watch the flashback continue in our midst as if it's a play and we're the audience. My younger self peeks through the trees at Donna and my father, and I narrate the memory that unfurls in my mind. "Donna says, 'Dr. Lennox, look what your son did to me!'" I'm the only one who can see her gesture at her naked, blood-smeared body, but her voice issues from my mouth. "'He raped me and then left me for dead.' She's crying. She's furious. She says, 'I'm going to tell my father. He'll have Brian arrested!'"

"Pure baloney," my father says calmly.

Brian's, Rory's, and Superintendent Van Pelt's faces show the opposite reaction: they believe me. Dr. Mara joins us, holding a small metal box that must contain the hypodermic syringes and vials of sedative that my father sent her to find. She looks from one person to the next, wondering what she missed.

I tell my father, "You said to Donna, 'No one will ever know.' Then you hit her on the head with your flashlight." I see his arm lash out, hear the thud of the heavy chrome cylinder striking her temple. "She fell on the ground." Her ghostly image lies before me, moaning, half conscious. I feel a sense of familiarity, a lack of surprise about what happened next. I've known it all along even though I didn't remember until now.

"Before she could get up, you attacked her," I tell my father.

I see his ghost throw himself upon Donna and close his hands around her neck. Lit by his fallen flashlight, they thrash together on the ground. Donna wheezes as her fingers try to pry my father's off her throat. Her eyes bulge with terror; her pale legs thrash. My father pins her down, tightens his grip. Her struggles weaken, then cease.

"You strangled her to shut her up," I say.

A disturbing change comes over my father. He's breathing hard; sweat glistens on his tanned face. His gaze turns inward, as if he's in a trance, reliving and aroused by the events of that night. A smile twitches his mouth, and his eyes gleam. The psychopath in him is showing, and I'm not the only one who sees it. Superintendent Van Pelt and Dr. Mara look aghast at him. I would have thought that two experienced psychiatrists would have perceived his true nature, but apparently not. Rory, stricken by new fear of my father, twists in his grasp.

Brian stares in dazed, open-mouthed shock. "*You* killed Donna."

CHAPTER 39

My father recovers from his trance; the mask slips back into place. "She's lying," he says smoothly. "Don't believe her. She's just trying to turn you against me."

But the air is pungent with the odor of the sweat exuded by the monster within him, and none of us can forget the transformation we just saw.

Fury reddens Brian's face. "You never told me you went to the woods that night. You never said you found Donna alive. You let me think I was a murderer. You kept me locked up for twelve years!"

"I did it to protect you," my father says. "You were a suspect."

"Don't bullshit me!" Loud with a temper I've never seen in him, Brian says, "It was for your own protection. You faked my death and let the police blame me for Donna's murder." Tears spill from his eyes, down his flushed cheeks. "I loved her. And you killed her."

"That's not all he did," I say.

My flashback isn't over. I'm in the woods, watching my father stand up after he strangled Donna. His chest heaves from the exertion. He bends over, feels her neck for a pulse, then retrieves his flashlight. Horrified by what I've just seen, I whimper. My father swings the flashlight in my direction. Our gazes meet.

"He caught me watching him kill Donna," I say.

The fury, revulsion, and hatred in my father's eyes is like a stake driven through my ribs. Then I'm running through the woods, sobbing in terror while the beam of his flashlight and sound of his footsteps pursue me. I follow the trail back to the house because Brian is there. Brian will protect me. My adult self understands that my father realizes where I'm going. He follows me like a dog herding a sheep. He wants me at the house; why not let me get there under my own steam? It's easier than carrying me. As I burst out of the woods, his hand lands on my shoulder.

"He chased me and caught me," I say.

The thud when he slams me face down onto the flagstone patio knocks the breath out of me. The flashback evaporates like mist at dawn.

"What did he tell you happened to me?" I ask Brian.

He shakes his head, addled by the torrent of disturbing news. "Nothing then. The last time I saw you was the morning before, at breakfast. I never got to tell you goodbye." Brian wipes away tears; his breath catches on a sob. "A few months later, while I was in the hospital in Switzerland, he sent me a telegram saying you'd died of TB."

"He must have drugged me too," I say. "The next thing I remember is him taking me to RKH."

I wonder how much of this my mother knew about and went along with. But I don't ask my father because it doesn't really matter. Her miserable death was punishment enough for whatever she'd done. My rage overflows onto Superintendent Van Pelt and Dr. Mara. "You erased my memory with shock treatments. How could you do such a thing?"

Dr. Mara looks appalled to have the spotlight of accusation turned on her and her husband. The superintendent gives me a weak version of his jovial smile. "We were only trying to help you, my dear."

"Baloney," I say. "What did he tell you that made you willing to do it?"

"He said you were schizophrenic and you were having hallucinations." Dr. Mara's husky voice is less firm than usual.

"He's a surgeon," I say. "He's not qualified to make psychiatric diagnoses. Did he show you any proof that I was schizophrenic? Perhaps a referral from a psychiatrist?" I add, "There's none in my file. I know because I've read it."

Superintendent Van Pelt licks his lips, raises his chin, and says in a lofty tone, "I didn't need proof from a trusted colleague."

"Adrian!" Dr. Mara says, dismayed.

Stung by her rebuke, Superintendent Van Pelt says to my father, "You didn't tell me you murdered that girl. You said your daughter saw your son do it and you wanted her to forget so she couldn't tell anyone."

"You didn't bother to question my story," my father says, as matter-of-fact as if they're discussing a real estate sale. "You were too eager to take the deal I offered—erase my daughter's memory in exchange for funding the research that you thought would put RKH on the cutting edge of psychiatry. That was a hundred thousand dollars of my money into your pocket."

The size of the bribe is staggering. Even Rory, from a rich family, looks impressed. Dr. Mara covers her mouth.

"A hundred thousand dollars down the drain," my father says. "Fever therapy was a bust. Your mad scientist killed two patients and almost killed my daughter."

I suppose fever therapy was intended to erase whatever memories persisted after my shock treatments.

Dr. Mara's pale skin turns paler. "I thought Dr. Franz's patients died of natural causes. Oh, God, Adrian, what have you done?"

"The hospital was near bankruptcy," Superintendent Van Pelt blusters. "I was trying to save it."

Seeing a possible ally in Dr. Mara, I say to her, "Your husband made himself, and you, accessories to murder after the fact."

"Yeah," Rory says, delighted to see her enemies compromised. "Wake up and smell the coffee, bitch."

"There's no use standing here arguing all night. Let's go back to RKH and sort things out." Incredibly, my father thinks he can smooth over the situation, keep everyone in line. His arrogance knows no bounds. He addresses Dr. Mara, who's still holding the medicine kit. "Inject the girl first. We'll get Brian and Caroline next."

Rory yells and begins struggling again. Dr. Mara stands motionless with horror. Brian says, "I'm not going with you!"

He charges at my father. The chain makes him slow and clumsy, but he catches my father by surprise: my father isn't accustomed to violent resistance from his previously docile prisoner. Brian throws himself on my father and seizes him around the neck. Instinctively putting up his hands to grab Brian's, my father lets go of Rory. Brian's weight knocks my father off balance and into her. Rory and my father fall against Superintendent Van Pelt. Dr. Mara drops the medicine kit and tries to steady her husband. They and Brian all go down in a heap. I rush to help Rory, but she's pinned under Brian and my father as they thrash and fight. Brian's leg hits me. I reel backward and sprawl on the floor. Superintendent Van Pelt and Dr. Mara squirm free of the melee. I crawl toward Rory and grab her hand, but Superintendent Van Pelt still has hold of her other arm. He and I stagger to our feet while yanking on Rory as if she's the rope in a tug-of-war. Rory shrieks, ducks her head, and bites the superintendent's hand.

He lets go of her. "Damn it!"

As Rory pulls me toward the door, I resist because I can't leave Brian. Dr. Mara blocks our way. Rory goes at her like a wild animal, punching, kicking, clawing. Dr. Mara, a veteran of the psych ward at Bellevue, captures Rory in a headlock. Rory screams and claws Dr. Mara's arm. I run behind Dr. Mara and dig my fingers into her armpits. Dr. Mara flinches and involuntarily lowers her arms. Rory breaks free.

"Stop right there!" Superintendent Van Pelt orders.

I turn to see him pointing a gun at Rory and me. Although he's committed or conspired in multiple murders and he spends his vacations hunting, I'm nonetheless shocked. I've never had a gun pointed at me. It's like a scene in a movie, unreal. But I've seen gunshot wounds, the blood-drenched victims rushed to Mount Sinai by ambulance only to die in the emergency room. At autopsies, I've seen the shattered bones, the ruptured organs. And I know Superintendent Van Pelt won't hesitate to pull the trigger. I see the same realization dawn on Rory. Eyes huge with fright, she sidles over to stand close beside me.

Superintendent Van Pelt's grandfatherly smile distorts into a grotesque caricature of itself. "Hands up, girls," he says, as if he's the sheriff in a Western. The twinkle in his eyes has a crazed gleam to it.

We obey and stand frozen. On the floor, Brian and my father grapple side by side. Brian has wrapped his chain around my father's neck. He's overweight and out of shape, but he's the younger, bigger, and more desperate of the two. Muscles tense, he pants as he pulls the chain tight. My father claws at the chain, his face red, mouth gasping. His legs kick the air. I watch, horrified by the violence yet thrilled to see my father get his just deserts.

"Adrian?" With her hat knocked off, blonde hair loosened from her chignon, and her eyes filled with alarm, Dr. Mara looks a far cry from her usual sleek, poised self. "You didn't tell me you were bringing a gun."

"I thought it might come in handy," her husband says, beaming at his own prescience.

"What are you going to do?" Dr. Mara asks.

Rory regards her with contempt. "He's going to shoot us, isn't it obvious?"

Superintendent Van Pelt tilts his head, contemplates Brian and my father. "I believe I'll let that matter take its course."

My father's struggles weaken; his heels drum the floor while Brian throttles him. Superintendent Van Pelt intends to simply stand by while his old friend dies. He too must have some degree of psychopathy.

"No! Stop them!" I hunger for revenge for Brian and myself. I want us both out from under my father's power, but not like this. By killing my father, Brian will become the murderer he's believed himself to be. "Brian, stop!"

Brian doesn't seem to hear me. Groaning, he pulls harder on the chain.

"Adrian," Dr. Mara repeats, confounded by the atrociousness of her husband's proposal. "How will we explain this away?"

"There was a quarrel, and the boy attacked his father." Superintendent Van Pelt aims his gun at Brian. "I killed the boy in an attempt to stop him."

After finding my brother alive, to have him murdered by the man who aided and abetted our father's crimes against us is horrible beyond belief. But I see that Superintendent Van Pelt isn't going to change his mind. It's to his advantage that both his partner in crime and Brian—a witness to tonight's goings-on—should die. Desperate, I appeal to Dr. Mara.

"You didn't know that Dr. Franz's experiments killed patients or that my father killed Donna Wright. You were an innocent bystander." Although I'm not sure that's really true, I'll say whatever I must. "But if you let your husband kill Brian, it's as good as pulling the trigger yourself. His blood will be on your hands too."

Dr. Mara alternately bites her lips and presses them together. Her face twitches; her eyes dart; she wrings her hands. She looks like Maureen Murray on the brink of a psychotic episode. My father's face is purple now. His body jerks feebly, spasmodically.

"You're a doctor," I tell Dr. Mara. "Can you live with this?"

"You won't get away with it." Rory taunts, "Dr. Mara, the jailbird, Dr. Mara, the jailbird."

Dr. Mara's face calms. She smooths her hair, and her blue eyes go cold and dead, reminding me of a corpse in anatomy lab. "We'll still have two other loose ends to tie up." She points to Rory and me.

In spite of everything Dr. Mara has learned about her husband, she's on his side. She's like Jean Norton and the other wives who are loyal to the end, dependent on their husbands for status and security. Dr. Mara won't risk her marriage, her professional position, or her cruises to save Rory and me. Superintendent Van Pelt aims his gun at us, then back at Brian; he can't decide who to shoot first.

This is the point at which I have nothing to lose.

I lunge at him and grab the wrist of his hand that holds the gun. We careen helter-skelter around the foyer while I claw and twist his wrist and Dr. Mara screams.

I call to Rory: "Run!"

But Dr. Mara is chasing her around the foyer. I can't make Superintendent Van Pelt drop the gun. He's old, but his muscles are like iron. Rory picks up the fallen medicine kit and hurls it at Dr. Mara. When Dr. Mara flings up her arms to shield her face, Rory tackles her around the knees. As they topple, the superintendent punches my eye. Pain explodes my vision into red stars and blackness. Knocked onto the floor, I hear thuds, metallic crashes, then a loud bang, then a cry of agony from Brian. I smell sulfur and smoke. Someone grabs my arm, hauls me to my feet.

"Dr. Kendall, let's go!" Rory says.

"I can't!"

Brian's been shot. Of the four doctors present, I'm the only one who wants him to live. But I'm weak and dizzy from the two blows to my head. The eye that Superintendent Van Pelt punched is already swollen shut, and the vision in the other is so blurred, I can't see anything except fuzzy shapes. Should I try to save Rory or Brian? It's like triage in the emergency room: to which seriously endangered patient should I give my attention?

"Go," I tell Rory, pointing toward the French doors at the back of the foyer. They lead to the dining room and the back door.

"I'm not leaving without you."

Somehow we've forged the bond that was impossible during her therapy. Rory drags me through the French doors. In the dining room, I have a brief, searing flashback of myself and my family seated around the table, my father criticizing my manners, my mother in an alcoholic stupor. Another bang shatters the window. Glass splinters pelt me.

"Jesus Christ, he's shooting at us," Rory says. "Come on!"

CHAPTER 40

Dear Dot and Maureen,

I know what it's like to think you would die for your family. So I understand why Dr. Kendall doesn't want to leave her brother. But staying with him will get her killed. She was the only doctor at RKH who tried to help me, so I have to save her if I can.

I drag her out the back door. She tries to break loose, crying, "I have to go back!"

I hang on tight. As I rush her down the steps, she trips, and we fall ass over teakettle onto the grass. There's another gunshot. The bullet whizzes over us and hits something in the distance. Oh, shit. *I've been hunting with Dad, and I've heard plenty of shots, but never aimed at me. I've never been a "loose end" before.*

Dr. Kendall moans. "Brian. Oh, God, Brian."

I saw the superintendent shoot him in the back. I don't know if he's dead, but I'm pretty sure Dr. Kendall is having a nervous breakdown. Just what we need. Clutching her arm, I run to our left, which I hope is the quickest route to the car. Suddenly the whole back yard lights up. I glance at the house and see Superintendent Van Pelt standing in the doorway. He's turned on the porch light. He can see us, plain as day. He raises his gun, tracking us. The lawn slopes down to the woods. I head there, pulling Dr. Kendall along, and dive into a gap between two trees just as a bullet smacks the one beside me. Then we're pushing through the woods, tripping on fallen branches, wading through dead leaves. I hear Superintendent Van Pelt and Dr. Mara chasing us. They have a flashlight. Its beam glances off the trees. I could easily outrun an old man and a woman who's wearing high heels, but not with my crazy psychiatrist in tow. And I'm lost.

"Which way back to the car?" I whisper to Dr. Kendall.

She just stumbles along with me, crying. Her hand is limp. I'm afraid that if I let go of it, she'll fall on the ground and lie there like a wounded deer, waiting to be put out of her misery. The scenery is all dense trees, thick undergrowth, rocks, fallen leaves and branches. Then the trees thin out and the sky opens up above us. I can see the moon and stars, but they're not bright enough for me to see what's up ahead. Superintendent Van Pelt and Dr. Mara are so close that I can hear them panting. I put on a burst of speed, dragging Dr. Kendall. Suddenly the ground drops off under our feet. Then we're tumbling down a steep slope, somersaulting and rolling. The flashlight beam flickers like crazy as Superintendent Van Pelt tries to get a bead on us. He fires more shots. Dirt kicks up from the ground. We fall off a cliff, into empty air.

I think of Niagara Falls and a story about a man who got killed going over in a barrel. Holy hell, we're gonna die*!*

Then I hit bottom, and somehow I roll out of a somersault and land on my feet. Dr. Kendall grunts as she thuds onto the ground beside me. There's a moment of relief before a gunshot cracks and the bullet punches my right calf. The pain is so God-awful that I shout, "Fuck!"

"Are you all right?" Dr. Kendall whispers. "Have you been shot?"

I crumple to the ground, gasping with agony. "Yeah."

She touches my leg, and it hurts so much, my whole body flinches. But I look up and see a round spot of light bouncing down the slope. Superintendent Van Pelt and Dr. Mara are coming. Their footsteps dislodge rocks that skitter toward us, then pause. I hear a metallic scrape and click. He's reloading his gun. He has at least seven new rounds, seven more chances to kill us. And I'm a sitting duck.

* * *

A preternatural clarity focuses my mind, sidelining all thoughts of the past and future, all my emotions and physical sensations. It happened in the emergency room at Mount Sinai when I was deluged with critically ill or injured patients. Racing from one to the next, I forgot that I was exhausted, hungry, and terrified that I would make a fatal mistake. I concentrated on what needed to be done. Now, with Rory injured and Superintendent Van Pelt bent on killing us, my single-minded focus homes in on what needs to be done. I forget Brian and my father. I don't think or plan. Fueled by adrenaline, I simply act.

I throw Rory's arm around my neck and hoist her as I stand up. She groans in pain, but she hops beside me on her good leg as I lead her along the bottom of the ravine. The moonlight shows me terrain that I explored when I was a child and know well even after twelve years. There was a low, shallow cave in the slope, partially hidden by overhanging vines and tree roots, where Brian and I used to play. It's still there. I ease Rory to the ground and drag her into the cave. I examine her leg as best I can in the dim light. It's bleeding profusely, but I don't think the bullet hit an artery. I unlace one of the sneakers Daniel loaned me and tie the lace around Rory's leg, a makeshift tourniquet.

"Stay here," I say.

I run back the way we came, stomping on twigs and in mud puddles, making as much noise as I can. I glance backward and see the light following me. I don't think about where I'm going. I'm barely conscious of the ache in my head, the dizziness, the pains in my knees where I scraped them while tumbling down the slope, and the fact that I can see, poorly, out of only one eye. All that matters is drawing Superintendent Van Pelt and Dr. Mara away from Rory. I can tell from the sound of their footsteps that they're both coming after me. I splash across the narrow creek in the bottom of the ravine. I know it's shallow, but the Van Pelts don't. I widen the distance between us as they follow more slowly and cautiously. The slope on the other side of the ravine is slick with wet leaves. I skid and grab tree trunks to keep from slipping backward. At the top is a trail, faintly lit by the moonlight that penetrates the leaf canopy. My energy flags, just as it did at the end of those busy shifts in the emergency room. I'm breathless from exertion; my head pounds with every step. Dizziness impairs my mental clarity like steam clouding a cold windowpane. It takes me a minute to realize that I'm on the same trail I took when I followed Brian that night.

The impulses of the unconscious mind, with its visceral desires, memories, and urges, are hard to subvert.

When I find myself in the clearing where I spied on Brian and Donna, it's an alignment of hidden forces that were put in play long ago.

Light shines into the clearing. Superintendent Van Pelt and Dr. Mara corner me there; I'm overcome by fatigue, unable to run anymore. Synchronicity brought us together yet again. Everything is going to end in the place where it began.

Dr. Mara stands on muddy bare feet; she's lost her shoes. Dirt covers the front of Superintendent Van Pelt's raincoat; he must have fallen. He holds the gun. They're breathing hard, their faces wet with sweat, but they smile triumphantly.

"You led us on a merry chase, Caroline," Superintendent Van Pelt says, as if humoring a child who lost a game of tag.

If I could catch my breath, I would tell him that he's a greedy bastard, a stupid sycophant, a disgrace to the medical profession. I would tell Dr. Mara that she's a fool who hitched her wagon to the wrong star. But all I can do is gaze at them in helpless rage.

Dr. Mara looks around, and her smile stiffens. "Where is Rosemary?"

It's as if I'm back in the emergency room and a new patient has arrived. I remember the time in the emergency room when I thought a woman's nausea and neck pain were symptoms of the flu, and the senior resident correctly diagnosed a heart attack. I can't afford a mistake when I answer Dr. Mara.

"Your husband shot Rory. She's dead." I imagine the grief and rage I would feel were it true. I channel those emotions into my voice. I have to make the Van Pelts believe me, so they won't go looking for her and she'll be safe until help arrives. *If* help arrives.

Dr. Mara's sigh exudes dismay and resignation. Superintendent Van Pelt looks unabashedly relieved. "That's one down, one to go." He aims the gun at me.

The adrenaline-rich blood racing through my veins stimulates my wits. I speak as quickly as I acted in the emergency room, where inaction can be as fatal as the wrong action. "How do you think you're going to explain Rory's death?"

In spite of his determination to eliminate me, he lets himself be sidetracked. "The girl was a dangerous psychotic. I shot her in self-defense."

"You might get away with claiming that you shot Brian to defend my father," I say, "but you shot Rory in the back while she was running away from you. That wasn't self-defense. It was pure, cold-blooded murder."

Superintendent Van Pelt scowls, vexed by my attempt to poke holes in his plan. "You won't be around to contradict me, Miss Smarty-pants."

"The evidence will. Rory's dead body in the ravine, with a bullet in her back. And mine here, with a bullet in *my* back. Because that's where you'll have to shoot me." I raise my hands and pivot.

It's the hardest thing I've ever done, letting him and his gun out of my sight. I imagine the loud bang, the bullet's impact knocking me down, the moment of agony before my heartbeat stops and the lack of blood flow to my brain obliterates my consciousness. The skin on my back flinches violently, pulling my shoulder blades together. My breath hisses in and out between my clenched teeth.

"Turn around!" Anger roughens Superintendent Van Pelt's voice.

No, the hardest thing is disobeying a man with a gun. I want to believe that if I do what he wants, he'll spare me. It takes all my will power to maintain my stance, to speak in spite of my fear. "Your friend the police chief might be willing to let you off." My voice is faint, my throat constricted. "But with three gunshot victims, don't be surprised if the state police and even the FBI get in on the act."

"Shut up! Do as I say!" Even Superintendent Van Pelt realizes that he could get in serious trouble for shooting two women in the back in addition to one man who's chained to the floor.

"I don't take orders from you." Despite my terror, I find satisfaction in defying him. "You fired me, remember? I don't work for you anymore."

"I'm warning you."

His voice is an ominous growl that would have slapped me back in line when I was afraid of losing my residency. Having nothing to lose is liberating. My mind races through possible tactics. *What does this patient need*? I'm my own patient now. It's my life I have to save.

"If you kill me, you'll be killing the only person who can help you and your wife out of this mess," I say. "You need me."

"Help us, how?" Dr. Mara cautiously moves in front of me to my right, so that she can see both her husband's face and mine.

"Don't listen to her, Mara," the superintendent says. "She's trying to trick us."

I can see her face too. I can see how scared she is, how eager for a peaceful resolution. "I'll back up your story about shooting Brian to save my father. I'll tell the police that you shot Rory because she attacked me and chased me into the woods. You saved two lives. You'll look like a hero instead of a murderer."

Doubt and hope argue in Dr. Mara's expression. "You would do that?"

Looking her straight in the eye, I lie with impassioned conviction, "Yes. If you let me live."

"Adrian?" Dr. Mara casts a pleading look at her husband.

Superintendent Van Pelt scoffs. "She knows too much. The minute she gets in front of the police, she'll spill everything."

Of course that's my intention, but I say, "No, I won't. I swear." I can see how much Dr. Mara wants to believe me. I say to her, "You're his subordinate because you're just his wife, just a woman, but you're the smarter one. To become a doctor, you had to be twice as smart and twice as good as all the men." Her gaze meets mine; we look back to a mutual past of long days and nights studying and working harder than our male classmates, enduring the indignities heaped on women in our profession.

"We can't trust her, Mara."

Morbidly aware of his growing desperation, of the gun pointed at my back, I press on. "He would be nothing without you helping him run his hospital. Don't let him take you down with him. Don't be another victim of his greed and stupidity."

"That's enough," Superintendent Van Pelt says impatiently. "Stand aside, Mara, unless you want her blood spattered all over you."

Defeat oozes through me like sidewalk slush, icy and gray. I've done my best, and my best isn't good enough. I've lost the patient.

"*I've* had enough," Dr. Mara bursts out, uncharacteristically shrill. "Stop telling me what to do, Adrian!"

I glance over my shoulder and see that Superintendent Van Pelt is just as surprised as I am that his wife is standing up to him. She says bitterly, "I warned you not to trust William Lennox. I told you he didn't care about us. But you wouldn't listen. You thought he was your friend. You're a goddamned fool!"

"Don't you talk to me like that!" Superintendent Van Pelt turns his anger on her.

"I'll talk to you however I want," Dr. Mara spits back at him. "You've made a hellacious mess and put me smack in the middle of it, God damn you!"

I stare, amazed at the raw fury I've unleashed from the poised, elegant Dr. Mara. It must have built up during her marriage, stoked by her husband's gross and minor offenses. She's like a marble statue broken open to reveal a hollow core filled with boiling acid.

"You're hysterical, Mara," Superintendent Van Pelt says in a patronizing tone.

Dr. Mara laughs giddily. "That's what men call a woman who won't kiss their asses. Well, I'm done kissing yours. I put up with you fucking the nurses. Do you think I don't know that Enid Norris is your mistress? Well, she can have you. After she helped you fake

Dr. Kendall's suicide attempt, you two deserve each other. I'm through!"

I had no idea about Superintendent Van Pelt and the Haven House charge nurse. I picture Enid Norris chasing me through the tunnels, catching me, and injecting me with Thorazine.

"Mara, go wait at the house while I finish this," Superintendent Van Pelt orders.

"Yes, go and sit like a good little girl while Daddy attends to important business," Dr. Mara says with a mocking simper. "The hell I will!" she shrieks. "Put that gun down, or I'll take it and use it on you!"

"Oh, for Christ's sake."

Out of the corner of my eye, I see Superintendent Van Pelt extend his arm, thrusting the gun's muzzle closer to my back. I exhale in despair, close my eyes, and try to visualize the people I care about and the memories I cherish, to make my last moment of life meaningful. But my mind is as blank as the dark space behind my eyelids. All I can do is wince and tremble, bracing for the shot.

There's a thud, as if from one large, hard object hitting another. The beam of the flashlight swings wildly as Superintendent Van Pelt grunts in pain. Then comes a deafening bang. I cry out. So does Dr. Mara. I fall face down, my arms and legs splayed, with a bone-jarring crash.

I can smell the gunpowder; I'm breathing.

I'm alive. I wasn't shot.

Amid a daze of relief and surprise, I hear yells, gasps, panting, and more thuds. Pushing myself to my hands and knees, I look at Dr. Mara. She lies crumpled on the ground, her body twisted, her face upturned. Her open mouth gasps. Her left hand clutches her stomach, which oozes blood. Superintendent Van Pelt shot her! Was he afraid she was so angry with him that she would tell the police everything that's happened? Even though I'm certain I'll be shot next, I swivel around to look at him instead of running for my life.

Superintendent Van Pelt is lying on his stomach, straddled by a small figure. It's Rory. She yells as she pounds his head and back with a large oblong rock. His white hair is bloodstained. His body jerks while his hand strains toward the gun he dropped. Rory pauses to grab the gun and hurl it into the woods. She looks up at me, her expression crazed with vengeful, gleeful triumph.

"I followed you." Gasps punctuate her words. "He was going to shoot you. I snuck up behind him." She pounds Superintendent Van Pelt again and again. "When he fired, I hit him, and he missed and got her instead." She jerks her chin toward Dr. Mara.

Dr. Mara groans in pain. Rory laughs, a high, exultant sound. "Serves them right." She lifts the rock high above Superintendent Van Pelt's head.

CHAPTER

41

A COLD WIND WHIPS the flag on the pole outside the county courthouse. It's October eighth, a cloudy morning, the ninth day of Brian Lennox's trial for the murder of Donna Wright. The Hudson Valley rarely sees murder cases as big as this. Spectators have packed the courtroom every day, lining up hours before it opens. There's an even bigger crowd than usual today. The prosecution and defense have finished their closing arguments, and the jury has been deliberating for three days. A verdict is expected soon.

Reporters have come from all over the country. Armed with notebooks and pencils, they mob the porch where I wait with Daniel Tanaka. Police officers keep them at bay while they shout questions at me.

"Dr. Kendall, what do you think the verdict will be? Do you really believe your brother is innocent?"

I should have stayed inside, but I couldn't bear the small, stuffy waiting room allotted to witnesses. It felt like the lockdown cell at RKH. I need space and fresh air, even at the cost of my privacy. Wherever I go, I attract unwanted attention. I've become a public figure since that night at the summer house.

* * *

That night, I dragged Rory off Superintendent Van Pelt before she could deliver the fatal blow. I couldn't let her kill him, no matter how much I wanted him punished for his part in the crimes against Rory and his other patients, Brian, and myself. That's the moment I truly became a doctor: I couldn't stand by and watch harm done to someone. The Hippocratic Oath was no longer an abstract concept but a code I live by. I said, "Rory, if you kill him, you'll go to jail." She might be spared the death penalty on account of her mental state and the abuse she suffered at RKH, but I doubt she could get off scot-free after bludgeoning a wealthy, prominent doctor to death in front of his wife, who would be the star witness against her. "You might never get out."

She gave in and huddled on the ground while I attended to Dr. Mara. The woman was in shock; she'd lost a lot of blood. I told Rory, "We have to call an ambulance."

After a long trudge, we stumbled out of the woods like refugees from a war, leaning against each other for support, Rory crippled by the bullet wound in her leg, I by an onslaught of grief for my brother, whom I'd lost for a second time. In the house, my father lay face up with Brian face down, overlapping him, both bodies motionless. Brian's pajama shirt was drenched with blood from the gunshot wound. The chain, gripped in Brian's hands, was wrapped around my father's neck. My father's face was swollen and purple, his eyes bulging, his mouth agape, his fingers clawed onto the chain links at his throat. I fell to my knees beside Brian, sobbing violently. Blinded by tears, I laid my hand on his back. His blood was wet, his body still warm.

I felt his back slowly rise, then fall. He was breathing.

Astonishment silenced my sobs. I whispered, "He's alive."

Rory cleared her throat. "Uh, so's your dad."

His bloodshot eyes rolled toward me, a wordless plea. I somehow got to the telephone in the second-floor hallway and dialed the operator. Somehow I managed to communicate the address of the house and the message that there were six seriously injured people. Eventually, police and ambulances arrived. The police cut Brian's chain. Medics loaded Brian, Rory, and my father into two of the ambulances while I led the police through the woods. We found the Van Pelts alive but unconscious. They were carried back to the house, and the third ambulance took them to the hospital. The police drove me there. I gave my statement while Brian, Rory, and Dr. Mara were in surgery and the doctors tended to Superintendent Van Pelt and my father.

I told the police everything, come what may. I'm sick of secrets and lies.

* * *

On the courthouse porch, flashbulbs explode. Daniel shields me from the photographers. I don't know what I would have done without him. He's been a constant, faithful source of support since I was discharged from the hospital.

Rory and I were in the hospital for three days—me for a concussion, Rory to recuperate from surgery to remove the bullet from her leg. When it was time to leave, I called Daniel. We didn't have anyone else. Rory's parents hadn't come when the police notified them that she'd been shot. Daniel borrowed a car, drove to the hospital, and picked us up. He found us the inexpensive motel, some ten miles north of Arden Spring, where Rory and I have been living ever since. He fetched our belongings and my car from RKH. He also retrieved his car and brushed off my apologies for abandoning it. I doubt there's much that he doesn't know about that night; the newspapers have been full of the story, and he came to the trial the day I testified. I don't know how he feels about me. We talk about everything except the personal. He brings me news from RKH.

The Van Pelts have resigned and vacated their mansion. The hospital is at the center of a scandal, its future uncertain. Many doctors, nurses, and other employees have quit. Daniel is staying temporarily because he feels an obligation to his patients. Joseph Mandel was caught stealing drugs, and the board gave him a choice: get help or face legal action. He's now a patient at a New York City hospital for drug addicts and alcoholics. Jean Norton discovered that her husband has been having an affair with one of the nurses. She's filed for divorce and begun a residency at the Boston Lying-in Hospital. Despite her lies about me, I'm happy for her because she's gotten some sense and she's fulfilling her dream of becoming an obstetrician. Good riddance to Ronald Norton, fired because his affair violated the morals clause in his contract.

Daniel phones me every day. On his days off, we hike the trails in the Hudson Highlands. We hold hands. We didn't talk about the future until last week. It was Sunday, court was adjourned until Monday, and we were picnicking in the Highlands. He told me that Agnes Van Pelt had called him into her office. I told him that she'd called me in too.

It was the only time I've been back to RKH. I swore never to set foot there again. I thought about ignoring the summons from Miss Van Pelt, the board member who had attended my disciplinary hearing. In the end, I went because I was curious. When I drove through the campus, I experienced no flashbacks. Learning the truth about the past has exorcised its power over me. In the flower bed where Rory crashed the truck, the ivy has been removed from the statue. The marble Greek goddess gazes tranquilly into the distance. She's not blind anymore. Like me. I'm free. Healed and whole, no longer fragmented by gaps in my memory, I can wash my hands of RKH and explore new horizons.

Miss Van Pelt received me in the superintendent's office. The throne-like leather chair and massive carved desk were gone, replaced by a folding table and chairs. Only dark rectangles on the walls remained of the oil paintings. The bookshelves were empty; so was the case that had held antique medical instruments. But I felt the presence of Superintendent Van Pelt, another ghost that haunts RKH.

Miss Van Pelt was formidable in her stern navy suit, her short silver hair crowned by a navy pillbox hat. "Thank you for coming, Dr. Kendall," she said, her voice as brisk and cool as her handshake.

I was glad she called me by my current name, recognizing me as an adult and a professional instead of a onetime teenage mental patient. "You're welcome."

Seated across from me at the table, Miss Van Pelt said, "Please allow me to apologize for the way you've been treated here."

Was she buttering me up for some nefarious reason? I gave her the benefit of the doubt. "Of course. I want to thank you for not voting to fire me."

Miss Van Pelt twisted her mouth, as if at the sour taste of the circumstances under which we first met. "That hearing was a disgrace. You were railroaded. I admit I disapproved of your concealing your identity, but I thought there must be more to the story than I was told. Which indeed there was."

The whole story had come out in my statement to the police and in the newspapers.

"The scandal has seriously damaged the reputation of RKH," Miss Van Pelt said. "Inspectors from the health department descended on it like vultures."

I think we have Daniel to thank for that.

"They found multiple violations, including buildings not up to code and inadequate drug security measures," Miss Van Pelt said. "They also cited RKH's treatment protocols. Their report called cold packs and hydrotherapy 'medieval,' and homosexual conversion therapy 'abusive and worthless.' They also noted 'short shrift given to psychotherapy' and 'excessive use of electroshock treatment.'"

I was glad, but I didn't understand why she was telling me all this.

"The responsibility for those faults lies with my brother Adrian." Miss Van Pelt's dislike of the superintendent was obvious from her frosty tone. "Whenever I pointed them out to him, he pooh-poohed me. He treats all women dismissively. Never mind that I'm a psychiatrist and I've kept up with the new developments in the field, which is more than he ever bothered to do."

Surprised, I said, "You're a psychiatrist?"

"In private practice for thirty years."

"But the superintendent introduced you as *Miss* Van Pelt." Not *Doctor*.

Dr. Van Pelt grinned. "Oh, yes, *Caroline Lennox*."

I grinned back. He'd tried to put her in her place with the same tactic my father had used to diminish me, but there we were, survivors.

Her expression turned serious again. "The situation at RKH was so bad that the board considered closing it. But it felt wrong to end its history on a bad note. We prefer to rehabilitate and build upon its legacy. And we've a duty to our patients. Therefore, RKH will continue to operate. But not in the usual way. We intend to address the problems at RKH and bring it into the modern age. We've begun a search for a new superintendent, new administrator, and head of research among the most progressive psychiatrists in the country."

"That sounds good." I was happy for the patients; they would benefit from the changes. "But shouldn't you be the superintendent?" And I still didn't see what any of this had to do with me.

"The other board members offered me the job. At one time, it was all I ever wanted." Dr. Van Pelt said bluntly, "Now I'm too old. RKH needs someone young and vigorous who can steer RKH for decades to come."

I sympathized with her, and I found myself liking her. I see her as my reflection in a distant mirror, my possible future self—an accomplished senior psychiatrist gracefully passing the baton to her juniors.

"I hope the changes I've described will be enough to convince you to come back and finish your residency, and to consider eventually joining our permanent staff," Dr. Van Pelt said.

I was stunned speechless. Just when I was ready to wash my hands of RKH, now I was invited to come back! To work at the place that almost destroyed me, when the whole world is mine to explore. Besides, I would have thought that since I was at the center of the scandal, I would be the last person RKH wanted.

"This isn't a pity offer. I'm not asking you back as compensation for your suffering or as a bribe to keep you from taking legal action against RKH," Dr. Van Pelt said.

Those were the only explanations that seemed plausible to me. "Then why?"

"Your education is top-notch. You're intelligent but not arrogant, sensitive but not weak. You care about your patients. You work hard to help them. You aren't afraid to stand up for them and do what you think is right even when the consequences could hurt you. All the staff and patients I asked about you said so. I think you have the makings of an excellent psychiatrist."

I thought of Rory and the conversion therapy session I interrupted. And it sounded as if Daniel Tanaka wasn't the only colleague who might have put in a good word for me. I had more supporters at RKH than I thought. I wasn't a total failure after all.

Dr. Van Pelt said, "Look, I realize that RKH has been languishing in the backwater of psychiatry for a long time, but I promise it will be on the cutting edge very soon. There won't be a better place for you to finish your training—or to make a name for yourself."

Astonishingly, she's trying to sell me on accepting her offer. Although I'm flattered, I say, "That's very kind of you, but . . ."

I've fulfilled my personal purpose at RKH—recovering my memory and learning the truth about my past. Perhaps that's all I ever really wanted from it. Perhaps it's a finished chapter of my life.

Dr. Van Pelt added icing to the cake. "You can restart the special program for girls and young women in Haven House."

That struck a receptive nerve. Rory isn't there anymore, but Dot and Maureen are. Here's my second chance with them and the other patients I think I can help—a greater temptation than the promise of working in a cutting-edge hospital and building my professional reputation.

Later, on a wooded cliff in the Highlands, with a panoramic view of the Hudson River below us, Daniel asked me, "What did you tell Dr. Van Pelt?"

"That I need time to think it over. What did you tell her when she asked you to stay?"

"The same."

* * *

Daniel has taken time off to wait out the jury's verdict with me. I've attended every day. I wanted to hear what the other witnesses said, and it's my only chance to see Brian. We haven't spoken since that night. The police wouldn't let me in his hospital room when he was recovering from surgery, and he isn't allowed to have visitors in jail. I only see him in court.

On the first day of the trial, I was astounded by the change in him. He's lost weight. Clean-shaven, with his blond hair neatly trimmed, he was handsome in a new navy blue suit. He looked both older and younger, as if the boy I knew had been resurrected in the body of the man. I sensed in him a core of inner peace, like the earth that holds steady in its orbit while storms, fires, and floods ravage its surface. When I was called to the witness stand, his calm presence lent me the courage to describe how I watched him come home covered with bloody scratches and tell our parents that he raped and killed Donna. I testified that I followed my father into the woods, where he found Donna alive and strangled her. I stood up to the prosecutor, who accused me of fabricating the memory. I didn't lose my composure when Superintendent Van Pelt took the stand.

"Caroline Lennox was psychotic and delusional," he said. "Her allegation that she was given electroconvulsive therapy at RKH in a deliberate effort to erase her memory is ludicrous." With his suave manner, in his well-tailored suit, he looked every inch the eminent psychiatrist. "Electroconvulsive therapy is the standard treatment for cases like hers. Memory loss is a common side effect, but such detailed, complex recollections don't suddenly pop up after twelve years. Caroline Lennox is still psychotic, still delusional, and lying to protect her brother."

When the defense forced him to admit that he was no longer the superintendent at RKH and that the state authorities were investigating him for malpractice and fraud, he became arrogant and blustery. He insisted that he had "voluntarily retired to pursue other interests."

My father wasn't able to testify in person. When Brian strangled him with the chain, his larynx was crushed. He underwent surgery to repair it but still hasn't regained his voice. He submitted a written statement, which said Brian killed Donna and the only thing he himself was guilty of was hiding his son from the law. He claimed I was a pathological liar. He threw Brian and me to the wolves to save himself. He currently lives in a private nursing home. He may never speak again. Muscle weakness and difficulty breathing and swallowing may be permanent too.

I never want to see him again, so I haven't visited him. Neither has his second family. The press interviewed his wife at their home in San Diego and reported that she filed for divorce and custody of their two sons. I feel no sympathy for him and no guilt about my lack of sympathy. Free of my childish desire for a loving father-daughter relationship, I'm glad that his infirmities should make him less able to manipulate people. But it's my word against his and Superintendent Van Pelt's. I'm a woman and former mental patient pitted against two important men. I can only hope that the jurors will recognize the truth, or if they don't, that justice will prevail in the other, related cases.

The Van Pelts were arrested along with Brian and my father that night. Their passports were confiscated so they can't flee the country. Dr. Mara has filed for divorce. They're out on bail, living separately. The authorities are still reviewing the entangled issues and deciding what charges to bring against whom. Meanwhile, the Van Pelts and my father have turned on one another. My father claims he entrusted me to the Van Pelts and my amnesia is entirely their fault. The Van Pelts say my father masterminded the cover-up of my family's role in Donna Wright's murder and he blackmailed them, threatening to report Dr. Franz's fatal experiment to the health department and have their medical licenses revoked unless they cooperated. The superintendent claims Dr. Mara killed Leonora Hirschfeld, Dr. Bullard, and Dr. Franz and attacked me. But Dr. Mara says her husband committed all four crimes, with help from his mistress.

The police are looking for Enid Norris. She's disappeared, a fact which doesn't argue in favor of her innocence. They're also looking for Nurse Janice, a potential witness. Her new job in California turns out to have been fictitious, and I'm afraid she was murdered to ensure her silence.

Due to the new developments, the murder charge against Rory has been dropped. The Van Pelts are now the prime suspects in the death of Dr. Bullard. And she won't face charges for assaulting the superintendent because the authorities believe that she acted in defense of herself and me.

Brian's lawyer predicts that, at the very least: my father will serve time for imprisoning Brian, Superintendent Van Pelt for shooting Brian and Rory, and Dr. Mara as an accessory.

* * *

At the courthouse, Rory pushes her way through the crowd to stand beside me. "Hi, Dr. Kendall. Hi, Dr. Tanaka."

The events of that night at the summer house have transformed the lives of everyone involved, not least of all Rory's. When she was discharged from the hospital, her parents tried to send her back to RKH, but she turned eighteen on that very day. Freed from their guardianship, with control over her trust fund, she can live wherever and however she chooses. Her dark hair has been cut into a short bob, and today she wears a dark gray trouser suit and white shirt, styled like a man's but tailored to fit her slim figure. She looks beautiful, neither masculine nor feminine but the best of both sexes and entirely herself.

Reporters besiege her with questions: "Did you try to kill Superintendent Van Pelt? Are you really a lesbian? Is that why you're wearing trousers?"

"Get lost." Rory pushes away a camera that a photographer thrusts at her.

She's come to court every day even though she wasn't called to testify because she didn't witness the events of the night that Donna Wright died and has no firsthand knowledge of the rape and murder. And because Brian pleaded guilty to the attempted murder of my father, the prosecutor didn't subpoena her to testify about that. She'll be a witness if and when the Van Pelts and my father stand trial. She's attended Brian's entire trial, certainly out of curiosity, but I think also to lend me moral support. I saved her and she saved me, or we saved each other. That's bound us together in a relationship less defined and more complicated than that of doctor and patient. And Rory and Daniel have discovered a mutual love of card games. While playing poker at the motel, they squabble like an older brother and kid sister, like Brian and me when we were children.

Now Rory holds up three Mounds bars she bought at the local store. "Want one?"

Daniel accepts, but I shake my head. Throughout the trial, I've suffered from indigestion. Daniel says, "You need to keep up your blood sugar level."

He's right. "Thanks," I tell him and Rory. I dutifully chew the sticky-sweet chocolate and coconut. They've been looking after me, and I mustn't faint on them when the verdict comes in.

Someone calls, "The jury is back."

We join the rush into the courtroom. The jurors are already seated in their box, nine men and three women. The pews behind the barrier that separates the defendant's and prosecution's tables from the audience are filling fast. Daniel, Rory, and I take our usual places closest to the defendant's table.

The bailiff escorts Brian into the courtroom. With his straight posture and stoic, far-sighted gaze, Brian looks like a soldier facing a firing squad, purged of fear, resigned. My heart aches with love and pride as I lean across the barrier toward him. He sees me, and a faint smile softens his expression before he sits down beside his attorney at their table. Brian was the last person to testify, to speak publicly about the most shameful act of his life. His voice was clear and strong even when tears filled his eyes.

"So you admit that you raped Donna Wright?" said his attorney, a young public defender who has proven surprisingly competent. "And you pleaded guilty?"

"Yes," Brian said.

"Why did you plead guilty?"

"Because I did it. Confessing is the right thing to do." To Donna's family and friends in the audience, Brian said, "I am so sorry. If I could change places with her, I would."

Donna's mother wept. Her father was grim; relatives glared. But Brian didn't quail as his attorney led him through a description of how he forced himself on Donna, she lashed out at him, he shoved her, and she fell and hit her head. Just as he begged me to help him do, Brian was owning his part of the responsibility for Donna's death.

"You also pleaded guilty to the attempted murder of your father. Why did you plead guilty to that charge?"

"Because I am guilty," Brian said. "I tried to strangle my father because he lied to me and kept me a prisoner for twelve years."

"And according to the terms of your plea bargain, you will serve two years for raping Donna Wright and two for your father's attempted murder, concurrently?"

"It's the least I can do."

"Did you kill Donna Wright?"

"I thought I did. My father told me I did. My sister said it was actually my father who killed Donna." Brian turned his clear-eyed, honest gaze to the jury. "It's up to you to decide."

The prosecutor is a pompous older man who, according to the newspapers, hopes to use a victory in this case as a stepping stone to the U.S. Congress. He grilled Brian mercilessly, but Brian stuck to his story, never letting the man provoke him to anger or to contradict himself. I was torn between pride in Brian's strength and regret that he hurt a young woman and his actions led to her death.

Now the bailiff says, "All rise."

Everyone stands as the judge strides into the courtroom, a middle-aged man with glasses and a receding hairline. "Mr. Foreman, has the jury reached a verdict?"

"Yes, Your Honor."

I hold tightly to Rory's hand. The bailiff delivers the jury's written verdict to the judge, who reads it silently, then says, "Regarding the charge of murder, what is your verdict?"

"Not guilty, Your Honor."

The courtroom explodes in wild, noisy clamor. Mrs. Wright sobs while her husband tries to comfort her and their friends and relatives shout angry protests. Brian solemnly thanks his attorney; the prosecutor shakes his head in disappointment. Spectators boo. Reporters run out to telephone the news to their editors. Rory and Daniel turn to me with smiles of relief and congratulation. I feel as if I've been drowning in the ocean with a heavy stone on my chest, and now the stone has rolled off, but it's chained to me like an anchor. Despite being acquitted of murder, Brian is a criminal and is going to jail.

The judge bangs his gavel, and the room quiets. "Thank you, jurors, for your service. "Brian Lennox, you are remanded to Sing Sing Prison to begin serving your sentence immediately. Let the record show that I commend Brian Lennox for his willingness to take responsibility for his actions, and that the brief length of his sentence takes into account the fact that he has already been held prisoner for twelve years. Court is adjourned."

People in the audience yell, "Murderer!" I rush through the gate in the barrier and fall into my brother's arms. He hugs me before the bailiff escorts him away. My eyes full of tears, I call, "I'll see you soon. Take care of yourself."

"You too, Cary," Brian calls over his shoulder.

As I walk out of the courtroom, Daniel and Rory shield me from the reporters, who call, "Do you really believe your own story?" "Don't you feel any guilt about helping a killer?"

Amid exploding flashbulbs, trailed by the mob, Daniel hurries Rory and me into his car. We drive away, leaving the uproar behind us. I sigh with relief as it sinks in. It's over.

Rory, in the back seat, leans forward between Daniel and me. "You can drop me off at the motel. I have to pack."

"Where are you going?" I knew we would part eventually, but I didn't expect it to be so soon.

"To New York City, tomorrow morning. I want to spend a few days there before I get on the ship to Europe."

"Wow," Daniel says.

I'm blindsided. Rory hadn't mentioned those plans. She says, "I was waiting for the trial to be over before I went."

I can see how eager she is to go, and I'm touched that she stayed to provide me companionship and moral support.

"Where in Europe?" Daniel asks.

"London. Then Paris," Rory says happily. "For a start. Maybe even Egypt and Madagascar someday."

"All by yourself?" I exchange worried glances with Daniel.

"Sure. I'll be okay. My law firm hired a travel agent to arrange everything for me. And if I get in trouble, there's always the American Embassy."

I forgot that she's an heiress with resources that other girls her age lack. "Have a wonderful time," I say. "And be sure to write. I want to hear all about it." I'm missing her already. She's become like family, the brave little sister I never had.

"Will do."

"When will you be back?" Daniel asks.

"Whenever they need me to testify at the other trials," Rory says. "After that . . . if I find someplace I like, I might move there permanently."

I sense her hope of a country, a town, a community that accepts people like her. "I think you'll find it," I say.

Daniel stops the car at the Cliffside Motel, a long, one-story brick building, painted pink with turquoise doors. Set on a wooded tract off the highway, it has a pool and a restaurant. I've grown fond of it. With Rory and Daniel for company, it feels more like home than anywhere else I've ever lived.

"We'll see you off tomorrow morning," Daniel tells Rory.

"We'll have a bon voyage party for you tonight," I say. "At the best place in town."

"I'd rather have one last hamburger here," Rory says, "and one last poker game." She opens her door and hops out. "Are you coming in?"

Daniel looks at me. I say, "Not yet. But wait a minute."

I get out of the car, put my arms around Rory, and we hug each other tight. I feel her practically vibrating with youthful, exuberant energy. My own spirits lift as I watch her skip toward her room. If superstition, paranoia, and insanity are contagious, so is *joie de vivre*.

Getting back in the car, I say to Daniel, "Can we just drive for a while?"

He steers the car onto the highway. The scenery flows past us, trucks and cars coming from the opposite direction, an orchard, woods and hills, a farmhouse and barn, cows in a pasture. Red and gold leaves are bright amid the green foliage. The crisp air blowing in the open windows smells of woodsmoke and apples. Everything seems sharper, clearer. I feel ready to think about the future.

"I'm going to accept Dr. Van Pelt's offer," I say. "I've decided to stay at RKH."

How odd that Resurrection Kill Hospital should turn out to be the place in the world that I always wanted.

Daniel turns to me. His smile lights up his eyes. "I'm so glad to hear that, Claire. I'm staying too."

"That's wonderful!" I hadn't given myself time to comprehend how much I was hoping he would stay or how sad it would be to go back to RKH without him. I remember my wishful thought about being half of a couple running a hospital together. "But I don't want to pressure you into staying if you don't really want to."

"You didn't. I already told Dr. Van Pelt."

I'm relieved that he isn't staking his career on my decision but disappointed because apparently he made his plans regardless of me. "Well, we need to finish our residencies."

Daniel refocuses his gaze on the road. "And while we're at it, we can help reshape RKH into a better modern institution."

"Yes. And I need to stay in New York so I can visit Brian regularly." Sing Sing Prison is only about thirty miles from RKH.

These are all good, practical reasons. But I experience again the sense that I can read Daniel's thoughts and he mine: Each of us hoped the other would stay. We each want to explore what the future holds for us personally, together, as well as professionally. Neither of us wants to spell it out because we both know it's too soon. New love is a fragile living thing that can't bear to be put under a microscope, probed, and dissected.

Our hands clasp. We smile as we look straight ahead at the road that extends toward the horizon.